OPERATION STARSEED

OPERATION STARSEED

J. M. Snyder

Writers Club Press
San Jose New York Lincoln Shanghai

Operation Starseed

All Rights Reserved © 2002 by Jeanette M. Snyder

No part of this book may be reproduced or transmitted in any form or by any means, graphic, electronic, or mechanical, including photocopying, recording, taping, or by any information storage retrieval system, without the permission in writing from the publisher.

Writers Club Press
an imprint of iUniverse, Inc.

For information address:
iUniverse, Inc.
5220 S. 16th St., Suite 200
Lincoln, NE 68512
www.iuniverse.com

This is a work of fiction. All events, locations, institutions, themes, persons, characters, and plot are completely fictional inventions of the author. Any resemblance to people living or deceased, actual places, or events is purely coincidental.

ISBN: 0-595-22262-5

Printed in the United States of America

For N, who was the first

Acknowledgements

So here's where the acceptance speech goes, no? I'd like to thank my parents, of course—without them, I would have never gotten this far. My brother and sister for encouraging me. Megan and Summer for helping me through these long chapters. Adam for combing over them one last time. The plethora of readers who, though they haven't read this one yet, gave me feedback on my web-published stories, necessary feedback that helped shape the writer I am today. I'd thank my editor, too, but I did that all myself.

Oh, and before I forget, I want to thank my muses, you know who you are. And hey, my cats. Why the hell not?

Part 1

It's a little after midnight and I'm the only one on the navigation deck when the call comes in. It's a mayday signal, loud and strong from the north sector, and I don't even think it could be him until I flip over the comm-link and his voice fills the cabin. "*Semper Fi* to Base," he says, his voice young and laced with static. For a heart-stopping moment I freeze, my hands hovering above the instrument panel, my breath caught in my throat. *Dylan?* My mind races and images of him tumble through me, memories I thought I had long since buried, his dark eyes and his full lips and the way his smile can eclipse the sun, it all comes flooding back. *My God, is that really you?*

"I repeat," he says, and I hear the weariness in his voice, it makes my fingers tremble. "*Semper Fi* to Base. Over." *You don't have to answer,* my mind whispers. *You can go get someone else, Tony maybe, just close the channel and go wake up Tony and tell him to start his shift an hour early, he'll do it, he's a good friend. Then let him come back here and hear the signal, let him talk to Dylan, you don't have to.* A burst of static fills the cabin and then I hear Dylan sigh, a lonely sound. I remember the way he touched my face the last time I saw him, his finger tracing the curve of my jaw when he told me good-bye. "Jesus Christ," he mutters, and I'm sure he doesn't realize he's still broadcasting. "Where the fuck is everyone tonight?"

Before I can give it too much thought, I lean on the transmit button and open the channel. My throat closes and I stare out the window at the black emptiness outside the station, the maw of space littered with stars so far away, I can't even believe they're real. *You made me feel like that, Dylan, when you left,* I think, listening to the open channel, the signal I'm sending, listening to my own breath. *That empty, that unreal.* I wonder what I possibly have to say to him now.

Luckily my professionalism kicks in and when I hear the words in my own voice tumble from my lips, they're almost foreign, they're that unexpected. "*Semper Fi*, this is Base, standing by."

I wait another two seconds and wonder if he's not going to reply before I realize I'm still leaning on the transmit. When I release it, static fills the cabin, a solar burst from the small sun just a few hundred thousand miles behind us. But beneath that I can hear his voice again, fading in and out through the static, cresting until I hear every word clearly and then ebbing away like the tide. "Neal?" he asks, and my name in his voice, I never thought I'd hear it again, it makes my knees weak and I'm glad I'm the only one on deck because I sink back into my seat and grip the arms of the chair until my fingers go numb. "Oh Jesus, Neal? Is that you? It's me, Dylan. Are you still there? Remember—"

I reach for the transmit again, push it harder than I should like it's to blame for the blood rushing through my ears, pounding in my brain. "Yes, I'm here," I say, and I don't tell him I remember even though I do, I never forgot. I don't tell him it's me and I don't say thank God it's him and I sure as hell don't tell him I was doing fine until I heard his voice and now I don't know if I'll ever be fine again. All of that is painfully clear in my own voice, tight and controlled, when I ask, "What is it you need, *Semper Fi*?" I refuse to even say his name.

Maybe it's my tone, but when I release the transmit again he doesn't respond right away. *Don't ask me if I still think about you, Dylan,* I pray. *You don't need to know the answer to that.* After a minute of silence I wonder if he's not going to respond at all—the first contact we've had with his unit since they've been out there and

I've gone and pissed the commander off, he's ignoring me now. Should I even bother to log the exchange? It wasn't much but the computer's recorded every word, backups are automatically made of every transmission, and I know myself well enough to know that before my shift's up I'm going to rewind the tape just to hear his voice again. I hate that. What's it say about me? About how far I've come since we broke up? *Not far at all.*

Another minute and I wonder if I've dropped the signal. Maybe he's drifted out of range—the coordinates on the screen tell me he's somewhere to the north and that's all uncharted right now, that's why his unit is out that way, they're mapping those stars and maybe he's too far out to come in clearly. He's not ignoring me, he's *not.*

Then static scratches across the speakers and his voice surrounds me. "Neal," he sighs. I close my eyes and lean back, hating the relief that courses through me, but I love his voice, the way it sometimes cracks a little even though he's already twenty, the way he can say my name and make me feel like a schoolboy all over again. "God, I'm glad it's you." I'm about to ask him again what he wants—the last thing I need is someone listening to the backup and hearing the two of us reminisce about what we used to have before they sent him out on this mission and he thought it'd be best if we just put *us* aside for awhile. Though now, here, tonight? Just hearing his voice again makes me realize how much I've missed him, how much I still feel for him, how much I want him back here and in my arms again, in my bed again, with *me. And he's got another what, two years out there? So wanting him isn't going to accomplish shit. He didn't WANT you pining for him, remember? That's why he suggested the break-up, he didn't want you to want for him, he wanted you to be happy if you could and how did he ever think you could be happy without him? I mean, really.* But just as I brush my thumb over the transmit, static crackles around me as he says, "We've sort of run into a situation out here, Neal."

It's been two months since I saw him last but I can still picture him in my mind, leaning over the radio, maybe running a hand through whatever hair has managed to grow back from the last time he cut it all off. He'd have a good length by now, a dark brown the color of rich chocolate, long in the front and clipped to the nape of his neck, that's the way he likes to wear it, and I clench my hands into fists because I can almost feel that soft length in my palms. His mouth would be close to the mike, he likes to keep it close so he can talk low—he used to call me on a secured channel when he did daily jaunts and he'd whisper over the signal, his voice sexy and wonderful and I'd turn it up as loud as I dared, put on the headset and press the receivers against my ears until it felt like he was speaking inside of me, my whole body vibrated beneath his words. Without realizing it I reach for the headset now, slip it on, switch over the signal and my voice sounds unbelievably deep to my own ears when I speak into the mouthpiece. "What kind of situation?"

"You recording this?" he answers, his voice filling my ears. *Keep talking to me*, I pray, leaning back in my chair. My body reacts to the sound of his voice, so close, so unbearably close, and even though I'm dressed in a loose-fitting jumpsuit, the area below my belt is suddenly feeling pretty damn tight.

"Yeah," I whisper. The mouthpiece touches my lips and I don't have to talk very loud for him to hear me. "What kind of situation, Dylan?"

"We've intercepted a signal—" he starts, and then he laughs. He has an infectious laugh, it makes me smile to hear it. "I almost forgot what you sound like."

I sigh. *He's not going to make this separation easy, is he?* I wonder. Even though it was his idea to start with—I was fine with him out there in space and me back here at the station, but he was the one who didn't want that. "Dylan," I warn. "What kind of signal?"

He must realize this isn't going to be the breathless reunion he was hoping for because he sighs and his voice is curt when he replies.

"From the Epsilon system." A cluster of stars well beyond the north sector—out past the range of their mission, which explains why he's calling it in. "It seems to be an archaic code but the computer's worked it out, says it's a welcome message, of sorts." I don't like the way he says *of sorts,* like he knows the computer can't be wrong but he doubts the validity of its findings all the same. "Seems there's life out there, Neal. Or was, I don't know, the source is pretty far away. Might be an old relayer stuck on endless repeat and everyone's dead, I just don't know." He takes a deep breath, lets it out slowly, and the rush fills my ears, I can almost feel it warm on my neck, my cheeks, my skin. "That's the situation. What do you think?"

What *is* there to think? "The computer translated the code?" I ask, trying to ignore the steady sound of his breathing in my ears. "It's not alien?"

"Morse," he says wryly. "Four hundred million miles away from home and there's Morse code out in them there stars, babe."

Babe. I sigh at the term of endearment and hate myself when I whisper, "Dylan, don't."

"Sorry," he mutters, but I can tell he's not, not really. How am I supposed to get over him when he calls me stuff like that? When he makes it sound like he's not yet over me? *Then why are we apart again?* I wonder. *Oh yes, his mission. He didn't want me sitting here wasting away, waiting for him to return. How could I forget?* When I don't answer immediately, he prompts, "Well?"

"I have to run this past Dixon," I remind him. I'm not the one here who makes the decisions, I'm just one of the tech crew who mans the nav deck every night, and it's been two months since the *Semper Fi* left with Dylan at her helm and he hasn't called in once on my shift, not *once*, even though he was instructed to keep the comm-link open at all times. I was beginning to think maybe he somehow knew my schedule and called in around it just to avoid talking to me. *But maybe he's just been busy,* my mind whispers, and I don't need to be thinking this shit, I don't need to be making up excuses for him and thinking how maybe we can get back together because he's out *there* and he's going to *stay* out there a good two years before I see him again and I don't need to want for him, he was right about that. "You know I don't call the shots around here."

He laughs again and I just want to curl up in the sound, it brings back all the times we spent together before he left. "I know *that*," he says coyly, and behind my closed eyes I can see the sardonic grin I hear in his voice. "I'm just asking for your thoughts, Neal, is all. What are you thinking about?"

You, I want to say, but I don't. *You called it quits, remember? You said you thought maybe things would be better if we went our separate ways and you wanted to stay friends but with this mission on the horizon, that's all you wanted to be, friends. So you don't need to know I'm thinking about you. You don't need to know I still ache for you, and you damn well don't need to know what hearing your voice tonight has done to me all over again.* I clear my throat and in a low voice tell him, "I'm thinking I need to get him in here to talk to you."

His sigh says that's not the reply he was hoping for, but he realizes I'm sticking to the script so he just says, "Yeah. But don't wake him up or nothing, I'm sure it's late there." I glance at the clock—it *is* late, and my shift ends in ten minutes. "Just get him to hail out here some time tomorrow, okay?"

"Sure." Behind me the door irises open and I glance up to see Tony, rubbing the sleep from his bleary eyes and nursing a steaming mug of hot coffee. His short dark hair sticks up in all directions—he didn't bother to smooth it down when he tumbled out of bed and now he runs a hand over his coarse beard as if to make sure it's still there, blinks owlishly at me for a few seconds, then drops into the seat beside mine. "I have to go," I say softly.

Dylan sighs again. "Okay," he whispers. As I click over the signal and take off the headset, his voice fills the cabin when he says, "You can always call out here, too. If you want."

We're just friends now, remember? I don't meet the look Tony gives me. Leaning on the transmit, I try to think of everything I want to tell Dylan, everything I've thought of since he's been gone, everything I never said while he was here. I want to tell him I thought I was over him but I'm not. I want to tell him that all I've done is pine for him and I just want to hear him say that when we broke up, we didn't throw away eight good months, we *didn't*. I want to hear that he misses *me* and I want to hear him say that he's sorry, he was wrong, he wants me back. Even though he's out in the north sector, I want to know he loves me still.

But Tony's watching me and this is being recorded, I can't say anything like that. So the only thing I murmur into the open channel is, "Night, Dylan."

His reply is just as brief, just as soft. "Night, Neal."

Then the connection breaks and the static dissolves around us, and Tony asks quietly, "Dylan?"

He knows we were lovers. He knows I fell for the boy the moment he walked onboard this station, cocky and confident, and when he winked at me that day, I fell like one of the stars out there, burning with lust and desire. Tony's my best friend, he *knows* all this, everything that happened, how Dylan was my first and how he made me feel like I was the only one who mattered and how proud I was when Dixon chose him for the mapping duty because out there among the stars, that's where he wanted to be. And I think he knows that I'm still missing him—he knows we broke up and he knows it wasn't what I wanted and he knows I pretend I'm over him but I still love him, I know he knows *that*. It's obvious when I can't quite meet his eye, when I nod and say, "Yeah," and my voice is thick because I still love him so damn much and hearing him tonight has me all choked up.

Carefully, Tony says, "We haven't had contact with that ship for awhile."

I shrug. I haven't been looking at the logs or listening to the backups because I don't want to accidentally hear his voice or see his name and have the wall I thought built up against his memories crumble apart again. *Too late,* I think. *Too damn late.* "What did he want?" Tony persists. Then, quickly, he adds, "Not that I'm prying. If it was just to talk—"

"They picked up a signal in the Epsilon system," I tell him. "Morse code. He thinks..." I shrug again—he didn't tell me what he thought about it but I know him, I've slept with him, loved him, I know how his mind works and I know he thinks it's something big if he called it in at this hour. Right now I think he's probably still sitting at the radio, staring out at the stars and thinking about me, the two of us, together. Probably remembering how I turned away when he tried to kiss me one last time before he left. I push that memory from my mind as I stand and stretch. "It's getting late, Tony," I say. "I'm not really up for this right now."

Tony nods. "I know," he concedes, sipping at his coffee. He winces but I don't know if it's because of the heat or the taste. "Did you log the call?"

"I will in the morning," I promise. "It's on the backup. Nothing personal, if you want to hear it."

He nods again and glances at the clock. "Get some sleep," he tells me. As I head for the door, though, he asks, "Are you okay with this?"

I force a laugh. The door irises open and I step out into the hall, thinking I'm not going to reply. Of course I'm not okay with this. I'm going to lie in my narrow bunk tonight and ache for Dylan, his touch, his kisses. I can still hear his breath in my ears, filling me up inside. But the door starts to close and I surprise myself by saying, "I'm going to have to be."

And that's all there is to it, really. I'm going to have to be.

❦   ❦   ❦

I dream of Dylan for the first time in weeks. In the dream he looks the same as he did the day I stood on the nav deck and watched him board the *Semper Fi* on the vidscreen. At the threshold of the ship he turned and I swear he looked right at me, through the security camera and at *me,* three decks above him because I was angry and didn't want to see him off. I didn't *want* to say goodbye. His hair was newly trimmed so short in the front, so unlike how he likes to wear it, and his face looked too pale on the vidscreen, his eyes too wide, too dark. Only a few years younger than me and in that instant when he looked back, when his eyes met mine, he looked so much older, his boyhood gone, left behind. *Like me.*

It's not so much a dream as a memory. In my mind I can see him again, the man who told me he loved me before he said he didn't want to tie me down. "I'll be out there for who knows how long," he said, his eyes pleading with me to listen to him. This was the day before he left and we sat on the bunk in my tiny room facing each other, my hands in his.

"Two years," I told him. That was the length of the mission, two years, and I could wait that long. For him? I could wait an eternity.

"I don't want you lonely," he said, licking his lips to wet them. I remember the feel of his hands in mine, rubbing my fingers, warming them. "What if I don't come back?"

I shook my head. "Don't say that," I whispered. "Why wouldn't you? Don't talk like that, Dylan—"

"I'm just saying things happen, baby." He kissed my fingertips, his lips soft and damp where his tongue had licked between them.

I asked if there was someone else, but he said no, only me. "Then why—"

"I want you happy," he told me. Tears faceted his eyes like jewels, and they sparkled like sapphires in the low lighting of my room. In the dream he's hurting, he doesn't want to do this, and I try to tell him that he doesn't have to, we don't need to break up when things are going so well—but even after all this time, I still can't find the words to say that. I still turn my face from his so he won't see my own tears. His lips still brush along my cheek in a thwarted kiss.

And then I wake up and he's still gone.

❄   ❄   ❄

My room's just a tiny cell on one of the lower levels of the station, large enough for a table and chair and my bunk, which slides into the wall as if that's going to free up any more space. It doesn't. Most times I don't even bother to put it away, who's going to see it? When Dylan was here we left it out because we were always in it, a tangle of limbs pressed together so comfortably, it makes me ache to remember the way we used to be. His hands on my body, his lips on my skin, his thick hair in my hands. For a moment I stare at the rumpled bed sheets and wonder if he's somehow managed to move on these past few months, if maybe he's found someone in his crew that he's sharing his nights with. I hope not—is that so bad? To hope he still wants me?

While I'm getting dressed, there's a knock on my door and then out in the hall, Dixon shouts my name. "James! Let me in." He doesn't go so far as to say *captain's orders*, but I swear I can hear the desire to do so in his voice. First thing in the morning—God, lucky me.

Dixon knocks again as I hit the power switch by the door and when it cycles open, he ducks into the room and glares at me, his lank black hair pulled back from his face and tied into a tight knot at his nape. His eyes are like shards of glass. "Why the hell didn't you log that call?" he asks.

"Hello to you, too," I mutter. Turning away from him, I pull a thermo-vest on over my jumpsuit, stomp my feet to settle them into my heavy boots, and do my best to ignore him. Tall and lean, Rick

Dixon is commander of the station and a royal asshole, and right now I don't feel like dealing with his shit.

I can see his reflection in the mirror above my bunk—he crosses his arms and leans against the doorway, watching me. A muscle in his jaw twitches in anger. "Well?" he asks. "I'm waiting. You know it's protocol to log every damn blip on that screen—"

"I know," I sigh. Looking at myself in the mirror, I run a hand through my disheveled hair in a lame attempt to comb it down. But it still sticks up from my head in defiant spikes because I cut it too short last time and it hasn't quite grown back in yet—it's a punkish look that I think Dixon hates because he's afraid it questions his authority, so I'm thinking I'll keep it this way a little while longer. "It was late—"

Dixon's reflection frowns at mine. "That's no excuse. All communications must be logged."

"So I'll log it now." Only I make no move to leave because I'll tell you, it's all Dixon's doing, this starmapping, and even though Dylan's the best pilot we have and even though he's great with his crew and he wants to be out there, I know he does—despite all that, I still blame Dixon for sending him, for *letting* him go. Mostly, though, I blame him for not transferring me to Dylan's crew. He knew we were lovers and I even came to him after we broke up, asked him again to put me on that ship. He said no.

So I didn't log the call last night, so what? I'll do it today. It's enough to know that I've managed to piss him off this morning. "James," he warns. "If you don't want me to listen to the backup—"

"Go ahead," I tell him. I'm sure Tony's the one who told him about the call and what the hell does he think, Dylan and I got frisky over the airwaves when we both knew the exchange was being recorded? "It's not cybersex, Dixon. We didn't get off on it."

In the mirror, Dixon's face hardens. *Touché,* I think, and I have to fight the urge to smirk at him. "I'll log the call, don't worry about it," I say. "When I get a chance. Jesus."

"In the meantime I'll just listen to the backup," Dixon grumbles. "I forgot he dumped you for this mission."

I glare at his reflection, and he *does* smirk because he knows that was low. "Get out," I tell him. When he doesn't move, I turn around and hit the power switch. The door tries to cycle shut but he's in the way and it aborts the attempt, eases open again. "I said—"

"Get out," Dixon echoes, stepping back. This time when I hit the switch, the door closes like the petals of a flower, silver swirls tightening into each other. Before he's gone completely, Dixon tells me, "I heard you."

"Fuck you," I mutter, but he's on the other side of the door now and doesn't hear me. *He didn't dump me for this mission,* I tell myself, but it's a cold assurance because Dylan's not here, is he?

He's out there in space somewhere and maybe Dixon's right after all. That thought makes me blame him all the more.

🍁   🍁   🍁

Tony's shift is over at nine and it's a little after ten when I finally make my way to the nav deck, so I know he's not going to be there. He'll be back in his room, snoring away, I know how he is. Won't rejoin the living until later this afternoon. I'm expecting one of the other techs to be on hand instead but I don't know who, I can't remember the schedule. It's me from five to one, Tony after me, then—

I catch a glimpse of Dixon as I step on deck and groan. He's the only one here at the moment, must have relieved the tech on duty. God, does he have to listen to the backup *now*? I deliberately waited another half hour thinking he'd be finished before I even got here. I should've known better.

Only it's not the backup he's playing, it's something else, staccato bursts of Morse code that fill the cabin and echo in the small room. He glances up at me and I ignore him as best I can, busy myself with the log chart and don't even look his way. On the sheet for last night,

I recognize Tony's thick writing—he logged the call for me. Probably didn't mention it to Dixon, and when the captain noticed the time was before Tony even crawled out of bed, he decided to come bitch at me. *Just because he saw Teague, D. J. on the log,* I think. The Morse code skips through me like a surrogate heartbeat, a series of dashes and dots I'm not paying any attention to, I couldn't even interpret it if I did. That code is so damn old, I'm surprised the computer even reads it anymore. On the log sheet, I scribble my initials by the call and hang the chart back up. I'm just about to leave when the code cuts off and a familiar voice comes over the link. "It repeats from there, sir."

Dylan. My heart stops in my chest.

In the window above the control panel, I see Dixon smirk. He tries to hide it behind his hand but I can see the gleam in his eye when he looks up at me and I know he's getting a kick out of this, the sick bastard. *Isn't that your boy?* he wants to say, I can almost hear the words out loud. *Oh no, wait, my bad. Not yours anymore, is he?*

"Sir?" Dylan's voice is tentative around us and I want to close my eyes, lose myself in its richness, but not with Dixon here. "You still—"

Dixon hits the transmit and says, "Right here, Teague. Say hi to Mr. James."

Asshole. "Hey, Neal," Dylan replies. I think he's going to say something else, something Dixon will snicker over, something the captain can throw back at me for the rest of the day, but he doesn't. When he speaks again, he's nothing but professional. "Remember the signal I was telling you about last night? Did you hear that just now?"

I push past Dixon and thumb the transmit button. "I caught the tail end of it," I tell him, staring at the coordinates screen so I don't have to look at the captain beside me. "That's the welcome message?"

When I don't release the transmit immediately, Dixon knocks my hand away. Dylan makes me do that, just lean on the control panel because I have so much I want to say, so much I *can't* say, and if I just leave the channel open then maybe I'll find the courage to say it somewhere along the way. "—S410," Dylan's saying. He didn't realize I had the transmit down. "Do you guys remember your history?"

"Repeat that, Teague," Dixon says, glaring at me. "We didn't copy."

Static accompanies Dylan's reply. "Operation Starseed, remember?" The name sounds vaguely familiar but I can't place it. "A dozen ships, a hundred terraformers each, dispersed what, twenty years ago? About that? Before my time."

But Dixon's nodding like he knows what Dylan's talking about. "Starseed?" I ask.

"Colonist effort," he explains.

Before he can say anything else, a sudden burst of static rips across the channel and I wince as I turn down the volume. Then Dylan's voice comes through, louder than before, but I can still hear the static beneath his words like an animal testing the length of its chain. "The message?" he says, and I nod as if he can possibly see me. "Have you decoded it yet?"

Dixon reaches the transmit before I do. "Not yet." Releasing it, he mutters, "Anxious, ain't he? Is he always quick like that?"

I ignore him—he's not getting another rise out of me, I swear I won't let him. When Dylan comes back across the channel, the static threatens to drown him out. "There's a part that says something about S410, and correct me if I'm wrong but isn't that similar to the naming convention used on the Starseed ships? I'm not sure—"

The rest of his transmission dissolves into scratchy bursts and a high whine like feedback that pierces right through me. "You're breaking up," Dixon tells him, and then, "Sounds like solar flares. We'll run the code through the computer here and see what we come up with. Hang tight for now, you hear me? Don't go chasing after this just yet—do you copy?"

Dylan tries to respond but we can't hear him through the static. "Dammit," Dixon mutters, closing the connection. "I don't want him jumping on that just yet."

"Don't tell me," I say. "Tell him." I want to ask him to rewind the backup, pretend I want to hear the signal, but I'd be lying if I said I didn't want to hear Dylan's voice again and I'm not going to give him anything to comment on. Heading for the door, I add, "Don't forget to log the call."

He doesn't answer, which is just as well.

※ ※ ※

"Operation Starseed," Tony drawls when I ask him about it in the cafeteria. He nods like he knows what he's talking about and doesn't look at me as he munches on the freeze-dried vegetables we're served with every meal.

I roll my eyes and sigh. "You don't know," I say. It's not a question.

"I've heard of it," he says, defensive. "I just don't remember what I heard. A colony or something, wasn't it?"

"Or something," I mutter, pushing the food around on my tray. "You're a big help, Tony."

He shrugs. "So check the annals. I'm a tech, not a historian, you know?"

Tell me about it. The annals are data disks that I don't think anyone's ever really gone through just because there's so much shit on them—histories of all the nations on Earth from the beginning of time, music and books and films, everything from the past three thousand years or so and who wants to sift through all that? There's no real order to the mess, nothing but a separate index disk, and it's just too much of a bother to look up anything. But I have all afternoon and by the time I have to be on the nav deck for my shift, I've found the disk with the Starseed data on it. On the deck I kick back in the seat, prop my feet up on the panel in front of me, slip on the headset and cue the disk. I scroll through the data, a cacophony of sounds and music and voices, and beneath it all I can hear the open channel, the empty space beyond my reflection in the window, the stars staring back at me.

Dylan's out there somewhere.

I wonder if he'll call in again tonight. I wonder if he heard Dixon's last transmission and he's just waiting out in the north sector, waiting for a directive, a command. But what'll Dixon do? Tell him to check it out, of course, he *has* to if he's going to map that sector. He's just stalling for time right now, wants to run through all the proper procedures, make sure his ass is covered before he goes sending a small map crew out into a system we all thought devoid of life. Dylan has what, four people on that ship? Navigator, radio tech, systems tech, and himself, that's it. No weapons because they're close enough for us to send out a patrol if we need to—and what if that signal isn't just an archaic relay, still transmitting after all this time? What then?

The disk stops spinning—I've gone too far, run through the whole thing without even paying attention to it. My mind's elsewhere, I'll admit, lost in thoughts of Dylan and how we used to be and damn Dixon for giving him this mission, damn him for taking it, damn me for letting him get to me all over again. *He was the one who wanted to call it quits,* I remind myself as I start the disk again. *Remember that, Neal. This was his idea, keep that in mind.* My fingers dance over the controls, flicker through four or five years and then stop, listen to whatever I get, start it up again. I'm not finding anything about Operation Starseed, or the S410, or the Epsilon system—

"*Semper Fi* calling Base."

It's faint and faraway and Dylan's voice, I'd recognize it anywhere. Clicking off the disk, I turn up the volume and press the mike to my lips. "Dylan?" I breathe with a quick glance behind me. I'm alone, no one else on deck but me, and the door is closed, there's no one here, no one to see when I gently run my hand over the panel and turn off the backup tape. They don't need to hear whatever we say to each other. "You there?"

His reply fills my whole world, it's so loud in my ears. I sit back in the seat and press the headset close, savoring each word. "I'm here," he sighs. "I was hoping you'd be on duty. God, Neal, I know you're recording this—"

"It's off," I whisper. When he doesn't answer immediately, I close my eyes and feel the hint of a smile tug at my lips. "It's just you and me, babe. What's on your mind?"

"You." It's a breathy rush and I know Dixon's wrong, Dylan *didn't* dump me for this mission, he *didn't*. There's a grin in his voice when he says, "I miss you something fierce, boy."

Tears sting my eyes and I don't trust myself to reply. "It's lonely out here," he continues, soft in my ears.

"It's lonely here, too," I sigh. "Dylan, why—"

"Shh," he admonishes, and I bite my lower lip to keep it from trembling. "Let's not talk about that right now, okay? Please?" I don't answer but I know what he means. I don't want to talk about it either, about us—or rather, about us not *being* us. If we don't mention it then maybe we can both pretend it didn't happen and we're still together and he's just on a routine jaunt, he'll be back in my arms in no time. *Two years*, my mind whispers, but I ignore it. "You still there?" he asks, unsure.

"Right here," I tell him. *I missed the sound of your voice*, I want to say, but don't. *I miss you, too, Dylan.* I don't say that, either.

For long moments we just listen to each other breathe, and with my eyes shut, I can imagine that he's beside me again, I can almost feel his fingers hovering above my skin, his lips almost touching mine. Almost. Finally he sighs and whispers, "Say something, Neal. Talk to me."

I press the eject button on the control panel and the data disk comes out into my hand. "Operation Starseed," I say, just because I can't think of anything that's not about the way we used to be together and I don't want him to go just yet. "You mentioned it to Dixon this morning? What was that, exactly?"

"I don't really remember," Dylan admits. "Did he tell you anything about it?"

I laugh at the thought of Dixon telling me anything. "We're not exactly best friends here, Dylan," I tell him, but that's as far as I'll go. He doesn't need to know that Dixon keeps kicking at me about this mission of his. "I'm looking in the annals but I can't really find anything."

Static scrapes across my ears. *Not yet,* I pray—he's so far out there, none of the transmissions last very long, it seems. A few precious minutes and then we're sabotaged by the stars and the sun behind us, and I lose him all over again. "Dylan?" I prompt.

"I heard it," he says. "Don't have much longer, do we? What's your shift now?"

"Five to one, every evening." *Why's it taken you two months to get back in touch with me?* I want to ask. *Why all of a sudden do you want to know when I'm on deck? Don't do this to me, Dylan. Please don't.* But we're not talking of that, are we? Only safe topics. Only things that don't concern the two of us. "Starseed was a colonist effort, right?"

More static, and through it I can make out Dylan's voice, growing distant again. "A dozen ships," he says, and I press the headset tight against my ears to hear every word. "I know one exploded shortly after take-off, thermonuclear reactor problem or some such shit. Three came back unsuccessful. A few of them landed in known systems—I want to say near Orion or the Horsehead, but don't quote me on that. Some disappeared."

A chill runs through me at the way he says the word, *disappeared*. "What do you mean?" I ask.

I can see him in my mind's eye—he's holding the headset to his ears like I am, to capture my every word. His eyes are closed and he shrugs now because he's not really interested in Starseed, no more than I am, it's just words to fill the silence between us and he's simply savoring my voice, my breath, me. He wants me—it's my daydream, I can tell myself that—he's aching for me and tonight in his lonely bunk he'll clutch himself and cry my name into his pillow and wish he never told me goodbye. "Neal," he sighs now, and static cuts off the rest of his sentence, if there's anything else he says. Then he comes back, strong, the channel clear. "The message mentions S410," he tells me, and maybe I'm wrong, maybe he's not thinking about me—or maybe he's just trying to convince himself he's not. "I'm thinking that's the way the ships were numbered, I'm not sure. They were fourth generation S-class starships and there *were* a dozen of them, you know?" Static prevents my reply but I nod, it makes sense. When he speaks again, there's a buzzing around the edges of his voice like a poorly tuned radio station. "What if this signal's from one of those ships?" he asks. "One of the ones that disappeared?"

"That was twenty years ago," I point out. Feedback whines through my head like a drill and I wince as I turn down the volume a bit. "You think those guys are still alive out there?"

"Maybe," Dylan says. "You're gonna hear it from Dixon for cutting off the backups."

I grin at that. I know. "Fuck him," I mutter, and Dylan laughs, a warm sound that fills the hollow spaces inside me. "Don't you go chasing after this, baby. Sit still and wait for his command, okay?" I don't like Dixon, I'll admit, but I don't want Dylan searching for the origin of that signal without any support. If Dixon's smart, he'll send a small unit of fighters out to the north sector to give the *Semper Fi* cover. I don't want Dylan jumping the gun on this and getting hurt because who am I kidding? I still love him.

At first I think he hasn't heard me. Then I think he's mad, he's not going to reply, he's probably already halfway to the signal's origin and anything he says will clue me in to the fact that he's not waiting around for anyone, he's going to find the lost colony and make a name for himself as the starmapper who located S410, whatever the hell it is. Maybe they'll name a star after him—I know that's gone through his mind, I know him so well and that's probably the first thing he thought of when he intercepted the signal. "Dylan?" I ask, nervous. "Don't tell me you're—"

"You called me baby," he whispers.

That makes me frown. "Did I?" I don't remember. *Freudian slip*, I think. *So much for him not knowing how you feel.* "Dylan, don't do anything without Dixon's go ahead, okay?"

"Sure," he murmurs. "Neal, I—"

Then the transmission dissolves into thick static and I listen to it a minute more, two minutes, three, trying to hear anything else he might have to say, but he's gone.

❦ ❦ ❦

The next day a steady pounding wakes me up, someone knocking on my door like they just might beat through the steel alloy with their bare fists. I roll over in the bed and think if it's Dixon again, I'm going to hurt the son of a bitch—

But it's Tony. "Neal!" he cries, his voice like a splash of cold water in my face. What's he doing up *now*? If his shift's over then it's after nine and he's usually back in his own room by this time, trying to catch another few hours shuteye. "Jesus, open this door already, I know you're in there. Neal!"

"Coming," I mutter. I wipe the sleep from my eyes and stumble for the door, hit the power switch with one hand as I try to disentangle myself from the sheets wrapped around my legs. As the door cycles open, I trip over the sheets and mumble, "Fuck it." This is too complicated for me this early in the morning so I'm just going to crawl back into the bed and pull the sheets up to my chin. They ward off the sudden blast of chilly air that blows through the open door.

Only Tony has other plans. "Get your lazy ass up," he says as he enters the room. He yanks the sheets off me and I grasp at them feebly, but he's bigger than I am and I just woke up, there's not much fight in me yet. "If I can't sleep," he says, "then you can't, either. Get out of bed."

He plops down on the end of my bunk and I draw my legs up to my chest just to move them out of his way. I'm sure he's not above pulling me out of the bed bodily if he has to. "So go to sleep," I tell him, punching my pillow back into shape. "Who's stopping you?"

"Dixon," Tony growls. I sigh and close my eyes. I don't want to hear this right now, I just want to go back to sleep and dream of the boy who used to be mine, is that too much to ask?

Apparently it is, because Tony slaps my thigh and rolls me over, out of the bed and onto the floor. "Fuck, Tony," I start, sitting up. The cold steel floor bites through my thin boxers, numbing my ass.

"Fuck nothing," Tony replies. "Next time you turn off the backup, how about you turn it back on when the call's over, hmm?"

Oh shit. "Is that what this is all about?" I ask, running a hand through my mussed hair. "Jeez, man, I'm sorry—"

"Sorry don't cut it." Now I notice Tony's rumpled jumpsuit, his bloodshot eyes, and I rub my elbow where I hit it as I fell out of bed. "Dixon's pissed to all hell—"

"Tell him it's my fault," I say, pulling myself up from the floor. My jumpsuit's hanging over my chair where I left it last night and I snag it now, step into it, one leg, then the other, as carefully as I can because I'm still woozy, not yet fully awake. "He *knows* it's me, right? What'd he do, chew your ass out about it?"

Tony laughs—the thought of him and Dixon going at it *is* a little humorous, Tony's the type who'll just nod in all the right places and Dixon wants reactions when he's yelling at you, it's not worth it if he can't get under your skin, which is why he hounds me much more than he does Tony. Tony's so laid back and easy going, it's hard to get him worked up about anything. Except girls, but there aren't many women on this station—most of them are on mapping crews and the few left, he's already had, or so he says. I don't ask for details—I don't want to know what goes on behind his closed door, especially not now when my own lover is gone and I'm not getting any myself.

That stops me, *my lover*—I haven't thought of Dylan as that since he left. *Watch yourself, James,* my mind warns. I zip up my jumpsuit slowly, my fingers numb. *You don't need to want him now. You were doing good, weren't you? You need to move on.*

And how am I supposed to do that if he's calling me again?

But moving on isn't turning off the backups so we can talk freely. Moving on isn't calling him *baby*—I didn't do that last night, did I? Moving on is forgetting the way we were, the way he looked beneath my sheets first thing in the morning, the way he would pull me back to the bed as I was getting dressed and kiss my knee, my hand, anything he could reach without having to get out from between the covers. "Come back here and love me," he'd say, and moving on isn't thinking about *that*, either, it doesn't help now, he's not here, is he? *Is he?*

No, he's not, Tony is, he's waiting for me and I'm still not sure why. As I pull on my boots, I ask, "What are you doing here again?"

Tony sighs. "Waking you up," he says, like I didn't know *that*. "Dixon's called a briefing on the situation. We have ten minutes to get to his office—"

"All I did was click the damn tape off," I tell him, shrugging into my thermo-vest. "Hell, it's not the end of the world. He needs to have a briefing about it? Can't he just bitch me out in private?"

"It's not just about you," Tony says with a smile. "He's got bigger things to worry about than you and your ex patching things up over the airwaves late at night." I kick his shin and he pulls his leg away. "Hey!"

"We weren't patching things up," I tell him. "Not that it's any of your damn business."

Tony rubs his leg and glares at me balefully. "Don't take it out on me. I was just kidding." It's nothing to kid about but I don't say that. I don't say anything at all—I'm just going to let it drop.

But he doesn't take the hint. "I didn't mean—"

"Fine," I say, cutting him off. "Just forget it, okay?"

"Fine," he mumbles. He favors his leg when he stands, like I hit him all that hard, and he actually hobbles to the door. "You coming? We've got eight minutes to get there."

I shove him through the door and out into the hall. "You want me to carry you?" I joke. Behind us, my door closes with a faint hum and I'd give anything to be back in the bed right now, Dylan's hands on me, even if only in my dreams. "I don't have to tell you I'm not looking forward to this," I say, giving Tony a push to get him moving.

"You think I am?" Tony asks. He blinks blearily and runs a hand down his scruffy face, pulling long furrows into his grizzled cheeks. No, I guess not.

We're the last to arrive at the briefing and everyone turns to look at us when we step into Dixon's office. A half-dozen fighter pilots, a handful of technicians, the medical crew and Dixon's staff, fifteen all tolled and Dixon's at the front of them with that insolent smirk of his. "Nice of you guys to decide to join us," he says, and there's something in his mocking tone of voice that makes me want to lunge at him, just for the satisfaction of seeing him flinch.

Tony runs a hand through his hair and grins that embarrassed grin of his, the one he's perfected that melts women's hearts and makes even the hardest men grin back. Without a word we slip into two chairs near the door. "We ready?" Dixon asks, and the others seem to lose interest in us, thank God, turning their attention to him. I wonder if he's told them about the backups—it's a silly gathering if that's what this is all about. The whole damn crew doesn't have to know about *that*.

But maybe Tony was right, maybe this *isn't* about me, because Dixon moves aside and turns on the screen behind his desk, where a map of the north sector lights up. A few familiar stars are labeled with ID numbers—once the entire sector is mapped, names will be assigned to them, but that's not our job. We're just here to punch in the coordinates, get them in the system. This sector can't be open for hypertravel until the stars are all pinned down and tagged, *then* they can run the cruise ships and heavy salvage barges through here. We have four crews out now—Dylan's to the north, two back behind us, and one in the Delta system, so close that we can sometimes catch a glimpse of their ship from the nav deck when we're angled the right way. There's enough pilots to send out more—the fighters don't mind going on short mapping jaunts, it's sitting around the station all day doing nothing that wears them down—but we're out of navigators. All crews need a navigator, it's space law, and we only have two left on the ship. One of them is Dixon's own who stays up on the bridge most days, I don't think I've seen her in weeks.

The other is me.

I'm a tech but I have nav training and I'm licensed, which pisses Dixon off to no end, I'm sure. He threw that up in my face when I asked to be transferred to Dylan's crew. "He already has a navigator," he told me. I said send me as a tech then, and he laughed. "And if something happens to one of my crews? If I *need* another navigator out there? What do I say, so sorry, he's out with his boyfriend, check back later? I don't think so."

Around us the lights dim and the stars on the screen seem to burn brighter. Dixon looks at me when he says, "The *Semper Fi* has picked up a signal out in the Epsilon system, here." With a laser pen, he points to a place off the screen, and the map scrolls to follow the little red dot. The Epsilon system is just a cluster of unmapped stars, not on our list of things to do because it's too far out there, no one cares about traveling out *that* way, so there's no need to map it just yet. Glancing around the room at the others gathered, Dixon continues. "It's in Morse, which suggests it's of human origin. From what we've managed to decode, it reads like a welcome message. There's a slim chance it might be one of the lost colonies of Operation Starseed—"

Soft murmurs erupt around the room. What, I'm the only one who never heard of it before? Raising his hands, Dixon calls for silence and waits until he has everyone's attention again. Beside me, Tony's still whispering to a cute redhead in front of him, one of the fighter pilots but I don't know her name, and when Dixon clears his throat, Tony sits back and mutters, "Sorry." The pilot grins and Tony starts to say something else but I elbow him quiet.

"We have to check it out," Dixon's saying, and I swear he keeps giving me a hateful look, like this signal is all my fault. "It's probably nothing more than an old relay stuck in a loop—" A few groans rise from the pilots. They're probably hoping for something more, some weird alien fleet that's trying to lure us into a trap, something so *Star Trek* that they can finally head out for something other than just maneuvers. Dixon forces a tight smile. "I know, child's play, but if we ignore it, then someone else coming through here later might pick it up and they'll want to know why we didn't investigate. We'll just send out a small crew, two fighters, that's it, just enough to cover the *Semper Fi* into Epsilon. I'm sure it'll just pan out—"

"Send Burke!" someone behind us calls out, and Dixon glares past me at the speaker as we all laugh. Eric Burke is a crackshot pilot, a real flying ace, but he's grounded for failure to obey orders. He can't seem to get it through his head when to come back onboard after the mock dogfights the pilots train at daily. The last time he lingered too long out there and Dixon laid into him, he turned his guns on *us*, and for a few hairy moments we all thought he'd actually try to take on a station like this with the turrets on his 778 starfighter. And he had the audacity to *laugh* when Dixon told him he was grounded, said he was kidding, couldn't we take a joke? Personally I wonder how funny he'd think it was if he *had* opened fire only to find that Dixon had the cannons manned and aimed at *him*. Basically that puts him on Dixon's shit list—his name's probably right up there under mine.

"Two fighters," Dixon says, and all six hands shoot up, including Burke's. But Dixon ignores them, holds up a piece of paper, rattles it like it's important and the hands go down, one by one. He's already made up his mind who he's sending out there, that much is obvious. "Milano and Parker, saddle up. You two get the honors this time."

Tessa Milano is a small woman with large blue eyes and long blonde hair—Tony says she visits him when he's on duty, I don't know how true that is, but she looks his type. She stands up and whoops loudly, high-fives Kitt Parker, who sits a few seats down from her. He's older than she is, one of those guys with a chiseled chin and thin hair that falls across his forehead, giving him a boyish air even though he's older than me. He and Dixon go way back—I'm sure that's how he got this pick. Dixon knows the pilots are getting restless for action and he could actually send all six of them, Burke included, they'd eat up the mission. But he doesn't play like that. He always likes to have someone left at the station in reserve, just in case one of the other crews runs into something out there. So Dylan gets only two fighters, that's it. I pray he doesn't even need that many. *Let it be a relay, nothing more,* I think. Beside me Tony's head drops to his chin and he shakes himself awake.

But Dixon's not through. Looking over the paper in his hands, he says, "Now the *Semper Fi* doesn't have a certified med tech onboard—"

"Our birds don't take passengers," Milano points out, as if Dixon doesn't know this. The star fighters are designed for one pilot, that's it. No gunner position, no navigator seat, nothing else.

Dixon silences her with a look. "You'll take one of the carriers," he tells her.

She flops back into her seat with a groan. "Those things are a bitch to fly," she mutters.

"Like piloting a brick," Parker adds. "Can't we just ditch the med?"

With a shake of his head, Dixon says, "We don't know how deep the origin is into Epsilon. Maybe a few klicks, maybe light years, we don't know. What I want is a carrier to meet up with the *Semper Fi*, and *then* you two take your birds, flank the ship into the system, fully loaded. You fly out there by yourselves and find the signal's deeper than we thought, then what? Where do you stop to refuel? What good are you to the crew then?"

That quiets them, but Milano slouches down into her seat and twists her gum like she's back in flight school and bored stiff during lecture, and Parker stares at the floor, chastised. With another glance at the paper, Dixon calls out, "Shanley." I hear Milano snort derisively. "You get this gig, too."

That's Evan Shanley, a male nurse with olive skin, soft doe eyes, and shoulder-length black hair he wears pulled back from his face in a tidy ponytail. Dixon likes him because he's quiet and doesn't talk back, does his job and doesn't worry about all the personal bullshit that goes on in a place like this. A good choice, if they're going to need a med tech, but I'm hoping it doesn't come to that. Just a relay, isn't that what Dixon said? For once I hope he's right.

Cracking her gum, Milano says, "Who else?" When Dixon doesn't answer immediately, she adds, "That's three, and we're on a carrier so we need a navigator, right? Space law—"

"James," he spits, and at first I don't realize he's talking about me. Then he tosses the paper down on his desk and turns off the star map. The screen goes blank, a stark white wall staring at us, and he brightens the lights. "Dismissed," he says. The shuffle of chairs seems muted to me, unreal. "I want you four ready to ship out in three hours—"

"Did he say me?" I ask Tony, who shrugs because he wasn't listening. *No, wait,* I want to say, but people are filing past me, heading for the door, and I can't seem to find my voice. *Me? I'm going out there for this? What—?*

At the front of the room Dixon laughs. "You wanted to be on that ship, didn't you?" he asks, throwing me a sadistic glance over one shoulder. "Here's your chance, tech. Live it up."

I wanted to go when I had Dylan, I think, but I'm not going to say that with this audience. I wait until the room clears out and then I hurry to Dixon's desk. He's already sliding in behind his console, probably going to send a message out to the *Semper Fi,* tell them to hold tight, we're on our way. *We.* What the hell am I doing going out there? And why the fuck is my heart hammering in my chest, my blood pounding in my ears? I'm not excited, I'm *not.* "Dixon."

He looks up at me and can't quite manage to hide that smirk of his before he says, "I'd suggest you get a move on, James. Three hours—"

"Do you find this funny?" I want to know. A few pilots lingering behind glance our way and I lean down over his desk, lower my voice so they won't overhear. "You're just doing this to be spiteful, aren't you? You *know* Dylan and I are—"

"I don't know shit about you two," Dixon interrupts. He turns back to his console and growls, "All I know is *someone* turned off the backup last night. The tape ends with the *Semper Fi* calling in and then nothing." The set of his jaw dares me to contradict him. I don't. "I've got a crew out there that needs support and space law says I need a navigator onboard any vessel I launch. I'm not giving up any more of my fighters than I have to so you're it."

Yeah, like this has *nothing* to do with the fact that he knows Dylan left me and he's banking that for all it's worth, he's doing this to make me uncomfortable, it's just another way for him to strike at me. "Fuck that," I mutter. "Do you get some perverse sense of joy out of doing this to me? How am I supposed to act when—"

Dixon sighs. "Try acting professional, James," he says, his voice hard. "Trust me, if I could send anyone else but you, I would. You can bitch and moan all you want but I think some part of you secretly enjoys this—"

"What?" I cry out, and behind me Tony rouses from his seat where he's falling asleep, mumbles my name. "You're fucking crazy if you think I *like* this shit. We broke up, Dixon. That's it, it's over between us, he said so himself and I thought I'd have time to get over that. The *last* thing I need is to be thrown into the lion's den."

"You're a navigator," Dixon reminds me. "It's your job. I don't care if you have a personal problem with the commander of the *Semper Fi*—I don't care that he dumped your ass or that you let him fuck you—"

"Just stop right there," I warn. My cheeks heat up and my head feels light, dizzy, my blood surges through my veins, making my hands shake and I have to curl them into fists so he doesn't see how badly he's gotten to me. "You don't want to touch that, I promise you."

He stares at me for a long moment as if weighing how far he can push me. *Not much farther, I'll guarantee,* I think, and maybe he reads that in my eyes because he turns back to the console, dismissing me. "You have a job to do," he says. "That's why you're here. Don't forget that."

"Dixon—" I start.

But he shakes his head. "I'm not hearing it, James. You're on that carrier in three hours or I'll have you brought up on charges for derelict duty, do you copy?"

I grind my teeth together to keep from saying anything I'll regret later. Glancing up at me, he asks, "Are we clear on this?"

I don't trust myself to speak. My jaw hurts, it's clenched so tight. But I manage a curt nod and storm from the room, Tony rushing to catch up.

Part 2

I hate the nervous thud of my heart in my throat as I stand with the others on the lower deck of the carrier and wait for the airlock to open. It took only two days' travel to reach the *Semper Fi* and another twelve hours positioning before we were lined up to receive the small ship. Through the intercom I could hear Dylan's voice as he guided the ship into our holding bay, joking with Milano to keep it steady and laughing when she told him to bite it. "Just get it in here already," she grumbled.

"That's what all the girls tell me," Dylan said with another laugh, and the cocky tone of his voice burned through me, eliciting a smile and a stirring in my groin that I refused to acknowledge.

The carrier shook slightly as the docking arms clamped onto the *Semper Fi* and it took all I had not to rush down to the airlock to see them at that moment. To see *him*—I'm terrified about this whole thing. He doesn't know I'm here, I didn't hail him *en route* and he didn't ask who all was on board, he only spoke with Milano and that was just when he docked. My only communications were with his own navigator, a sassy girl who worked with me on the coordinates to keep us off a collision course with each other, that was it. As far as I know, he's going to be surprised to see me. *Just let him be happy I'm here*, I pray as I stand behind Milano, who leans against the wall with her arms crossed, tapping one foot impatiently. *Don't let him look at me and groan, don't let him ignore me. That's all I ask.*

Beside us Shanley and Parker check the DAQ screens, running diagnostics on the *Semper Fi* and her crew to make sure they can safely come aboard. It's standard procedure, checking for contamination or structure damage, but I want to just hit the override button and get them in here *now*. On the vidscreen I can see the crew inside the airlock, two women and two men. Dylan's closest to the door and despite the security camera's poor quality, I can see his hair has grown longer, it's parted in the middle and hangs down either side of his face in a soft swag—I love that. *I love him*, I tell myself, but I'm still not admitting it and when the thought is gone, I don't pursue it.

Finally Shanley gets a green light on his medcam. "It's a go," he says, his voice almost feminine, it's so soft, and I wonder whoever told him that was a cool phrase to use, *it's a go*—they should be shot. Folding out the handheld bio-scanner he'll use to examine the crew more closely, he says, "If your systems check out—"

Parker nods. "They do." With another nod to Milano, he tells her, "Let them in."

All this just to open the damn door. I keep back as the hydraulics start to whine and there's a slight *pop* when the seals separate, then the hatch slides open. Dylan is the first through the door, his head down, watching his step over the lip of the door frame. "Jesus," he sighs. The other crew members file in behind him and I know their names from the log—service tech Leena Chen, navigator Vallery Andrews, radio tech Mike Johnson—but I can't put the faces to them. Except for Mike, I'm assuming he's the guy with the short blonde hair twisted into the beginnings of dreadlocks that hang in his eyes. And then there's Dylan Teague, pilot and commander and my ex-lover, and just seeing him again makes my chest hurt with each shallow breath I take. With a quick smile at his crew, he says, "I thought you guys were gonna make us sit out there all day—"

Then he looks up, sees me, and the rest of his words die, his smile freezes, he stops. *Surprise*, I feel like saying, but that would be mean.

Instead I force a lopsided grin, one corner of my mouth wanting to smile and the other not quite following its lead. This close he's everything I remembered and more, gorgeous, those eyes, that smile, the scruff of hair along his jaw where he hasn't been shaving—that makes him look old, older than the boy I knew, and maybe I was wrong, maybe we *have* changed and it's a good thing we broke up because maybe he's moved on without me.

But there's something in his eyes that tells me he's still just as lost in me as I am in him, and I have to look away so I don't drown in that gaze. "Hey Dylan," I mumble. It's the most I can come up with right now.

Everyone else disappears. Vaguely I'm aware of Shanley and that stupid scanner of his as he runs it up and down and all over the crew members like a metal detector. He hovers around Dylan like a pesky fly, but Dylan stares at me, at *me*, and he still hasn't said anything yet. *He's speechless*, I think, and I press my lips into a thin line so I don't smile at that thought. I like to think I've done this to him, I've made him this way, me. "Arms up," Shanley says, and Dylan raises his arms at his side mechanically. "Turn around."

Somehow he manages to do that without taking his eyes off me. "Neal?" he finally asks, and when the scanner in Shanley's hand beeps, he pushes past the med tech and closes the distance between us, his hand already reaching for mine. It stops above my wrist like he's just remembered we're not dating anymore, he doesn't have a right to touch me like that, it's over between us. *Your fault, Dylan*, I think, staring into his eyes. He's just inches from me and I have to look up at him, he's a head taller and I can't seem to look past his lips, I can feel the memory of them pressed against mine. I know the way his skin feels, so soft, his unshaven jaw like the downy flesh of a peach, my fingers can still feel it. "God," he sighs, reaching for me again, but when I don't respond, he stops and his hands drift to his waist, prop up on his hips just for something to do. "What the hell are you doing here?"

"Navigator," I whisper, and Dylan laughs. The surprise is gone now, replaced with an eagerness I thought I'd never see again. "They needed someone—"

"So they sent you." His eyes widen and he lets his gaze drift down my chest, my waist, lower—I can almost *feel* that look he's giving me, like a hand on my body, tender and hungry at the same time. "Damn, you look good."

Well, no, I don't, I know I don't. I've been on this carrier going on three days now and I must look like shit. But look at him, he's been on the *Semper Fi* for two months and in my eyes he looks like a god, beautiful and amazing. I feel awkward beside him, I always have, because he's such a pretty boy with a smile like the sun and laughing eyes and strong hands, thin muscles, hard sculpted planes along his face and chest and thighs. An athlete's build, slim, and he used to tell me he loved my thicker frame, my round ass, my fleshy biceps. He used to say he felt safe when I held him, like a little boy hiding away from the rest of the world, and he'd snuggle up against me in the bed and wrap his arms around my waist, hold on tight like he'd never let me go. *Only you did,* I think as he stares at me, devouring me with his gaze. *And now you're looking at me like that and what am I supposed to think, Dylan? You're practically undressing me in your mind here and how the hell are we supposed to be just friends when simply looking at you again makes me so hard it hurts? How can we be friends when I still want so much more than that from you?*

I wish I could ask him, but I don't.

❦ ❦ ❦

Once the crew is settled into the carrier, I retreat to the safety of the nav deck. I can't sit in the cafeteria with seven other people and pretend Dylan's not there, not when he looks at me the way he does, the hint of a smile on his face matching the promise I see in his eyes. Every time he opens his mouth to speak, I feel like a gawkish teenager, and I know the others see this, they *must*. The way he makes me feel, the way I stare at him, the way he watches me, like he didn't sit on my bunk two months ago and tell me we shouldn't be exclusive, at least not right now. Every time he laughs, I smile at him. Every time he winks at me, I flush. When his knee nudges mine beneath the table, I almost knock over my glass of water, I'm that jittery. I have to get out of here.

So I mumble some lame excuse and hurry to the nav deck, where it's dark like a womb and I can hide away from everyone else for a little while, at least. The only lights come from the displays on the control panel and the few stars beyond the console window. Leaning back in my seat, I stare out at those stars and hope Dixon's getting a good laugh out of this. God, I feel like I did when I first met Dylan and he was so untouchable, I could have cried for wanting him. I can still close my eyes and remember how he caught up to me in the corridor one day, shortly after take-off. "I see the way you look at me," he said, and at that moment I wished the floor would open up beneath my feet, swallow me whole. *He knows,* I remember thinking. *He knows*—"It's okay," he told me then, lowering his voice. He rubbed a hand down my arm and my skin tingled beneath his touch. "I just wanted to let you know that I'm interested," he whispered. "If you are."

"In what?" I managed to ask. He's like a drug, heady, numbing, and at the time I couldn't imagine actually touching him, kissing him, loving him. It was too much—the image of the two of us locked together in throes of passion, it was enough to drive me insane.

He simply smiled that sunny grin of his and with a quick wink, said, "You know in what." I must've looked shocked, or scared, or both, because he laughed. "Yes, *that.*" Sobering up, he leaned closer and breathed, "My room's on the lower deck. If you want—"

"Mine's just down the hall," I replied.

That's all it took, I think now, settling back into the plush chair in front of the control panel. I can hear the steady blip of the nav system, honing in on the coordinates I plugged in earlier, and beneath that is the constant Morse code message, stuttering quietly to itself. One night and I was his, we were inseparable. Eight months later I thought nothing could come between us, and then he said goodbye.

Behind me the door cycles open and someone enters the deck. *Vallery*, I think, it has to be—the *Semper Fi*'s navigator is a young woman Dylan's age, with long brown hair she wears pulled back in a ponytail that falls halfway down her back. She has pretty eyes, bright and dark, and an almost careless air about her, like she doesn't quite realize just how attractive she is. But she's smart, I'll give her that. She helped me program the carrier to follow the signal and then laughed when I thanked her like it was nothing. "Dylan tells me you know Tony," she said, and I wondered what *else* Dylan told her—I wonder if she knows about him and me. "I hear he likes the ladies." I said he did and she laughed again. "When we get back, you introduce me to him, okay?" As if she needs my help—Tony will be all over a girl like her the minute she's onboard the station.

The door eases shut with a muted hiss and I glance up, only it's not Vallery standing over me, it's Dylan, and we're finally alone now, the two of us in this darkened room and damn him for sneaking in on me like this. "Hey," he murmurs. He comes around in front of me and leans back on the control panel, crosses his ankles, dares to touch my knee. His hand is warm through my jumpsuit, which is suddenly too thin and growing hot beneath his touch. "I wondered where you ran off to."

"I didn't run off," I tell him, but who am I kidding? I'm avoiding him, or at least, I was. His hand moves a little ways up my thigh and I sigh, a shaky sound between us. "Dylan, don't."

He pulls his hand away. I feel naked without his touch and I want to tell him I didn't mean for him to stop, not *really*, but I can't, not until I know where we stand. He lowers his chin to his chest and picks at the zipper on his jumpsuit, and I don't have to see his face to know he's pouting. He's got a childish streak in him that I want to hide away from the rest of the world, an innocence I want to protect.

"I didn't," he starts, and then he falls silent again, like he's changed his mind about what he wants to say. "Neal."

"Yes?" I ask. I'm falling back on my professional air, it keeps the distance open, keeps us apart. When he doesn't answer, I add, "We're on a steady course. The signal's getting stronger. I don't think it'll take too long to get to the origin—"

He sighs as if I'm boring him. "Is that all we have to say to each other?" he wants to know.

I shrug. *It's your fault,* I think. It's easier to lay all the blame on him. Trying to steer the conversation to something more personal, he asks, "How have you been doing?"

"Okay," I lie, but I'm sure he sees right through that one, it's in the way I can't quite meet his eyes. "You?"

"Okay," he echoes. Now we're both lying to each other, has it come to this? Softly, he asks, "Are you, I don't know…is there someone else? I mean—" He presses his lips together as if it pains him to even say the words. "Are you seeing anyone?"

My heart twists in my chest. "No," I whisper.

Relief floods his features and before I can say anything else, he's kneeling beside my chair, his hands holding my own where they rest in my lap. "Please," he says, and it's almost a sob in the darkness. His eyes shine like the stars out the window behind him and he kisses my knuckles, his flesh against mine so soft, so warm, just as I remembered. "God, Neal, I'm sorry. I don't know what I was thinking, I didn't want to lose you, I didn't—"

"How did you put it?" I ask, trying to extract my hands from his, but he won't let go. "Something might happen to me, isn't that what you said? I don't want you lonely—weren't those your words?"

"I was wrong," he whispers, his lips on my wrist. *I'm not buying this,* I tell myself, *I'm not,* but I can't seem to find the strength to pull away. "Neal, I was wrong, okay? You're all I think about, you're all I *care* about, please—"

"Because I'm here now," I say. He shakes his head, the wings of his hair brushing against my fingers, and when did I start to stroke through it? He holds one of my hands in both of his and the other's roaming through his soft hair and wait a minute here, this isn't what I want, is it? *Bullshit,* my mind whispers, and my fingers clench in his hair. I hate that I'm so weak against him. *This is exactly what I want.* "You never called in, not once."

Dylan buries his head in my lap, a familiar, comfortable weight, and his faint breath tickles across my crotch. "I was scared," he admits. "So scared, Neal, I thought I'd ruined the best thing I'll ever have. I didn't want to call in and hear your voice, I wasn't ready for that. I thought I was doing what was right, you know? I thought it wasn't fair to go off and leave you there and that's why I said we should cool things down a bit. And I knew you didn't think so, you tried to tell me and I just wouldn't listen, and the last thing I wanted was to call in and hear your voice and have you turn me away just because I was an ass. I know I was, okay? I'm sorry, baby, I didn't mean it, I was an ass and I'm so sorry, please…"

"Shh," I whisper, and he presses my fingers to his mouth to keep quiet.

"I'm sorry," he breathes. His voice cracks slightly and it hurts to hear him like this, it hurts to know that he aches for me just as much as I do for him, and if we could've just talked this out before he left then we wouldn't be here now, trying to salvage something we both tried so desperately to put behind us. "Neal—"

"Shh," I whisper again. I pull him to his feet and into my lap. His heavy weight settles against my hips and thighs and pushes into the beginning of an erection at my crotch. He leans his head on my chest, wraps his arms around my waist, holds me tight. With trembling hands I smooth down his jumpsuit where it's bunched around his shoulders, brush my fingers along his neck. He feels so right here, in my arms. Why did I ever let him go? "It's okay, Dylan." Here, in the dark, just the two of us, he's so young again, needy and trusting like a little boy clinging to me. I love how he lets his defenses down around me, how he lets me see him like this, when he's his most vulnerable. I hug him close and sigh his name against his temple. He smells so strong, the thick musk cologne he favors surrounding us in a warm haze, and I know I've forgiven him, there's nothing *to* forgive. "I love you," I tell him.

His hands bunch into fists at my sides. "I was an ass," he murmurs against my throat. "Take me back, Neal, please. I'm not asking you to wait two years if you don't want to but please—"

"I told you I'd wait forever," I remind him. He looks at me and whatever else I was going to say is lost when he presses his lips to mine.

🍁   🍁   🍁

He doesn't ask to stay with me, just takes my hand when he rises from my lap and pulls me to my feet, eases his arms around my waist, kisses me with such tenderness that my knees go weak and the only thing holding me up is him. And I thought I could live without this man? He thought he could make it without me?

He follows me from the nav deck, down the corridor, to the room where I sleep. Inside the bunk is already pulled out, the sheets twisted together in a heap in the middle of the mattress where I left them this morning. I don't even bother to turn on the light, just hit the switch to close the door behind us and then his hands are on me, relearning the contours of my body. They fumble with my zipper, ease my jumpsuit off my shoulders, push the confining material down and out of the way and to the floor. His lips are hungry on my skin, leaving damp trails along my jaw and neck, his tongue licking its way to my mouth. Without a word he leads me to the bunk, and when he sits down, I stand above him, unzip his jumpsuit, push him back to the mattress and climb onto him, this is all so familiar to me, this is the way we're meant to be.

His hands erase the past two months, the lonely nights, the sad memories and distant dreams. His kisses remind me of how much he loves me—he whispers the words into the hollows of my body, hidden places he finds again, my secrets that are his. Soon the sweaty sheets cling to our naked bodies, twine around us until we're one moving in an ancient rhythm, a dance of lust and desire and need that consumes our souls. I love him, this man beneath me, in me, part of me, and when he arches against me, my name a breathless rush from his lips, I press him back against my pillow and kiss his neck, my hands fisted in his hair. "Don't do that to me again," I sigh, and he nods, clinging to me as our hearts beat together, slowing down, our former ardor passed. "Don't leave me again, Dylan. I won't let you."

His reply is a kiss, two, five, a hundred that become just his mouth on mine, his hands on my body, and I breathe his name as he rolls onto me, unsatiated, wanting more, wanting *me,* and I can't deny him that because all I want, all I've ever wanted, is him.

✤   ✤   ✤

In the morning he's there beside me, curled against my back. It's a glorious feeling, waking to him again. I feel his hands flat along my stomach, his knees pressed against my thighs, his head tucked into the space between my shoulder blades where I'd have wings if I could fly. As I shift beneath the covers, he tightens his arms around me and murmurs my name. When I kiss it from his lips, he squeezes his eyes shut and scrunches up his face like a little kid. "Go back to sleep," he sighs. "It's too early to be up."

"That's easy for you to say," I tell him, punctuating my words with another kiss. Now that his ship's docked in our bay, he's just a passenger until Milano and Parker take to their fighters and he's left to pilot the carrier. But me? I'm the navigator here, I've got to get up and check the systems and make sure we're still on course. I try to disentangle myself from his arms but every time I pull one hand away, the other finds another part of my body to hold onto, until we're both awake and giggling, hands all over each other. "Dylan."

"What?" he asks, as if he doesn't know. He has a slow, sly grin that makes me laugh, and that makes him raise his eyebrows, curious. "What?" he asks again.

"Nothing," I say, resting against him. He holds me close and this is the first morning I can remember in a long time that I've woken up and wanted to stay awake. It's the first day I've felt alive since he left me and even now that memory is fading like a bad dream, the past two months are gone, they didn't happen, they don't exist. It's just me and him and anything without the two of us in it isn't worth remembering anymore.

I wait until he cuddles up to me, relaxing, his eyes already slipping shut again, before I sit up quick. He's not expecting it and I manage to slide from the bed and dance out of his reach when he grabs for me. "Come back here," he growls, playful.

I laugh defiantly at him. "Come get me," I say, picking up my jumpsuit from the floor.

I manage to step into it and pull it over my ass before he takes me up on my offer. He tumbles from the bed, the sheets falling away from his nakedness, and wraps his arms around my waist, pulls me to him. "I'm not letting you go," he whispers into my hair, and I laugh again, try to twist away, but it's only a halfhearted gesture, I don't *want* him to let me go. I'm thinking we can maybe steal another half hour—it *is* early, and maybe no one else is up yet. Even if they are, surely they can run the damn ship without our help for a little while longer. Dylan's hands slip lower, cupping my budding erection through the open zipper of my suit, and maybe we *can* spare another few minutes at least.

We only make it as far as the bed when someone knocks on the door, interrupting us. Above me Dylan drops his head to my shoulder and sighs. "Maybe if we're really quiet, they'll go away," he murmurs. Somehow I don't think so.

The knock comes again and I push against his chest, rolling him off of me. "I'll get rid of them," I promise. I want him as badly as he wants me, it's obvious when I stand up, he can *see* my need before I wrap the sheet around my waist to cover my crotch. When I hit the switch, the door cycles out of the way and Vallery's standing there, her hair yanked back from her face so severely, her eyes look slanted. She takes one look at me, naked except for the sheet draped across my groin—then she looks behind me, sees Dylan curled in my covers, and it's times like this when I hate these automatic doors that reveal everything. Whoever thought these contraptions were an improvement over manual doors never had a lover stretched out in his bed when someone came calling. "Hey, Val," I murmur.

"I'm sorry," she stammers, and it's enough that her cheeks pink and she looks away, embarrassed. "I didn't know—"

"It's okay," Dylan tells her. "I'd say it's not what you think but I'd be lying."

Placing a hand above her eyes to shield them, she looks at the ground and mumbles, "I'm not thinking anything right now, trust me."

Behind me, Dylan laughs. "You just come for the show?" he asks, and I swear her cheeks turn a brighter shade of red. "Or was there something else you needed?"

"Dylan," I admonish softly. He reaches out from the bed and I don't know how he manages to stretch so far, but he tugs at the sheet I wear. Slapping his hand away, I try to glare at him and can't quite manage it, not when he winks my way. I turn back to the door and start, "Val—"

"We've traced the origin," she says, speaking quickly. "You're sort of in the middle of things here, I understand, it can wait." She holds up one hand to cut off my protest. "No, really. Just stop by the nav deck when you're…when you're done." She hurries away down the corridor before I can reply.

Laughing, I lean on the switch, hold it down as the door irises shut. "The mood's shot anyway," I start.

But I turn and see Dylan's smoldering eyes, shining with naked lust, and he grabs hold of the sheet around me, reels me to him, and maybe I'm wrong, maybe we can still get things going here after all. When I'm close enough to the bed, he tears the sheet away, tosses it to the ground, and pulls me down beside him. "It's not *completely* shot," he whispers, his lips closing over a part of me that agrees. "She said it can wait. I can't."

"Remind me to thank Dixon next time I radio the station," I say, losing myself in him again. Much as I hate to admit it, this is all his fault, too, the two of us getting back together. I'm sure he's going to love to hear *that*.

When we finally make it to the deck, Vallery has the signal turned up and a quick glance at the data screen tells me we've picked up speed. Out the window I can see the nose of one of the fighters to our left, flanking us. "What's up?" I ask, sinking into an empty chair in front of the control panel beside Vallery's.

She points up in the air to draw my attention to the signal. "It's changed," she says as Dylan sits on the arm of my seat. "Last ten minutes or so, right after we homed in on the source." Dylan cocks his head to one side and frowns, as if he's trying to make out the meaning beneath the staccato bursts of code. "Nothing to be alarmed about," Vallery continues, handing me a log sheet. On it the new message is printed out—a series of lengthy coordinates pinpointing a course through the Epsilon system. "I think it's sort of like a welcome mat, you know?" Dylan leans against my shoulder to read the message, and despite the matter at hand I can't ignore the warmth of his body against mine. I love him, have I mentioned that? "They know we're tracking the signal so they're making it easy for us, giving us a road map to guide us through the stars."

"That would suggest it's not a relay, then," Dylan murmurs. Stretching an arm across the back of my chair to support himself, Dylan looks at me with an eager grin on his face. "Maybe it *is* one of the lost colony ships."

Vallery laughs, excited. "Maybe it's an alien society," she offers. I see the gleam in her eyes, it matches the one in Dylan's, and they're getting carried away with this, just a little, aren't they? "Maybe they learned Morse code from our transmissions or something. There are so many radio signals out there, just bouncing around for years and years. Who's to say something else hasn't found one and learned our language and is now trying to communicate with us?"

"Who's to say it's anything like that?" I counter, handing the sheet back to her. I lean back in my seat and avoid looking at either of them, I don't want to see the disappointment I've put in their eyes. Running an arm around Dylan's waist, my hand resting high on his thigh, I tell them, "It could still be a relay, we just don't know. Maybe it's configured to change the signal when someone's locked into it." At Vallery's sigh, I add, "I don't think it's aliens. Nothing in the annals ever corroborated the idea of intelligent life out here. I seriously doubt we'll be the ones to find it after all this time."

Vallery pouts prettily and smoothes her hands over the log sheet as if the message is written in Braille and she can read it with her fingertips. "You never know," she mumbles.

"Do you think it might be one of the Starseed ships?" Dylan asks, leaning back beside me. He scoots down until he can rest his head on top of mine, a heavy, welcome weight.

I shrug, noncommittal. "If it is, they're all dead by now, I'm sure." It's been twenty years since that mission, right? I can't imagine any colonist effort setting out with enough supplies for all this time, not for a hundred terraformers. In a quiet voice, I tell him, "Chances are they ran out of fuel or food before they found an inhabitable planet and this signal's all that's left." When neither of them answer, I sigh.

"I'm sorry, guys. I just don't think it's going to turn out to be anything all that exciting."

Suddenly Vallery slaps my arm. "Well," she says, flipping her ponytail over one shoulder, "at least let us *pretend* it's gonna be cool. I mean, until we know for sure, okay?"

Surprised, Dylan and I start to laugh. She's a cute girl, Tony's going to love her when we get back, I just know he will. She smacks me again and I catch her wrist, hold it until she manages to twist free from my grip. "Okay, fine," I say, grinning at her. She wants to think it's aliens out there? Fine, if that's what makes her happy. "What's our ETA?" I ask, hoping to steer the subject away from little green men. I haven't really studied the screens and with Dylan leaning against me the way he is, I don't feel like moving just yet.

"Two days," she says, "tops. I replotted our course with these coords once the computer spat them out and it's not as far out there as we assumed it would be. Tessa says we're so close, she wanted to take up a position, so she's switching with Parker every hour on the hour. They want to keep one fighter in the sky at all times. Once we get within a few thousand klicks, they'll both get out there." Leaning forward, Vallery fiddles with a few buttons, nothing major, just something to keep herself busy. I rub a smooth spot into Dylan's thigh and he takes my hand in both of his, laces his fingers through mine. When he brushes my knuckles across his lips, I grin up at him and he blows me a kiss. I see Vallery's reflection in the window—she glances at us, then looks away, a slight smile on her face. I wonder if he told her about me during those two months they spent together on the *Semper Fi*. I wonder if he told her he still loved me, he missed me, he wanted me back. She doesn't seem too surprised that we're together, even if she did interrupt us earlier, so I'm sure he must have mentioned me before. "Two days," she says again, "if that. I added a little thrust to the boosters just because it's closer than we thought. If you're right and it's nothing to write home about—"

"It's not," I assure her as Dylan picks at the hairs along the back of my wrist.

"Then we'll be back at the station in no time," she says, flashing us a quick grin before turning back to the panel. *Only now I don't want to return,* I think. I squeeze Dylan's hand in mine and wonder how we'll ever manage to part when this whole thing is over and I have to leave him again.

❦   ❦   ❦

The carrier's still on course, the signal growing stronger every hour, and by midnight Vallery all but throws us off the nav deck, telling us to go get some sleep, come back in the morning. "Just don't come knocking when I'm getting my groove on," Dylan says with a wink.

"Don't worry," she promises, "I won't."

Back in my room we lie together on my bed, wrapped around each other so comfortably, I don't think either of us will get up any time soon. "I told her about you," Dylan says when I ask him about Vallery. With a laugh, he adds, "Jesus, how do you think I made it through these past few months? There were times I was ready to just turn the *Semper Fi* around and race back to your arms, mission be damned. And then I'd think you never wanted to see me again and God, I would've gone insane if she didn't let me dump it all out on her."

"Poor girl," I murmur, and he laughs at me, kisses my cheek, pulls me closer. I wonder what that was like, though, having someone to talk with about us. I never mentioned it to anyone, not really—the most I told Tony was that it was over between us when he asked why I wasn't on hand to see the *Semper Fi* off. Everything else he clued in on his own. He's very perceptive, not as stupid as he likes people to think, but he plays well at the bumbling, self-depreciating oaf, and the girls fall for his *aw shucks* act so I guess it works for him. He's just not the type to ask me what I'm going through, and I'm not one to offer. When I get back to the station he might ask me how things went out here with Dylan, he might not. If he does, I'll just say we got it straight, end of story.

But Dylan's not like that—he bleeds emotions, rage and anger and love and desire, it's all raw to him, all real, and if he can't feel it completely, if it doesn't consume him, then it's not worth feeling at all. He's told me he likes me the way I am, closed off almost, because it makes prying beneath my shell and getting inside all the more worthwhile. Personally, I like him inside, deep inside me where he'll never resurface and I'm the world to him. He's the only one I allow in that far, and when I stare into his deep blue eyes, I feel like giving in, giving up, giving him anything his heart desires because he's my world, too. He's all that matters to me.

His other two crew members know about us, too, Mike and Leena. The systems tech has short blonde hair cut close to her scalp that stands up in wiry spikes, and when I run into her in the corridor, she bumps me with her hip and says, "I told him he was wrong to let a boy like you slip away. I'm Leena—" She holds out a hand which I shake warily. "You keep a tight rein on that one, you hear? A guy like him doesn't know what he's got til it's gone. He's damn lucky you took him back."

I laugh. "What'd he do, tell the whole crew about me?"

"You know how he is," she says, and I nod because yes, I do know, all too well. He's vocal and outspoken and he loves me, he shouts it in the corridors when he sees me, his voice echoing off the steel walls and I'm glad there's only eight of us on this damn carrier, I'm glad there's not a whole ship full of people who can hear him.

Most of all, I'm glad *Dixon* can't hear him, I'd never live *that* down. You'd think we'd be further than such petty bigotry after all this time, all these years, but I guess not. He's the only person I've ever met who had a problem with me being the way I am—liking boys, the way I do. Liking *Dylan*. I think that's what bothers him the most, actually, not that I get it on with a guy but that it's his star pilot who's schmooping over me like a lovesick puppy. *That* pisses the hell out of him. If I was with Tony or anyone else, he wouldn't give two shits about me. Dylan falls in love and bam, I'm public enemy number one.

But now we're back together, I tell myself, and I can live with Dixon's ignorant remarks because I know Dylan didn't leave me for the mission, I know Dylan *loves* me. I for one am going to love the look on Dixon's face when he hears that we're back together again. I hope I'm there to see it, and I won't hide my smirk then, oh God no. I can hardly wait.

❦   ❦   ❦

The next day finds me alone on the nav deck, leaning back in my chair and staring out at the stars, thinking about my boy and how he's in the med lab right this minute with Shanley, going over the inventory. If I sit up, I can see the nose of Parker's bird out to our right, giving the carrier a wide berth as he keeps a steady watch. Around me the deck is filled with the incessant *beep beep blip beep* of the signal, a tuneless rhythm I begin to tap out on my knees, steady, regular, unending.

Then it changes. I wouldn't have noticed if I wasn't keeping time and my fingers missed a beat, another, a third. "What the—?" I mutter, sitting up slowly. The code *sounds* the same to me, mostly, but there are a *few* inconsistencies, and I've heard of relays programmed to switch to another signal when detected but what prompted *this* change? Quickly, I type in the commands to decode the signal again. At the far end of the control panel, a printer comes to life and starts to spit out the translation.

I snatch up the log sheet and study it—the code *has* changed. There's the welcome message, the "Greetings, all who hear this" bit that played over and over when Dylan first intercepted the signal.

Then the coordinates follow, the course we've been on since the code changed the day before. Out of habit I check the computer's compass, just to make sure we're still on track.

We are. Another thirteen hours until we reach the origin, according to the timestamp, and as I watch the display, the green digital numbers flicker from *13:00:04* and down, counting down, until it's only *13:00:00* and then it's *12:59:59*. We'll get there soon enough.

Beneath the coordinates on the log sheet is the new message. At first I think it's a variation of the first message, nothing more. "Welcome, traveler," it reads, and then, "S410 eagerly awaits your arrival. Comm-link will open three hours before you land. Hope to speak with you then. Unarmed and are at your mercy. Repeat, no weapons. No defense. Request the following decontamination procedures be implemented ASAP."

Decontamination procedures. They're outlined in quick bursts like bullets. Micronuclear bioscan. Dermafollicle cleansing. Hemothermal sterilization. I don't know what any of this means but it sounds unnecessary to me—each of us has been through the bioscans when we boarded this ship. We're all clean. Why should we do it all over again? *Nine hours and we'll find out,* I think, glancing over the message a second time. I assume they plan to contact us when we near the origin, whoever *they* turn out to be. They're opening a comm-link to us, right? *It's just a relay,* I remind myself, *no one waiting for us, nothing but a computer someone forgot to turn off long ago, calling out to anyone who's listening.*

Still, I have to admit I'm feeling a little excited now—maybe the S410 *is* a part of Operation Starseed, and even if the colonists are all dead and gone, something out there's working, sending us these signals, right? Something's "eagerly awaiting our arrival," as they put it, and the least I can do is show the decontamination wish list to Shanley. He *is* the med tech, after all. This sort of stuff should be right up his alley.

With a final glance over the control panel to make sure everything's still going strong, I duck through the door before it irises open fully and hurry down the corridor, log sheet in hand.

❦   ❦   ❦

When I enter the med lab, Dylan is in one of the patient's chairs, the ones with metal trays built into their armrests and a spotlight clipped to the back. He looks up from the box of unopened lancets he's riffling through and gives me one of his sunshine grins. Nearby Shanley squats on the ground with a clipboard on his lap—he glances up as I enter. "Neal," he says in that soft voice of his. "Dylan was just talking about you."

"Hey, baby," Dylan murmurs, and I lean down to give him a quick kiss but he has other plans and his tongue slips between my lips, he grabs the front of my jumpsuit, holds me down and doesn't want to let me go. "You miss me?"

I laugh and run a hand through his wayward hair. "You know I did." I keep my voice low so Shanley doesn't overhear. "What've you been saying about me?"

"Just how much I love you," Dylan replies. He makes no effort to keep his voice down, but Shanley isn't listening, he's busy with the inventory. *At least someone is,* I think, watching Dylan play with the supplies. He picks up a handful of the tiny lancets, little nubs no bigger than the tip of his thumb, each one wrapped in a plastic seal that crinkles when he lets them fall between his splayed fingers. It's obvious he's contributing as little as possible to this whole inventory effort, and he's just looking for a way out of the next few hours of counting pills and bandages and sutures with no one but Shanley for company. Kissing me again, he asks, "Evan? Don't you have someplace else you can go?"

Without looking up from his clipboard, Shanley counters, "Don't you?"

Dylan sighs lustily and rolls his eyes, as if this is all a big inconvenience to him. "No privacy," he mutters, and he sounds so sincere, I have to laugh. That makes him grin. "There's an examining table in the back," he says with a wink. "Fifteen minutes, baby, please? I need a break."

To be honest? I'd love to, and the thought of stretching him out on the table back there, the coated paper rustling beneath him, noisy and loud as we make love…it's tempting. But Shanley's busy and he's right, we don't need to be getting it on *here* when we have my room for that, even if it's not quite as adventurous. Remembering the log sheet in my hand, I hold it up like it's the only thing stopping me from a midday tryst. "Much as I'd love to, I can't," I tell him, speaking quietly. "*Some* of us have work to do."

He cuts me off with another kiss. "Since when?" he wants to know, taking the sheet from me. "What's this?"

"The signal's changed again." A slight frown creases his forehead as he reads through the new message. Leaning over his shoulder, I point at the decontamination procedures and add, "This part strikes me as odd."

Dylan laughs. "Only that part? What about the rest of it? They're going to open a comm-link? What the fuck?" I see the shine in his eyes when he glances up at me and I know what he's thinking before he even speaks. "And you're still sticking to this relay theory, aren't you?"

I shrug—I don't want to tell him that I've been thinking maybe, just maybe, there's a slim chance someone might be out there. It's improbable as hell and I don't want to get his hopes up, I know he wants this to be something big, and if I tell him he might be right, the S410 *might* be a colony ship, part of Operation Starseed, and one or two people *might* still be alive onboard, sending us those signals, *maybe*, then he'll get carried away with the idea and I don't want him crushed when it turns out Dixon's right after all and it *is* just a relay, nothing else. I don't want to do that to him, so I mumble, "I don't know what I think."

He studies me a moment longer and I can tell he knows I'm holding out on him, but then he looks away and doesn't push it further. He might later, when we're alone and I'm holding him close and he has me right where he wants me, when he's the only thing that exists and I'm his completely, but he lets it drop for now. "What's hemothermal sterilization?" he asks, turning back to the log sheet.

"That's what I'm here to find out," I tell him. With a distracting kiss on his cheek, I pluck the sheet from his hands and walk around his chair to Shanley. Handing him the sheet, I say, "You might want to take a look at this."

Shanley stands, takes the sheet, studies it for so long that I'm almost afraid he's fallen asleep on his feet. Behind me, Dylan runs a hand along the small of my back, lower, lower, until it cups between my buttocks and I slap at it. "Not now," I whisper. But he does it again, his fingers rubbing against hidden flesh, and when I reach for him a second time, he pulls away. "Stop it," I hiss over my shoulder. He only winks back, blows me a kiss. I try to glare at him, but who am I kidding here? He's adorable and he's mine. Once again, he's mine.

Beside me, Shanley frowns. "What's our window here?" he asks. He turns the paper over as if there might be something written on the other side but there isn't, so he turns it back and rereads the message when he finds that's all there is. "These procedures are pretty extensive—"

"Twelve hours," I tell him. "Less than that, now. What are these things?"

"Micronuclear bioscan," Shanley says, pointing at the words on the sheet, "that's a fairly standard procedure. Just a little more intensive than what we go through clearing into the ship, but it doesn't take long. Fifteen minutes each, tops. But with eight people—"

"That's two hours," Dylan says behind us. His hand snakes between my legs again and this time I catch his wrist, pull his arm around my waist, lace my fingers through his and hold him tight. Standing, he comes up behind me, presses his body against mine, rests his chin on my shoulder and looks at the sheet in Shanley's hands. "It's just a scan, that's it?" he asks. Shanley nods. "What about the other two?"

Shanley's frown deepens and he stares at the sheet, doesn't look up as Dylan's other arm slips around my waist and he holds me close. I'm not a public person, not like Dylan is, all touchy-feely in front of others, but I've been without him for so long and I never thought we'd be like this again, I never dreamed we'd be together so soon, and Shanley doesn't seem to mind so I don't let it bother me. "Dermafollicle cleansing," he reads, and then, "Hemothermal sterilization. The cleansing's easy enough, just submersion in an antiseptic solution, nothing much. The hemo though, that'll take time. In med school we called it the boil. Not fun."

"How much time?" I want to know.

Behind me, Dylan sighs. "It sounds painful. I don't like that *s* word."

A smile flitters across Shanley's thin lips. "It's not what you're thinking, trust me," he says, handing the sheet back. "Uncomfortable, yes, and it might make you sick for a few hours, but nothing too bad. Basically it's a laser field that boils the impurities out of your blood—antigens, viruses, bacteria, anything traveling through your veins that's not supposed to be there. It became standard op after the ID scare a few years back." At the blank looks on our faces, he explains, "The Immune Deficiency scare? You're old enough to remember that chalky pink syrup, right? Three times a day to boost your immune system? Everyone had to take it, *everyone*. Remember?"

Vaguely. I remember taking medicine when I was little, lots of it, after every meal and before I went to bed, syrup for the longest time and then pills when I was old enough to swallow them. I took those less frequently, though, and by puberty I didn't take them at all. I don't even remember what they looked like, really, just that I used to choke on them sometimes. I could only take them with water and they never seemed to go down completely—I always imagined I could still feel the pill lodged in my throat afterwards, no matter how much I ate or drank. "The pills?" I ask.

Shanley nods. "Those were part of it, near the end."

Dylan hugs me tighter, his breath ticklish on my neck. "I remember those," he says softly. "Not exactly what *I* like to swallow, though, if you catch my drift."

I do so I hit his arm and he laughs, but Shanley ignores his suggestive tone, thank God. "For a while there it was touch and go," he says. "Too many people dying from mutated strains of germs we conquered decades ago. The mandatory hemothermal sterilization procedures got rid of most of that threat before we were even born, and then the medicine cleaned up the rest of it. We've still got an HTS onboard—all ships with a med lab are required to be equipped with one, even now. But if we're going to run everyone through these processes, we should get started soon. Twelve hours?" I nod, and he shakes his head. "That's barely enough time."

"Why would they want us to go through all this trouble?" Dylan asks, looking at the sheet in my hands.

"Someone wants to make sure we don't contaminate them with anything we might be carrying," Shanley replies. "It's a good idea, actually, but I think a bioscan would suffice, in all honesty. The dermofol is really unnecessary, if you ask me. I mean, it's great if you have crabs or lice or the rash but that's about it. And the HTS? That's really going overboard. I've never even actually run one outside of med school. Most everyone's been clean for years."

Now he glances at Dylan's hands around my waist, and I can almost read his thoughts, he's wondering if *we're* clean, I know he is. *Most everyone's been clean*—true, though there have been isolated cases where the immune deficiency diseases popped up again, I can recall two or three, usually a fast run of Ebola or HyperHIV or something like that sweeping through a whole ship and killing everything in its wake, but those are few and far between, and they aren't very effective, usually burn themselves out before the contagion can spread. Still, I want him to ask if we're clean because I'll tell him we are—Dylan was my first and he only had one other lover before me but he's told me all about the guy and I know they used protection. We did at first, too, but after a while he told me he wanted to love *only* me and I trust him completely so we did the whole bioscan thing and came up clean. We've never bothered with protection since and look at us—no bugs, no disease, neither of us *pregnant*, of course, so why bother with it, you know? That's my feeling, at least, and sometimes Dylan gets so anxious, it's better this way, we don't have to stop in the middle of things and figure out what he did with the condoms. So I'm cool with this whole decontamination procedure, really. I've been there, done that, more or less, and I know there's nothing to find, anyway. We're both clean.

But Shanley doesn't ask, and neither of us offers up the information. "You sure this isn't going to hurt much?" Dylan asks.

I elbow him playfully. "Buck up, baby," I tell him. "You've done it before."

"But that sterilization thing," he starts, and then he shakes his head. "I don't like the sound of that."

"It's not bad," Shanley promises, but I can tell Dylan's not so sure.

Shanley wants someone expendable to run through the procedures first, just in case anything goes wrong. He doesn't say that, of course, but when Milano volunteers, he tells her no. "We need you to pilot one of the fighters," he says.

She glares at him but doesn't protest because she knows he's right. We need everyone, really—she and Parker to run the fighters, Dylan to pilot the carrier, Chen is the only service tech and Johnson's the only radio tech and that leaves me and Val, both navigators. So it's got to be one of us. "I'll do it," I volunteer. If anything happens—if the HTS is so old, it fries my blood in my veins and the dermofol solution eats away my flesh, at least Vallery can still guide the ship. At least there's that.

But it's not that bad—all that hype for nothing, really. I spend fifteen minutes lying in the full-body bioscanner, listening to it hum in my ears like the buzzing of a million flickering light bulbs, then another fifteen in the dermofol tank, my whole body tingling as tiny bubbles cleanse the impurities from my skin. By that time Milano's already stripped and lying in the bioscanner, Parker and Dylan in line behind her. As I climb into the HTS, she dives into the dermofol tank like it's a swimming pool and this is nothing more than downtime for us. Piece of cake, really.

But the next half hour I spend upright in the HTS, feeling like an entombed mummy, protective gauze wrapped around my eyes, my ears, my mouth. I wear a heavy lead drape over my genitals—when Dylan first saw it, he laughed, called it a chastity belt. "For all the good it'll do you," he joked.

"It'll keep you out," I replied.

Dylan shook his head. "I'll find a way in," he promised. At the time I was glad for the heavy drape, though, because it pressed against the swell at my groin and deterred the erection beginning to grow at the tease in his voice.

Inside the HTS it's dark and even though my eyes are closed, bandaged shut, I believe I can see red beams dancing around me, lasers sterilizing my blood—it's a queasy feeling, almost like sinking very fast or maybe standing too quickly, it's sudden like that, makes me lightheaded and dizzy and my stomach churns sickly. Shanley said it makes some people sick, didn't he? I remember him saying that.

When I hear the latches unlock and strong hands guide me out of the HTS chamber, I stumble into a chair, bend over my knees, curl into myself and tell my body I'm not going to vomit, I won't get ill, I can't. Gentle fingers unwrap the gauze from my head and then Dylan's kissing my cheek, his voice soft and his hands warm as he covers me with a thermal blanket. "You okay, hon?" he asks, and I nod numbly even though I don't feel okay, I feel like I'm dying, I just want to be dead. He rubs my shoulders and whispers that he loves me, and when someone calls his name, says it's his turn for the tank, I almost ask him not to go. *Hold me*, I want to tell him. *Dylan, please, don't leave me.*

But we don't have much time so I just wrap the blanket tight around myself and sip at the sugary orange drink Shanley gives me. When Dylan's out of the tank, he sits next to me, holds my hand. By the time he's up for the HTS, my stomach's settled and I can sit upright again without feeling like my head's too heavy to hold up.

I dress into my jumpsuit and wait for him to come out. When he does, he's pale and weak and it breaks my heart to see him like this, frail and sickly and hurting. I take him in my arms, lead him to my chair, sit him down and warm him up and unwrap the gauze that hides his pretty eyes from me, his lovely lips. "Neal," he sighs. "Jesus."

I hold a cup to his mouth and force him to sip at the orange drink. "It helps you feel better, baby," I tell him, and he nods, chokes on the drink, runs his hands over his face until long furrows gouge his cheeks. "It's not the best procedure in the world, is it?"

He shakes his head. "Not at all," he mutters. I hold him tight and wait for him to feel better. "I'm going to die," he croaks at one point, his hands fisted against my back and his lips hot where they're pressed to my neck.

I'm kneeling on the floor in front of the chair and he's hugging me like a small child, clinging to me, really, almost unable to let go. "You won't die," I promise, rocking gently to soothe him. He's been through two glasses of the orange crap and it's not helping, he still feels sick. Milano's already back in the pilot's seat and Parker's out on a recon flight, just to take a quick look around, make sure the sky's still clear around us, which it is, and Vallery's just come out of the HTS—we're more than halfway finished with the decontamination procedures now, less than ten hours until we reach the origin. The next time Shanley passes by us, I look up at him and say, "He's still nauseous."

"Sometimes the boil's like that," he tells me, as if that's any consolation. "Take him back to his bunk for a while—he needs some rest."

I don't need to mention that Dylan can't pilot the carrier if he feels like this—he can't even hold his head up without moaning. Carefully, I get him to his feet and help him dress into his jumpsuit. "Come on, baby," I murmur, holding his pants as he steps into them, leaning heavily against me to keep from staggering. "You just need some sleep, that's all." I zip up his jumpsuit and he leans into me, my arm holding him up as I help him from the med lab and back to my room.

There I lie him down on my bunk, pull the sheets up to his chin, smooth his hair back from his face and press my lips to his forehead like my mother used to do to me when I was a little boy and sick with a fever. His skin is hot, flushed and pink and feverish, too damn warm. "Hot," he sighs, tugging at the sheets. "Get these off me."

I take off the sheets and he starts to unzip his jumpsuit. "Dylan—"

"It's hot," he complains. "Take it off, Neal, please. Take it—" The zipper catches in the fabric and he tugs at it, hard yanks that threaten to tear the material before I manage to catch his hands and hold him still. "Take it off," he sighs. His breath is like a furnace against my cheek. "Please, baby, I'm dying here."

"You're not dying," I tell him, but he *is* warm so I unzip his jumpsuit and help him out of it. Then he tears at his boxers, trying to take those off, as well. "Dylan," I warn.

"Off," he says. "Baby—"

So I ease the boxers down and he kicks them away. Then he lies back on the bed, spread-eagle, no limb touching any other part of his body and his breath coming in short, quick gasps as he stares at the ceiling. "It's still hot," he mutters.

I suppress a laugh. "You can't take off anything else," I tell him. I sit down beside him and stare openly at the trail of hair pointing the way down his abdomen to the dark triangle of curls between his legs, the thick red flesh, the hidden skin below. Gently, I reach out and begin to stroke him, slowly, softly, just long motions that aren't meant to turn him on, not really. I just want to soothe him, that's all, my fingers stroking over his cock and balls and hips lightly, and he closes his eyes, breathes my name, tells me he loves me.

When he starts to get hard, I move my hand, rub at the hollows of his hips, where the hair ends and there's just smooth flesh, cool to the touch. "Lay with me," he says, and he rolls onto his side, making room for me on the bunk.

I lie down behind him, curl against his body and pull him to me. "Is this okay?" I whisper, wrapping my arms around his waist. "You're not too hot—"

"I'm feeling better now," he tells me, covering my hands with his where they rest on his stomach. "A little chilly, actually. I'm naked."

"No, really?" I ask, and that makes him laugh. He sounds much better, and when I stand up, he turns, looks at me over his shoulder, watches wordlessly as I slip out of my own jumpsuit and boxers. Then I lay down again, pulling the sheets up over the both of us, cuddling up to him and holding him tight. "You feeling better?" I ask, burying my head into the nape of his neck.

"Much better," he sighs, snuggling back against me.

Part 3

The timestamp on the nav deck reads *02:48:23*. The numbers aren't green anymore but yellow, a warning that we're close to the signal's origin. Another forty-eight minutes and they'll be an angry red, two hours from landing. Outside all I can see are the boosters of Milano's fighter, flying point now, straight ahead of us. They look like twin suns in the distance, but I can make out the vague shape of her bird, the dark wings almost invisible against the dark sky, and I know she's out there, I hear her breath through the open comm-link we're maintaining. Her stats fill one of the vidscreens, and beside them are Parker's, in his fighter behind us. Every now and then the two of them talk to each other in clipped tones to keep a low radio presence, and their pilot speak is a code I almost understand, but not quite.

"What's your twenty, Parker?" Milano asks, her voice tight, strained. She's nervous—we all are. It's twelve minutes past the three hour window and the signal's still the same, there's no comm-link, no hail of welcome, nothing else to tell us more about this whole situation. Nothing at all.

"I'm on your six," Parker says. I glance at the vidscreen for the rear cam and see the faint ripple of space where his fighter is, his cloaking shields at half power. "Any word yet from the welcome wagon?"

I click on my mike and shake my head, even though they can't see the gesture. "Negative," I tell them. I'm alone on the deck right now, waiting for Val to come back from the cafeteria so I can go down and get something to eat. I plan to stop by the cockpit on my way back—I'll pick up two plates and make sure Dylan gets something to eat before we land. He's finally recovered from the HTS but he's still woozy, hasn't kept anything down since Shanley tried to get him to finish another glass of that supplement drink of his. Four hours ago that was, and God, it was so awful, I held Dylan's head in my hands as he vomited orange sugar into the toilet, retching so damn hard I was afraid he'd tear something and start throwing up blood. "It's okay, baby," I cooed, but I didn't know if he could hear me or not. "It's okay, you're going to be fine, it's okay."

He laid his head in my lap and I held him tightly, his shoulders trembling, his whole body shaking. "It's not going to be okay," he muttered, his arms around my waist, holding me tight. "I feel like shit. Don't let Evan near me again, you hear? When I see him, I'm gonna kick his ass for doing this to me, I swear I will."

It wasn't Shanley's fault, not really, but I didn't feel like arguing with him, not when he was sick like that. Fortunately he fell asleep there in my arms and I half dragged, half carried him back to my bunk, where I tucked him beneath the covers and sat beside him, a hand on his fevered brow. When he woke up a few hours later, he still felt weak and unsteady but at least the sickness had passed. Shanley stopped by to check on him one last time—I told him Dylan was doing much better and turned him away. "I'm still going to hurt him," Dylan promised, glaring at the closed door after the med tech left.

But he *is* better, has been for a while and now he's in the cockpit, keeping the carrier on a steady course and waiting. We're all waiting. I glance at the timestamp again and find that it's almost a half hour past the three hour mark. They're late, whoever *they* are. Behind me I hear the soft hiss of the door as it irises open and I see Vallery's reflection in the window above me when she enters the deck. *I told you so*, I think—didn't I say this signal was nothing more than an old relay? There's no one out there and all we're going to find is the wreck of an abandoned ship, the computer stuck in an endless loop, nothing more.

"Your turn," she says, falling into her seat on the nav deck. She's holding a tray with a bowl full of thick green soup and a stack of crackers on it, which she balances precariously on her knees. "It's broccoli soup or some lump of meat, I wouldn't try that if I were you. It's scary looking." When I laugh, she grins at me and blows on the soup, which is already starting to congeal. "Anything from our friends out there yet?"

"Not yet," I say, rising to my feet. "Didn't I tell you guys—"

The comm-link buzzes. Val looks up at me, her pursed lips curving into a self-satisfied smirk. "Didn't you tell us what?"

"Don't be like that," I warn her, trying not to smile myself. "It's not becoming."

"Like what?" she wants to know, but I just shake my head and turn to the control panel so I don't have to look at her if I have to say she was right.

But it's not an external call, it's Dylan. When I click on the vid-screen, I see him lounging in the pilot's chair, one leg slung over the armrest and his hand stroking along his inner thigh, so close to his crotch that I almost want to ask Vallery to turn away, she shouldn't be seeing this. With a sexy grin, he stares right at me, through the screen at *me*, and purrs, "You coming up here sometime today, baby?" His voice is low and throaty and it turns me on just hearing it. I want to pull on my headset and lose myself in his words, his image, but I can't—Vallery's here. "I miss you."

"I'm going to get us some dinner," I tell him. "I'll be right there."

Raising her voice, Vallery calls out, "Don't eat the meat, Dylan. Go for the soup, trust me."

Dylan laughs, an infectious sound that fills the deck and makes me smile at Val over my shoulder, such a wonderful sound. I love that boy something fierce. "I'm hoping for something more filling than that," he drawls, cupping his dick with one hand. "Neal knows what I'm talking about, don't you, baby?"

I duck my head to hide the thin blush creeping into my cheeks—Jesus, he knows how to touch me in all the right places, doesn't he? "I'll be right there," I tell him, and before I can cut off the comm-link, he whoops loudly. "That boy," I start with a shaky laugh. *He makes me hard,* I think, but I'm not telling Vallery that. Hell, from the way she's grinning at me, I don't think I need to say anything at all, she's picked up on that one herself. "I better get going," I tell her, embarrassed because she knows where I'm going, her eyes say she knows exactly what we'll probably end up doing, and this isn't something I really want people to think about, you know? Dylan and me wrapped together and making love and his lips on mine, his hands on me, and…clicking off the vidscreen to the cockpit, I tell her, "I'll be back."

"Take your time," she says with a wink, sipping at her soup.

God.

❧   ❧   ❧

She's right, the soup's the safest bet, and I carry two trays of it up to the cockpit, one on top of the other, walking carefully to avoid spilling any. On the captain's bridge, I hit the door switch with my elbow and stand back as the door cycles out of my way. I step onto the deck and as the door closes behind me, I announce, "Soup's on."

There are two seats in the cockpit, the pilot's chair that Dylan is stretched out in and the copilot's seat, which is empty. Turning, Dylan smiles when he sees me, stands and takes the top tray from me as he plants a quick kiss on my lips. "I thought you'd never get here," he murmurs, kissing me again, lingering this time, his lips soft and his tongue insistent where it presses into my mouth. "I was afraid you were holding out on me."

I laugh and step back so he doesn't knock into the soup, my elbow hitting the door behind me. "Dylan," I say, "dinner's gonna get cold—"

"Let it," he tells me. Setting his tray down on the floor, he takes the other one as well, places it beside his own, then leans me back against the wall, a hand on either side of my head and his hips grinding into mine. "I need you," he sighs, kissing my neck. I let my eyes slip closed and fist my hands into his jumpsuit.

"Right now?" I ask, hoping it sounds coy and teasing and not the least bit like my blood's on fire for this boy in my arms, pinning me up to the door, but he thrusts into me and I know he feels that hard thickness at my groin, aching at the confines of my jumpsuit—I know he feels it against his own erection because *that* rubs along my thigh, as eager as his lips that cover mine.

"Now," he breathes, and the hum of my zipper when he pulls it down is lost in my low moan. His knee presses between my legs and into my crotch, and then his hands are slipping into my open zipper, smoothing along my naked chest, cupping my erection through my thin boxers and then easing around my hips, beneath the fabric, until he has one arm wrapped around my waist, one hand cradling my bare ass, kneading hungrily. He buries his face in my throat and I hug him close, my arms around his neck, my lips in his hair and I moan his name again, he's kissing me and rubbing me and he's right, what's wrong with right here, right now? Somehow I get a hand between us and trail it down his chest, trace the zipper down to the bulge at his groin, take the hardness in my palm and squeeze it, making him gasp and thrust into me again. "Oh Jesus, *now*," he sighs.

I like him like this, so needy, so *mine*. "I like it when you call me Jesus," I murmur, but he kisses me quiet because he's done playing, he wants me and he's going to have me and he's getting no argument from me there.

I have him unzipped and in my hand, already damp where he's starting to come, and he's working my boxers down, trying to get into them without either of us taking the time to get fully undressed, when the vidscreen flares to life behind him and Vallery's face appears. I can see her over Dylan's shoulder. "Hate to interrupt—" she starts.

"Vallery!" Dylan cries. He tugs my jumpsuit closed, covering my chest but parts of me peek out below as I scramble to tuck him back into his suit. I don't know what all she sees but her eyes widen and suddenly the screen goes blank, she's turned off the cam. Still, I turn towards the door, his body blocking mine as I snap my boxers back together and fumble with the zipper to close my suit. "Fuck, you *knew* we were getting it on here—"

"I'm sorry," she mumbles, her voice filling the room. "I didn't mean to...I mean, I thought you'd—I didn't see anything much, I swear."

"You saw enough," I mutter. Dylan runs a shaky hand through his hair and we're going to have to talk about this, this is the second time she's done this to us, and now I'm going to be hard until I get with him tonight. We won't be able to get the moment back now, not with me thinking she might bust in on us all over again. This time I zip my jumpsuit all the way to my chin, and when I turn around Dylan has his only halfway closed, the collar crooked. I can still see his bare chest, smooth and muscled, and I straighten his collar, pull the zipper up all the way, whisper to him, "This is getting old."

"Val, we're busy here," he says, his arms slipping around my waist again until I'm caught once more in his embrace, but now my hands are between us, keeping us apart, and when he leans down to kiss me, I turn away. With a lusty sigh, he rests his forehead on mine and raises his voice as he calls out, "Well? What do you want? Make it quick so we don't have to."

"Oh, hey, I forgot," she says, her tone of voice making me grin at the frustration that flitters across Dylan's face. "This is just a pleasure cruise, right? We're only here so you two can kiss and make up—"

"Stop it," Dylan growls. Pressing his lips to my cheek, he whispers, "They don't understand how much I need you, baby." I do—I can feel his need curled against my hip, but Vallery's right, this *can* wait. I try to push away but Dylan's stronger than me and he holds me close. "Where do you think you're going?" His breath is hot and exciting along my skin. "Val—"

"Hello, you guys?" she calls, as if we're not listening. "You think I'm doing this just to harass you?" Dylan opens his mouth like that's exactly what he's thinking, but I cover his lips with mine to silence him. "There's an incoming signal on the comm-link. Or are you two not interested in that anymore?"

I don't know about Dylan, but *I'm* interested. "Be right there," I tell her, and with another kiss, another squeeze and a promise to pick this up later where we left off, Dylan follows me from the cockpit. *An incoming signal*—I don't even let myself think about what it might be.

The others are already crammed on the nav deck when we show up—Vallery in her seat and Leena in mine, Shanley and Johnson leaning against the wall on either side of the door. A steady *blip blip blip* signals an incoming transmission, but they're waiting for us to arrive before accepting it. All four crew members turn as we enter, and Leena hops from my seat to Vallery's knee, where she perches, waiting. They're all waiting. When I sink into my chair, Dylan sits on the armrest and I flash Vallery a tight grin. "Well," I start, but I can't think of anything else to say so I turn to the control panel, watch the blinking light on the transmit button. I wait.

"The fighters are patched in," Vallery tells me. I nod, that's good, they'll hear the transmission too, but I have no clue what happens next. *You hit the transmit,* a voice inside me whispers. *You say hello. It's not that hard, is it?*

No, not in theory. But who's on the other end of that signal? What voice will answer mine? I don't know, and that's what terrifies me. I glance up at Dylan—he's the captain so this is his show, right?

He nods at me and takes a deep breath. "Here goes," he says, and before he can think it through, he hits the transmit and opens the comm-link. Empty space yawns around us, the open channel waiting like baited breath, *waiting*—for a moment I think he's not going to speak, for the first time since I've known him he doesn't know what to say, and I place a comforting hand on his knee. He slips his fingers into mine and clears his throat, and it's his strong, authoritative voice that says, "*Semper Fi*, standing by."

Static crackles through the room. Dylan's hand tightens in mine, and I don't even realize I'm holding my breath until a young, male voice comes across the comm-link. "*Semper Fi*, this is S410. Welcome."

Relief floods through me and Leena claps, Vallery laughs, even Johnson grins at Shanley and they both step closer to lean over the backs of our seats. Clicking on the intercom, I ask the pilots, "You guys hearing this?"

"Ten four," Milano says, and Parker murmurs his assent.

A quick glance at the stats screen shows her pulse rate's up, Parker's too, their veins are flooded with adrenaline right now. I'm about to tell them to take it easy, these are humans we're talking with—not a forgotten relay, not aliens, *humans* and Dylan's been right all along, this *is* one of the Starseed colonies and I'm going to kiss him silly tonight, tell him he was right, he's amazing, they'll name a star after him for this for sure—but another burst of static grates across the comm-link and then the stranger speaks again. "I repeat, *Semper Fi*, this is S410. Welcome."

Johnson gives Dylan a playful shove. "Answer him," he says, grinning like a cat.

Dylan glares at him. "What should I say?"

"Ask him if he's cute," Leena offers.

"Leena!" Vallery squeals, but she's laughing and we're all relieved, this is turning into something incredible, there are *humans* out there!

Leena looks around at us and shrugs, perplexed. "What?" she wants to know. Shanley grins and Johnson laughs. "What'd I say?"

I hush them as Dylan leans on the transmit. With deliberate care, he speaks slowly, his voice even and sure. "S410, my name's Teague. I'm the captain of *Semper Fi*. We picked up your signal just outside of the Epsilon system and were sent to investigate. We're in this region on a two year star-map jaunt and...um..." He turns to me for help.

"Are you cute?" Vallery whispers, and Leena falls back against her, giggling. Dylan kicks her shin to shut her up.

"Tell them we're on our way," I suggest.

He nods. "We picked up your signal—"

"You said that already," Johnson mutters. Dylan glares at him and God, they're going to think we're the most unorganized ship in the fleet if we keep this shit up. *At least lay off the transmit*, I think. *They don't need to hear the comments from the peanut gallery.*

When there's no reply, Dylan adds, "We're under the belief that this is uninhabited space. Our annals show no life in this sector." With a grin at me, he adds, "Some of our crew think you guys are all dead."

Still no reply. "Great," I whisper. "You've pissed them off."

"I didn't," Dylan starts.

Then I realize he's still on the transmit and I take his hand in mine, hold it down in my lap. Now the channel flares to life again, a barrage of static lacing the masculine voice, already in midsentence. "—much alive, we assure you. Forty-two strong and ten of our women are expecting. What union are you affiliated with, Captain Teague?"

Dylan laughs. "I like the sound of that, *Captain* Teague. Finally getting some respect," he says, but Leena slaps the back of his head and he ducks out of reach with another laugh. "No union," he transmits. "You have a name, kid?"

"Conlan," comes the reply. "What union—"

"No union," Dylan repeats. Dixon runs his own station, hiring out to whoever pays the biggest commission, and everyone signs up for each individual run, if it's something they want. This is my second stint with him and Dylan's first. Dixon likes to keep a young crew, no one over thirty. Starmapping can take its toll on a body, long, lonely hours out in uncharted space, you need fast reflexes and most riggers don't like to hire anyone handicapped or sick or old, not if they can help it. Dixon stays out of the union and doesn't have to follow EOE guidelines, keeps his station the way he likes it and changes crews each trip, almost. I already sense he's not going to offer me a position on the next run, even though I know he wants Dylan to pilot again. We'll see how *that* works out.

"No union," Conlan echoes, as if repeating it for someone else. Then he asks, "What's your armament?"

When Dylan reaches for the transmit, Milano's voice fills the cabin. "Don't you dare tell him that, Teague. The fucker doesn't *need* to know."

He looks at me and I nod. "She's right," I say. It's an odd question—does this guy seriously think we're going to tell him what we're packing here? We're assuming he's friendly but we can't bank on that. "Don't—"

"Light artillery," Dylan says into the channel. "D-5 right now, no threat detected. I repeat, defcon-5 currently activated. We're not aiming for you boys, just covering our asses."

Another long pause. I check to make sure the comm-link's still open and it is. Behind me Johnson shifts nervously and in the other seat, Vallery picks at her nails. We watch the console as if we can will a reply with the weight of our collective gaze alone. In a soft voice, Shanley suggests, "Maybe that's not what they wanted to hear."

Suddenly static erupts from the speakers and we can hear Conlan beneath the white noise. "I repeat," he starts.

Dylan rolls his eyes. "Jesus," he whispers, leaning back against me. "He doesn't clue in too quick, does he?"

"What is your armament?" Conlan continues. I fiddle with the controls, trying to diminish the interference, and as he speaks, his voice grows louder then falls away, swings towards us, grows quiet. "We need an accurate count of weaponry and personnel before we can issue clearance into the colony—"

"They have a colony?" Leena asks, awed. "You know this puts us in the annals, right? Operation Starseed actually *worked*."

I shake my head. "We don't know that," I tell her—we don't know this is a Starseed colony, we don't know *anything* yet, but I can look around at the others and know they're already believing this, we're already heroes in their minds, I can read the visions of glory in their eyes. Dylan's especially, and I want to take him in my arms, turn him around, make him *look* at me and *listen* to me and make him realize we can't be jumping to conclusions right yet, we can't be celebrating this when we don't even really know what *this* is.

If we were alone, just the two of us, I'd do just that. But it's not only us here, it's the whole crew, and Dylan's not hearing me, he's arguing with Milano over the intercom. "If we're going to land," he tells her, "he says he needs an inventory—"

"Bullshit." The word is spat angrily, and I can picture her frowning face in my mind, she's the only one of us cautious about this whole thing. "Tell him we have fighters and that's it, Dylan. You can't compromise our position just because he says so."

"Fuck," he mutters, because he knows she's right. Into the comm-link, he says, "We have eight crew members, two fighters. I'm not at liberty to say anything more, but this is a peace mission. We're starmappers, not space pirates or militia men. No unnecessary weaponry."

Parker's voice comes over the intercom. "Shut him up, James," he growls, and I ease a protective arm around Dylan's waist. "Tessa's right, they don't need to know what we're carrying. Jesus, what if they're out there aiming at *us*?"

"I'm not—" Dylan starts, but I tighten my arm around him and he falls silent. In the window in front of us, I can see his reflection, the furrow of his brow, the pout on his lips. "If we're going to land—"

"Who said anything about landing?" Vallery counters.

Dylan glares at her, then at Leena, on her lap. Then he turns, his gaze falling on Johnson, on me, on Shanley behind us, anger and confusion warring on his face. I want to kiss it all away but I can't, not here, not in front of the others. *Tonight*, I tell myself, and I hope he can read that promise in my eyes. *Tonight I'll hold you, baby, and kiss you and make it all better. I'll let you be right.* "If we're not landing," he asks, looking at me like he expects me to be the one to answer him, "then what the hell are we doing out here, anyway?"

"We're landing," I assure him. "Dixon wants this checked out, that means we land."

Conlan speaks again, the static in his voice scratching his syllables. "Eight crew," he confirms, and then, "We need certification that the decontamination procedures have been implemented for each member."

Leaning past us, Shanley presses the transmit, raises his soft voice and speaks clearly, slowly. "I am Dr. Evan Shanley," he says, his words unmistakable. "The crew medical files record the results of the decon tests. If you have a DAQ-185 compatible system, I can transmit the information to you."

"We do, thank you." Conlan's reply this time is quick, unhesitating. "But we have to set up the system first. We'll contact you in a half hour's time for the transmit, and then the committee can review the findings before you land. S410 out."

The static disappears as the connection is closed. "Bye to you, too," Leena mumbles. She looks around the room and her gaze stops on Shanley, kneeling by the console and already setting up our DAQ system to transmit the files the next time Conlan calls. "They're real keen on knowing all they can find out about us, aren't they? What's your armament? What're the results of your decon tests? But what did we learn about them?"

"Nothing," Johnson says. Vallery nods in agreement and Johnson glares at me like it's my fault, I should've talked to the guy, not Dylan. "We didn't learn shit."

"Forty-two colonists," Dylan says. With one hand he traces the seam of my jumpsuit along my inner thigh. When I try to cover the spot nonchalantly, he begins to pick at the seam, pulling the material up around my fingers because he's bored and restless and he wants to get this party started, he doesn't want to wait another two hours until we land, he doesn't want to *talk* about this anymore. Where he leans against me, I can feel his body hum with unspent energy. "Didn't he say that? Ten pregnant women. That's why they want to make sure we're not a threat."

But Johnson shakes his head. "I don't like this," he declares. "Let me talk next time, I'll pump them for information. What are we gonna tell Dixon when we call this in? Oh, we don't know anything about them, we forgot to ask?"

"We don't have to call it in yet," I remind him. "Not until we have something concrete. We're probably too far out to transmit back to the station anyway—"

"We should at least try." Johnson pins me with a hard stare but I look away. I'm not calling Dixon. I don't want to hear any cracks he's going to make about Dylan and me now that we're back together. When I don't answer him, Johnson sighs dramatically. "All I'm saying is maybe he should know what we're about to do."

"He *knows* what we're going to do," Vallery points out. Johnson glances over his shoulder at her and then sighs again, stalks away from my chair and throws himself against the wall by the door, angry. Vallery looks at me as if for confirmation. "This was his idea, wasn't it? Sending you guys, sending the fighters—he knows we're going in."

From the far side of the nav deck, Johnson mutters, "I still think we should give him a heads up."

Dylan opens his mouth to reply, a hot retort on his lips, when Shanley's soft voice silences him, stopping us all. "There's really nothing to call in yet, Mike." In his corner, Johnson makes a sardonic noise in the back of his throat. "If we call him, he's going to ask what we know, and what is that, exactly? I mean, at this point—"

"At this point, we know nothing," Leena says, and Shanley nods, turns back to the control panel, where he's configuring the DAQ system. Leena watches him for a moment before she looks up at Johnson. "If we call him, Dixon's just going to tell us to wait another few hours, you know how he is. Wait til we get down to the colony and know something more, *then* call it in."

Johnson glares at us as if he knows we're right, there's no reason to contact the station yet, and he hates that. He hates that none of us agree with him on this, I can see the way it's eating at him, it's in his angry frown, his glittering eyes. "Fine," he says, hitting the power switch to open the door. The steel irises out of his way as he steps into the corridor. When the door starts to close, he adds, "But I get a chance at them, next call. We need to know as much about them as they do about us before we land."

"Fine," Dylan agrees. The door shuts Johnson out of the deck and we can hear his boot heels ring off the steel corridor as he storms away. "Can we go back to our food now?" he asks no one in particular. "We've got a half hour—"

"Twenty minutes," Leena corrects, standing. She stretches languidly and rubs at her already tousled hair, mussing it up further. "Going on fifteen. I hope you boys can make it fast."

Dylan leaps up, pulls me to my feet. "You heard her," he says, steering me towards the door. The intense look on his face and the way he smacks the power switch to open the door, ducking through the steel partition before it even fully opens, tells me he's hoping to finish what we started *now*, he doesn't want to wait until tonight.

Out in the corridor, the two of us finally alone, I let him wrap his arms around my waist and nuzzle my neck. "My room," I tell him. I don't want any interruptions this time.

We're still twined together in my sweaty sheets when they page us to the nav deck. No vidscreens this time, just our names echoing through the ship as we hurry to dress, and I get one of the jumpsuits up to my hips before I realize it's too tight along my thighs, it's not mine. "Here," I say, tugging it down as Dylan starts to zip up the jumpsuit he's wearing, *my* suit. "This one's yours."

The page comes again. "We're on our way," he mutters to no one in particular, stepping into his own jumpsuit. He stands in the open doorway, watches me zip up, waits while I pull on my boots. I can feel the weight of his gaze on my ass, my legs, when I bend over to scoop the sheets back onto the bed. "I love you," he says suddenly. "Just so you know."

"I know," I tell him, waving my hand dismissively as I walk past him out into the corridor. He grabs my waist, pulls me back against him, kisses me hungrily. "Hey!" I laugh, twisting out of his arms.

Vallery's voice comes over the intercom. "Don't make me call you boys again," she threatens.

On the deck, Val's already in her chair, Leena beside her, and Johnson's in my seat, watching Shanley punch coordinates into the computer. "About time," he mutters as we enter, and I get the feeling he's still pissed about this whole deal. He gets up and pushes past me, glares at Dylan when he stops him with a hand on his shoulder. "Get off me, Teague."

"Watch it," Dylan growls. He gives Johnson a shove out of his way, and when Johnson shoves back, I think they're going to get into it, right here—I catch Dylan's arm, whisper it's okay, we don't need to be fighting amongst ourselves, but Johnson backs away. "You have a problem?" Dylan wants to know. Johnson crosses his arms and shakes his head and avoids looking at either of us.

I start to tell Dylan to forget it, he doesn't need this added stress, none of us do, but the transmit starts to beep, signaling an incoming call, and I sink into my chair as Vallery opens the channel. Leaning over my shoulder, Dylan holds his breath until Conlan's voice cuts through the ever-present static. "S410 to *Semper Fi*, over. I repeat—"

"I repeat," Dylan mocks, but Leena slaps his shoulder and he laughs at her. "What? It's annoying."

"S410 to *Semper Fi*," Conlan says, unaware of Dylan's teasing. "Request transmission of personnel medical files. I repeat—"

Dylan presses down the transmit button before anyone can stop him. "We heard you the first time," he says, ducking around my seat to avoid Leena's stinging hand. "Shanley's about ready to send the files—" He looks over his shoulder at the med tech. "Are you?" With a nod, Shanley gives Dylan a thumbs up. Jeez, is he for real? But Dylan only claps him on the back as he stands and says, "It's your show, then."

Shanley leans close to the transmit as he says, "Conlan, I need your DAQ coords—"

Suddenly Johnson's there, pushing Shanley away. "What's *your* armament?" he wants to know, his voice bitter and fast. "You have forty-two colonists, where are *their* med files? What's the terrain like down there? What's the condition of your craft? We don't know shit about you guys—we need *this* info before we land—" Dylan grapples with Johnson, trying to pull him back, and Leena wedges herself between the radio tech and the control panel, knocking his hand from the transmit and shoving him away. "Get off me!" Johnson cries, struggling, but Dylan's stronger than he is and Leena's scrappy, she manages to avoid his flailing arms and helps Dylan get Johnson behind the seats until he's up against the door and sputtering in anger. "We need to know what we're getting into," he says, trying to extract himself from his crewmates. "We're flying into this thing *blind*, can't you see that? We don't know—"

Leena hits the power switch and the door irises open, spilling Johnson and Dylan out into the corridor, where they land in a tangled heap on the floor. Then she hurries through the closing door, helping Dylan haul Johnson to his feet. Over his shoulder, Dylan calls out, "Evan, make sure those files go across." The door shuts on Johnson's protests as he's dragged away from the nav deck.

"Well," Vallery says, taking a deep breath, "that could've been handled better."

"No, you think?" I ask with a shaky laugh. Shanley looks at me and I nod. "You heard him, send the files. If they still want them."

Conlan speaks tentatively, unsure. "Um, Captain Teague? You must understand that we cannot give that kind of information out just yet. Ours is a very precarious position…" He trails off, as if these aren't his words but someone else's and he's listening to the next prompt. "Once the committee has verified the medical condition of your crew, then we may be able to exchange the information you…have requested. But until that time…"

I press the transmit just to stop his halting speech. "Captain Teague is preoccupied," I tell him. "I'm the navigator, Neal James, and I apologize for that outburst, that was our radio tech and his opinions do not reflect those of the rest of the crew—" I hear Milano mutter, "Bullshit," over the intercom, but it's low enough that I can ignore it for now. "If you are ready, Dr. Shanley will send the medical files now."

A long pause, and I'm almost sure that Conlan heard Milano's comment, he *must* have, and he probably doubts the validity of my apology, he's wondering where Dylan's gone off to, he's wondering what the hell kind of command we have if the radio tech can just interrupt the transmission like that but none of us expected it, I know *I* sure as hell didn't. I'm about to apologize again, beg him to believe me if I have to, we can't come this far and be denied the chance to land and check out this colony, Dixon will kill us if we let this slip by, fire us on the spot, but then Conlan says, "Our DAQ coords are as follows—" and I know it's going to go right this time, I know we'll get down there and we'll land, we'll be the first to find one of the lost Starseed colonies, and Dylan will finally get his name on a star.

❦   ❦   ❦

Conlan tells us it'll take another hour or so for the committee to meet and discuss our records, and he'll get back in touch with us after that. Which means we wait, Vallery and I on the nav deck and the others scattered throughout the ship—Shanley to find something to calm Johnson down and Dylan back in the cockpit, Leena running a systems check, Parker and Milano still flanking us in their fighters. Vallery keeps asking me what I think we're going to find at this colony, as if I might know something more than she does, as if I'm holding out on her here. "What about this committee of theirs?" she asks, and I shrug because I don't know. She's just trying to fill the silence with something, words, conversation, *anything* to make the time pass. "What kind of committee do you think it might be?"

"One with people on it?" I offer.

She slaps my arm and sighs. "You know what I mean. Are we talking a government here? Concerned colonists? Do they make laws and enforce them or just suggest things that need to be done? Are these people elected—"

"Jeez, Val!" I cry, laughing at her. "I know as much as you do about this whole thing."

She thinks that over and then says, "Maybe we *should* let Mike talk to these people." Her voice is soft, barely audible, like she's afraid of speaking too loud. "Just to find out what we *are* getting into here. Maybe—"

"Think about it," I tell her, trying to steer the talk away from Johnson, because there's a part of me that wonders if maybe he's right and we *should* listen to him, but I don't want to go against Dylan, he's my lover and captain of this ship, his word is carved in stone as long as we're in flight, I can't side against him. "If this is Starseed—"

"Isn't it?" Vallery asks. "I mean, haven't we sort of agreed that it is?"

I nod, then remind her, "But we don't know for sure yet. We *assume* it is, but they've never come out and *said* so, have they?"

Chewing on her lower lip thoughtfully, Vallery admits, "Not in so many words."

"It might *not* be Starseed," I tell her. "We just don't know. It might be another ship out there, lost and stranded and don't give me that look, it *might*."

"But it's not," she says. "You know it's not, I know it's not, we all *know* this is one of the colony ships."

"Let's say it is," I concede, "just for the sake of argument. Let's say there's a ship out there that held a hundred people twenty years ago. It got off course somehow and ended up here, and we're the first contact they've had in that time." Vallery nods—she's with me so far. *Wherever I'm at,* I think, because I'm not really sure myself. I'm just making this up as I go along. "So. They've been cut off from civilization for the past two decades. If we're thinking this is a Starseed ship, then we have to assume they have the supplies and terraforming equipment all of the ships left with, which should have been enough to get them started. So they should have a whole system set up by now, don't you think? A steady food source, a community structure—it should all be in place already." She nods again. "So why shouldn't they have a committee of some sort? Maybe it *is* a government, I don't know, but I'd be more surprised if they *didn't* have some kind of representation, some sort of figurehead, someone calling the shots." When she doesn't answer immediately, I add, "You know?"

"Maybe," she says, but that's not really an agreement, is it? I don't like the frown on her face or the way she toys with a tiny hole in the leather armrest of her seat, like she's thinking something she's not too happy about.

"Maybe?" I ask. When she shrugs, I prompt, "But what? Tell me."

"But they had a hundred people," she whispers. *Now* she looks up at me, her eyes wide and scared. "They're down to what, forty-two? And Conlan made a point to tell us ten women are pregnant, like he was *proud* of the fact. Like it meant something special. What happened to the other colonists, Neal?" she asks. "If it's been twenty years, you'd think a hundred people would have multiplied, the colony would have grown, but it didn't. What happened to the others?"

I don't know. And I don't have to say that, she can see the answer in my eyes. I just don't know.

"I see it," Milano says, her voice hushed over the intercom. Vallery and I exchange a quick glance and she turns up the volume, the open channel a loud hiss around us. "Small planet, possible moon, I'm not sure. There appears to be an atmosphere cover. No defense systems in place—none that I can see, anyway."

Vallery pulls up Milano's system through the computer link and data splashes across our vidscreens, radar signals and flight information and her vital stats, everything we need to know about the fighter and its pilot. We can see the planet's mass on the radar. I look out the window but all I see are stars and Milano's boosters, that's it. "Any fighters?" I ask her. "Anything out there that might be gunning for us?"

"Negative," she tells us. "I'm flying solo up here, guys. Looks like Conan was telling the truth."

"Conlan," I correct, but I keep my voice down and don't think she hears me.

Parker's voice comes over the intercom. "So we landing here or what?"

"Still waiting on the green light," I remind him. It's been almost an hour since Conlan's last broadcast—how long is this going to take? What are we going to do if we get right up on the colony and there's still no contact? Circle until they tell us we can land? Clicking over the intercom, I buzz Dylan in the cockpit. "You hanging in there, flyboy?"

I can hear the grin in his voice when he comes back across the speakers and purrs, "Come up here and see how I'm hanging, babe."

"Oh God," Vallery giggles. "How do you put up with him?"

With a smile, I say, "I like him like that." Though sometimes I wish he wouldn't be so open, not when he knows there are others around. True, it's only Vallery, but what if we were back at the station and Dixon overheard him? I know he's been talked to about it before—right before he left on this mission, Dixon called him into his office and I'm sure it was me he wanted to talk about. Dylan spent all his free time in my room—he was the reason I was late for my shift most of the time, even though Tony covered for me. He wanted Dixon to change my schedule to accommodate his, he wanted clearance to the nav deck when I was on duty, he wanted me transferred to the pilot's quarters and Dixon drew the line at that. I couldn't seem to make Dylan understand that he wasn't helping matters, Dixon didn't *like* me, he didn't like that we were together and nothing I said seemed to get through that boy. He loved me, he *loves* me, and that's the only thing that matters to him some days. He thinks it should be as simple as that. I wish it were.

❦   ❦   ❦

The planet's just as Milano described it, small and almost moon-like, red and green through the gaseous cloud cover—it reminds me of a glass ball on a Christmas tree, and it fills me with the same sense of awe and wonder. Parker takes a quick look around and reports that this is just one in a cluster of small planets, all smaller than our moon back on Earth, which means nothing to me because I've lived all my life on space stations out here in the far reaches of the galaxy, I've never *seen* the Terran moon. But Vallery oohs like she knows what he's talking about and when she looks at me, I nod, too, why not? We're here, aren't we? I'm nervous and excited and can't stop grinning—we're really *here*. S410. Leena's right, we're going in the annals for this.

We're close—the timestamp reads *00:42:23*, less than an hour before we're in position to land—when the transmit beeps again, an incoming call. *Conlan,* I think as Vallery opens the channel. "*Semper Fi,*" she says, her voice bright and pretty. "Navigator Vallery Andrews, standing by."

But it's not Conlan who replies. "Benjamin Ellington," the stranger says, introducing himself. "The committee has reviewed your crew med files and the decision has been made to grant you permission to land in the S410 colony."

"Where's Conlan?" I whisper.

Vallery shrugs. "Off duty?" she asks. "I don't know."

"In response to your request," Ellington continues, "I'm sending you eight random files from the colony's med lab, along with information about the colony itself. There is no armament to speak of—I believe Jeremy told you that much—"

"Jeremy?" Vallery asks, cutting him off.

"Conlan," he adds. "You spoke with him previously?"

He waits. When it's apparent he's waiting on *us*, I hit the transmit and tell him, "Yes, he's been in contact with us since the comm-link opened." Data fills the screen in front of me, the files he's downloading to our DAQ system. "Get Shanley in here to look at this," I whisper, and with a curt nod, Vallery leaves the nav deck. Into the transmit, I laugh and admit, "You know, we're all very excited about this." Less than a half hour now and we'll be down there, shaking hands with these guys, making history.

"As are we," Ellington replies, but his voice is dry and almost insincere, like he's reading a script. Before I can question him about it, though, he says, "Someone will contact you when you're ready to land."

And then the connection closes and he's gone.

🍁   🍁   🍁

Eight files. Shanley prints out hard copies and hands them around to the five of us gathered on the nav deck—Dylan's still in the cockpit and the two fighters still flank the carrier, but they're connected to us with an open intercom so they hear everything we say. "He said these were random colonists?" Shanley asks, handing me two of the files.

I glance at the names. *Conlan, Jeremy S.*, the first one reads, and I wonder just how random the selection process was. "That's what he said," I tell him, flipping to the next file. *Thomas, Marie J.* "I have Conlan and a girl, Marie."

From the seat beside mine, Vallery says, "I have that Ellington dude. He's kind of cute." She holds up the file for me to look at the blurry, pixilated image that might be something vaguely resembling a human, but I'm not sure. It might also be just a bunch of ASCII letters clumped together on the page. "You sort of have to squint," she explains.

They've sent us five men, three women, the same makeup as our crew. Two of the women are with child—"Her third pregnancy," Johnson reads from his file. Turning over the paper in his hand, he frowns and adds, "Doesn't say anything about the kids, though. Just that she's expecting another one. At twenty-five! Damn, these girls are young."

"They're all young," Shanley points out. Then he reads off the names, the ages, what he's been scribbling down while we leafed through the files. "Conlan, male, twenty-five. Maclin, male, twenty-four. Thomas, female, pregnant, twenty-eight. Ellington, male, thirty—he's the oldest so far. Walker, female, pregnant, twenty-five. Corey, male, twenty. Martin, male, nineteen. Mayes, female, eighteen. They're all so young." He glances at the files in Leena's hands and says, "Most of the pertinent information has been edited out of these. We have birth records for the ones born in the colony, and hospital scans for the rest, but there's nothing here about their formative years. They go from infants to adults, nothing in between. No colds, no broken bones, nothing."

"Maybe there's nothing to report," I suggest.

But Shanley shakes his head. "This is a colony, Neal," he reminds me. "They're starting over again, doing it all for the first time. This is all completely new to them, so they'd *want* to keep extensive records on every single person. The tiniest scrape, a toothache, irregular menstruation cycles, it'd all be written down."

"What about the children?" Leena asks. When we turn to look at her, she shrugs, explains, "The kids. These two women are pregnant and it's not their first time, neither of them. This is one girl's second and the other's what, on her third?" Johnson and I glance at each other and nod. We have those files. "So what happened to their other kids? I don't think there *are* any others."

"What?" Vallery asks, and I shake my head, hold up the file in my hand, point to it and remind her, "It says this is her second one—"

"Second *pregnancy*," Leena points out. Crossing the deck, she takes the file from me and scans it quickly. Then she taps the paper and says, "See? Right here, second pregnancy. Not second child." As she hands the file back, she asks, "What happened to the first one? There's nothing in this about the first pregnancy, is there?"

She's right, there's not. The file should be thick, full of ultrasound results and the baby's statistics and the mother's vitals, and none of that's here. Apparently Johnson's file's the same way, because he starts tearing through it, almost angry, looking for anything about the previous two pregnancies, anything at all. "Fuck," he mutters. He throws the file down in disgust and the papers flutter to the floor by his feet. Kicking at them, he glares at Shanley like this is all his fault. "What the hell is this shit? This…this *censorship*? Is this some kind of game for them?"

Over the intercom, Dylan says, "We're their first contact, Johnson. Some of those kids down there were born in the colony, weren't they? We'll be the first people outside S410 that they've ever seen. Of *course* they're going to be cautious."

Johnson doesn't respond. In an effort to diffuse the situation, Shanley hands him the last file, the one full of planetary statistics. "Take a look at this," he says softly. "Let me know what you think."

What *he* thinks should be of no consequence—he's the radio tech, not a navigator, but I don't say that, I know Shanley's only trying to calm the kid down. *Kid*, as if he's not the same age as my lover, but he acts so damn childish sometimes, worse than Dylan in full pouting glory. Glancing over the file, Johnson shrugs, noncommittal. "I'm not even really sure what I'm looking at here," he admits grudgingly.

I hold out a hand for the file, and I'm surprised when he actually gives it to me. It's about what I expect, really—mostly hard clay, which makes the planet look red from this height. Stunted grass, some shallow riverbeds, an almost continuous rainy season, sixteen hour day/night cycle—"Sixteen hours?" I say with a grin. "That's going to take some getting used to."

Shanley nods at the file in my hands. "What do you think?"

"I think it's probably not going to make a list of the best vacation spots in the galaxy," I tell him, and Vallery laughs. "Lots of clay, always rainy, probably not very good for crops, if they've managed to grow any." Browsing through the file, I find a section about their original spacecraft, and I read it out loud. "The S410, one of twelve colony ships in Operation Starseed—"

"Whoo!" Vallery cries, surging to her feet. She catches Johnson's arms and twirls around him, wiggling her hips as she dances. "What did I tell you, Neal?" she asks. When Johnson doesn't fall into step with her, she turns to Leena, who dances up on her, the two of them twisting to an imaginary beat. "I told you so," she sings. "I told you so—"

"Vallery, please," I say, but it's hard to watch her and Leena dance and maintain a straight face, they're so cute, so *happy*. "Don't—"

"I *told* you so," she says again.

I laugh and tell her, "Yeah, you did. Sit down already, will you? You're making me nervous." She sticks her tongue out at me but sinks back into her chair, Leena sitting on the armrest. "Can I finish reading this?" I ask.

"Go ahead," Vallery concedes. Under her breath, she mumbles, "I told you so."

Ignoring that, I turn back to the file. "The S410 was badly damaged in a meteor shower," I tell them, paraphrasing the text. The last thing I want is another little bump and grind because this really is one of the Starseed ships out there. "It was programmed for a course closer to Sol, which would have put them back near Earth, but the interference from the shower threw them off course."

"Pretty far off course, if you ask me," Johnson mutters.

No one did, I think, but I hold my tongue. "The damage took out one wing of the ship, killing fifteen colonists instantly. The navigation system was also shot—their shields, radar, all gone. They thought maybe they'd turn around, head back for the station outside of Orion, but they got lost and wound up here, in the Epsilon system. Something happened..." I frown at the file in my hands—this doesn't make sense. *We picked up the planetoid on our vidscreens,* the text reads, *and landed with difficulties resulting from the meteor damage. Early efforts at terraforming proved fruitless, but the ship was inhabitable and the survivors*—"Of what?" I ask out loud. Looking around at the crew, my gaze falls on Shanley, who watches me closely. "The survivors decided to maintain a colony aboard the ship, but the survivors of what?"

"The meteor shower?" Leena suggested.

"Only fifteen people died in that," I remind her. "I don't think that's enough to classify everyone else as *survivors*, do you?"

She shrugs and leans back against Vallery, who shrugs, as well. "We weren't there," she points out. "Maybe to them it *was* survival."

I'm not buying that. "To me it suggests something else happened," I tell her. "They had a hundred people, lost fifteen, and now are down to forty-two? In twenty years, and the women are fertile—two of the ones pregnant now, this isn't their first time. It just doesn't add up for me. Don't tell me you guys are okay with this." Vallery shrugs again and Leena looks away, doesn't meet my eyes. Johnson stares at the floor and frowns, I know he's thinking the same things I'm thinking, I know this bothers him, too.

Shanley starts to gather the files together. When he gets to me, I hold onto the file, force him to look at me, at *me*, and he sighs. "We'll just have to ask them when we get there," he tells me. "We're in a delicate situation here, Neal. They don't trust us as it is. If we press them too far, they may deny us landing clearance altogether."

"How?" I counter. I'm just playing the other side here, I tell myself. I know Shanley's right, but Johnson's right, too, and that bothers me. These files, they don't tell us anything more than what we already knew, which wasn't a whole hell of a lot to begin with. The only thing we've learned for certain is that they *are* one of the Starseed ships, that's it, and we suspected that all along. "If they're defenseless like they keep saying they are, how will they keep us from landing? That doesn't make any sense."

Taking a deep breath, Shanley says, "We're not out to make enemies here, Neal. Another thirty minutes and we'll be able to ask them these things in person."

I nod and let him have the files. He's right. We'll be down there soon enough.

❦   ❦   ❦

In the end we decide that only four of us should go down, that's it. Dylan, because he's the captain and he *wants* to go—"You can't keep me from this," he tells us as Vallery configures the landing system. He leans back against the control panel, one foot propped up on my chair by my thigh, his arms folded across his chest. "I earned this. It's my signal, they spoke to me first, I deserve to go down there."

"Fine," Johnson says. "You go. I ain't." He looks around at the rest of us as if defying someone to challenge him. "I'm going to see if I can set up a long-range transmission from this carrier. Dixon needs to know what's going on."

"Fine," Dylan says. "You do that. I'm going down there."

I touch his ankle, a quick gesture no one else sees. "You said that. Who else?"

"One of the fighters," Leena says, and over the intercom, Milano interrupts, "Not me. I'm gonna stay up here and keep my finger on the trigger, if you know what I mean. Take Parker."

From the other fighter, Parker sighs. "Can I fly my bird down there?"

"And give them all heart failure?" Dylan asks. "We'll take the *Semper Fi*. It's less intimidating."

"It's unarmed," Parker points out.

Dylan ignores him. "Me and Parker, who else? We need a navigator…" He nudges me with his foot. "You don't want to go down there, do you, Val? I mean, not *really*, right?"

Vallery laughs. "Take your boy," she tells him, winking at me.

"You don't want to go?" I ask her. Me, I *want* to go down there, check out the land and these colonists and the ship, see what's kept them planet-bound for the last twenty years, get answers to the plethora of questions tearing through my mind right now. But if she has her heart set on going, I'll give up my seat. If I *have* to.

But she shakes her head. "I can stay here," she says. "Honest."

"Maybe we can go in shifts," I suggest. "Four the first time, four the next. If you want—"

"Maybe we can just send one party and get this over with, okay?" Johnson mutters, and Dylan stiffens beside me. He's so protective at times, and right now he doesn't need to get into another argument. I cover his boot with my hand, shake my head, *not now*.

Johnson continues. "We're just here to check out the signal, remember, people? Ask them to turn it off or maybe get the frequency on file, we're mapping for a stellar bypass nearby—can't have that blip of theirs pulling anyone out of hyperdrive now, can we? This isn't a fucking vacation, you know."

"I'd like to go," Shanley says, and thank God he's here, his soft speech and quiet manners easily diffuse Johnson's bristly demeanor. "If no one objects—"

Leena shakes her head. "You *should* go, you know what questions to ask about all this." With a grin, she elbows Johnson and says, "It's just you and us girls, boy. Isn't this going to be fun?"

The way he rolls his eyes and grunts suggests he thinks she has a warped idea of what fun really is.

So it's just Dylan and me in the airlock, waiting for Shanley. Parker is already out by the *Semper Fi*—he landed his bird in the hangar and didn't bother going through the decon procedures, not to enter the ship when he's just going out there again anyway. I lean back against one of the cold, white walls of the airlock, and I can feel the steel bite through the thick jacket I wear over my jumpsuit. I toy with the zipper and then stop myself, I'm not nervous, I'm *not*. These are humans, just like us. If anything, they're probably terrified—who knows what they're expecting? Some of them have never even *seen* another living creature outside of their tiny little planet, we're their first contact with anyone else. If anyone should be nervous, it's them, not us. Not me.

Dylan closes the airlock door and sighs. "What the hell's taking him so long?" he mutters, but I don't know so I don't answer. He walks over to where I stand and steps in front of me, presses his lips to my forehead, murmurs against my skin, "I love you, babe."

My arms find their way around his waist and I hug him tight. "Love you, too," I breathe against his neck. "What do you think we're getting into here?"

He shrugs, a gesture that settles his body closer into mine, and his arms wrap around my shoulders, pull me to him, hold me close. "I'm not sure," he admits. His lips are soft against my temple, and when he kisses me again, I close my eyes and savor the touch. "Mike's right, we're not staying long. Just a few days, I'm guessing. Just long enough for the novelty to wear off." I laugh at that, and I feel his mouth pull into a grin. "Dixon will want info but just enough to pass on to the Worlds Council. I don't think there's anything else he can really do, anything he'll *want* to do. He's all about mapping this region, that's it."

"He's not getting paid to waste time with this little colony," I point out.

Dylan laughs, breathless against my ear, and then kisses my neck. "Exactly," he purrs. His fingers pick at my jumpsuit's zipper, pulling it down slightly, tickling beneath the separated fabric, tracing the curve of my collarbone, the hollow of my throat. So soft, that touch. So amazingly gentle. "If Shanley's going to be awhile," he starts, kissing my jaw.

The door slides open and Shanley steps out into the airlock. "I'm right here," he says. On the vidscreen behind him, I can see Vallery setting the DAQ system up for the decon. "If you guys don't mind," he adds, the hint of a smile on his face, "maybe you could wait until later tonight to do…whatever it is you're about to do?"

I laugh and push Dylan away, but he manages one last quick kiss and then the light above the outer door buzzes green and the door slides away to reveal the hangar and Parker, already waiting for us. "Later, then," Dylan promises as he leads the way to the *Semper Fi*.

Part 4

Dylan takes us in low and steady, keeping the *Semper Fi* above the spotty cloud cover until Vallery patches in the landing coordinates. Then he plunges into the planet's atmosphere, into a steady, driving drizzle that fogs up our external screens and leaves us flying blind because he's going too fast. "I hate it here already," he mutters. The *Semper Fi* is small and the nav deck is merely an extension of the cockpit, so I'm sitting where a co-pilot would on the carrier, all my nav screens right here in front of me, but we still wear headsets and when he speaks, I hear his words echo deep within me. Parker and Shanley are strapped down behind us, in the tiny corridor that leads from the cockpit to the crew quarters. Twin benches line the walls back there, and rigging keeps the shocks and bumps of a landing to a minimum. As we hit a pocket of turbulence and I feel the seat beneath me jolt suddenly, I wonder why whoever made this craft didn't put that rigging in the cockpit, as well. "I can't see where I'm going—"

"Slow down," I tell him. I'm not looking out the window, I can't see shit through the thin fog and rain, but on my data screen I see we're nearing the landing strip that Ellington told Vallery would be open for us, and the way we're flying, we're going to skip right over it. "Dylan, you have to slow down a bit—"

"I'm the damn pilot," he reminds me. "Don't tell me how to fucking fly."

I ignore that. He's tense, we all are—we don't know what we're flying into, Johnson was right, those files told us *nothing*, and when Dylan gets like this, he's irritable and says shit he doesn't mean. He'll apologize later, I know he will, and he's so much a part of me, of my soul, that I can't be mad at him for long, not when he'll be holding my hands in his tonight and kissing me and saying he's sorry. He's my weakness, I hate to admit it but it's true.

And he knows he's flying too fast because I feel him cut the throttle and the engines whine as the *Semper Fi* starts to slow down a bit. *Told you so,* I think, but I'm not going to say that. It'll make him madder still and then *I'll* have to be the one to apologize, and I don't want that. This mood of his isn't my fault.

Vallery's clear voice comes across the intercom. "I'm going to switch the channel over," she announces. "Ben says he has you on his screens. He says you're coming in too fast so rein it in some, boys. You're going to shoot right past the colony."

"I never have that problem," Dylan mutters, and I grin because at least he's joking now. He pulls the yoke in and slows down even more, until it's just a few klicks a minute and that's where I need him to be. "Ask Neal. I never miss when I come."

"I so did not need to know that," she says. He laughs and winks at me, and see how easy that was for him? He hasn't even said the words and I already forgive him. "I'm switching over now. Try not to say anything to scare these kids off, okay? Please?"

"Whatever you say," Dylan mumbles. Leaning across the space between our chairs, he plants a quick kiss on my cheek and breathes, "You thought it was funny, didn't you?"

Grinning, I tell him, "Yes, I did. Hilarious."

He studies me for a minute like he's not sure if I'm playing with him or not, but then he kisses the corner of my mouth and whispers, "Come closer."

"Dylan," I warn. On the screen in front of me, a little red light starts to blink. "We're losing altitude, babe."

"I'm on it," he swears, but the ship dips away below us and from the corridor, Parker hollers at him to watch what the hell he's doing. Dylan straightens up and jerks hard on the yoke, bringing the *Semper Fi*'s nose up, and then he slouches in his chair and pouts. "I said I had it covered. Jesus."

Now I lean across to him and place my lips against his ear, and I whisper, "I know you did," before I kiss him lightly. As I sit back in my seat, he turns and smiles at me and this is why I love him, this is what I live for, these small moments where his smile lights up my entire world. "Just keep her steady, hon," I tell him, opening the channel Vallery's switched over. "Ellington?" I ask—didn't she say Ben was the one who had us in sight? Not Conlan, the other guy, the older one. "You with us here?"

"Standing by," comes the reply. It strikes me that these colonists are all very curt, very professional—almost humorless. I wonder what we're going to find down there when we land...*but look at what they've gone through,* I remind myself. More than half of their original number gone, and we're not sure why but something like that's got to take a toll on a person, no? Maybe what I'm mistaking for a lack of humor is just a grim outlook. Maybe for them, there *is* nothing to joke about here. "I have you on the screens," Ellington says, his voice free of static now that we're in the planet's atmosphere. "You're coming in a little too fast—"

I speak before Dylan can make one of his randy comments. "We've cut the thrust," I tell him, even as Dylan lets up on the boosters. "I have the landing strip on my vids but I can't see it. Are we on course?"

"You're almost on top of us," he says, and Dylan cuts the thrust off completely, lets the ship coast through the rain. Locking the coordinates into the nav system, I rise to my feet and lean down over the control panel, try to look through the clouds to see...

The land begins to materialize below us. "Hold her steady," I breathe, and behind me Dylan makes a noncommittal noise in the back of his throat, a grunt that's his way of answering when he's busy. He's flying without the boosters now, and the engines are only at half-cycle, I can hear them churning through this nasty weather, and it's going to be a touchy landing, I can tell that already. We can't see shit out there, and as I lean over the panel dangerously, trying to look down the side of the ship and see the ground, I find there's nothing really *to* see. Just short, dried grass clinging desperately to red clay, a muddy stream running with blood-colored earth and swollen along its banks, a row of half-formed crops, haggard and bent beneath the steady rain. "This is not a pretty place," I murmur.

"Sit down, babe," Dylan tells me. "You've got a great ass but it's in my way."

I laugh and plop back down into my chair. "You're just easily distracted," I counter. On my data screen the landing strip is coming right up on us. "Five degrees to the east. Turn it slow."

"Any slower and we'll fall asleep," Dylan replies. Beneath us the ship starts to curve, and the fog ahead grows dense, dark. As we approach, the shape solidifies into the hulking remains of a colony craft, a huge starship twice the size of Dixon's station. Dylan pushes his mouthpiece up, clicking off the open channel, and whispers to me, "I'm going to take her around once. Just to see what we're dealing with here."

"Good idea," I breathe. He flies in close and we can see the battered hull, an ugly, dingy color, the steel pocked and dented. Along the bottom, a tenacious vine clings stubbornly to the landing gear, a dark, almost reddish growth like cancer that's spread along the lower portion of the ship. The ship's name stands out on the hull, the paint flecked, each character easily the height of the *Semper Fi* itself. *S410*. And below it, in letters that would tower over us if we stood beside them, the words, *Operation Starseed*. "I'm not believing this." Paging the carrier, I ask, "Val? You getting this on the backup?"

"I'm getting it," she replies. "Nice hunk of junk they've got there."

Ellington's voice cuts her off. "Captain Teague, you've missed the landing strip—"

"No shit," Dylan mutters. Thank God his headset's turned off. "Tell him to keep his shirt on, we're just looking. Jeez."

Yeah, that'll go over big. Into the comm-link, I say, "We overshot the strip. You were right—coming in too fast. We're trying for another approach."

"Bullshit," Dylan whispers, but he angles around the ship and starts back towards the landing strip. "How big you think this mother is?"

I shrug. "The stats file said what, almost five hundred meters long? That sound about right?" Small interior rooms, only about two hundred square feet per person, if I remember correctly. Not much space at all, but with their reduced population, the ship's probably a perfect home for those who remain.

As we come around the stern to the starboard side, we can see the wreckage mentioned in the file—a huge, gaping hole torn into the hull, cabling like sutures dangling from the open wound. The rooms beyond are gray, dead, empty. Fifteen people were killed when this happened, twenty years ago. I wonder if they were sleeping in these rooms at the time, or if this was part of the working area of the ship, not living quarters. *And what about the others?* my mind whispers. *The forty-some people who started out on this ship and aren't among the living now? What happened to them?*

Dylan glides past the damage, coming back to the landing strip, and now I can see it, a patch of cleared land where the clay is packed down in a long, narrow run. "There," I tell him, and he nods, eases the craft down. It shakes around us, reluctant, and for a moment I think we're not going to be able to hold the position, the skids slip in the clay and we're going to have to lift off again, we're not going to be able to land, but then Dylan digs in and we touch down. The engines die and I can hear the *tap tap* of rain against our hull. Beneath us the

Semper Fi settles into the clay, the ship creaking around us, and I glance over at Dylan, flash him a quick grin. "You rock," I tell him.

He sighs loftily. "I know," he says, and when I punch his arm playfully, he laughs and pulls away.

In the corridor behind us, Parker unhooks his riggings, stands and stretches to the ceiling, stomps his feet as if to wake up his legs and says, "I'm flying us outta here. You're a hazard with that stick in your hand."

"I got us down, didn't I?" Dylan asks, defensive. He tears off his headset and stretches in his seat. With a wink my way, he asks me, "Do you think I'm a hazard, baby?"

I busy myself with transmitting the final coordinates to Vallery and mumble, "No comment." Parker laughs at that and Dylan pouts, but I'll kiss that away later. On my screens I see a hatch open on the S410 and then three people step out, each covered in a plastic poncho that's wrapped around them to ward off the rain. "Heads up, guys," I tell them. "Looks like the welcoming committee's on its way."

Parker leans past me and squints out the window. "We gotta go out in that shit?" he asks softly. "Can't we wait til it lets up a bit?"

"I don't think it ever lets up," I tell him. "What did the file say?"

From the corridor, Shanley speaks up over the jingle of riggings as he tries to extract himself. "Almost continual precipitation. This is probably the best you're going to get."

There's a knock on the hatch and Dylan glances at me. "You scared of a little rain?" he asks, grinning at Parker, "or can I let them in already?"

This is it. Dylan and Parker head to the back of the ship, where the hatch is. Shanley follows them, and as I finish up with the coords, I click on the intercom again. "We're leaving the ship," I tell Vallery, speaking low into my headset. "I'll let you know when we get to their comm center."

"Take care," she says, and then the connection closes and I toss my headset aside, trying to ignore the nervous roil of my stomach as I follow the others.

🍁   🍁   🍁

The three men stand back as the hatch opens—farther away than necessary, in my opinion, since the raised door could provide some relief from the rain, but they don't take advantage of it. Instead they wear clear plastic ponchos with hoods pulled up over their heads and they watch us exit the *Semper Fi*, exchanging wary glances when I seal the hatch behind me. "Only four?" one of them asks. He's shorter than the other two and stands slightly in front of them, as if in charge. A mess of poorly chopped locks above his dark eyes lead down into thick sideburns that point to a smooth chin dripping with rain. He squints in the downpour and frowns at us, and I recognize his thin voice immediately. Ellington, *has* to be, and if I hadn't seen his med file myself, I wouldn't believe this man's thirty, he doesn't look that old. He looks like a surly kid, actually, playing the leader with his hands on his hips and the rain runneling down his cheeks like tears.

Before anyone can answer his question, he nods as if this is what he's expected all along and says to no one in particular, "That's good, really. Four's good." He looks us over and I try not to squirm, but it's chilly out here and even beneath the overhang of the ship, water spits at me, a fine spray that covers my face and hands and seems to trickle down my collar into my jumpsuit. Finally his gaze rests on Parker, the oldest of our group, and he asks, "Which one of you is Teague?"

"That would be me," Dylan says, stepping forward. He holds his hand out and for a breathless moment, I think Ellington's not going to shake it. The look on his face is what, contempt? Fear? I'm not sure, it's hard to read, and it might just be a product of my imagination, a trick of the clouded light, because then he takes Dylan's hand and pumps it once, hard, before letting go. Pointing behind him,

Dylan introduces the rest of us. "Parker's one of our fighter pilots. Shanley's the med tech, and James here is the navigator." With a bawdy wink my way, he nudges Ellington and grins. "Damn good one, too, if you know what I mean."

"I'm sure he doesn't need to know," I say, rolling my eyes. *Didn't Vallery tell you to lay off the comments?* I want to ask, but I don't. When he catches my eye, I shake my head. "Dylan," I warn.

He sighs and there's an awkward moment where we wait for them to say something, anything, just to cover the rush of rain around us. Dylan takes a step back out of the drizzle and I place a hand against the small of his back to keep him from stepping into me. In the *Semper Fi*'s flood lights, his hair sparkles wetly as if studded with diamonds. He starts to turn, the hint of a smile already pulling at his lips, and I know he's going to say something low and provocative that's going to make me blush, he's good at things like that, especially in front of other people—he doesn't care who knows we're together, can't understand that it's not always the time and place to mention sex, he's only twenty and still a teenager at heart. He says it's me that does it to him, makes him horny 24/7, and the last thing we need is one of these guys to take offense at whatever he's about to say. I force a tight grin and through clenched teeth mutter, "Don't."

Ellington's frown deepens as he watches us. "Benjamin Ellington," he says by way of introduction, and I wonder if that long name's his way of compensating for his small stature. He turns slightly, jerks a thumb at the tall, lanky man to his right, whose pale skin stands in sharp contrast to the dark aviator shades that hide his eyes. I don't like the lean, hungry grin on his thin lips. "Seth Maclin." The guy nods, the briefest of gestures. He reminds me of a wolf watching sheep, waiting for a chance to pounce, and all I know is I don't want him behind me when we head into the S410. I don't want that man anywhere near me.

"Caleb Henry." Ellington turns to his other side, jerks his thumb at the large, stocky man to his left. His skin's the color of rich mahogany, shiny as if oiled by the rain, and he has a wide nose, a wider mouth, large eyes that stare at us, into us, into *me. Guards,* I think randomly—these two men have the appearance of guards, even though they're both unarmed and their hands are shoved beneath the plastic ponchos, hidden in deep pockets we can't see. But there's something in the way they stand, the way they watch us, the way they don't speak and defer to Ellington and sort of stand *around* him, protective almost, that reminds me of bodyguards. I don't like that.

Another awkward pause. I study the ground, the wet clay smearing my boots in long, bloody stripes, and then Ellington pulls out a handheld scanner, fiddles with the display. The guys with him never let their gazes waver from us and I can't seem to meet their eyes, I don't like what I can't read there. Almost reflexively, I clench my fist into Dylan's jacket, grabbing a handful of the material to keep him close to me. No, I don't like this at all, not one bit.

"Just a precaution," Ellington's mumbling, only half speaking to us. He holds the scanner up and it beeps once, an angry sound. "Low grade detector, nothing major, just looking for knives and blasters and you know, things like that." The scanner beeps again and he glances up at the *Semper Fi*, that perpetual frown on his face deepening. "You're going to have to come out from under there, I think. The hull's screwing with the readings."

Disgust flickers across Parker's face. "It's raining," he mutters, as if this is something no one else has realized yet.

With a wry grin, Ellington tells him, "It's *always* raining. You get used to it. Who's first?"

Dylan steps forward and I let him go. As he raises his arms out at his sides, Ellington holds the scanner in front of his chest, runs it down his legs, his arms, tells him to turn around. Dylan puts a little twist in his hips as he turns, and when he looks at me, he's grinning again, this is *fun* for him. The scanner remains silent in Ellington's hands. Leaning his head back, Dylan blinks up into the cloudy sky, the rain coursing down his cheeks, his arms spread wide, and in that instant I have to catch my breath, he's so beautiful, so amazing, and he's mine. All mine.

"Clean," Ellington grunts. He sounds almost disappointed. Dylan stands in the rain on the other side of Ellington's companions—*bodyguards,* my mind whispers, *they're bodyguards and they're here to keep us away, if we're not what we claim to be.* I don't like that they're between us, they've managed to separate us and I step forward for their little security check, I want to be on the other side of those men. I want to be where Dylan is.

But Shanley steps up, too, and I let him go first. Dylan winks at me from behind Maclin and Henry. "Love you," he mouths, and I smile and look away. Johnson was right, we don't have to stay here long. I'm already looking forward to climbing back into the *Semper Fi* and leaving this dreary planet behind.

❦ ❦ ❦

They hurry us through the rain to the wreck of the S410—Ellington at the head of our small troupe, then Parker grumbling about the weather to Shanley, who shields his eyes with one hand and keeps his head down as he walks. Maclin is next, the roll of his hips like the lope of a wolf on the prowl. I don't like that man, there's something slick about him, something I just can't put my finger on and I tell myself I don't *want* to find out what it is, I don't care that much. I walk behind him, trying to keep some distance between us—the last thing I need is for someone to stop up ahead and I'll run smack into him, I don't want that at *all.*

Dylan walks beside me, holding onto the sleeve of my jumpsuit. His fingers are cold where they rest against my wrist, and I want to take his hand in mine, warm it up with my breath, kiss his clammy knuckles until they're pinked again, but I can't. Not here, not now. Not with Henry behind us like a storm-cloud, dark and brooding. With my head down, I glance back at him once and he's staring at Dylan's hand on my arm, his brows drawn together. He sees me looking and shifts inside the plastic poncho he wears, but he stays silent. I don't like the look in his eyes, I've seen it before, it's the way Dixon looks at me when Dylan's around. Like it's my fault he loves me. Like there's something wrong with that. Lowering my voice, I lean close to Dylan and whisper, "Can't we stay back at the ship?"

"It's not that bad," Dylan replies with a playful tug on my sleeve. I don't know.

The S410 looms above us, a monolith in the foggy sky. The path leading up to the ship is slippery, the clay sliding out beneath my boots every now and then, and at one point I fall to the hard ground. Suddenly Dylan's there, his strong hands lifting me up, holding me around the waist, concern written across his face. "Watch it, babe. You okay?"

"Fine," I tell him, wiping my hands on my thighs and leaving red earth smeared along my jumpsuit. When he tries to look at my hands, I curl them into fists—they sting, but I'm all right. "I'm fine, Dylan, really."

With a glance over his shoulder at us, Parker calls out, "Hello? It's raining here, people."

Dylan ignores him, takes my hands in his and pries them open. The skin is scraped and raw but there's no blood. "See?" I tell him, folding my fingers into my palms. "I'm fine."

I don't think he's so sure. He looks at Henry, who's watching us intently, warily, but then Maclin asks, "What's the holdup?" and Dylan lets me go. I keep my hands in fists and step carefully, following the others, and I feel Dylan's hands on my hips, he's right behind me. As I pass Maclin, I don't look up at him. "You want to watch it out here," he tells me, his voice deceptively soft.

"I'm fine," I tell him, though I do slip a second time but Dylan's right behind me and he catches me before I go down. "Have I mentioned that I hate this place yet?" I mutter as we approach the colony ship.

"Not in so many words," Dylan says with that infectious smile of his, which brightens the day and makes the rain disappear, the clouds break, the sun shine down around us for just the moment he looks my way. In the shadow of the S410, we huddle with the others for warmth, trying to squeeze beneath the ship's bulk to keep the rain away while Ellington opens the hatch. Here there are no security codes—he simply leans against the hatch, then shoulders it aside as the metal squeals in protest. I don't think he's going to get the thing open, he's just one man, but the hatch slides into the wall just enough for us to enter. Henry and Maclin reseal the hatch behind us.

We're in an airlock but it's old and the walls are cracked, it's not exactly sterile anymore. Still, Ellington runs the system through a standard decontamination bioscan just to be safe. *Overly safe,* I think, because he knows we're all clean. As we wait for the decon scan to cycle through its course, Shanley comes over to me and holds up a small bottle of antiseptic spray. "Let me see your hands," he says.

I hold them out, palms up, and now they've begun to bleed, drops of dark red blood beading along the scratches, not very pretty at all. The spray Shanley coats them with is cold and numbing, and as I watch, the white antiseptic dissolves away, leaving my skin itchy and damp. I'm all too aware of Ellington watching us as he pushes the hood of his poncho back, his companions following suit. They stand against the far wall by the inner door and stare at me as if I might have caught something out there, I'm sick of all this staring. I know we're the first people they've ever met from offworld but they're so damn cautious, it's spooky. "Thanks," I mutter, fighting the urge to wipe the medicine away.

Parker laughs. "That's going to put a damper on your private time," he says. "Both hands, kid? You had to scrape up *both* hands?"

"That's what I'm here for," Dylan tells him, bumping my hip with his.

I see the look the colonists exchange and God, these guys, they're out to embarrass me to death, aren't they? "Dylan—"

He sighs. "I know, I know. Not *now*."

"This is unprecedented," Ellington says suddenly, snagging our attention. "Your visit. Some of the colonists have been fighting the use of the signal for years now. Some don't think it matters, it's never been intercepted before. Some say you're just here to tear this down all over again, all we've finally managed to build up." *It's not that much*, I think, but I bite my tongue so the words don't slip free. Ellington's eyes are dark, unreadable, and he pins each of us in place with his gaze, I feel weary from the weight of it. "Some people didn't want you to land."

"We're not here to tear anything down," Dylan says. "We're starmappers, that's it. They're putting in a bypass soon and the guy we work for, he's been hired to tag this whole sector. I just happened to pick up your signal on our lower band. We had to check it out to make sure we do a thorough sweep of the area, that's all." He laughs, a disarming sound, and is that a smile on Ellington's face? Like he wants to believe us but he's still not sure. He never did say which group *he* fell into, if he was one of those who didn't even want us to land. Dylan continues. "If we just let it slide and years down the line someone comes through here, hears the signal, checks it out and gets slaughtered by aliens—well shit, that's a lawsuit right there, you know?"

Henry glances at Ellington and then back at Dylan. "So you're saying you want us to cut it off?" His voice is deeper than I expected, a rumble like thunder in the distance. "That's why you guys are here?"

With a shrug, Dylan admits, "We thought it was just an old relay and I guess we were going to dismantle it, or maybe map the frequency so it's on file, or…" He trails off and nudges me, wanting me to pick up where he left off.

"Did you know you're the only Starseed colony to take hold?" I ask. The way their eyes widen, I can tell that this is news to them.

"There were twelve ships, right? I'm not sure of the statistics but we can get them for you, if you want. Basically you're the only ship that succeeded."

Now Ellington laughs but it's a wry, haunting sound. "You call this success?" he asks. "Did you read the files we sent you?"

Shanley says, "They were carefully censored."

Above the inner door, a green light blinks silently. Pushing away from the wall, Ellington heads for the door, his companions falling easily into place behind him, one on either side like guards. Bodyguards. "Some colonists didn't want you here," he says, and he stops in front of the closed door, turns and frowns at us each in turn. I swear he stares at me the hardest, me and Dylan, who's so close beside me, his hand rests against my hip with the lightest of touches. "Some argued that we can't keep you away. We're defenseless, as you probably noticed on your flight around the ship. So you're welcome to stay, discuss the signal with the committee, I guess, come up with a solution that won't compromise the integrity of your bypass." Dylan opens his mouth and I know he's going to say it's not our bypass, but my elbow in his stomach keeps him quiet. "But this is *our* colony. We have our own laws, our own safety regulations, and they work for us. All we ask is that you follow them while you're here."

"That's not an unreasonable request," Shanley says, and we all nod in agreement, sure, we can do that. In front of Ellington, the door slides open, a little stiffly but on its own, and he enters the ship. His companions stand on either side of the door and wait for us to follow.

※　　　　※　　　　※

I don't know what I'm expecting—people lining the corridors, maybe, craning their necks to gawk at us. But there *are* no people, and the corridors are empty. Our boot heels echo off the steel with a hollow sound that seems to fill the whole ship and the place feels deserted, like we're the only ones here. "Where is everybody?" Dylan asks. He walks beside me and I can feel his hand hovering near my back protectively.

Ellington walks ahead, setting a fast pace. "This part of the ship's closed off," he explains, leading us away from the airlock. The lights around us are dimmed, at half power—I thought maybe they were simulating evening, but apparently not. "It takes a lot to keep a ship this size running, as you can imagine, and we only have two power supplies—one up now, the other on standby. When one goes down, it takes about two months for it to recharge." He glances over his shoulder to make sure we're keeping up.

Shanley is right behind him and then Parker, then me and Dylan, then Henry and Maclin, whom I just think of as *the guards*. Satisfied we're still with him, Ellington continues. "So we only use what we absolutely need to survive—the labs, mostly, a few of the sleeping quarters, that's about it. Everything else is shut down. Some parts are even sealed off, like the damaged wing. You can't get there from inside the ship."

The corridor twists into the heart of the ship, and as we walk, I realize the lights grow steadily brighter, until we come to a sealed door that bars our way. "The committee's going to want to meet you," Ellington says as he stops in front of a security box. He types in a code, blocking our view of the box with his body so we don't see the key sequence, and there's a shrill alarm that cuts off as the door slides open. He steps through the door and waits on the other side for us to follow. "Welcome to S410."

We come out into the ship's commons. Dixon's station has a room like this, a place for the crew to unwind, filled with vidscreens and holograms and video games, exercise equipment, books, audio disks, a bar in one corner, tables along the walls. Only this room is much larger than the R&R deck on *his* ship, this is *huge*. The ceiling stretches away above us and I look up at the railings lining the balconies, wonder how many of those rooms are being used now—the lights are dim on the second deck and above the third is nothing but darkness. Beneath our feet are ceramic tiles faded to the color of worn denim, and the steel hull of the ship can be seen through cracks running across the tiles here and there. An eatery counter runs along the far wall and behind that there's a doorway that probably leads to the kitchens, tables are scattered all over the place, there's a fountain off to one side, its spray of water tainted with the reddish clay from this planet's surface. But the electronic entertainment has been dismantled—large plants grow up from the hologram pads and the vidscreens have been painted over, probably so they won't be used, won't drain the ship's resources.

And we're not the only ones here.

A young woman pushes a broom slowly across the tiles, moving with deliberate care—she looks no older than Dylan, if that. She looks up as we enter, stops what she's doing, openly stares at us and if she's that young, she's probably never seen anyone outside of the colony before, no one like us. Near her two men sit at a table playing cards—when they look up I see that they, too, are young, our age, they're all so young here. Another man stands by the fountain, a woman sitting beside him, her belly swollen with child and one hand in the water. They're all looking at us and this is what I thought it'd be like, this sudden feeling of being on display, of being seen, of being known.

Two more women come into the commons from the kitchen behind the counter, wiping their hands on thin towels, and one of them points at us, her eyes wide. They're all dressed in plain, handmade clothes, the same pattern, the same materials. Shirts with sleeves that end at their elbows and scoop necklines, pants that fall straight from their hips to their ankles, socks on their feet instead of shoes. They remind me of kids at a slumber party—the outfits look like pajamas. They're all the same utilitarian colors, drab blue and gray and green, as if made from whatever sheets and blankets could be found in the ship's linen supply. Now I notice our guides wear similar garb, hidden beneath the plastic ponchos they still have on, which drip rainwater into a trail of little puddles behind them. They have on boots that click across the tiles but everyone else moves silently, almost gliding away like ghosts as we walk through the commons.

With each step we take, heads turn, people stop, they stare, and I catch half-whispered words and quiet phrases—*They let them land…I'm not going…This was stupid, what if they're carrying? What then?* "Carrying what?" Dylan whispers, taking a step closer to me. His arm eases around my waist, his hand fisting at my side, and behind us Maclin clears his throat. I turn around to find him glaring at us but Dylan ignores him. "Neal, what—"

"I don't know," I tell him. This wasn't a good idea at all, us coming here, what were we thinking? Some of these people look at us like we have a plague, or we're here to…what did Ellington say? Tear down everything they've built up, destroy their way of life, but we're not, that's not it at all. *What is it, then?* a voice inside my mind whispers.

It's just the signal, I reply. *We have to get that mapped so it doesn't interfere later on down the line, that's it, that's all.* I don't like the way these faces harden when we walk by, the way they whisper behind our backs, the way Ellington seems to be holding his breath, waiting for something to happen, and his companions—his *guards*—they close the distance between us until I swear they're right up on me, the only thing keeping them off my back is Dylan's arm around my waist, that's it. "I don't like this," I mutter.

Ahead, Parker curls his hands into useless fists at his sides and I know he's feeling the same way, he's wanting his fighter right about now. "The committee should still be gathered together," Ellington says, heading down a corridor that branches off the commons. I can still feel the people watching us, I know they're talking about us, and if they're all unarmed then why does this whole thing frighten the hell out of me?

The corridor ends at a large conference room. A wooden table fills up most of the room, and behind it sits one person, a man, that's it.

Some committee, I think, and beside me Dylan leans closer, I know he's thinking the same thing. Before he can remark on it, though, the man looks up and frowns at us. "Only four?" he asks, echoing Ellington's earlier comment. "What did you do with the others?"

"They didn't come," Ellington says. Pointing to Dylan, he adds, "That's Teague."

The man rises to his feet and extends a hand across the table. He's painfully thin, almost gaunt, with dark wavy hair and cheekbones I swear would cut glass. As Dylan shakes his hand, I notice his shirt pulls up, exposing bony hips and a smooth stomach. "Conlan," he tells us, running his other hand through his hair to push it out of his face—he has so *much* of it.

"Don't tell me you're the whole committee," Dylan jokes.

His arm's still around my waist, he's holding on like he's afraid I'm going to disappear, and when Conlan sees that, he frowns, glances at Ellington, Parker and Shanley and the doorway, then back at Dylan. With a noncommittal shrug, Ellington slips out of his poncho, shakes water from the plastic, doesn't look our way. "I thought everyone was still here," he says softly. Behind us there's a slight rustle as Henry and Maclin take off their ponchos, as well. "The committee—"

"Adjourned," Conlan says. He pumps Dylan's hand again and lets go. "So who's who here?"

"Neal James," I tell him, stepping forward. He shakes my hand, a quick jerk, and does the same with Parker and Shanley. Tentatively, I say to Ellington, "You weren't kidding when you said some people don't want us here."

Parker laughs. "Warm welcome we got back there, eh?"

"I think the term I would use," Shanley suggests, "is veiled hostility."

Conlan exchanges another glance with Ellington, who shrugs again. "It's not that bad," he mumbles, and then he starts for the doorway. "Let me go see if I can't round up some of the others." He ducks out into the corridor and is gone, Maclin right behind him.

Henry debates following them but doesn't. Instead he leans back against the wall, crosses his arms in front of his chest, watches us down the length of his nose like he suspects the four of us will gang up on Conlan here if he takes his eyes off us. *We won't,* I want to tell him. *Trust us, please, for once.* But why should they? I mean, really?

Sinking back into his seat, Conlan motions at the other chairs scattered around the table. We each sit down, Parker on the other side of Dylan and Shanley beside me, and Dylan pulls my chair close to his so he can keep a hand on my thigh. For once I'm glad he's so clingy, it's reassuring to feel him touching me at a time like this. Across from us, Conlan folds his hands together, steeples his fingers and rests his chin on his fingertips as he watches us, waiting for…Ellington to return? Something else? I'm not sure. For long moments we sit there, silent, Dylan's hand kneading my thigh with a slow, gentle rhythm and my hands twisting nervously in my lap. I don't even look at Conlan, just stare past him at the nondescript wall and wait.

Finally Conlan clears his throat and I jump, am I that wound up? I didn't realize it, and I smooth my jumpsuit down over my thighs, brush Dylan's hand and then ease mine beneath it, curving my fingers around his. When Conlan opens his mouth to say something, though, it's Shanley who speaks. "Where are the children?" he asks.

We all turn towards him. "The children?" Dylan asks. "What—"

Shanley meets Conlan's steady gaze and explains. "Two of the files you sent us belonged to pregnant women, neither with their first child. So where are the others? In classes, maybe? I didn't see any in the commons."

"There are no children," Conlan says. His voice is quiet and sad. "None of our women have ever carried to term."

Silence. "None?" Dylan asks with a frown. "Why not?"

"Did you read the files we sent?" Conlan asks.

Shanley nods. "There was nothing in them. Nothing explicit—"

"We called it the bleed," Conlan tells us. He looks at his hands, folded as if in prayer, and he speaks so softly, we have to strain to listen. "It was about half a year after the meteor shower, when the ship started to feel the strain of the damage, I guess you'd say, and we started looking for a place to land." With a wry smile, he adds, "I was only like five at the time, so this is just what's in the logs. I don't have any real memories of it."

"Of what?" Dylan asks. I tighten my hand in his.

"The bleed," Conlan says again. "You have to remember, we left on this mission as a hundred terraformers—men and women and their families. There were a lot of families, and a number of children, maybe as many thirty—almost a third of the people who started out on this ship were kids. And we all underwent rigorous decon because of the ID problems back then. The slightest hint of disease and you were removed from the roster, someone else got your position." I think of the decontamination procedures we had to go through just to get here, the bioscan and the dermofol and the HTS. From the look of disgust that flitters across Dylan's face, he's probably thinking the same thing. "We weren't supposed to get sick, none of us. We couldn't."

"But?" Shanley prompts.

Conlan sighs. "We're not sure," he admits. "Maybe it entered the ship once the hull was breeched, maybe it's indigenous to this planet, we just don't know. And we didn't think anything of it at first—just a cold, that's all we thought it was. A case of the sniffles, that's it." With a shuddery breath, he says, "It gets worse, um…" His mouth trembles and he blinks back tears. "You die. What more can I tell you? I don't know how it works but you get sick and you die. Within days—no more than a week, tops. Most everyone died."

Most everyone… "Except a few of you," I whisper.

He nods and takes a deep breath to steady himself. "The kids survived. Ben was the oldest, only fifteen at the time." *Fifteen years ago, I* think. How old is Conlan again? I don't recall but he said he was just five then so that'd make him three years older than me. Only three, and his eyes have a haunting quality to them I hope I never see in a mirror. "We got sick and got over it, you know how kids are. They just shake off colds and bounce right back. But the others..." He trails off, stares at his hands as if the story's written there in his long, thin fingers. "It's like the flu, at first. Muscle aches and a stuffy nose, runny eyes, just a feeling of ugh, something you can't quite shake. Only it doesn't go away, and you get this fever that seems to burn up everything inside of you until you don't even *care* if you ever get better. And then you start to bleed. That's the end, when you start to bleed and it just rushes out of you, the virus and your life and everything just...just bleeds out."

"A filovirus," Shanley announces. I glance over at him and he nods at me, then looks at Conlan, conviction giving his voice an unusual strength. "The symptoms are synonymous with Earth's Marburg or Ebola viruses, or maybe a mutated strain of Frakes. That ran unchecked back during the ID years."

Conlan shakes his head, his hair falling into his eyes. He brushes it roughly away. "We were clean," he explains. "There was nothing on this ship when we left on this mission—not the flu, not Frakes, not even a common cold, *nothing*. We were in space almost a hundred and twenty days before the meteor shower, and more than that before we landed here. The disease didn't crop up until after we set down on this planet."

"How long after?" I want to know.

"About a month," Conlan says, "before the first person died. Before we knew there was a problem." Suddenly I'm thinking of my little fall on the way to the ship, my bloodied palms and how long ago did the last person die of this disease? How is it contacted? What if I get it—what if I have it? What if—*stop it*, I caution. Beside me, Dylan frowns, he sees something in my face that worries him. *Just stop it right now, you slipped and you weren't even bleeding all that bad so don't think about shit like that.*

"And the last person?" I prompt. My voice cracks slightly and I hate that, I hate this fear pounding through my veins. "How does it spread?"

"It's mostly eradicated now," Conlan says with a grim smile. "No one left to catch it, I guess. It's…we're not real sure how it jumps around. Airborne, the strain we all caught as children, had to be. But the adults—maybe the deadly strain is sexually transmitted? We don't really know. You have to keep in mind most of us were just little when it happened—I think I was twelve the last time someone died of it and by then it was almost expected. The precautions we took to isolate the infected were second nature."

"So what, nine years now?" Dylan asks. "And this place is safe? You don't think we're going to catch it, do you?"

Conlan shakes his head. "If there was even the slightest chance of reinfection, I would've cut the signal when we figured out you had locked onto it and you would've never found us. You wouldn't have clearance to land and you wouldn't have access to the colony." *You have no weaponry,* I think, watching him. He glances at each of us nervously, as if he can hear our thoughts and knows we're all thinking the same thing. *You couldn't stop us from landing if we wanted to. Your little door back there with the key code might not have kept us out, if we really wanted to gain access.* "The virus is gone," he assures us. "I promise you."

From the other side of Dylan, Parker speaks up. "Why can't your women have babies then?" *Good question.*

"We don't know," Conlan says again. Another sigh, so painful, so heart-wrenching. "Most of us can't seem to conceive. When we do, the child dies *in utero*, usually by the end of the second trimester, and the women miscarry. We're not…we can't seem to—the colony's going to die out, you realize this, don't you? We can't procreate. We're not going to survive."

I drop my gaze to the table and remain silent. Dylan shifts beside me, suddenly uncomfortable, and Parker shuffles his feet along the floor, Shanley clears his throat—we don't know what to say. *Nothing*, I think. There's nothing *to* say.

Finally Conlan tells us, "But we're trying. We have...laws, I guess you'd say. Regulations, to prevent it from cropping up again. For the most part we've sort of agreed that it's carried through...bodily fluids, um..." He shifts in his seat and doesn't look at Dylan or me. I get the impression he knows about our hands laced together beneath the table. "We have a quarantine area set up in one of the med labs and this is very awkward to talk about with strangers, I'm sorry—"

"Don't be," Shanley assures him. "We're simply visitors here. We have to know your laws if we're expected to follow them."

Conlan takes a deep breath and nods. "No unauthorized sexual relations," he says abruptly. With a wan smile, he adds, "That sounds bad, I know, but we don't know if it's still out there and we can't take the risk of it spreading again. We're only a handful of people here. We have safe zones set up for...for *that*, but both partners have to be screened and the woman has to be ovulating, *has* to be. We need to carry on, if we can."

Dylan laughs, a dry, humorless sound. "No heat of the moment stuff for you guys, huh?" He winks at me. "How romantic."

"We don't have the luxury of romance," Conlan tells him, his voice hardening. "We are dying out. This is our home and we're not interested in moving offworld because we've come this far and we can make this work, we *know* we can. We just can't afford to lose what we've done here. Surely you must appreciate that. You must understand the reasoning here." *Now* he looks at me, at Dylan, pins us in place with an unwavering gaze. "You must respect it, if we all expect to keep this disease under control. You *must*."

❦   ❦   ❦

When Ellington comes back, he's alone. Maclin isn't even with him anymore, and he slides into a chair beside Conlan, gives us all a wan smile. "They're getting together in another hour or so," he explains. He must mean the committee. Conlan nods, and Ellington lowers his voice but I'm sitting right in front of him and can hear him well enough. "Marie's having contractions—"

"Now?" Conlan asks, half rising from his seat. "It's too early—"

Ellington pulls him down, holds his arm to keep him from running off. "She's on the terbute. There's nothing you'll be able to do, sit back down." Conlan doesn't look so sure. "You're just going to worry her—"

Beside me, Shanley clears his throat. "Excuse me," he interrupts, leaning across the table. "I'm sorry, but you said one of the women is in labor?" Ellington nods and Conlan covers his face with shaky hands. "How far along is she?"

"Seventeen weeks," Conlan whispers, his voice muffled through his fingers. "God, Ben, she can't be—"

"And she's on terbute?" Shanley interrupts. Ellington nods again. "Do you mind if I take a look at her?"

Before Ellington can answer, Conlan rises to his feet. "I'll take you to her." Ellington starts to speak but Conlan shakes his head. "Which lab is she in?" When Ellington doesn't answer immediately, he prompts, "Ben? Which lab?"

"Two," Ellington mumbles. "I don't think it's a good idea—"

Conlan doesn't let him finish. "You coming?" he asks Shanley as he hurries from the conference room. Shanley pushes back his chair, scraping the legs across the steel floor, and follows after him.

"That's not very far along, is it?" Dylan whispers. I shake my head. Seventeen weeks is only what, four months? Turning to Ellington, Dylan asks, "Is she going to be okay?"

Ellington shrugs. "I don't know," he admits. "This..." He sighs and closes his eyes, pinches the bridge of his nose as if he's too tired to even really think about it right now. "She lost her first baby at fifteen weeks but she's been doing so well this time..." He trails off and God, what the hell do you say to something like that? Somehow *I'm sorry* just doesn't seem like enough.

But Dylan tries anyway. "I'm sorry," he says, and Ellington forces a tight smile and nods, like he knows we'd apologize even though it isn't our fault. Beneath the table, Dylan's hand tightens in mine and I rub my other hand along his wrist, up his forearm, in slow, even strokes. "Evan's a good doctor, best med tech I've worked with, I'm sure he can help. If there's anything he can do, I know he'll help out. I mean—"

"Hon, hush," I admonish, keeping my voice low so Ellington doesn't hear. Sometimes Dylan doesn't know when to stop—he gets nervous about things like this, sad things where he doesn't know what to say but he feels he needs to say *something* and he thinks if he keeps talking, he'll eventually stumble upon something comforting. Only it doesn't work that way, and I'm sure Ellington doesn't want to be talking about this with us, it's not really any of our business. We're here about the signal, that's it. They coped with these problems before we showed up and they're going to have to deal with them once we leave, there's nothing we can say or do to change that, no matter how good a doctor Shanley is.

"I just thought—" Dylan starts again.

"Don't," I murmur, rubbing his hand between both of mine. "Please." He falls silent, and I whisper, "I know you're only trying to help but now's probably not a good time, baby."

Ellington frowns—I know he heard that, I can tell from the way his brows furrow together and an awkward silence falls around us, the only sound the nervous scruff of Parker's shoes along the floor. Finally Ellington looks up at Henry, still standing like a sentinel by the doorway. "He told you about the bleed," he says, and when I nod, he nods, too. "About…the precautions we take now?"

"He mentioned some," I tell him.

He nods again. "Basically it boils down to this." His gaze shifts to me, to Dylan, then back to me, as he searches for the words to say what he's thinking. I think I know where he's trying to go with this. *No unauthorized sexual relations,* isn't that what Conlan said? Yes, I know what he wants to say, I can see it in his frown, his eyes, the muscle that twitches in his jaw. "This is hard for me to say. You're going to stay here awhile, I assume. Maybe a day or two? I don't know." Dylan shrugs and beside him, Parker grunts, we don't know either. "We have a few rooms you can use but he told you our policy, right? He told you the virus is probably sexually transmitted, right?"

With a short laugh, Parker asks, "So what, you don't want us porking your girls? No problem. We weren't really planning on it—"

"Shut up," I tell him. That's not what he's talking about, not at all. If this were about the women here, he wouldn't be looking at me the way he is, he wouldn't have a problem telling us hands off. "You mean me and Dylan."

Ellington nods, relieved. "You have to understand our position here—"

"What about us?" Dylan asks, confused. "Are you saying—I thought he said the virus is gone now. I thought—"

"We don't know," Ellington says. "*We* don't have it—everyone gets a monthly bioscan, and the women are monitored every week when they're expecting. I'm not saying it's disappeared but we make damn sure we're not going to lose anyone else to it. As far as we know, it hasn't resurfaced in almost ten years but we're not about to take any chances. We can't."

"So what are you saying?" Dylan wants to know. He looks from me to Ellington and back again. "Neal, what—"

"We have laws," Ellington tells us. "Men and women stay in separate quarters. Any relations you have with a woman stay in the quarantine lab. It's a safe zone, and you both have to be screened—Jeremy told you this, right?"

I nod. "There's no unauthorized sex," I say. "No romance, no love. Let me guess, nothing between members of the same sex either, right?" Dylan's fingers clench mine so tight, my fingertips go numb.

Ellington sighs. "I'm sorry," he whispers. "You have to understand our position here. We can't afford the risks involved."

"You mean—" Dylan starts, but I cut him off. "We understand," I assure him, squeezing Dylan's hand in mine to keep him quiet. "This is your colony, your laws. We understand."

"Just so you do," Ellington says softly.

※   ※   ※

Ellington suggests a tour of the colony—he seems more at ease around us now that we've talked, even though we just skirted around the whole issue of Dylan and me together. As we follow Ellington down the corridor to the med labs, I hang back behind the others and catch Dylan's elbow, pull him back with me. "He's basically saying he doesn't want us to get freaky while we're here," I whisper, watching the others in front of us, Ellington and Henry and Parker. "Because of the bleed—"

"We don't have it," Dylan mutters. A slight pout pulls at his lips and I know he was hoping for some downtime alone tonight, it's in his sigh. "This isn't a good idea, baby. Let's go back to the ship, okay? Just tell Dixon we checked it out and there's nothing to see."

I laugh. "You just want some loving tonight—"

"Damn straight!" he hollers, and the others turn around to see what's going on. *Nothing to see,* I think, flashing them a quick grin as I pinch his arm. It doesn't work—he twists free and says, "Don't do that, hon, that hurts."

"Keep it down, okay?" He pouts at me, one of those little boy looks of his that makes my heart twist in my chest, makes me want to catch him in my arms and hug him tight, kiss him and make everything bad go away. Only I can't, not here, not as long as we're inside the S410 and I wonder how bad it would look if we asked to stay onboard the *Semper Fi* tonight. Ahead of us is the med lab and Ellington stops in front of a long, low window so we can catch up with the others. "It's just one night," I whisper to Dylan. "Don't pout. One night won't kill you."

"It might," Dylan replies.

"What about the last two months?" I remind him, trying to lighten the mood. "You aren't dead yet."

Dylan laughs. "You don't know how close I came some days," he says.

As we approach, Ellington glances at my hand on Dylan's arm and there's something in that look that makes me let go. He's my lover, I hate that I can't even touch him here, but I said I understood, didn't I? I can see where he's coming from and it *is* only one night, two at the most, that's it. We'll talk to the committee soon and then we'll head back to the carrier, and after that we'll be apart *again* because I'm going to have to return to the station, Dylan will be on his mission, and I won't think about that, I won't. *Just one night,* I promise myself. *If we have to stay longer, we'll stay in the Semper Fi, I don't care how that looks. He's mine.* Hell, I'll sleep in their damn quarantine lab if I have to, just to be with him.

Ellington points at the window and the three of us crowd together to peer inside. A woman lies on a bed in the center of the room, the skin around her closed eyes as dark as bruises in her pale face and her hair like seaweed spread out on the white pillow. She's hooked up to a monitor of some sort, which beeps quietly beside the bed, and on the other side is a straight-backed chair where Conlan sits, his elbows on his knees, his chin in his hands, watching her, waiting. Shanley and another man hover by the monitor, talking low. Conlan doesn't seem to notice them—he just stares at the woman, nothing else exists for him. "Marie," Ellington whispers behind us.

"She doesn't look too good," Dylan murmurs, resting a hand on the window.

I stop him before he can tap on the glass. "Dylan, don't."

Beside me, Ellington leans his head against the window and sighs. "If she loses this one…" He shakes his head. "It's times like this that I simply don't know how we manage to go on."

"It's his, isn't it?" I ask. That's why Conlan wanted to rush to her side when he heard she was having contractions—the child is his.

Ellington nods. "We don't have partners, *per se*," he explains. "No marriage, nothing like that. But you were wrong when you said there's no love here. There is—look in there and tell me you don't see it."

I *was* wrong—I *can* see it, a sweet tenderness that makes me ache. It's in Conlan's jaw, bunched in helpless anger. In Marie's hand, protective across her swollen belly. In the way she reaches out and he takes her hand in both of his. But I don't like the sadness I see in her eyes, the defeat I see in his shoulders, that makes this—everything around us, everything here—more real.

"The statistics are in their favor," Ellington says, his voice quiet. "She's conceived both times she's been with him, right away, *both times*. And we were so sure this would be the one, you know? We just knew it had to be." Lowering his voice, he whispers, "It *has* to be."

Dylan's hand finds mine. In the med lab, Shanley flips through her chart as the other doctor begins to set up for an ultrasound, but they don't exist for Conlan, they're not there. The only thing that matters to him is the woman and the child she carries, *his* child. They're the world to him, the way Dylan is to me, and it's a selfish thought but I wish Dylan had never heard that damn signal in the first place. I wish we had never come out to this forgotten colony—there's nothing we can do here, nothing at all, and I hate the way I feel right now, useless and impotent and guilty because there's a part of me that's glad it isn't me in there, sitting where Conlan is. I wrap an arm around Dylan's waist and lean against him and thank God it's not me.

Part 5

The sleeping quarters are on an upper deck, above the labs and the commons area. There's one stairwell at the far end of the ship and this time when we cross the commons, colonists line the walls to see us. *This* is what I expected, but I don't like the closed looks on their faces, the undisguised fear, the hostility and anger. Dylan keeps a hand on my wrist and glares around us distrustfully, like he thinks someone's going to come up and snatch me away. "It's okay," I tell him, but I don't believe that myself. *They think we're here to make them leave with us,* I think, watching one woman shrink back as we pass. *Or they think we've brought our own diseases and they'll go through the sickness and death all over again. Or we're just the first, and others will follow, and they're scared.* I don't blame them. If I were them? I'd be terrified.

And alone, I think, relishing Dylan's slight, possessive touch. *Because they don't let men love other men here and what would I be without Dylan? Would I be like Conlan back in the med lab, sitting by a lover's bedside, waiting for a child of mine to die?* I don't think I could live like that. God, no.

Our boots ring out in the stairwell, echoing around us in a rising crescendo until I have to look back to make sure it's only the five of us and not half the colony trekking up the steps behind us. At the top of the stairs Dylan trips over the lip of the doorway and curses beneath his breath. "Fucking shit," he mutters, and it's just one thing after another here, isn't it? Nothing's going right and he gets all bent out of shape over a little stumble and it's just too cute, that frown that creases his brow and pulls his lips into his signature pout and I can't help it, I have to laugh. It starts with a tiny giggle that I can't suppress and by the time he turns around to look at me, I can't stop, I'm laughing so hard. "You think that's funny?" he asks, but there's that smile I love and then he starts to laugh, too. "Oh fuck."

I lean on his shoulder and his arm comes up around my waist, he holds me as we laugh, my breath hot against his neck and I know this isn't the time or the place but suddenly I want him, this boy holding me tight, I want him so bad, my whole body trills with a heady rush and I know he can feel what he does to me, my budding erection presses into his thigh and he pulls me closer, his hands smoothing along my back and we can't stop laughing, this isn't funny, it *isn't*. I'm going to ache all night for him now, dammit the hell. "Dylan," I sigh into his hair. "Oh God, I'm sorry."

Behind us, Parker asks, "You about finished here?"

He's not just annoyed—he sounds *pissed*, and I pull away from Dylan reluctantly, wipe tears from my eyes, take deep, hitching breaths and try to stifle my laughter. Ellington and Henry exchange a worried glance that sobers me up. "I'm sorry," I say again, louder this time, and I shrug Dylan's arm off as I step away from him. "It just struck me as funny, that's all. I'm sorry."

Dylan's giggles taper off and I nudge him with an elbow. "Me too," he mumbles. "Sorry, guys. Jesus."

Ellington gives us a withering look that diffuses any laughter still within me, then turns and starts down the corridor at a quick pace, Parker right behind him. Henry watches us, waiting, but I turn slightly and whisper to Dylan, "I told you about calling me Jesus."

That makes him start again, a snorted chuckle and he covers his mouth with the back of his hand as if to keep it in. "Stop it," he says, giving me a playful shove. "You're going to get us both kicked out of here."

"Me?" I ask, indignant. I want to remind him that I'm not the one who tripped. I've stopped laughing, haven't I? Well, mostly, anyway. When I try to push him back, though, he catches my hand and laces his fingers through mine. With a glance at Henry, I try to shake him free and can't. "Dylan—"

He hurries after the others, tugging me along. "Come on, babe," he says, giving Henry his most disarming grin. The guy doesn't smile back—they're like statues, these colonists, *damn.* "We're missing the tour."

Henry falls in after us and we catch up with Ellington at the end of the corridor. I ignore the look Parker gives us—what can I possibly say that will explain to him how giddy Dylan can make me? He would never understand how just one look from the boy can set everything right in the world, how he can make everything else disappear for me until there's only him, that's it, that's all I need. So I don't meet his angry gaze and I put on my best *paying attention* face, and when Ellington sweeps an arm out to indicate that we should enter the open doorway into the room beyond, I'm the first through, Dylan's hand in mine pulling him in after me. "The men's sleeping quarters," Ellington announces.

It's one in a series of rooms interconnected by low, doorless portals. Bunks are doubled up along the walls in dormitory fashion, six to a room and then a cluster of narrow lockers beside a makeshift bathroom—a sink with a mirror above it, a shower, a toilet stall. A portal on either side of our room shows more of the same, stretching out in either direction, easily fifty bunks in both directions. Pointing at the bunks that form an aisle beside me, Ellington explains, "These are empty here and here—" He indicates the two across from us as well, flush against the wall. "Take your pick."

Dylan frowns at the portals and turns, takes in the open doorway behind us. "No privacy, is there?" he asks. I squeeze his hand in what I hope is a comforting gesture—*I know, baby,* I want to tell him. My groin throbs for him—*trust me, I know.*

But Ellington just shrugs. "We can't afford it," he says, and I nod, yeah, I understand. Maybe if I keep telling myself that, I'll start to believe it.

※　　　　　※　　　　　※

Next Ellington leads us to the communications center, at the heart of the ship. It's a large lab beneath the commons—computers line all four walls and in the center of the room is a clear glass tube that runs from floor to ceiling, clay-laced water like blood rushing through its length. It takes me a minute to realize we're directly below the fountain. "This is what you came to see, isn't it?" Ellington asks, gesturing at the consoles that beep quietly to themselves, the printers spewing out reams of data, the large processors humming with life. It's warm down here, surrounded by all this machinery, and vidscreens around the room show us the fog and rain outside, dark space above the planet, a tiny winking dot that might be our carrier, might just be an errant star, I'm not sure. There are a few radio techs here, a girl and two guys who glance up as we enter and then turn back to their stations and pretend we're not even there. "The signal's origin," he continues. "It's broadcasting at only a third of its potential because we don't want to waste power. We never really thought anyone would pick it up."

"Nobody would've," Dylan says, leaning over a shoulder of one of the radio techs to get a closer look at her screen. She throws Ellington an annoyed glance and then moves over, lets Dylan lean in close to the console. "There's no reason for anyone to be out in this system, really. Not til we get the stars mapped out this way. What's this?" He points at data scrolling across the screen.

"System specs," the radio tech tells him, but she doesn't elaborate.

I turn to Ellington, who's watching us like he thinks we're going to break something. "Can I call the carrier from here?" I ask. "Just to let them know what's going on."

"What *is* going on?" Parker mutters, tapping on the glass fountain in the middle of the room. "When can we meet this committee of yours and get going?"

"They said an hour," Ellington reminds us, "but with Marie like she is, maybe not tonight. Not until…" He trails off and frowns at me, but I can read the unfinished sentence in his haunted eyes. *Not until the labor stops or the baby dies,* that's what he was going to say. I'm glad he didn't. I don't want to hear the words out loud.

Shaking the thought away, he nods at the computer where Dylan's standing. "Sure, hail your friends. You can operate one of these?"

I glance at the radio controls and tell him, "Yeah, I think so. It's an older model but it can't be too hard." His frown deepens and jeez, don't these people *ever* smile? "I'm just kidding."

Dylan grins over his shoulder at me and says, "Show him how you can work it, baby. You're—" I shake my head and his smile disappears. "Sorry," he mumbles, turning back to the console.

I come up behind him and run my hand down his back—I can feel the curve of his spine beneath my fingers and I want him again, it's painful how bad he can make me ache. "It's okay," I say softly, busying myself with the radio before Ellington even makes that damn noise in the back of his throat, the one that tells me he doesn't like the way my hand rests on my lover's waist. I want to whisper *tonight* but I can't, that's not a promise I can keep, so I lose myself in the radio and try to ignore the way my jumpsuit bites into my erection, the way Dylan's hand brushes mine when he moves, the way Ellington watches the two of us like he seriously thinks we're going to get it on right here. "So is Marie on the committee?" I ask as I search through the frequencies for an open channel.

"No," Ellington says. "Jeremy is—don't play with that." He takes a tachometer from Parker, sets it down again, but when he turns away, Parker picks it back up to study it. Ellington doesn't notice—he's too busy watching Dylan to make sure he doesn't press anything accidentally. "I don't know what you're thinking about when we say committee but it's not really a government or anything, just six people at a time. It's sort of a revolving position, six months each so we all get our say. Everyone's on it at one time or another. Jeremy is committee chair right now and can you stand back some? Please?" He eases between Dylan and the console, easing him away from the controls. "Just stand there, okay? Don't touch anything."

"I'm not—" Dylan starts, but before he can argue, a burst of static erupts from the speakers and then Vallery's voice fills the room. *"Semper Fi,"* she says, excited. *"Neal, is that you?"*

I grin at Dylan and hold down the transmit button. "How'd you guess?" I ask. Her laughter's a happy reply. *We should've let her come down here,* I think, *liven these people up some.* "What's shaking, girlfriend?"

She sighs, a sound that ends in a breathless giggle. *"We were beginning to wonder what happened to you guys,"* she says. *"Tessa's all about flying down there and saving your sorry asses—"*

And there's that disapproving look in Ellington's eyes—what, these people don't even cuss? "This isn't a secured channel," I warn her. "I'm just checking in…"

"Oh, right! Sorry, guys. Sorry." I can picture her in my mind, her hair pulled back in that severe ponytail she favors, and it'd toss from shoulder to shoulder as she shakes her head, apologizing. *"I didn't mean it, promise. You know I've got bad timing—"*

Dylan pushes past me and hits the transmit. "That's putting it mildly, sister," he growls, laughing as I push him away. "It's true!" he cries.

"I know it is," I tell him, nodding at Ellington. That quiets him. I can't bear the chastised look on his face, so I wink at him quickly, then turn back to the radio, but not before I see the hint of his sunny smile. "Everything going okay up there?" I ask Vallery. *Tell us to come back,* I pray. *It's horrible down here, so much death, not enough life, just tell us to come on back and forget all about this, okay?*

But she doesn't. "Everything's fine," she says brightly, and then laughs again. "Mike's about to go crazy, says we're hen-pecking him, I don't know *what* he means by that. He's just in a shitty mood—oops! I didn't mean that, sorry. Sorry." Before I can reply, she asks, "How's it going down on your end? Dylan behaving himself?"

"Hey!" he cries, but I laugh and tell her, "More or less. You know how he is." Then I give her a brief overview of the situation, choosing my words carefully because I get the impression that Ellington's listening a little too closely to what I have to say. So I tell her about the committee and how we're supposed to meet with them tonight and how we might not, glossing over the complications that have arisen with Marie's pregnancy because that's really none of our concern. "Shanley's helping out," is all I say. I don't mention the surly demeanor of the colonists or the virus that decimated so much of the ship's population, and I sure as hell don't tell her that Dylan's mad because they won't give us a room to ourselves and he's not going to get a piece of me tonight, she *really* doesn't need to know *that*. But I describe the planet's surface and the S410 and when she asks if it's still raining, I tell her it is. "Far as I know, anyway. They say it's always raining here."

"I'll let Tessa know," Val laughs. "She was mad you didn't take her down there instead of Parker but when I mentioned the rain, you should've seen the face she made. Tough as nails pilot she may be, but heaven forbid those curls of hers start to frizz."

I've decided I quite like Vallery. When she's finished this mission with the *Semper Fi*, I hope she hangs around the station a little while. She'd be fun on the nav deck and I know Tony's going to love her. I'm going to talk her up until he's as anxious for her to get back as I will be for my boy. Catching Ellington's slight sigh, I tell her, "I have to get off this channel, Val. I'll let you know what happens when it does."

"And don't forget to give us a heads up when you're on your way back," she says. "Tessa might shoot you out of the sky otherwise. That girl's trigger happy." Another laugh—such an infectious sound, I wish we *had* brought her instead of Parker, even if she has an uncanny knack of interrupting Dylan and me when we're getting busy—and then she says, "Over and out," like she's a little kid, playing space games.

I give Ellington a wan grin and move away from the radio before he can suggest it. "Thanks," I say.

He nods as he takes the log book away from Dylan, who's leafing through it, only half interested. "Let me take you guys back to the men's quarters. Hey, can you—no, don't—" He snaps his fingers at Parker, playing with the ship's nav controls as if they're joysticks for a video game. I can even hear the little fighter noises he makes beneath his breath—the ship's grounded, what harm can he do? I don't know, but when he sees Ellington frowning at him, he backs away guiltily and shoves his hands deep into his pockets. "I'm going to check with the committee," Ellington says, leading us from the comm center with obvious relief. "Just wait in the quarters—I don't think it's a good idea if you go wandering about, you know?"

Back in the commons, among the colonists with their silent, baleful stares, I miss Vallery's bubbly laugh—yes, I know exactly what he means.

※ ※ ※

When we get to the men's quarters, Dylan vaults onto the upper bunk against the wall and pats the space beside him like he wants me to jump up there, too. "Careful," Ellington warns as Parker picks the other bunk, the one by the door—he falls into the lower bed with an awful groan from the mattress springs. "Look, try not to—"

"When's dinner?" Parker asks, folding his hands behind his head and closing his eyes. A true fighter, he's already napping, going to take advantage of whatever downtime he can get.

Ellington frowns at me like he thinks I'm going to tear apart one of the other bunks. "A few more hours," he tells us. "I'll let you know when." The way he's doing this, walking us around and being so damn evasive when answering our questions, it's aggravating, his distrust in us. I feel as if there's nothing I can do to possibly make him see we're not as awful as he seems to think.

"Neal," Dylan says. As Ellington turns to leave, Dylan cups his crotch and winks at me. "Up here, baby."

Ellington's step falters, and for a moment I think he's going to say something, remind us of the whole unauthorized sex bit, and *just don't*, I pray, climbing onto the lower bunk beneath Dylan to give myself some leverage to hoist myself up beside him. *Don't say it again, we don't need to hear it, we already KNOW.*

He doesn't, thank God. As he leaves, I swing one leg up onto the upper bunk and Dylan's hand curves around my thigh, slips between my legs, beneath my ass, gentle and firm and he's not helping one bit here but I'm not about to tell him to stop. "Up here," he says again, playful, and somehow I make it up onto the bunk despite his hand in places that make me weak to think about it.

When I lean back against the wall, he lies down on his side, head in my lap, and looks up at me with those dark eyes that eclipse the rest of the world. The way he stares up at me, his thick eyebrows pulled together in consternation, his chapped lips a thin, pink line—"Dylan," I sigh. I have to remember we're not alone, Parker's on the other bunk, we can't do anything, we *can't*.

But Dylan seems to forget this, and he shifts his gaze to the slight bulge at my crotch, where the zipper of my jumpsuit puckers out like an exaggerated erection. With one long finger he traces the zipper's path, pushing the fabric down until I can feel his touch along hardening flesh. "Dylan, don't," I tell him, catching his hand in mine. I don't need him to turn me on any worse than I already am.

He sighs and props himself up on one elbow, pouts up at me with that puppy-dog look he's perfected because he knows what it does to me. "Why not?" he wants to know, and before I can answer, he fists his hand in the front of my jumpsuit and pulls me down to him. "Kiss me," he whispers as his lips close over mine.

Somehow I manage to mumble, "Parker." Then his mouth cuts off the rest of whatever it is I want to say, his tongue licks into me, and I forget that we shouldn't be stealing these tender kisses at a time like this.

Dylan presses into me, hungry. "He's asleep," he breathes, his fingers fumbling with the collar of my jumpsuit. "Please—"

"I'm not asleep," Parker mutters from the other bunk. "You two knock that shit off."

Letting go of my jumpsuit, Dylan rolls onto his back and punches the mattress beneath us angrily. "You go somewhere else," he suggests, but he lies down again, his head on my thighs, and glares at the ceiling like it's going to do any good. "Baby, I *want* you," he whines. A twenty year old man whining like a child, it's not a pretty sight.

You're not the only one, I think, trailing my fingers through his bangs. In a high, mocking voice, Parker mimics, "Baby, I *want* you."

"Shut up," Dylan growls. "Nobody asked you."

"Nobody had to," Parker counters.

When Dylan opens his mouth to reply, I cover it with one hand—this could go on all day, talking shit back and forth, just picking at each other, Dylan's done it before. Always has to have the last word. "Just drop it," I tell him. He stares up at me with wide eyes and then I feel his tongue on my palm, licking my hand. If he thinks that's going to get to me—

"Yeck!" he grimaces, pushing my hand away. Holding my wrist, he looks at my open palm and says, "I forgot Evan sprayed you with that medicine crap."

"Taste bad?" I laugh at the face he makes, simply priceless.

"I need kisses," he tells me, struggling to sit up, "to make it all better."

I press my hand to his chest to keep him down. "I ain't kissing you with that stuff on your mouth."

Dylan wipes his lips with the sleeve of his jumpsuit and looks up at me, hopeful, but I shake my head. With an exasperated sigh he rolls his eyes and presses back against my crotch, just to be spiteful—I know him too well. "It's gone," he mutters, but didn't I tell Ellington he didn't have to worry about us? It's only one night, tops—we'll meet with the committee later this evening or first thing in the morning, we'll talk about the signal, and we'll leave. Back on the carrier we can lock the door to my room and turn off all the vidscreens and disable the damn intercom if we have to, and I won't even think about what's going to happen when I have to leave for the station again. I don't let my mind go any farther than the two of us in my bunk back on the carrier, twined together beneath my sheets, finally finding a release for all this tension that's building between us now.

When I don't answer him, Dylan sighs again and closes his eyes, his forehead still furrowed. Gently I rub his stomach, flat and hard through his jumpsuit. I wait until his breathing slows and his brow smoothes out, and then I ease his zipper down, just a little bit, just enough to slip my hand inside. He moans softly and burrows his head against the swell of my erection. "Neal," he sighs, and I rub his chest in long, slow strokes, trace circles around his nipples, trail my fingers up and down the planes of muscle that lead to his stomach. The zipper works its way down beneath my wrist, pushed out of the way the further I go. I rub along his abdomen, his hips, his erection that strains the fabric of his boxers, and he thrusts up into my hand with another moan, this one loud enough that across the room Parker opens one eye to see what's going on.

I flash him a quick smile and lie down alongside Dylan, shifting as little as I possibly can so I don't disturb him but he looks at me anyway, his eyes dulled and shiny with lust. "Where are you going?" he murmurs, sitting as I prop myself up on one elbow and curl my legs onto the bed. "Neal—"

"Lie back down," I tell him. He obeys, resting his head on my legs, and then he rolls onto his side so he's facing me, his back to the rest of the room and his unzipped jumpsuit falling open to reveal smooth, pale skin. "You're so beautiful," I breathe, running a hand along his muscled chest. He brings his knees up as I fold my arm beneath my head, and now we're an unending circle, an eternity, just us two. A perfect position, actually, if we were alone. But we're not.

He watches me as I rub his exposed flesh, my hand sure along his body, the contours more familiar to me than my own. When I brush across the front of his boxers, his eyes slip closed again and he bites his lower lip to keep quiet. I trace the outlines of his swollen dick, smooth the fabric down beneath my hands, press at him and stroke and knead until he gasps my name breathlessly. *Oh no,* I think, savoring the way his body responds to my touch. What did I tell Ellington? *You don't have to worry about us, we can control ourselves—heh, yeah right. So much for that.*

And Parker's just in the other bunk. "See what you make me do?" I murmur. Beneath my hand, Dylan's boxers are growing damp, almost transparent, and he nods but doesn't trust himself to speak. "You're so bad."

He nods again. "Neal," he sighs, reaching out to stroke my own erection, still confined in my jumpsuit. His fingers work at me, make me hard, make me ache, and I can't stop myself from leaning forward, pressing my mouth against the thin material that hides him from me, closing my lips around his thick shaft through his boxers. With my tongue I trace the head of his dick, and this time he sinks his teeth into my thigh to keep from crying out—I feel him bite a mouth full of my jumpsuit as I lick across the salty tip, my breath cooling the path my tongue leaves behind.

Suddenly footsteps ring out from the corridor and I glance up over Dylan's hip to see Shanley enter the room, his face lined with exhaustion. I sit up a little too quickly—damn, what are we *doing*? Here where anyone can see us, I'm not usually like this, I swear I'm not, but before I can even think to apologize, Dylan leans back to glance over his shoulder and rolls right over the edge of the bunk.

"Dylan!" I look down—he landed on his feet, thank God, but he shakes his head like he's dazed and the front of his jumpsuit gaps open, his erection tenting his boxers obscenely, there's no *way* Parker and Shanley don't know what we were just up to, not when he's up like *that*. Covering my face with my hands, I lie back against the mattress and wish I could just sink into it completely and disappear. "God," I mutter. "Are you alright?"

I hear the insidious hiss of his zipper as he says, "I'm fine—"

"I'm sorry," I tell anyone who cares to listen. "It's not what you think, really it's not."

Parker doesn't answer—he's already asleep. But Shanley admonishes, "You shouldn't," and I nod, yes, I know we shouldn't. Not here. Not after I *told* them we wouldn't. With a soft sigh, he climbs into the bunk above Parker's and stretches out on the mattress. I wait for him to say something else but he doesn't.

"Move over," Dylan says, climbing up beside me again. I scoot over as far as I can, until the cold steel wall is flat against my back, and he lies on his stomach, his arms folded beneath him—he sleeps like that when he's hard and he's trying to will an erection away. *He's not the only one*, I think, and I don't want to touch him again, look what it led to last time, but I can't lie here beside him and not do anything, it's impossible, I'm not that strong. So I rest a hand on the space between his shoulder blades, that's it, that's all, nothing more. "Well?" he asks, not the least bit embarrassed that Shanley walked in on us. "How's that girl doing?"

"Marie." Shanley rolls onto his side so he can look at us—I can see how tired he is, it's written in his haggard cheeks, his hooded eyes. "She's a trooper but I'm not sure the baby's going to make it."

Well, *that* kills the mood. Beneath my hand Dylan stiffens and I start smoothing a slow circle into his back. "You can't help her?" he asks in a childlike voice. Sometimes I forget how young he really is—how young we *both* are.

Shanley sighs. "Terbute isn't really what she needs," he explains. "It's mostly for first trimester labor pains but she's further along than that. These colonists aren't doctors. They're just kids who've managed to make due with what they have."

"So she's going to lose this one, too?" I ask. I can't imagine how that would make me feel—I hope I never have to know. In my mind I see Conlan sitting by her bedside again and I *know* I can't go through whatever it is he must be feeling right now. I rub along Dylan's back and he makes a little contented noise, a sort of rumbly purr, that I can feel beneath my hand. "There's *nothing* you can do?"

"Nothing short of getting her out of here," Shanley replies, "and that's not an option. They don't want to leave, any of them—have you talked to the people here?" When I shake my head, he tells us, "They're too proud to ask for help, and now that they know this is the only colony that worked? They'll never leave it. It's the only home any of them has ever really known."

"So that's it then," Dylan mumbles, his face half-buried in his pillow. I can tell from the sleepy tone of his voice that his eyes are probably closed and he's so relaxed beneath my gentle massage, he's going to end up like Parker in a few more minutes. "What are we doing here if they don't want our help?"

"The signal," I remind him. He murmurs something incoherent and nods, settling closer to me. Look at this—so damn horny one minute, ready to pass out the next. He's usually like that after sex, just wants to cuddle up and zonk, he's out like a light. No sweet talk for him. Just holds me as tight as he can without strangling me, buries his head against my chest, and falls asleep.

Shanley starts to roll away from us, like he wants to give us at least a tiny semblance of privacy if he can, but I stop him with a question. "You asked her to leave?"

He nods. "Just to the carrier, even, and she won't. I don't blame her, actually—she shouldn't be out of bed, shouldn't really move around at all. But I have briox in the lab there. That's what she needs, not the terbute." He closes his eyes and doesn't say anything else for so long, I nuzzle against Dylan's shoulder and kiss him quickly, close my own eyes, a nap would be good right about now. When Shanley does speak again, his voice is softer than usual, almost thoughtful. "I'm surprised their medication's any good after all this time. I could stitch her cervix but with the risk of infection floating around, that's not such a good idea. If I had the briox, I wouldn't *have* to do that. It'd stop the contractions and…" He trails off, probably thinks I've fallen asleep like the others.

But I haven't. Opening one eye, I look across the room at him, also dozing, and ask, "Why can't someone bring the medicine down here?"

He stares at me as if he hadn't thought of *that*. "Tessa," he says, and I nod, I can see the excitement light up his tired eyes. "She could fly one of the fighters down—it'd just take a few hours, right? Not very long at all, and she's already gone through the decon procedures so that shouldn't be any problem. She can—"

Beside me Dylan rouses himself and asks, "Who's going to fly the carrier?" Shanley's smile vanishes. "She's the only pilot up there," Dylan continues. "So that won't work."

"You could go get it," I suggest, reluctant to abandon the idea completely. "We have two pilots right here—take one of them and the *Semper Fi*, go back to the carrier, get the medicine, and return. If you leave tonight, you can be back first thing in the morning. She'll be able to hold out that long, right?"

"I'll go," Dylan says, sitting up. Then he winks at me and adds, "You come, too. We'll need a navigator—"

I shake my head. "He needs to go, he knows what he's going for. I won't know briox from aspirin." At Dylan's sigh, I remind him, "Two people in a space craft don't need a navigator. A licensed pilot can run the nav deck. You still want to go?"

"No." Dylan drops his head back to the pillow with such force that it surprises me he doesn't hurt himself. "Take Parker. He wants to get out of here."

"We all do," I say softly. I kiss his ear where it peeks out from beneath his hair and look up to meet Shanley's gaze. "Will that work?" I ask him. "If you go back and get the medicine for her?" Maybe then they'll start to trust us, they'll see we're not here to hurt them or tear their colony down. These people here, they're *my* age. For all the talk I'm spouting about the signal, I'd be lying if I said I don't want them to succeed. They're our neighbors out here for the next five years or however long it takes to map this system, and I won't be able to eat, live, and breathe on the station knowing there's a group of kids out this way dying for want of what I'm taking for granted.

The hope I see in Shanley's face tells me he's thinking the same thing. "Kitt can fly the *Semper Fi*?" he asks. I nod, I'm sure he can. "How long did it take to get down here?"

I think back to the nav stats displayed on the vidscreens when we landed. "Three hours, almost four," I tell him. "So let's say we meet with the committee tonight, you tell them the plan, they let you go and you can be back at the carrier by midnight, right?" He nods tentatively, but yeah, that sounds about right. "You just need to get some supplies, that won't take long—"

"I know where everything is," he says, excited again. "I just finished inventory, remember?"

Beside me, Dylan mumbles, "I helped."

I kiss his hair, soft like raw cotton. "I know, baby," I whisper. He takes a deep breath and lets it out slowly, a long, drawn-out sigh.

"Another three hours or so and you'll be back. No more than eight altogether. Will Marie last that long?"

Shanley shrugs, unsure. "We can try it," he says. "Heck, it's *worth* trying. If it works..." *The first baby in this dying colony,* I think. And we thought just finding this place would put us in the annals? *Shit.* "We *have* to do it," Shanley declares. "There's no other option."

※　　　　　※　　　　　※

I don't even realize I doze off until Maclin is there, waking us up because it's time to eat. Dinner is served in the commons area—colonists line the counter in front of the kitchen to pick up a tray and then find seats at the tables or by the fountain. They keep to small groups, two or three to a table, and they don't talk loud, none of them do. Their whispers are like the fall of water in the fountain, soft and subdued and somehow out of place in this ship. Standing in line for my own tray, I can feel the weight of the S410 press down on me, emptiness like the ache of a rotten tooth stabbing through me, and I can't believe the small handful of people gathered here is all that exists in this world.

The food is a salad full of thick greens and onions, a baked potato, a bowl of thin soup and a handful of crackers, a tall glass of cloudy water, that's it. "Hmm," Dylan murmurs behind me as he takes one of the trays, but I don't know if he's being sarcastic or not. He doesn't elaborate.

"At least it's something," I whisper. "They don't have to feed us." With tray in hand, I weave through the tables, looking for a place to sit. I have a feeling that if I try to take one of the empty chairs at any of the colonists' tables, they might just get up and walk away and I don't want that kind of open rejection. As long as they're only watching us with wary eyes, as long as they keep their talk about us low enough that I can't hear it, I can pretend that we're not intruding here, we're not a threat to their way of life. Only all the tables are taken, and no one looks up as I walk around, no one gives me a warm smile, no one offers me an empty seat. I just want to put the tray down now and go back to the *Semper Fi*, is that too much to ask?

Dylan presses his tray into my back. "Over there," he says, nodding to a table near the fountain where Conlan sits, alone. "Isn't that what's his face?"

"Conlan," I say. I turn and catch Shanley's attention, nod over to the table, then start in that direction. Dylan follows me and as I set my tray down, Conlan glances up at us. "Hey there," I say, sliding into the seat across from him. "Mind if we join you?"

He frowns as Dylan sits down beside me and then turns back to his tray, the food on it pushed around as if he's trying to eat but isn't quite succeeding. "Not at all," he says, his voice soft, his eyes tired. His hair is beginning to get oily near his scalp where he keeps pushing it out of his face, and thin lines etch his mouth. He looks exhausted—*you should get some rest*, I want to tell him, but I know that's probably not going to happen. As if remembering we're his guests here, he asks, "How are you guys doing so far?"

"Fine," Dylan tells him, and he nods to emphasize the point. I dip a spoon into my soup and watch steam curl up from the liquid—it warms my face and it's too hot to eat so I just crumble the crackers into it and start on the salad as Shanley and Parker come up to us. Shanley sinks into the seat next to mine and Parker takes an empty chair from another table, pulls it up to ours, sits down next to Conlan. "How's your girl?" Dylan asks. It's the question on all of our minds, I think, and leave it to him to be blunt about it.

Conlan doesn't answer right away, just shrugs and stares into his bowl, his lower lip trembling. "Fine," he whispers, but I don't believe it. I don't think any of us do. Composing himself, Conlan clears his throat and raises his voice, looks at us and nods. "She'll be fine."

"What about the—" Dylan starts, but I kick him beneath the table and he shuts up quickly. The last thing he needs to ask about now is the baby. Stirring his soup, he mumbles, "That's good, I guess. That she's fine."

"Yeah," Conlan says. I get the feeling we're keeping him from…well, from whatever he was doing before we came over here. He glances at Shanley and chews the inside of his lip before he asks, "Have you been to see her again?" Shanley shakes his head. With a sigh, Conlan asks, "That surgery you mentioned, stitching her up inside? Will that work?"

"It might," Shanley says, sipping at his soup. "Or it might not, I'll have to be honest with you here. There's a ten percent chance that the laser will break the placenta and she'll lose the baby."

Conlan pushes his tray aside and folds his arms in front of him, stares at his food, and his voice is distant when he answers. "Ten percent's not that bad." His gaze shifts to Shanley again as if for confirmation. "It's better than what she has right now, isn't it? I mean, the baby's going to die if we don't do something, right?"

Now Shanley looks at me and raises one questioning eyebrow. I nod and turn to Conlan, but how should I start? *It doesn't have to be like this,* but like what? *We can save her*—but can we really? Finally I settle for a simple, "We've been thinking," and that gets his attention. He sits up a little taller and glances at me, at Dylan and then back at me again. "Maybe there's something we can do."

"Like what?" Conlan's eyes narrow suspiciously.

Beside me, Shanley speaks up. "The drug I mentioned earlier, briox?" When Conlan nods, Shanley continues. "I have some back at the carrier. Neal was thinking we could go back and get it—"

Optimism flares in Conlan's eyes for a moment, but then fades and dies. "You're running away," he says softly, as if he's not quite believing it. "You said you'd help and now you're just going to leave—"

"No," Dylan says, shaking his head. "That's the stuff she needs, this briox, not whatever it is she's taking now."

Shanley nods. "I'm not going to let your child die without a fight," he promises. "Kitt and I could go back to the carrier—" Parker looks up from his food, glances at us for a moment, then turns back to his salad, that's the extent of his participation in this conversation. "We can leave tonight," Shanley assures Conlan, "and be back by morning. It won't take long at all and we'll come back, I swear we will." At the uncertainty written across Conlan's face, Shanley adds, "With the briox, Marie's chances of carrying to term are increased eight to one. Those are better odds, don't you think?"

Conlan doesn't answer right away. He twists his hands together and a muscle in his jaw clenches angrily. When he finally speaks, his voice is quiet and carefully neutral. "You're saying with this…this briox, she won't need the surgery?" Shanley nods. "And the baby will live?"

"I can't promise that," Shanley says, but there's a hope in Conlan's eyes that wasn't there before. "But this way at least the baby has a chance, Jeremy. It's safer than the surgery. It's a non-invasive pill that she takes twice a day and it stops the contractions, tightens the cervix, all this has been proven in medical journals for years now. There's a lot less risk involved, you must see that."

"I do," Conlan murmurs. "If you leave now—"

"They'll be back by morning," Dylan assures him.

Conlan glances at him. "You're not going?" Dylan shakes his head and Conlan looks at me, so I shake my head, too. "You're staying here? Both of you?"

"Is that okay?" I ask. When Dylan opens his mouth to answer, I kick him beneath the table again and he doesn't speak. "Think of it as sort of a guarantee," I explain. We're not going to just leave like this, tell them we'll be right back and then high-tail it out of here, leave them waiting for us to return. "Almost four hours to get back to the carrier, maybe an hour prep time there to get the drug, and then another four hours here."

"What's there to lose?" Dylan asks.

Conlan studies his hands and doesn't say that there's a *lot* to lose, for him at least. There's Marie and her second child, *his* child, and that's too much, no one should have to give up that, no one should be forced to. "I'll have to talk to the committee," he tells us. "We didn't…none of us thought you were staying for long but I guess we sort of thought you'd stay together, you know? People might not understand if they see only half of you leave. They'll think you're staying here for good, maybe, to settle in here, and they—" He sighs. "*We* don't want that. We're all a little worried about the bleed resurfacing again, now that you're here, or maybe something different, something you're carrying that we've never been exposed to. You don't know how hard I argued to get them to let you guys land."

I wonder again how they could've possibly stopped us, unarmed as they are, but before I can ask, Shanley says, "You have to understand how it is for us, too. This is the chance of a lifetime. Yours is the only colony to succeed from Operation Starseed and the fact that you've made it this far amazes me. But you're dying out—you don't need me to tell you this." Conlan nods in agreement. "If there's the slightest chance that we can help you, the thinnest hope—don't you think we all deserve to seize it?"

"If the baby lives," Conlan starts, but his voice breaks slightly and he doesn't continue that thought. Instead he nods and presses his lips together until they're just a white line in his face, and he sighs. "Alright. We were going to get the committee together tomorrow so you could—" He gestures with one hand like he's not sure what we were going to do, exactly, but then again, neither do we. "I guess talk to them? About the signal. But if you think this drug will work, if you think it'll help Marie—"

"It will," Dylan assures him, even though we don't know that for certain. I nudge his foot with mine but when he frowns at me, I feel bad, he's only trying to help. So I wink at him and turn back to my soup, and beneath the table I feel his hand rub along my thigh. "At least it's worth a try."

Conlan nods again. "I'll talk to the committee," he says, rising to his feet. He scoops his tray up and shoves his chair in with one bony hip. "Are you sure you can be back by morning? Marie probably can't hold out much longer than that."

"The briox takes effect almost immediately," Shanley tells him. "The sooner we leave, the sooner we'll be back."

And that's cheesy as hell but that's how he is, and for once I'm glad he has this plethora of one-liners because that one makes Conlan grin. It's a ghost of a real smile, but there's a hope in his face that wasn't there before and I pray that Dylan's right, I pray this medicine *does* work. These colonists deserve that much, after all they've been through.

❦   ❦   ❦

Before we finish eating, Conlan is back. His hand shakes as he runs it through his hair to push it out of his eyes and he doesn't even sit down, just leans over the table, breathless with wild eyes. "Fifteen minutes," he tells us. "We're meeting in the conference room down the corridor, you know which one?" He doesn't wait for a reply, just hurries on excitedly. "This isn't about the signal, not yet—the general consensus is to let you guys stay a day or two if you want, get a feel for what we've got going here, before we start talking about what to do about that. But I told them your plan and it's a good one, they're all excited about it, fifteen minutes, okay?" Shanley and I exchange a glance and he nods. Then I look at Parker, who's still eating, and finally at Dylan, who shrugs, *why not?* "Okay," Conlan says. He claps his hands together and then laughs, a quick sound that he stifles before it can get away from him. "Fifteen minutes. Okay."

As he hurries away, I notice Ellington headed towards our table, but Conlan intercepts him, drapes an arm around his shoulders, leads him in the direction of the conference room where we first met earlier. Ellington glances over his shoulder at us, at *me*, since I'm watching him and for a minute I see something in his eyes that I can't read and don't like. *He doesn't believe us*, I think, which surprises me. *He doesn't believe we'll come back with the briox, or he* doesn't think it's going to work, and he doesn't like this sudden hope that has Conlan bumbling and spastic, he doesn't like that one bit because he's thinking about what's going to happen if the pill DOESN'T work, what's that going to do to his friend? I don't know—I don't *want* to know, and I'm grateful that Conlan drags him away before he can come over here and ask those questions out loud so we don't have to answer them.

Fifteen minutes. I can't finish eating and when it looks like Dylan's done, I stand with my tray in hand and head back to the counter. Dylan follows me. "You think this is going to work?" he asks as I set my tray among the others on the counter, waiting to be cleared.

"I don't know," I tell him. I step aside and wait while he stacks his tray on top of mine. It wobbles precariously but doesn't fall.

I glance back at our table, where Shanley is now getting to his feet and Parker is shoveling the rest of his food into his mouth as quickly as he can. "I think it might," Dylan says. I get the feeling he's only trying to fill the silence that envelops us, close this distance that the colonists have sort of forced upon us. "Do you think Shanley will get back in time?"

"Dylan," I sigh as the others head our way. "I don't know."

Beside me, Dylan frowns slightly and I'm about to apologize for snapping at him, he knows I don't know the answers to his questions but he just wants to talk and I shouldn't be short with him, I love him, I'm just a little anxious right now about this whole damn thing, but before I can say anything, he slips his hand into mine and squeezes gently as if to say he knows. "I know you don't," he whispers, and fuck the colonists who are watching us now with their judgmental eyes, fuck their righteous stares and their indignant frowns. *Mine,* I want to tell them as I tighten my fingers around his. *This boy's mine, I can hold his hand if I want to, I can kiss him and love him if I want to.*

And I *do* want to, but I know better than that. So I extract my hand from his as the others approach and I want to promise him something later but can't. Dammit the *hell*, I can't. "Well?" Shanley asks, setting his tray on the counter. "Should we head on over there?"

He leads the way to the corridor where it's just the four of us and it feels wonderful to be out of the constant spotlight of the colonists' sight. Dylan falls into step beside Parker and snags a handful of my jumpsuit to keep me close as I walk in front of him. "You sure you can handle the *Semper Fi*?" he asks. "She can be a little temperamental at times—"

"I was flying before you were *born*," Parker brags, and I laugh because that's a lie, the guy's only a year or two older than me. "I'll handle her fine, don't you worry about it. She won't *want* you in the cockpit when I'm through."

With a playful tug on my jumpsuit, Dylan says, "I don't know about that. Why don't you tell him how good I am, Neal?"

"How about I don't?" I counter. I see Shanley's amused grin and have to duck my head to hide the color that creeps into my cheeks.

"Aww, baby," Dylan starts, and he eases his arms around my waist, pulls me back to him in a quick hug. "Don't be like that," he murmurs against my neck.

"Dylan," I complain, twisting away—well, not *complain*, not *really*, but this isn't the time or place and he *knows* this—

"It's just us," he mutters, but he lets go when he sees the open doorway of the conference room up ahead. Low voices drift out to us, someone laughs, someone else says, "No, I don't—" but the rest is lost, covered over with other words that blend together into a busy buzz of conversation. I think I hear Ellington's high voice, strident and bitter, he's arguing with someone but I can't make out the words. Then we step into the room and the half dozen colonists gathered around the table fall silent, turn as one and look up at us, through us, and I fight the urge to turn around to see what they're looking at. *It's just us,* I think, hearing Dylan's words echo through my head, and this time when his hands fist at my sides, I don't push him away.

Ellington was right—the committee isn't what I expected, not at all. Just six people, that's it. Ellington himself sits by Conlan, the two of them leaning together as if they were talking privately seconds before we walked in. For an awkward moment we stare at each other, waiting, and I'm just about to apologize and back out into the corridor, we shouldn't just bust in like this, it's not polite, when Conlan rises to his feet, smiles at us, and says, "Hey, you're early." *No shit,* I think, but Conlan's holding his arm out to us, indicating the chairs we sat in earlier, and it would be rude to just walk out now. "Have a seat, guys."

The noise of our chairs scruffing against the floor is unbelievably loud in the quiet room. No one else speaks to us, no one looks away, they pin us to the seats with their silent gazes and I can't look at any of them, not even Ellington. Only Conlan, even though I don't like the way he's grinning at us—he's got too much riding on our plan and what happens if we fail? What then?

"The committee," he says, sweeping his arm around the table at the other colonists gathered. "You know Ben—" Ellington sits back in his seat and crosses his arms, his face closed, but he nods at us anyway. On his other side is a woman with long, blonde curls whose mouth draws down into a tight bow as she watches us, her eyes large and round and dark against honeyed skin. Conlan introduces her as Holly, and then there's Maclin, who leans against the wall between them, his eyes hidden behind those dark shades he still has on and his hair covered with a battered cap. I didn't expect him to be on the committee, to be honest, but didn't Ellington say everyone got a chance? Six months at a time, if I remember correctly.

Then there's another woman, this one pregnant and beginning to show, I can tell by the way she sits back from the table, her hands folded across top of her belly protectively. Her name is Kelly, and she has short black hair so dark it's almost burgundy in spots and skin like chocolate, she's very pretty. I wonder if this is her first child. If the briox works for Marie, will there be enough for the other women? Ten in all—what kind of supply does Shanley have on the carrier?

Next to Kelly is a man Conlan introduces as Ramsey—there's something authoritative about him, something almost scary. He looks older than the rest of us, with red hair cropped as short as it can possibly be, tight against his scalp, so light that it's almost translucent near the top. He has ruddy skin and icy eyes that I swear pierce into me, and a perpetual scowl that deepens when Conlan says his name. As Conlan introduces us, Dylan's hand takes mine beneath the table and Ramsey glares at us as if he can see that touch and he knows we're lovers. I'm sure they all know—Ellington probably told them, or Conlan, I think he suspects it. Hell, I think the whole damn colony knows, and I've never felt this self-conscious before, not about my sexuality and not about someone I love more than life itself, not about Dylan. I want to tell them all to just grow up and get over it already. So men love other men, so what? It's not a foreign concept, and it's not what caused that virus of theirs to wipe out more than half the population, and it's not what's killing their babies, it's *not*.

But Conlan jumps right to the heart of the matter. "Tell them about the briox," he says, sitting back down. "Tell them what you told me."

Beside me, Shanley rises to his feet and clears his throat, looks around at the committee members. Dylan squeezes my hand reassuringly, pulling it into his lap so he can wrap both hands around mine. "Briox is a neuromuscular inhibidilator," Shanley explains, and he's already lost me, I don't know what he's talking about. But Conlan nods happily as if this is exactly the sort of information he wanted to know and he glances over his shoulder at Ellington, who glares our way and doesn't look at his friend. I stare at the table in front of me and refuse to meet the weight of that gaze. "It has the ability to prohibit premature labor in late trimester pregnancies," Shanley continues. "Basically it tightens the muscles of the uterus and cervix, preventing contractions. It's much safer than the surgical procedure I spoke with Jeremy about this afternoon and Marie's chances of carrying to term with the briox increase almost tenfold. She's the perfect candidate for the medicine—"

"It's on their carrier," Conlan interrupts. He looks at Shanley for confirmation and he nods. "The ship with the rest of the crew? So if someone goes out there and gets it—"

"Why can't they come here?" the woman named Kelly asks. "It'll take less time."

"There's only one pilot left on the carrier," Dylan explains.

From his position against the wall, Maclin speaks up, his voice deceptively soft. "Look what happened when they landed. You want to go through that again?" The committee members look at each other and nod—*what happened?* I wonder. He must see the question written on my face because he smirks and asks, "You saw the fountain? That red clay in the water, that's your fault."

"Wait a minute—" Dylan starts, indignant.

Conlan holds up a hand and explains, "Our filtration system is used to cleaning out the silt from the rains. But your landing stirred up more than it can handle. We sort of expected that, really, and we managed to bottle some water for meals until the clay settles to normal levels again."

"You take off, you stir that shit up," Ramsey mutters. I don't like that man, he makes me nervous, with his angry voice and hard eyes. "It takes half a day to clear out and then you land again, what the hell are we supposed to drink til then?"

"It's the only way, Ramsey," Conlan argues. He pushes the hair off the back of his neck and sighs like they've been over this already, before we even showed up. "They have a pilot here that can fly their ship to the carrier, get the drug, come back—"

"We don't even know if it's going to work," Ramsey reminds him. "I don't think we should chance it. Let's get to the damn signal already and they can just leave."

Conlan's voice is soft, a stark contrast to Ramsey's anger. "And my child dies," he says, so sadly that Ramsey has to look away, he can't meet his friend's eyes anymore. "And then what, your child, too? When Kelly goes through the same thing in another month or two. You're not thinking of the colony, Ramsey—"

"I'm thinking of the water supply," Ramsey tells him. Suddenly everyone else has ceased to exist, it's just the two of them, and the rest of us hold our breath, afraid to speak as we watch the two men. Ramsey scares me—*terrifies* me, to be honest, looks like the kind of guy you avoid running into after dark if you want to stay alive, and Conlan is half my size, so damn thin, Ramsey could easily break him in two, and if things get out of hand, will any of us be able to stop a fight between them? I seriously doubt it. "I'm thinking of the goddamn colony, Jeremy," Ramsey cries. "I'm thinking of the forty-some other people we have to worry about here, and not just one kid—"

"*My* kid," Conlan corrects, but he doesn't raise his voice, doesn't let whatever anger is probably swirling through his veins show. "And yours, Ramsey. And Seth's, and the other seven fathers here, the ten mothers, the *future* of our colony. If we don't take this chance just because we're going to be without water for a few days..." Lowering his voice as if Ramsey's the only other person in the room, Conlan suggests, "I think you're scared it might not work."

"I'm not scared of shit," Ramsey growls. He pushes his chair back, the legs screeching across the floor, and when he stands the chair rams into the wall, an clash of metal on metal that rings through the room. "I'm not like you, Jeremy. I can't just trust these guys—" He flings a hand in our direction and I want to duck beneath the table, away from his terrible gaze. "We don't know shit about them or this drug of theirs. What if it kills Marie and the baby, what then?"

"It won't," Dylan interrupts.

Ramsey turns towards us as if seeing us for the first time and *God, Dylan*, I think, watching the bunched muscles in Ramsey's jaw twitch. *Can't you just keep your damn mouth shut for once? Please?*

Beneath the table I squeeze his hand in a death grip and pray that this guy loses interest in us. *You're fighting with Conlan, remember? Not us, him. Not us.* "Who the fuck asked you?" he wants to know.

"Ramsey," Conlan says. Ramsey doesn't reply, just stares at Dylan until I'm sure he's going to come across the table at him, he's going to tear him apart and I won't be able to stop him, I can't take on someone like him, even if I try. "Ramsey, listen—"

"Sit down," Kelly says, her voice as soft as Conlan's. For a moment Ramsey wavers, I see the uncertainty flicker in his eyes, and then she takes his hand and pulls him down beside her. He sinks into his seat abruptly, as if his legs fall out from under him. Kelly closes her fingers around his and whispers, "We can't say no to this, babe. If the drug works—"

"We don't know it will," Ramsey grumbles, dropping his gaze to where their hands are laced together on the table. "We don't know shit about it."

"It's a chance we have to take," Kelly tells him. Conlan nods and despite Ellington's unwavering stare, I think Ramsey's probably the hardest one on this committee to sell on the idea. *What about your own child?* I want to ask him, but I'm not that brave. I can't get the way he glared at Dylan out of my mind, that's a look that's going to haunt me all night, and I don't want that evil gaze turned my way again. "Ramsey," Kelly says gently. "It's a chance *I'm* willing to take."

Part 6

I radio Vallery to let her know the *Semper Fi* is heading back. Then the four of us follow Ellington, Maclin, and Conlan across the commons to the doorway leading through the abandoned hulk of the ship to the airlock where we first entered. "You have to watch it when you're docking," Dylan tells Parker as we walk. Both Parker and Shanley wear plastic ponchos that crinkle with each step, and Dylan keeps a hand on the small of my back, rubbing gently now and then. I'm glad we're behind everyone else, so no one sees that touch.

An ache opens in my chest and I want to be dressed in one of those ponchos, I want to be on the *Semper Fi* and heading back to the carrier—I want to be able to sleep with my lover tonight. I want his hands and lips to erase the wrongness and doubt these colonists have so effectively made me feel with the way they look at us, the way they talk about us. *We're helping you,* I want to say. But I don't, I keep silent, it's not my place to say anything at all and in another day or two, we'll leave this prejudice behind. Though, to be honest? Then I'll have to leave Dylan again and at least this way we're together, even if we're not able to love each other the way we want to. At least we can touch and at least I can see his smile again, at least there's that. And I can hear his voice, though right now I wish he'd shut up about that damn spacecraft. "She sort of pulls to the left—"

"I know this, Teague," Parker growls. "Tell me again. I know how to fly."

"I'm telling you how to land," Dylan explains. "You have to hold it steady when you're going in—"

With a glance over his shoulder, Parker winks at me and asks, "Did you teach him that?"

Oh God. "No," I mutter. I may love my boy to death, I may have no qualms telling people he's mine, but I've never been one for randy jokes and bawdy innuendos. I get too easily embarrassed, and I hate the blush that colors my cheeks, I hate that I've never been comfortable joking about sex.

Dylan laughs and rubs my back. "You're so cute," he murmurs, leaning close to kiss my shoulder. *And this is why the colonists don't like us,* I should point out. It's one thing to be discreet and another thing altogether to flaunt it.

We round a corner and the airlock's up ahead, closed like an accusation. Conlan stops and stands aside to let Shanley and Parker pass. I get the impression he's hanging back for a reason, so I stop beside him and Dylan leans against the wall, pulls me into the space between his legs, wraps his arms around my waist even as I try to keep some distance between us. It doesn't work, and even though we're not alone, he thrusts against me with a breathless giggle, holds me tight, won't let me go. "Dylan," I warn. I don't like the way Conlan can't quite look at us—he watches Ellington set up the decon cycle for the airlock, stares at the ceiling, the floor, anywhere but across the corridor where we are. I catch Dylan's hands as they smooth down my hips and extract myself from his embrace. "Not right now," I tell him.

He sighs, a sound so forlorn that I want to kiss him and make it better and I can't. I just lean against the wall beside him, my hands folded behind my back, and try my hardest to ignore his wounded pout. "So," I say, hoping to disperse the awkwardness that hangs across the corridor between the two of us and Conlan. It doesn't work—he still doesn't look our way. "Why didn't you mention our landing would ruin your water supply?" I ask. "We didn't *have* to land, if it was going to inconvenience you…"

Conlan shrugs. "It was a risk I was willing to take," he says softly. He's turned away from me as he watches the others at the airlock and I can see thin lines carved around his mouth and eyes, worried into him, making him older than he should be. "Ramsey's wrong, the take-off won't taint the water that much more. It shouldn't, really, and by the time they land again, the filtration system might even be able to handle it, we'll see."

A few feet away, Maclin opens the airlock door, holds it while Shanley and Parker enter. Shanley gives us a thumbs up before he disappears into the chamber—an actual thumbs up, how scary is that? "You watch how you handle my ship," Dylan calls out but Parker dismisses that with a wave of his hand. "He's going to wreck it," Dylan mutters to no one in particular. "I should be going." He nudges my foot with his and adds, "You, too."

I give him a wan smile and shake my head. *Not now,* I think, and he must get my drift because he sighs and glares at the floor, occupies himself with picking at the leg of my jumpsuit like a kid—pulling the fabric out so it tents beneath his fingers, then letting it fall back into place against my thigh. As Maclin closes the door and Ellington starts up the decon cycle, I tell Conlan, "A few hours, nothing more. How's Marie holding up?"

"Fine," Conlan whispers.

I don't know what else to say. A dull whine starts up in the airlock, the cycle kicking into full force, and Dylan nudges my foot again but I don't pay him any attention. "It's worth the risk," he mumbles, pick pick picking at my jumpsuit, and when I do look at him, he's frowning at the material as he lets it fall from his fingers. "You could've told us we'd fuck up your water," he says, so low that I'm not sure if he's talking to himself or Conlan. "We didn't have to land. Then no one would hate us—"

"We had your med files," Conlan explains. "We knew Shanley was a physician. To me, that's all that mattered. We've never...you have to understand, we've never *had* a physician here before. The colony med team died from the bleed like everyone else. We get by with what we have, the annals and data logs, but we don't really know what we're doing." With a bitter laugh, he says, "Just kids playing doctor, that's all we are."

That makes Dylan smile. Turning to me so Conlan can't hear him, he takes my hand and pulls me closer, his eyes sparkling. "You ever play that when you were little?" he asks, and the wicked way he's grinning at me, the way he rubs up against me so I can *feel* what he's thinking, it's coiled below his waist and pressing into my hip, that makes it so hard to keep him at bay.

Clearing his throat, Conlan continues as if Dylan's not all over me right this second. "If this briox works, it'll be worth a few hours' thirst."

I lace my fingers through Dylan's so I can keep him in check. He leans against me and rests his head on my shoulder, his arms snaking around my waist, and as long as he's not planning on going further, we can stay like this, that's fine. Even though Conlan glances at us and quickly looks away. Even though Ellington frowns at us and Maclin smirks, I can live with that. "That one guy doesn't think so," I tell him.

"Ramsey," Dylan says softly, only he sings it, *RAM-see*, and I think if that guy back in the conference room could hear him now, Dylan wouldn't play like that. I know *I* wouldn't—that guy didn't look like the playing type. Apparently Dylan thinks so, too, because he hugs me and mumbles into my neck, "That guy's a dick."

"Hush," I tell him, glancing around as if Ramsey might somehow appear and fly into a fit of rage at Dylan's words. *Then Shanley and Parker come back here to find us dead because you're just being silly,* I think, running my hands along Dylan's strong arm. *That would not be a good turn of events.*

Across from us, Conlan forces a thin smile and says, "He's not that bad." *Yeah, right,* I think. *Here it comes—"you have to understand…"* Surprisingly not. "He's just a little rough around the edges," Conlan explains. "He's…he and Ben are the oldest here." With a nod, he indicates Ellington, who is still fiddling with the airlock, Maclin nearby as if standing guard. "When we first started getting sick, I was just a little kid. I have no memory of the first wave, I guess you'd call it. When my parents died? That's gone. Marie's mother took me in and I don't even really remember what happened when *she* died, either, and I was what, twelve at the time? It just seemed natural by then, all the death." He takes a shuddery breath and now he turns to us, lowers his voice as if afraid his friends might overhear. "Ben and Ramsey, Marie, a handful of the others, they were almost ten when we started out. They can remember a time before this, something…*other*, a world that isn't just death and dying and sickness. Ben wants us to get back to that, he wants it so bad, and Ramsey—" Conlan's smile grows sad, his eyes distant. "Well, some of us have just given up hope, I guess. I'm not apologizing for him—"

"No," Dylan murmurs, "of course not." I frown at him but can't tell if he's being facetious or not. For a long moment I consider kicking him in the shin but he's not smirking or anything, just stares at the floor and scuffs his boot against mine, so I lean back against him and he tightens his arms around me. I hate this talk of the bleed. I hate to even think about that happening here, where I stand now, so long ago and these colonists still haven't managed to heal, they keep their rigid rules and strict laws against sex and maybe they've grown older these past twenty years but they haven't yet learned how to move on. With a sigh, Dylan tells him, "You don't have to explain."

"You don't know what it was like," Conlan says as Ellington and Maclin head our way. "You don't *want* to know, trust me. It's his way of coping, you have to understand."

You keep saying that, I think. Glancing at us distrustfully, Ellington walks by, back towards the heart of the ship, Maclin behind him, sneering at the way Dylan holds me, and how can I understand that? I know I wasn't here, I know I don't struggle at this day to day existence they have, but I can't understand how they can be so dead set against us, against this love we have, against our very life itself. I can't understand that at all.

Conlan waits for us to follow, and with him behind us, the others in front, Dylan's hands fall away from me and we barely touch as we trek back through the corridor, our steps echoing around us, solemn, like the steps of condemned men. *Is it too late to change our minds?* I want to know. *To just leave with the others? Please?*

Only Ellington sets a steady pace and Conlan is between us and the airlock, and when I feel the silent rumble of the world beneath my feet, aftershocks from the *Semper Fi*'s boosters, I already know the answer to that.

❧ ❧ ❧

The commons are empty now, the lights dim, the subtle splash of the fountain the only sound in this make-believe evening. As we follow Ellington and Maclin, Dylan's hand slips into mine and he starts to slow his pace, pulling away from the others. At the fountain, he trails his fingers through the water and lingers, tightening his grip so I have to wait for him. "Dylan," I say softly, tugging at his hand. "Come on, hon. It's been a long day."

"Just a few minutes," he says. He glances up at Conlan, lost in his own thoughts as he drifts by—he doesn't realize we're not following anymore. "I just need you all to myself for a little bit." Dylan wipes his damp hand on his leg, then takes my wrist, his cold touch warming as he rubs beneath the sleeve of my jumpsuit. Pulling me closer, he kisses the exposed skin above my collar and murmurs, "Five minutes, can't you give me that?"

"Right here?" I reply, but it's a hollow argument because there's no one else right here, it's just us. The only sounds are the steady splash of the fountain and the muted clack of footsteps on the tiled floor, the others heading for the men's sleeping quarters. And Dylan's lips are impossibly soft behind my ear, his tongue hot and wet, licking at me, sucking, hungry. His arms ease around my waist, his hands smooth down the curve of my ass and cup my buttocks, he moans against me as he pulls me to him, and I can't stop myself from running my hands up his chest and around his neck and I lean into him, I love him, I want him so bad—

Behind us someone clears his throat and I turn in Dylan's arms to see Ellington there, hands on his hips, watching, waiting. In the dim light I can't see his eyes but I don't have to, I can tell what he's thinking by the set of his mouth. *Damn you*, I think, pushing Dylan away. *Are you happy? You've managed to make me feel dirty and horrid and I hope that makes you fucking thrilled, I hope that's what you wanted. Damn you.* And if I were a stronger man, I would say that, but I don't—instead I just look at the tiles beneath my feet, a few drops of water from the fountain beading by my boots, reflecting the low lights, and I murmur an apology, I'm not even quite sure what I say, I can't hear it myself.

Before he can say anything, though, Conlan's voice carries over to us from where he waits by Maclin. "You know, I think I should check on Marie." Ellington turns and Dylan's hands find my waist again, a tentative touch that makes me angry, he shouldn't have to feel unsure and awkward with me, *we* shouldn't be made to feel like this, like we're doing something evil and wrong. Conlan points towards the corridor that leads to the med lab and shrugs halfheartedly. "Just to say goodnight, you know. Tell her to hold on. They'll be back soon, right?"

He looks at me and for the first time I realize what he's doing. Distracting Ellington, he *has* to be doing this on purpose, because now all the attention's on him and not us and *thank you, Conlan*, I think. He's waiting on an answer. "Yeah," I tell him, then I raise my voice a little, nod and say, "They should be back by morning."

"So I'll tell her that," Conlan says. He starts to move away from us, towards the corridor. "You guys go on ahead, I'll be right up. Just want to tell her…" He trails off, and when Ellington starts to say something, he turns away from us and hurries across the commons. "Just to say goodnight. I won't be long."

"Jeremy," Ellington begins, and then he sighs, crosses his arms and rubs at his eyes with one hand, pinches the bridge of his nose until he's got to be tearing up, that has to hurt. "Fuck."

Oh, wait, what was that? I think the word surprised him, too, because he runs his hand down his face and sighs. "Didn't we agree not to tell her?" he asks. At first I'm sure he's talking to me but he's not facing us, he's staring at Maclin, who shrugs as if to say, *Don't look at me, talk to HIM.* Another sigh, and then Ellington mutters, "She doesn't need this kind of stress." He turns and glares at us, like this is our fault. "If she doesn't know and this pill doesn't work, then there's no harm done, you know? But now you've got him all riled up on hopes and he's going to get her excited and *that's* not good, she doesn't need to know…" Raising his voice, he tells Maclin, "Go see if you can stop him, will you?"

Maclin nods and trots off after Conlan, his steps fading away down the corridor. *Leaving Dylan and me and you,* I think, watching the anger and defeat war on Ellington's face. I'm afraid to speak, afraid to get his attention turned back our way, I don't want that. Finally, without looking at either of us, he says, "I know you're hating me right now."

"What—" Dylan starts, but I elbow him and he presses his mouth against my shoulder to keep silent.

"We just need a little quiet time alone," I explain. Ellington glares after his friends and Dylan's strong arms around me somehow give me the courage to say, "Everyone keeps telling us to understand, and believe me, I do. But you've got to understand *us,* too. Dylan's been mapping the north sector for the past two months—this is the first real time we've had together since he left the station. I'm not saying bend your rules for us—"

Ellington snorts derisively. "Good."

A dull anger rises in me but I tamp it down. "I'm just saying give us a few minutes, that's all," I tell him. "Please. Just enough time to say goodnight." How can he say no to that? *He's sent Maclin after Conlan,* a voice in my mind whispers, *just because he wants to see his girl one last time before going to sleep, and you think he's going to let you and Dylan make out? You're joking, right?*

Dylan holds his breath and I slip my fingers through his, squeeze as tight as I dare. *Please,* I pray, but I'm not going to say it, I'm on thin ice here as it is and another word might be too much. *Please—*

"Not here." Ellington glances around furtively, as if there's someone just out of sight who might be watching us. "Anyone can see you—"

"There's no one here," Dylan begins, but my elbow in his stomach stops him.

With a sardonic glance at us over his shoulder, Ellington launches himself across the commons, setting a quick, brisk pace. "Keep up," he says.

We almost trip over each other in our haste to follow him. In the stairwell, he slows down enough to quiet his steps and we tiptoe after him, Dylan's hand curved around the back of my thigh possessively. At the top of the steps, that hand slides between my leg, rubbing at hidden flesh, and this time it's *me* who stumbles through the doorway, I can't seem to remember how to walk. "Watch it, babe," Dylan purrs. I don't have to turn around to see his smile—I can hear it in his voice.

Ahead, Ellington storms down the darkened corridor towards the men's quarters and Dylan pulls me along after him. But before we reach the sleeping room, Ellington turns and disappears into a narrow serviceway. "Where—" I start, but Dylan ducks around the corner, me right behind him. I try to stand my ground and can't. "Dylan, wait."

The serviceway is pitch black, so dark my eyes almost hurt and I look behind me to make sure I haven't been rendered blind. There's the corridor, though, only now the dimmed lighting looks as bright as day compared to this night around us. I clutch Dylan's hand and pray he doesn't let go, I'll never find him again in this.

Suddenly he stops, and I run into him, his body hard and warm and so achingly familiar against my own. I can smell the clean scent of his hair, the musk cologne he put on this morning when we both crawled out of my bunk back on the *Semper Fi*—God, how long ago was that? I don't even know. He reaches back for me, his hands fumbling at my waist before he gets a good grip on my jumpsuit. "Sorry," I mumble, daring to snuggle against him in the darkness where no one will see.

"It's okay," he tells me. I kiss the nape of his neck and knead his shoulders just to prove to myself he's here.

Then Ellington speaks, surprisingly close, his voice an insidious hiss. "Listen," he says, and because I don't know where he is, I blink in the direction of the sound. I can't even see his eyes glisten, it's that dark. "I want you to know I don't condone this, not at all. I'm giving you ten minutes, you hear me? Ten, that's it. Starting now—"

"Starting when you leave," Dylan interrupts, but already I feel his hands along my hips and he turns around in front of me, his breath tickling my face. "Unless you're staying for the show."

Dylan's lips close over mine and I close my eyes, give in to his tongue and his hands, even though we're not yet alone. When he moans my name into my mouth, I hear someone shuffle down the serviceway, back towards the corridor. "Ten minutes," Ellington reminds us. "Keep it clean, you understand?"

"Just go away," Dylan sighs. He presses against me, pins me to the wall, his fingers already tugging at the zipper of my jumpsuit. For a moment Ellington's silhouette blocks the light from the corridor, then he turns towards the sleeping quarters and is gone. *Gone.* We're alone, for the first time in what seems like forever, and it's such a foreign concept that I don't even know where to start.

Luckily Dylan doesn't have that problem. He unzips my jumpsuit, eases it down over my shoulders, kisses the hollow of my throat as I fist my hands in his jumpsuit, pull him close, sigh his name into his thick hair. His mouth is damp and his breath hot against my skin, a promise of all that he wants from me, all that I'm willing to give.

He moves lower, kissing his way down my chest until he licks one nipple through the thin undershirt I wear. I hiss in pleasure when his lips close over it through the material, his tongue working the tender bud into a hard nugget, his hands on my back pressing me into him. "Dylan," I sigh—this is only supposed to be a goodnight kiss, right? Not a quick release, not *sex*. But his knee comes up between my legs, a sweet pressure at my crotch, and I'm hard for him, he can feel that, his fingers work my zipper down further and slip into my boxers and encircle my thick cock and he squeezes me, rubs me, cradles my balls in his hands and I'm going to throb all night now, thank you very much. He's so strong against me, holding me up when my knees threaten to buckle, my feet slide further apart, I arch into his hand and his fingers do delicious things down there, dance over secret flesh, push into me until I have to bite his shoulder to keep from crying out. The only words I know are *yes* and *God* and *Dylan*, and they run together in a delirious rush that he cuts off with another kiss.

"I need you," he says, and before I can stop him, he's on his knees, taking me into his mouth. His tongue swirls down my length and I thrust into him, grab fists full of his long bangs, push into him as far as I can go, over and over again. His hands are the supports that keep me standing, the world beneath me, it's only him, and he does such wicked things with his tongue and lips, licking me like I'm all he's ever wanted and sucking, humming, kneading until I come. That's when I melt into his arms, trembling against him, spent. His lips find mine in the darkness and he tastes so sweet, his mouth alive with my juices, his hands smoothing my fevered skin, my fluttering stomach. "I love you," he tells me, like he always does when he takes me into him.

I kiss the words away. We don't have much time and I don't want to waste it.

❦ ❦ ❦

Ellington is waiting for us when I lead Dylan out of the serviceway. He's giddy and breathless and can't keep his hands to himself—just the way I like him. I do this to him, make him this boyish man who holds my hands and rubs up against me, keeps me close to him, kisses me with little pecks on my cheek whenever he bumps into me. "I love you," he sighs—I did that to him, took his breath away, because we didn't *keep it clean*, like Ellington wanted. Dylan likes the things I did to him with my tongue, the way I licked and sucked and loved him as he whimpered my name—I didn't want anyone else to hear so I put the flat of my hand in his mouth, and when he came, he bit down so hard, I still have his teeth marks in my skin.

But by the time we step into the main corridor, our jumpsuits are zipped again. Ellington glares at us like we've been doing something wrong and Dylan's hands fist at my waist, he hates that look, we both do. "It was only ten minutes," Dylan says, his voice tight, defensive, "more or less."

Ellington doesn't rise to the bait, just turns and leads the way to the men's sleeping quarters. Behind me, Dylan giggles. "Shh," I admonish, but he takes my hand and presses my fingers into his crotch, where he's hardening again and I so didn't need to know that because it turns me on, too. So I pull my hand away and frown at him over my shoulder, with his disheveled hair and shiny eyes and his kiss-swollen, red-rimmed lips—*that doesn't help any,* I think, my heart twisting in my chest because he's so damn beautiful to me. "Dylan," I start, but he kisses me quick and I stumble into Ellington when he stops just inside the sleeping quarters. "Sorry," I mutter, backing away.

Into Dylan, who's waiting for this chance. He rests his head on my shoulder and wraps his arms around my waist and right now he's like an octopus, all hands, all over me. "I get the top," he declares, extracting himself from me to vault into the upper bunk. From his safe perch, he beams down at me and winks. "You're the bottom tonight, babe."

No comment, either from me or Ellington, and Dylan flops back against the pillow and sighs. It's dark here, the only light a softly glowing tube that runs above the sink, casting the rest of the room in shadow, and I can't see his face but I know he's pouting. Coming over to the bunks, I whisper, "Don't."

"Don't what?" he mopes.

I don't answer. Instead I sit on the lower bunk and toy with my zipper, wondering if I should strip down to my boxers and undershirt—would that be offensive? I don't have the soft linens the colonists wear and I don't really want to sleep in this jumpsuit, that's going to be uncomfortable. But when I look up at Ellington, he simply shrugs. "Do you mind if we—" I start, and I don't get any further before Dylan flings his jumpsuit onto the floor.

So much for modesty. The jumpsuit lands at my feet like shed skin. Dylan peeks over the edge of his bunk and grins. "Take it off, baby," he says. "Show him what you've got."

And there's that noise Ellington makes, the one where he sort of clears his throat, sort of growls, like he thinks we might have forgotten he's standing right here with us. So I smack the top of Dylan's head and he disappears back into his bed, and when I stand to unzip my jumpsuit, he's already burrowed beneath his blankets like a little boy, the covers fisted under his chin, watching me with wide eyes. "Be good," I tell him, shrugging out of my jumpsuit.

"The doors stay open," Ellington reminds us, nodding at the doorways that link our room to the ones on either side. He speaks quietly, as if he doesn't want to disturb anyone. *Except us,* I think as I kick off my boots and step out of my jumpsuit. It covers Dylan's on the floor. *You're all about busting our rhythm, aren't you?*

Ellington jerks his thumb at the empty bunks where Parker and Shanley napped this afternoon. Beyond them I can see another set of bunks, a sleeping shape on each. He doesn't have to say anything else—I can read the words clear enough in his shadowed eyes. *You're not alone,* that look says, *so don't fool around.* "Breakfast is served in the commons at eight," he says. "Hopefully your friends will be back by then."

"Hopefully," I echo. He waits until I crawl into my bunk, pull the covers up over myself, turn away from him and face the wall before he walks away. Sure, there are two other people asleep in this room. Sure, we're not alone. But right now I'm just glad he's not sleeping here, too. *You have to understand,* a voice in my mind whispers, and it sounds suspiciously like Conlan's. *He's been through a lot. They all have.*

I know. I know already, okay? I know, and I'm sorry. I'm sorry Dylan ever picked up their stupid little signal. I'm sorry he called it in. I'm sorry Dixon wanted us to check it out, and I'm sorry he sent me out to this dying colony.

You're lying. Here, in the darkness, with Dylan in the bunk above me, the springs creaking slightly and someone snoring in a distant room, here I can be honest—I'm sorry these people have had it rough. I'm sorry their babies are dying. I'm sorry Conlan's girl is depending on Shanley to get back here in time with the medicine. I'm sorry we're not on the *Semper Fi* tonight, lying in my own bunk with my lover, lying together satiated. I'm sorry we had to hide a few stolen moments in a dark serviceway like a dirty secret—but I *am* glad Dylan heard the signal. I'm happy he called it in and I'm almost delirious over the fact that Dixon sent me, *me,* to check it out, because now we're together again and the past two months have dissolved into nothing, it's just us now, that's it.

Above me Dylan shifts. Then he whispers my name, so low that at first I think I'm dreaming. When it comes again, a little louder, I hiss, "Get to sleep."

"I can't," he replies. Like he's been up there tossing and turning for hours already. "Neal," he whines. "Talk to me."

I sigh. "You're going to get us in trouble—"

"He's gone," Dylan tells me. *What about the others?* I want to ask him, but I don't. Maybe if I ignore him, he'll fall asleep.

The springs squeal as he moves around up there, then I hear a soft thud, something falling to the ground, and when I roll over, it's him, crawling into my bed. "Dylan," I start, but I hold the blankets open for him. I can't deny him anything. "Do you know what they're going to say—"

"I don't care." He cuddles up against me, his hands slipping over my stomach to cover my crotch, his touch arousing me all over again. Kissing my neck, he murmurs, "I love you, baby. I can't get enough of you, you know that. Now hush up and get to bed."

Because I love him, too, and because he's so damn irresistible, I scoot back until our bodies lie as one, me spooned in his embrace. Maybe *now* we can both get some sleep.

🍁   🍁   🍁

"Will you fucking *look* at this?"

The voice is hard and stings like a slap in the face. I feel Dylan roll over and then suddenly his hands are stripped away from me, his touch is gone, and he cries out, "Hey! Get off me—"

Harsh hands grip my shoulders, drag me from the bed. Out of the shade of the lower bunk, the world is too bright—I can't see, and when I try to wipe the sleep from my eyes someone twists my hands behind my back. "What—" That's as far as I get before I'm shoved against the upper bunk, a fist clenched in my hair, burying my face into the mattress. I struggle but my wrists are held fast behind me, someone kicks apart my feet, I can barely breathe and just what the *hell* is going on here?

I hear Dylan snarl, "Don't you dare touch him, let me go—" Then there's a faint scuffle and his arguments grow indistinct, muffled—they must have him against one of the other bunks, holding him down like they have me. *Don't fight, baby,* I want to tell him, but the words are only in my head. When I try to open my mouth all that comes out is an angry roar and whoever is pinning me down stifles it, grinding my face into the mattress. *Don't fight them, this is just a misunderstanding, it has to be.*

"What's going on here?" That's Conlan's voice, thick with sleep, and I'm glad he's here because that's what *I'd* like to know. "Ben—"

"You know the rules," Ellington says. There's no sympathy in his words—what happened to the guy who gave us ten minutes in the dark last night? Where is he now?

Rough hands turn me around, someone I don't know, a guy my age with thick, dark hair matted into ratty curls that frame his face. There's a gleam in his eyes that I don't like and he pinches my arm where he holds me. Someone else has my wrists, someone I can't see, but that Ramsey guy is on Dylan, bending his arms behind his back at awkward angles, and Maclin's hand fists in those long bangs I love. "Let him go," I growl, watching as Dylan struggles helplessly against his captors. I pull against the arms holding me back and kick out, my bare feet ineffectual. *Give me my boots,* I think, trying to twist away. I see the other guy now, the one holding me back, and it's Henry, his face neutral and his gaze somewhere distant, far away, not on me at all. *Give me my fucking clothes and at least let me wake up a bit here, Jesus.* I'm in my boxers, undershirt, and socks, and I've never felt so naked in my life.

Half of the colony crowds into the room—the whole committee, Ellington with his arms crossed in front of his chest, Conlan running a hand through his tousled hair and blinking owlishly, Kelly and Holly at the doorway peering in. The rest is a sea of faces I recognize from the commons, the other colonists, men I don't know who stare at me with undisguised hate and anger and what the *hell* did I do? *Nothing,* I think, and before I can stop myself, the words tumble from my lips. "We didn't *do* anything," I tell them. I don't like the plea I hear in my own voice, is that really me? "Jesus, people, we just shared a bed. He's my *lover.* We didn't have sex—"

Ellington steps forward and I turn to him, beseeching. "Tell them. Please. We didn't do anything, you know we didn't, I told you we wouldn't—"

"And I told *you* we had laws here," Ellington spits. He points to Conlan, who tries to shrink back into the crowd and when I look at him, he turns away. "Jeremy told you *why* we have to live like this, you said you understood—"

"I do," I mumble. I twist my wrists but Henry squeezes them tight, the bones grinding in his hands. "We kept it clean, like you said." Behind him, Dylan's stopped struggling, and it breaks my heart to see him like this. "He can't breathe," I tell them. Maclin glares at me, pushes Dylan's face into the mattress hard, he's doing it to spite me. From the corner of my eye I see Conlan cover his face with his hand and he shakes his head—he can't believe this is happening. *Me either.* "Can't you see you're hurting him? Let him up at least." Maclin doesn't move and Ramsey scowls at me. When I lunge for them, Henry and this other guy hold me back. "Stop it!" I cry. "Jesus fucking *Christ*—"

"Let him up," Ellington says.

Maclin grinds Dylan into the mattress for a moment longer, then releases his grip. *God*—Dylan's face is mottled and red and he gasps for breath in huge, hungry gulps. "Neal," he sighs, and he tries to wrestle free from the men holding him but it's useless. "Get your fucking hands off him, asshole. If they hurt you, baby—"

When he looks at me, winded and indignant, I spring forward again, trying to break away, trying to reach him, he's *mine,* they can't keep me from him, they *can't.* The move surprises the men behind me, surprises Ellington, whose eyes go wide and he takes a step back, out of reach. Then the hands tighten on me, pull me away, keep me from my lover. "Dylan," I sob. *Just let me go already,* I pray. *Just let me go to him, please.*

"Ben, what's going on here?" Conlan asks again.

Ellington nods at Ramsey, who starts to drag Dylan from the room. "No!" I cry out, but Ramsey just gives me a hateful grin as he pulls Dylan kicking and yelling my name through the door and out into the corridor. Kelly and Holly stand aside, let them through, and for a moment Kelly puts her hand out as if to stop him, but she doesn't. *Please,* I pray, but she simply turns away, like she's not seeing this. When Dylan strikes out with his feet, Maclin grabs his ankles in both hands, lifts him from the floor, the two of them carry him out and *can't we get any decency here?* I wonder. "Dylan! Where are you taking him? Someone tell me what the *fuck* is going on, *please*—"

No reply. Ellington nods at Henry and I'm pulled through the crowd, towards the doorway. Then Conlan steps up, *finally*, puts a hand on my chest and stops them. "Ben," he starts, "what—"

"They broke the law, Jeremy!" Ellington pushes past me, knocks Conlan's hand aside. "No sharing bunks, you *know* this. One thing leads to another and the next thing you know, the bleed is back, *we're* the ones dying this time—we had the respiratory strain but the one that killed everyone else, you *know* we might still get that one, you *know* it's out there, it *has* to be."

"They don't know the law," Conlan counters. "Ben, he says they didn't..." His voice trails off and he glances at me for confirmation.

I nod vigorously. "We *didn't*," I tell them. "Swear to God we didn't, all we did was sleep, that's *it*—"

Ellington doesn't care. "If I let you do it," he hisses, poking me in the chest with one stubby finger, "then *they're* going to want to do it, and I can't have that. We've worked too damn hard for this, and it might not be much to you but it's all we have. It's all *I* have, and I'm not going to let you stroll in here and tear it apart." For a long moment his eyes meet mine and I see the challenge in those dark depths, I see the *want* of a fight stewing in him. *He's not going to let you win,* my mind whispers. *Anything you say, you'll regret, he'll see to that.* When I don't respond, Ellington steps aside and mutters, "Go on."

Conlan looks like he has something more to say, and I give him my most pleading look, *please,* I want to beg of him, *we didn't know, please help us, please*—but I don't. I can't.

As I'm pulled through the crowd, I can't think of one damn thing to say in my own defense.

🍁 🍁 🍁

I don't fight—what's the use? Just let Henry and this other kid lead the way, down the stairwell and across the commons to a hatch that stands open. *Where they took Dylan,* I think, and I tell myself that it'll be okay once I'm with him again. Everything will work itself out once we're together.

Only that's not part of the plan. Beyond the hatch is another stairwell, this one leading down into the bowels of the ship, down below the comm center and further, until I'm sure we're in the very earth itself, the bottom deck of the ship that I know has to have settled into the ground over the past twenty years, the way it rains here. And this ship is so huge, so deserted. I've never felt so alone.

On the bottom deck, they lead me to a door protected by thick steel beams that slide away when Henry enters a code into the keypad. *So this part of the ship's still working*—I wonder why they keep it up, if they don't want to drain their power source. *Reinforcement. Can't rule without an element of terror so they keep this as a reminder, a prison.* I wonder how often they use it, and if we're going to be the only ones down here.

When the door opens, we enter a guardroom of sorts—a communications panel is set up on one side, a rather sophisticated system for a colony ship, but I guess they had to police it somehow. Tiny monitors above the panel display the rest of the ship—most of them are black now, looking out at darkened corridors and unlit rooms, but the few that are on show the quarters, the commons, the med lab, a few empty jail cells. Behind the panel sits a thin, nervous man with skin as dark as some of the monitor screens. He doesn't look up at us, just nods towards the far side of the room, where a wall of steel bars separates this from the rest of the prison. "Cell D6," he says in a gravelly voice. On the panel in front of him is a switchboard of sorts, a grid of buttons, hundreds of them, it seems. He presses one and it lights up green, a safe color, so why don't I feel safe right now? Then he reaches beneath the panel, hits a secret switch that I can't see, and the bars in front of us separate to create a doorway. "Fourth door on your right," the guard explains. "It should be open."

"Where's Dylan?" I ask as Henry leads me through the doorway. I try to dig in my heels, keep them from pulling me through, but it's no use, they're both stronger than I am. I'm all too aware that all I have on is my undershirt and boxers—goose bumps cover my arms and I'm beginning to shiver, it's chilly down here. Beneath my socks, the ridged steel floor is cold and bumpy, like walking on stones in winter. Would it be asking too much for some clothes? Who am I kidding? They won't even tell me where my boy is. "Can't you answer me? Where's Dylan?"

"Down here," Henry growls. He's still not looking at me, and when I try to resist, he practically lifts me up, his hands as strong, as uncompromising as the thick bars that close behind us, sealing us in. Locking *me* in.

We pass one door on the left, go another three feet and pass another door, this one on the right. Another three feet, another door—they're made of bars like the one behind us, this is a prison, it hits me all at once and I feel a cold dread settle into my stomach—a *prison*. "Please—"

"Fucking queer," my other captor mutters.

I stop and stare at him, this freak with the nasty curls who has the audacity to judge me. Suddenly his touch burns my skin. Where did they learn this language of hate? "You didn't just—"

"Shut up, Tobin." Henry tugs me forward roughly and I almost fall to my knees.

I try again. "Where's Dylan?"

Henry closes his hands around my arm, tightens them, until I can feel each pulse that carries blood from my shoulder to my wrist, each beat of my heart caught in his viselike grip, and my fingers tingle, he's cutting off my circulation, he's holding on so damn tight. "Please," I sob, and am I crying? I don't know. I don't care. My eyes sting and my hands are going numb and how can I fight back if I can't even clench them into fists? I'm cold, too cold, and my legs stumble out from beneath me, tears burn my face. I barely see the opened door they pull me through, I hardly notice the cells that line this new corridor, each one empty. "Dylan," and the name is a bitter shout, a hoarse cry. I try to pull back towards the door, away from these men and these cells and I can't, I just can't. "God."

At the end of the corridor, one of the cells is unlocked, the door open like an invitation. Henry throws me in and I fall to the floor, the steel biting into the bare skin of my knees and calves. "Dylan," I moan—*oh God, where is he?* I'd give anything to know that. *Just don't hurt him, please don't hurt him, please.*

Then the door to the cell slides shut behind me, trapping me here, locking me away like a criminal. I hear someone laugh—that Tobin kid, must be, because it's nothing like Henry's deep voice. I don't even have the strength to defend myself, they've taken Dylan from me, they've taken my life away, my lover, and my mind is a whirlwind of rage and impotence and hurt, wounded pride, disbelief. This isn't happening, not to *me*.

Footsteps echo away down the corridor, then the door to this wing closes with a metallic thud, and I'm left alone. Utterly, completely alone.

There's no sense of time. Nothing marks its passing. Ten minutes, hours, days, they're all the same to me. At some point my knees go numb. My shoulders ache, my head buried in the cold darkness where my arms are crossed in front of me, my brow pressed to the floor and steel like ice picking its way through my skin. *Dylan.* It's the only word I know. Sometimes, just to prove that I still exist, I whisper his name but I don't like the scrape of sound that's now my voice. It scares me. *Dylan.*

When I trust my legs, I try to stand. My forehead hurts—I can feel the hatched pattern of the floor pressed into my skin and I rub at it just for something to do. I'm in a cell. Arrested. Detained. That still hasn't quite sunk in completely yet.

My knees wobble but hold my weight, thank God. If I fall, I think I'll just lie there, I don't have the strength to pick myself up again. I'm alone. I hate being alone.

There's a bunk in the cell, a thin mattress, sparse blankets, a flat pillow at either end. A sink in one corner by a cracked toilet, that's it. Behind me is nothing but bars, thick and close together to keep me in. A narrow slot cuts through the door, a little more than waist high, and a thin shelf juts out from the slot into my room. The walls are the same dull metal as the rest of the ship, and the only light comes from the halogens that shine along the corridor, so my whole world now is cast into shade, the shadows of the bars segmenting my cell, my bed, me.

My cell. I don't like how easily that word comes to me. It's not mine, just a misunderstanding, that's all. When Shanley comes back we'll get this straightened out and they'll let us go, we'll leave and never come back, ever. *My cell.*

I wrap my arms around myself, shivering, and turn in a slow circle in the center of the cell, trying to look everywhere at once. Those monitors in the guardroom, one of them must show me here, but I can't see anything that might be a lens. In a corner somewhere maybe, set up high near the ceiling, I don't know. Is someone watching me? That guy at the control panel, Henry, Tobin? Can't they see me standing here half naked? Hugging myself for warmth, these thin boxers clinging to me? Or are they enjoying this?

That thought pisses me off. Enjoying *this*—they probably have two monitors set up, one into my cell and one into Dylan's, and they're laughing at this separation they've enforced upon us. I hate them, all of them. "Fuck you all!" I shout, angry as hell. I don't know who I'm talking to but I know they can hear me, they must. "I hope the rest of my crew doesn't get back in time and I hope all your babies die. They deserve it, you all do, fuck you." Lowering my voice, I fight back tears that threaten to come and mutter, "Fuck you."

That was hateful. I don't wish that on anyone, I'm just mad, but the words ring around me, I swear I hear them still, echoing off the walls and reverberating through my cell until I wish I never set them free. *I don't mean it,* I think, but I'm not saying I'm sorry, not out loud, because then *those* words will sear into my brain and I don't need to hear the apology forever. "I'm cold," I mutter, and that ricochets around me, *old old old*.

On the bunk I find that what I thought was a second pillow at the foot of the bed is really a small pile of clothes, like the linens the colonists wear, folded neatly. Those soft slipper-shoes with soles that sort of cushion the bottoms of my feet. A long-sleeved shirt made from some kind of worsted cotton, it feels like I'm wearing a blanket and the sleeves are too long but I roll them up and at least they're warm. A pair of pants that are tight across my butt because I'm rounder than most men—Dylan *loves* my ass, loves to knead it in his hands, smack it playfully, kiss the mounds of flesh, nip at the soft skin. Thinking of him brings the anger back, the indignation, the hate. I still can't quite believe they just took him away from me, tore him from my bed, while we slept—how could we guard against that?

I didn't think there was anything *to* guard against. I thought we were safe.

How stupid could I have been?

I crawl onto the bunk, cram myself back in the corner and pull my knees up tight to my chest, until I'm taking up as little of this damn cell as I possibly can. Maybe I can cease to be here. Maybe I can live wholly in my mind, my heart, my soul, where Dylan is. *They can't keep me here,* I tell myself. *I'm free if I don't let them get into me.*

I should've seen this coming. The dirty looks whenever Dylan touched me. The harsh whispers when we passed. The way Conlan and Ellington both skirted around the subject, using oblique references and obscure terms, trying to tell us with their eyes alone that they didn't want us together. For the good of the colony.

But we're clean. They've seen our med files, they *know* this. I've never had another lover and Dylan's not carrying anything, I know he isn't. And what did they think we would do? Grow bored with each other and cruise the colonists? Start a trend? Like our love is a disease they have to crush the moment it blooms. Like it's unnatural or wrong to feel the way we do—how can love be wrong? How can it be a bad thing for me to love him? *You have to understand,* Conlan's voice whispers, and fuck that, I don't understand shit, I don't *have* to. *They* are the ones who have to understand. Dylan is mine. I want him back.

Easy for you to say but look around you, James. Look at the walls, they're steel. Look at the bars, they're solid iron, you're not getting through them any time soon.

I lower my head to my knees and tell myself I'm not crying. I'm not going to cry. I'm stronger than that.

But how can I hold myself together without Dylan? *He's my strength and you've taken him away from me. Damn you all to hell.*

Later, but I'm not sure when. At one point I fancy I hear Dylan calling my name but it's just in the chambers of my heart, the beat of my veins, it's not real. He's not in this cell block, he's somewhere else, they're keeping him as far away from me as possible and I hate them for that. All of them—Ellington with his smug air, Maclin's damn smirk, Ramsey's mean streak that made him rough with Dylan. The memory of their hands on my boy makes me tremble because there was nothing, nothing, *nothing* I could do. I hate them all, even Conlan, though he's the only one who tried to stop them from taking us. *Didn't try hard enough.*

Down the corridor, out of sight, I hear the quiet hiss of a barred door opening. I don't bother getting up. I've sat in this corner for so long now, I don't think I can move if I want to. Soft footsteps shuffle towards my cell, moving slowly enough that I'm sure it's someone carrying a tray full of food. I tell myself I'm not hungry, but starving myself won't accomplish anything. They won't care.

For some reason, it doesn't surprise me to see Conlan step into view, a tray of pancakes in his hands. He looks up at me through the bars and forces a faint smile. "Breakfast," he says, setting the tray into the slot in the door. I stare at it where it sits on the shelf and tell myself again I'm not hungry, even as my stomach begins to growl. I can smell the thick syrup, the melted butter. Conlan toys with the silverware through the slot, trying to line the fork and knife up on my napkin just so. He's nervous.

Without moving I ask, "Why you?"

Conlan shrugs and doesn't quite meet my gaze. "I volunteered," he tells me. "I wanted to tell you…" He shrugs again and whispers, "I don't think this is right."

I force a laugh. "Imagine that," I say. "I've got news for you, kid. Me either." His smile tightens but he doesn't move, doesn't leave. I hold my breath and dare to ask, "Where's Dylan?"

"Another cell," Conlan answers evasively.

"Is he okay?" I want to know. *Please,* I pray.

Conlan tears at the corner of the napkin on my tray. Why's he so nervous all of a sudden around me? *It's not catching,* I should tell him. *Don't worry about that.* When I'm about to speak, though, he murmurs, "He'll be fine."

I don't like the sound of that. This is Conlan, whose girl lies in the med lab in premature labor four months too soon and he thinks *she'll* be fine, too. "If those jackasses hurt him—"

"He bit Seth," Conlan admits. He talks to the pancakes on my tray, not to me. I feel like I'm eavesdropping, he speaks so low. "Ramsey bloodied his nose, is all." One corner of his mouth pulls into a half-hearted grin. "He yelled himself hoarse, you know. Your name, that's all he said. He's asleep now. It's so quiet down that hall."

"I want him," I announce. Conlan's smile disappears. "I want him here, with me. You can keep us down here if you think it's what's best but I want him—"

"I can't do that." Conlan leans against the bars like he's the one in the cell and he's looking out at me. "You're not in any real position to make demands, you know that, right?" Like he has to remind me. "Everyone's really scared right now—"

"We didn't *do* anything!" I cry, and that comes out harsher than I intended. Taking a shaky breath, I add, "He's my lover. As in I love him. Do you have that here? Love?" When he starts to answer, I cut him off. "It's not just sex or fucking or fooling around. It's not just making babies or feeling good. He's a part of me, *you* have to understand *that.*"

"I do," Conlan whispers.

"Then why—"

"One of the women miscarried," Conlan tells me. I stare at him, shocked, and before I can ask him, he says, "Not Marie. It was Shauna, she's not that far along and this is her third child. It was sort of expected, you know? She lost the other two and we all saw this one coming but there was nothing we could really do."

Except go into panic mode. "How far along was she?" I ask.

Conlan mumbles, "Couple weeks. Still in the first trimester, I think. It happened thing this morning and there were…complications…"

"Like what?" I prompt. I need something to explain the witch hunt that put me here.

"I'm not sure," Conlan says. "Ben was there, not me. He said there was—" He sighs, gathers his thoughts, blinks up at the ceiling of my cell like it's all written out there and he can just read it aloud to me. I glance up but it's only dim light and bars of shade, that's all *I* see. "Lots of blood," he explains. "He got scared. So much blood, it's a wonder she's still alive."

And for this you jailed us? "But she is—"

Conlan nods, conceding, "She is, yeah."

"So what's the problem again?" That sounds callous, so I add, "I'm sorry she lost the baby."

"Me too," Conlan whispers. "Your friend Evan? He said she was going good when he looked at her yesterday, real good, and then she miscarried and now she's got a low-grade fever and the chills. That might not mean much to you—"

"But that's how the bleed starts," I finish for him, and he nods. Beneath the warm clothes I wear, my skin prickles with a sudden fear. "Oh shit."

"Oh shit," Conlan echoes. The words sound awkward in his voice, foreign, odd. "Exactly."

Silence. It drapes around us like a shroud, deadening the faint clank of my silverware on the tray that Conlan repositions to busy himself. "I'm sorry," I whisper. *That thing about the babies dying? I didn't mean it. I swear I didn't, I take it back.*

Conlan presses his lips together until there's nothing but a white line where his mouth is, and his hair hangs in front of his eyes but he's not looking at me, he's still playing with my pancakes. "So we're sort of on high alert here," he whispers. "Ben and Ramsey decided you guys should stay in another part of the ship, somewhere safe—"

"Behind bars?" I ask with a laugh. How fucking safe is that?

"When they came to get you," Conlan continues, as if I didn't interrupt, "and they saw you in the bunk together, well, things got out of hand. Just a little."

"I'd say." Out of hand? *You call being dragged bodily out of bed, your lover's touch ripped from you, you think that's just a little out of hand?* This guy's got the gift of understatement, to say the least.

With a desolate sigh, Conlan murmurs, "I'm sorry."

Me too. "So now what?" I ask him. That's what I'd really like to know. "When can I see Dylan again? When the *Semper Fi* lands?"

"It won't." Conlan lets the words sink in, and just as I'm about to ask him what he means by that, he explains. "We don't know what's going on right now. Does Shauna have the bleed? If so, does that mean we'll all get it again? Does it mean this time it's going to be lethal? Is this the deadly strain? We don't know. Who else has it? We don't know." Fear like a cold hand grips my heart, squeezes until it skips a beat, and I have to lace my hands together to keep them from trembling uncontrollably. "But you've never had it," he continues, and I can see where he's going with this, I don't want to hear it, I don't even want to *think* it. "None of your crew has. We can't just let your friends back in here—you have to understand—"

"They could get infected," I breathe. Conlan frowns at my pancakes and nods. "We could all get it this time." He nods again. "We could die."

"You could," he agrees. That's not exactly what I want to hear. With a wry grin, he adds, "This might be the best place for you right now."

"Not without Dylan," I tell him, and his smile fades. "Can't you move him in here—"

"No."

I try to rein in my anger. "Not even to this corridor? Please—"

But Conlan shakes his head, adamant. "I can't. You have to understand—"

"Stop *saying* that!" I cry, and before I can stop myself I grab the pillow beside me, launch it across the room at him. It falls miserably short, though, landing in the middle of my cell. "Jesus, stop telling me to understand. What the hell is it you want me to get? That I'm supposed to rot in this damn cell until you think it's safe to let my friends in to save me? That I'm supposed to stay here alone? What happens if you all die out—what happens to me then? To Dylan?"

Conlan's voice is as indignant as a little kid's when he mutters, "It might not be the bleed this time. It might not even be fatal, we don't know yet—"

"Then you should let Shanley land. He's a physician, remember?" I remind him. "Maybe he can help you."

"I'll have to talk to the committee," Conlan says.

"Can't you do anything on your own?" I ask him. "It's all about that fucking committee for you, and look what good they've done. They're the ones that have us locked in here. They're the ones who've decided the rest of my crew can't come in, can't rescue us, can't help your girl—" Conlan's frown deepens—that hit a nerve. Lowering my voice, I plead with him. "They'll say no, you know that. They'll argue this out until you're all dead, or they'll hem and haw and come to find out it's not the bleed but Marie loses your baby because they waited too long to get her help." In almost a whisper, I say, "This isn't your first child." Conlan shakes his head, no, it isn't, and he brushes the hair back from his face, wipes his eyes. He's heartsick about this poor kid, he has so much to lose if Shanley doesn't come back, we both do. "Don't let them take this one from you, too," I whisper.

For a moment I can almost see the indecision war across his face. He wants to help me, true, but he wants to help himself more, he wants this baby to live, he wants it so bad, I see the emotions rage through him, what's law versus what's right. *Please,* I pray silently. *You have to understand—*

"I need to talk to the committee," he mumbles. I let out a breath I didn't know I was holding, disappointment eating into me. He backs away from the cell, stumbles, catches himself before he can fall. "I'm sorry. Please, I'm…I'm sorry."

And then he's gone.

Part 7

I sit on my bunk, in the corner, folded into myself for hours. I don't get up to eat the pancakes and they grow cold, the smell of syrup cloying, I'm sure it's congealed by now. I'm not going to eat them. I have to think.

I stare at the blank wall above the toilet and see Conlan's face again, the way his eyes grew distant when I mentioned the child Marie carries. He knows Shanley can help her. He knows it may be her only hope—how much longer does she have before the terbute doesn't work anymore and she goes into labor? And loses another child. He can't go through that again, I know he can't. Shanley needs to be able to land.

And get us out of here, I add silently. *Shanley lands and he'll talk sense into these people. They'll have to release us and let us leave. Didn't Conlan say they only wanted to keep us here until our friends arrived?*

Only now they aren't going to. And Marie's child dies. And if this is the bleed again? *Then we all die, Dylan and me included, and we die alone because they won't let us share the same cell.*

I'm not going to let that happen. I have to think.

Conlan—he's the only one who tried to stand in the way when we were arrested. I have to smile at that word, *arrested*, because they don't have weapons, no police, nothing but brute force and I feel like I'm a kid again, caught up in a game of cops and robbers and locked away in a coat closet because it's the only place we can think of to use as a jail. But I can't forget the bars that stripe along the floor, cut across my bunk, *those* are real, this isn't just a game of make-believe. No one's going to come down here and laugh when they find us, ask, "What are you doing in here?" and set us free, that's not going to happen because they won't let the *Semper Fi* land. They won't let the rest of our crew back in the colony.

They won't let us go.

I have to think.

Conlan knows this is wrong, he told me that. He knows I don't belong here. He knows the way I feel for Dylan and he says he understands the feeling, he's the only one here who does—love is a foreign concept to these colonists. But there's Marie, whose mother took him in when his own parents died. More sister to him than lover, I'd imagine, but she's carried his children, both of them, and that has to mean something. That has to create some kind of bond, regardless of what everyone else here seems to think, what *Ellington* seems to think. Conlan's lost one child already. I suspect he's harnessed too much hope on Shanley's briox to let another go without a fight.

I still remember the struggle I saw in his face, Ellington's words battling with mine, what the colony needs versus what *he* needs, and he almost won that time, *almost*. I could *see* it, the way he wanted to listen to me, he *wanted* to say that his child is more important because to him that's *all* that matters, that's all he cares about, he *knows* this. And it scares the hell out of him, that's why he ran away. He's been listening to that damn committee of his for so long now that he thinks they must be right, no matter what. He doesn't want to admit that maybe, just this one time, maybe they're not.

That terrifies him.

What if I can convince him otherwise, though? What if I can get him to go against their judgment for his child's sake? *Then he lets Shanley in here. He gets us out, too. I can get Dylan back. If he'll only listen to me.*

Somehow, I have to make him listen to me.

No one else visits for a long time. I can't believe they've already forgotten about us, but maybe with everything else going on, we've slipped their minds. I wonder how Dylan's doing, my poor baby boy. Crying himself hoarse for me, that makes me livid, I'm going to hurt that Ramsey for hitting him. *I love you,* I think, imagining my words a telepathic projection that breaks through these walls of steel and finds him, envelops him, comforts him. I imagine him lying curled up on his bunk, baleful and bitter, and then my thoughts cover over him like a blanket, warm him, smooth out the lines that crease his forehead, the pout that tugs at his lips. *I love you.* I can almost hear his reply. *Me too, baby. I love you, too.*

I don't move. I hope whoever's in the guardroom is watching me on the monitor, wondering if I'm still alive, I've sat in this same position for so long, and I hope I'm boring them to tears, I hope they're hating this duty they're on, whoever it is. I hope Dylan's as motionless as me, because there's nothing to see here, nothing to write home about, move along now. *Let us go. We're not animals in a zoo, there's nothing interesting about us, nothing wrong or perverted or diseased. It's called love, people. It's called forever. Look into it.*

It feels like years later when my stomach starts to growl. There's a slight pain in my temples, a headache because I haven't eaten, and I eye those ice-cold pancakes from the safety of my bunk. I wonder how fast the bleed works—what if they're all dead by now? How would we ever know?

It hasn't been that long, I assure myself. *Wait a little while longer. Another hour, that's all. No one comes by then, you can eat those pancakes. They're cold but they're still edible.* Another hour and those pancakes will start to look damn good, I'm sure.

But I don't have to wait that long. I silently count off fifteen minutes and am about to say fuck it and just eat the breakfast when I hear the door at the end of the corridor open. *Thank you,* I pray. It'll be Conlan, and I can talk with him again, ask about Marie and see what he knows about the *Semper Fi*, and maybe get a little closer to actually getting out of here. He's the key to this, I know he is.

But it's not him, it's that kid Tobin who shuffles into view, his head down over a tray. I can see steam rise from a bowl of soup and my stomach churns hungrily—that looks *so* much better than those pancakes do.

Tobin looks at me through the long curls that hang in front of his eyes and there's something in his expression that I don't like. *Fucking queer,* isn't that what he called me? The words are still there, written on his face, stifling whatever happiness I might have felt to have company. *Go away,* I think. I'm not getting up from my bunk until he leaves. "Hey," he says. Seeing the breakfast tray, untouched, he asks, "Didn't you like the pancakes?"

I'm not shooting the shit with this kid. As he sets the tray he carries on the floor and removes the breakfast tray from the slot in the door, I frown at him and ask, "Where's Conlan?"

"What do you want him for?" Tobin counters. He places the breakfast tray on the floor by his feet and then lifts the one he carried in, eases it into the slot. "You getting lonely in there?"

Oh God, just go away. He makes me sick.

But he doesn't leave. Instead he curls his hands around the bars and presses his face against them, leers in at me. "Hey," he says again, lowering his voice. I glance up—I hate that grin of his, that unhealthy shine in his eyes. "Come here."

"No," I tell him. "Go away."

Tobin leans against the bars, rubs his groin along the hard steel, and his eyes slip closed in pleasure. *Don't even tell me he's getting off on this.* "I said come here," he moans, one of his hands sliding down the bar until it cups the slight bulge at his crotch. His fingers curve beneath his erection, working himself hard. "I know you want it."

Not from you. I turn away, disgusted. "Go jerk off someplace else."

"Maybe your boy's getting lonely," he suggests. A dull anger rises in me—*oh no, you didn't,* I think, balling my hands into fists. "What's his name? Maybe he'll want—"

That's as far as he gets before I spring up from the bunk and cross the cell, two steps, that's all it takes for me to reach him. I grab a fist full of those skank curls and pull him against the bars so hard, they ring with the impact. Before I can stop myself, I grab the bread knife from my tray, jam it against his throat. His skin turns white beneath the blade. "Don't you even *think* shit like that," I growl, punctuating my words with another tug on his hair. His eyes go wide at the sight of the knife, pressed just below his Adam's apple. "You say his name and I'll slice your throat, you hear? You touch him in *any* way and you're dead. Understand *that*?"

He tries to nod but the knife scratches his throat and he just settles for a high-pitched, "Uh-huh." His eyes roll wildly, and when his gaze flits up to the corner where the bars meet the right wall of the cell, I know I've found the camera that peers in on me.

I yank on the curls until both of his hands grip the bars and he tries to pull away. Then I turn to the corner where the camera must be. The knife is still at Tobin's throat, threatening to cut deeper each second, and he doesn't struggle for fear of injury. "And you have *me* locked up," I say, loud enough that whoever is watching can hear. "Not an asshole like *this*."

"Stop," Tobin sobs. "I didn't mean—"

I let him go. He staggers back, surprised, and trips over the breakfast tray, landing in the pancakes when he falls on his ass. The front of his pants still tents where he got a rise out of this, out of *me*, he actually thought I'd jump to fuck him, is that it? That *Dylan* would? I know my boy—if Tobin tried this with him, he'd get more than a sore head, a knife at his throat. Dylan's quick with his temper and he's the jealous type, this freak would simply have to *think* about sticking it to me and Dylan would rip his dick out with his bare hands, shove it down his throat, feed him his own balls for dessert. *And he thought...* I don't even want to go there.

Anger clouds my mind and I shove my lunch tray through the slot in the door, hard. It flies out into the corridor, clatters to the floor, hot soup splashing across Tobin's legs and crotch. "Fuck!" he cries, scrambling to his feet. He holds his suddenly wet pants out, they must be scalding, steam rises from them and that *had* to hurt. "You *faggot*—"

I still hold the knife. Leveling it through the bars at him, I promise, "You don't want to come down here again. Send Conlan." I raise my voice so whoever's in the guardroom will overhear. "Anyone else and they'll get this knife thrown at them. You think I'm kidding?" I notice Tobin's smirk, but it fades when I raise the knife threateningly. "I want to talk to Conlan. Have him bring me more soup." As Tobin fans his pants to dry them, I yell, "Now!"

He backs away like he doesn't trust me not to throw the knife when he turns around. That's not a bad idea, actually, but my anger's already passing. He's just lucky he didn't try this with Dylan, that's all I have to say. When he's finally out of sight, I hear him start to run.

Back on the bunk, I sit in the corner again, my legs to my chest, and clench the knife in a tight fist as I wait.

❦   ❦   ❦

More footsteps. I don't bother to look up until Conlan says, "I hear you tried to kill Tobin."

"Is that what he's saying?" I ask. Conlan carries another tray, slides it through the slot in the door, more soup. No knife this time, I notice, but I still have the other one in my hand. I feel like a petulant child when I tell him, "He started it."

Conlan only nods. "I know."

He busies himself with cleaning up the spilled trays that litter the floor and doesn't look at me. Carefully, I ask, "How's that girl doing?"

He lifts the pancakes by their soggy edges and flops them onto the tray, picking each one up with two fingers, grimacing as he holds it away from him and syrup drips to the floor. "Not good," he says. He doesn't elaborate.

"I'm sorry," I whisper. Conlan nods, yes, he is, too. "Have you heard from the *Semper Fi*?"

Silverware clatters to the floor as Conlan drops it, a spoon, forks, the knife from breakfast. The noise echoes down the corridor. "This morning," he whispers, glancing up through the bars of my cell to where the camera is hidden. I follow his gaze but don't see anything. Still, I get his drift and hop down from the bunk, come over to the bars, start to stir the soup. It's a thick stew, not as hot as the last bowl. Lowering his voice, Conlan tells me, "They called in right after...I'm not sure when exactly, sometime after—" He sighs. "After you guys were detained." *Detained*, I think, amused at his choice of words. Like this is just an inconvenience for me. "I didn't talk to them," he continues, "Ben did. They wanted landing coordinates and he told them no."

"Did he tell them why?" I ask. I sip at the soup, surprised at how hungry I suddenly am. The spoon shakes in my hands, making the soup splash. When's the last time I ate anything? Has Dylan eaten yet? "How's Dylan doing?"

"He's fine," Conlan mumbles. Scooping the trays together, he picks them up and stands, syrup running in a thin strand from the bottom of one tray to pool on the floor. "Mostly he's just lying down. Sleeping, I think." He nods as if confirming this, Dylan's sleeping, yes. That sounds good. Then Conlan laughs. "He's got a mouth on him, though—" I grin at that. "Doesn't he? When we bring him a meal he starts talking all this trash. Demands to see you. Swears he's going to tear this place down to get you back."

"That's my baby," I say with a smile. God, I miss him. It's an ache in my heart, so painful it almost makes me choke.

"I'll tell you one thing," Conlan admits. "I'm not going to be anywhere near here when they let him out. He's going to hurt someone."

I nod. "Possibly." This is Dylan—I *know* he's going to hurt someone when they finally open the doors to these cells. He'll go ballistic until he finds me. I'm thinking they should probably release me first, then I can catch him when he erupts from the cell, try to contain the dervish, hold him tight until he stops raging. *Like they're going to listen to me*, I tell myself, sipping at the soup. If I had my way, we'd be out of here already. Still, it doesn't hurt to hope.

He hasn't answered my other question, though. "What did the crew say?" I want to know. "When you told them they couldn't land?"

Conlan shrugs, unsure. "The transmission broke up, according to Ben." *Yeah, right,* I think. *You believe that one?* "They haven't contacted us again. I don't know if they're still at the carrier or maybe on their way, orbiting the planet, I just don't know."

"Can you find out?" He shrugs again and starts to back away—I'm treading on shaky ground here. He believes Ellington, I can see that in the way he frowns. To snag his attention, I ask, "How's Marie?"

The trays fumble in his hands but they don't fall—he catches them in time. "Fine," he sighs, and that's a lie, it's written all over his face. "She's...she'll be okay. She's fine."

"She needs the briox," I tell him.

"I know," he replies. A fork falls from one of the trays, pings off the floor at his feet. With deliberate care, Conlan bends his knees, sinks down to pick it up.

I try again. "Shanley can help her—"

"I *know*." The trays slide out of his hands, tumble to the ground. "Dammit," he mutters, trying to gather up the plates again, the bowl, the silverware and cold pancakes and napkins. I feel like I should apologize for making him do this but they should've sent Tobin to clean up this mess, it's *his* fault. Before I can say anything, though, Conlan murmurs, "We have to wait a few days to see how Shauna progresses. Right now she's in quarantine. Could be this is just a cold, nothing more. Could be she's going to get better. We just have to wait and see."

A few days. Is that how long we're going to be stuck down here? I can't stand this forced separation, I can't stand knowing Dylan's locked away somewhere, locked away from me. "How long has it been already?" Days, it feels like, but I know that's wrong. Still, it has to be nighttime by now. I've been in here forever.

"Few hours," Conlan says, surprising me. "She's starting to cough up blood and one of the other women thinks she has it, too. Alison? She's not...well, she's not pregnant, and Ben says she's just scared, we all are. She was with Shauna when she miscarried and now she's saying she's infected, too."

"Is she?" Fear floods through me. I no longer taste the soup, just feel the warmth as it trails down my throat. *If it's spread already then maybe it IS the bleed. Maybe they'll all die. And then we will, too.* No, I won't let that happen. Not without seeing Dylan again, I *won't*.

"I don't know," Conlan whispers, standing. "I hope not. Shauna sat with Marie for a while yesterday. If she's got something that's contagious..." He trails off, shrugs again, picks at a soiled napkin on the tray he holds and sighs. "We could really use your friend right about now."

Softly, I suggest, "Why don't you talk to the committee? See if you can get them to let—"

"They won't," Conlan says, his voice hard. "I already asked. They're not—heh, Seth says they're not entertaining the idea at this time."

Yeah, that sounds like committee-speak to me. "But you guys need a physician down here," I remind him. "Marie needs the briox—"

"I know." He glares at the tray in his hands and his words take on an angry tint. "Don't you think I know this already? There's nothing I can do."

But I don't give up, I can't. I have too much at stake here now, too much to lose. *Dylan.* "I'm sure—"

"It's the committee's decision," he tells me, backing away. He's leaving again and my chance is slipping away, he has to help me, he has to see what needs to be done, why can't he *see*? "Not mine, Neal," he tells me, and his eyes plead with me to understand. "I'm just one man, I can't do anything about this. I'm sorry."

Then he turns and hurries down the corridor. "Wait!" I call out, but he's already gone.

❦ ❦ ❦

He doesn't come back for the lunch tray when I'm through—Maclin does. I stare at him balefully from my bunk and wonder if this is a test, if they're waiting to see if I'm going to attack him. I wonder if I will. "Where's Conlan?" I ask when it's obvious he's not going to speak first.

He grabs the tray, his hand hitting the empty soup bowl, almost knocking it off the narrow shelf, but he catches it before it can fall to the floor. "Don't worry," he tells me, as if I might be. His voice is seductively soft. "I ain't gonna put the moves on you. You're not my type."

That's not the answer I'm looking for. "Conlan?" I ask again.

Maclin pushes those dark shades up onto his forehead, revealing hard, brown eyes. "Go ahead and throw that knife you got," he purrs. He talks like I imagine a cat would, with a slow drawl that belies the alertness I sense about him. He nods at the knife I still hold in my hand and it seems silly now, not much of a threat. "Or don't, doesn't matter much one way or the other. Your boy already tried to kill me."

Now I notice a bandage covering the sensitive skin near the crook of his right arm. *I'm sorry,* I almost say, but I bite the words back because Ramsey struck Dylan and that still pisses the hell out of me. "You gonna eat any more of this?" Maclin asks, giving the tray a slight shove.

I ignore that. "You should let the ship land," I tell him. I don't know the name of his girl but didn't someone mention that he was one of the expecting fathers? Maybe I can reason with him, maybe he's stronger than Conlan. "How can you hope to survive if you can't reproduce?"

"That's none of your concern," Maclin growls. "You stop talking that shit to Jeremy. He doesn't need to hear it."

So that's why you're here instead of him. What, Ellington's worried Conlan might actually start listening to me? *Ooh, free thought, can't have that.* "We can help you," I try instead. "If it's not the bleed—"

Maclin drops his shades back into place over his hardened eyes. "That's a chance we can't take."

He turns to leave, tray in hand, and I cry out, "What about Marie? If she doesn't get the drug, she'll lose the baby, you know that."

"One child," he says, his voice insidious. "When it might save the whole colony to keep strangers out right now? She's young enough. She'll bear more."

"What if it was *your* child?" I want to know. "Christ, you can't be that heartless—"

Maclin shrugs. "My girl's not that far along," he admits. "Once this whole scare blows over, we'll let your friends land, get the drug, the other babies will live." *MY child will live,* that's what he's thinking, I can see it in the smug expression on his thin face.

"What about Conlan?" I press. "You can't tell me his child means nothing to you."

Lowering his shades, Maclin peers at me over the top of the frames and says, "It means nothing to me."

"Fuck you then," I mutter. If everyone in this damn colony feels the same way he does, they all deserve whatever they get.

❦ ❦ ❦

My hand has molded to the knife handle. I don't even feel it anymore, it's an extension of my arm, I couldn't throw it now if I tried. I hear nothing, nothing at all—these walls must absorb sound, there's nothing to tell me I'm still here, nothing to tell me I'm still alive but the steady beat of my heart in my ears and even that might be imagined at this point. The *Semper Fi* will leave without us, return to the carrier, return to the station and we'll be stuck here forever. Apart, forever.

And if it's the bleed...

I don't want to think about that. It's not the bleed, it *can't* be. *But it's spreading*, my mind whispers. *It's spreading already—two girls have it now, isn't that what Conlan said? How many more were exposed before they quarantined them?* He mentioned Marie, didn't he? Said the girl sat with Marie for a while and so *she* might have it now, right? If it's the airborne strain, if it's contagious—

Shanley.

The name drifts through my mind, looking for something to attach to, numbing me and I'm not sure why, I can't seem to follow that thought. *He can't help us now*, I tell myself, but suddenly it's like his name is a blinding light, so bright that I can't see anything else, I can't think anything else, everything circles back to him. *Shanley. He's on the Semper Fi, not here. How long will it be before they decide to leave without us?* I don't think Vallery would let them and she's the navigator, but what if they run low on fuel? What if Johnson gets the radio to reach out to the station and Dixon calls them back? He won't want to lose a pilot like Dylan but I know he'd just as soon leave me here to rot so he'll call them back and—

Shanley.

I hear Conlan's words again. When he brought me breakfast, first told me about the scare. *"Your friend Evan? He said she was doing good when he looked at her yesterday, real good, and then she miscarried and now she's got a low-grade fever and the chills. That might not mean much to you—"*

And now another woman has it, right? Or thinks she does, at any rate, and Conlan's worried Marie might catch it because she was with the girl yesterday, too, and what happens if this *is* an airborne strain of the virus? What if it *is* the bleed in respiratory form?

Then Shanley has it, too.

The thought washes over me like ice water through my veins. *If it's the bleed and spreads like they say, then Shanley has it, and he's probably already infected Parker and the crew of the carrier and if they head back to the station then everyone there will get it, too, they'll all die, someone has to warn them, someone has to—*

Then it hits me, so hard that my head reels from the thought. There's no reason the *Semper Fi can't* land, not if Shanley's already exposed to the virus. There's no reason he can't come back into the colony with the briox now, no reason at all.

Before I can stop myself, I jump off the bunk, press my face against the bars, try to see down the empty corridor. "Hey!" I yell, and my voice rings off the steel walls. "Hey! I need to talk to somebody!"

No answer. Just my own voice, echoing away. Can they even hear me? I doubt it. If Dylan's down another corridor and he cried himself hoarse and I didn't hear a breath of it, chances are I'm just wasting my time. I try to rattle the bars but they don't budge, they're set too deep into the floor and ceiling. Then I try to run the knife across them, like I've seen criminals do in the old holovids from Earth, but the thin blade just plinks over the steel, doesn't make any real sound at all. Anger makes me cry out again, "Hey!" Top of my lungs, long and drawn out until I run out of breath and my voice warbles off and still nothing. No one hears me. No one cares.

For a few frantic moments I wave my arms at the corner where the camera is—maybe someone in the guardroom will see me, maybe they'll come down here to check on me, see what the problem is, and then I can ask to speak to Ellington. He's the one I need to appeal to here. Conlan may be committee chair but it's just a puppet position, I'm almost sure of it, Ellington's the oldest in the colony. He sort of took over this whole thing from the moment we got the go-ahead to land, always keeping an eye on us, quick to point out that we're not wanted here, so eager for tight control over everything we say and do. We only saw the parts of the ship *he* took us to, the parts *he* wanted us to see. And he's hated this briox idea of Shanley's since we suggested it, glared at us during the meeting while Conlan argued for it, told Conlan not to get his hopes up, told him not to excite Marie, told us to keep it *clean*, for Christ's sake, did he really expect Dylan to keep it clean? Ten minutes is a *challenge* to that boy. Back at the station once he got it in his head that he wanted me on the nav deck, despite the fact that I was on duty and Tony had just run down to the cafeteria for a snack. He wasn't gone five minutes and we didn't even get undressed and Dylan *still* managed to make me cry out his name when I came. Ellington couldn't have been serious about that *keep it clean* remark, no way, no how.

But a blowjob's no reason to imprison us, and it was his idea anyway, those few stolen moments in the dark serviceway, and his was the first face I saw this morning when they arrested us. He wouldn't listen to me even though he *knew* we didn't do anything, he *had* to have known. Jesus, how many times a night does he think I can get it up? *No, wait, don't answer that,* my mind whispers, because if they didn't have that stupid *no sex* rule then Dylan and I would have probably been all too eager to see just how many times we *could* love each other, I know I would have given anything to find that one out last night. *Two months,* I think. *Two whole months without him, wanting him, needing him, and now he's mine again and I can't have him and if Ellington's so gung-ho about this colony succeeding, then why hasn't he considered the possibility that Shanley's infected?*

Maybe he's already thought of it, though. *Then why won't he let them land?*

❦ ❦ ❦

I can't sit back down, not with all these thoughts whirling through my head, clawing to get out. If Shanley's infected, he *needs* to come down here, he can't go back to the station, none of the crew can, not if this is the bleed. And they need to land soon, they need to land *now*, because if they die up there in the carrier, how will Dylan and I ever get back? Assuming we don't catch the virus, and assuming we get out of these cells.

I don't like assumptions, they never pan out, they're just false hopes and I don't need those cluttering my mind. I need to focus. I need to stay alert.

I pace the cell like a caged animal, trying to work off the excess energy that makes my hands tremble, my heart race. With the colonists' soft shoes on, I can barely hear my footsteps, and when I reach one wall and turn towards the other, I scuff my feet just to make sure I'm still walking. It takes ten steps to cross the room, turn, ten back, turn, ten again. I widen the steps, pick up the pace, walk faster and faster until I can close the distance in seven steps so far apart, they're almost leaps. My breath catches in my throat, my blood pounds in my ears, the noise of my shoes scraping along the steel the only sound and I turn again—

And freeze as the door to my cell pops open.

The bars separate just an inch, and then as I watch, they begin to retract, drawing into the side of the wall, *opening*, and I don't care why, I don't care how, I'm already reaching through to my freedom when I hear footsteps down the corridor, heavy footsteps, *lots* of them, a whole army headed this way. For a second I wonder what my chances are, if I just throw myself through the opening and barrel down the corridor—I wonder how far I'll get before I'm stopped. *I can still try it,* I think, watching the gap in the bars widen slowly.

Then Ellington steps into view, and Ramsey's behind him, his cold, blue eyes chilling all thoughts of escape. And Maclin's with them, and Henry, they block the corridor like a human wall, there's no *way* I could break through their defense. And Conlan—he stands behind them, stares at the floor, doesn't even look at me. At my side, I clench the knife tight in my hand and ask, "What's this all about?"

"Put it down," Ellington says, nodding at the knife.

My fingers tighten around it. "Or what?" I want to know.

Ramsey starts through the door of the cell and I take an involuntary step back, I don't like the hateful way he stares at me—*touch me and this goes through your chest,* I think wildly, but who am I kidding? This bread knife will barely scratch his skin. *But you hit my boy, I'm going to make you pay for that.*

"Ramsey, stop." Ellington's high voice cuts through the tension in the room and Ramsey's step falters. "Get back here." When Ramsey doesn't listen, Ellington sighs. I can see him pinch the bridge of his nose in that way he has because this is spiraling out of his control.

Conlan speaks up. "Ramsey," he warns.

To my surprise, Ramsey stops. He throws himself back against the bars, crosses his arms, glares at me. Then, his voice soft, Conlan tells me, "Neal, please. Put the knife down. We're not here to hurt you."

I want to believe him, but he's not alone. "What do you want, then?" I ask.

It's Ellington who answers me. "Your friends want to talk to you."

Shanley and Parker. "They're on the radio?" I ask, hope blossoming in me. "Listen, I was thinking, if this is the bleed—"

"We don't know if it is or not," Ellington says. "It's too soon to tell."

"But if it *is*," I say, excited, "if it *is* then Shanley must have it, too, right? He was with that girl yesterday and if he's infected, then he has to come back here, don't you see?" Behind Ellington, Conlan's eyes light up and he looks at me, he didn't think about that, maybe none of them did. "If he's infected, there's no reason he can't come down here, no reason he can't help Marie—"

Ellington cuts me off. "We don't know what it is," he growls, angry.

"Ben—" Conlan starts.

"We don't *know*," Ellington repeats, and Conlan falls silent. *Dammit!* How can Conlan let him *do* that? "Look, the *Semper Fi* is standing by. I don't know how long the transmission will last—you know how these storms can be." He motions down the corridor and behind him the others stand aside, showing me a clear path. "Can we talk about this later?"

I don't trust this. "Is Dylan coming?" I want to know.

Maclin sighs and Ramsey rolls his eyes, Henry bends his neck from side to side quickly, loosening the muscles, I can hear the crack from here. Conlan frowns at Ellington, who tells me, "I don't think that's a good idea—"

"Then I'm not going." Not without Dylan.

The way Ellington looks at me almost breaks my resolve. "I'm not asking here," he says. He doesn't have to mention the men behind him—Maclin is just skin and bones but there's a toughness like leather about him, and if he managed to help Ramsey carry Dylan, then I think he can probably force me to the comm center, him and Ramsey and Henry, the three of them would have no problems at all dragging my ass out of this cell and down these corridors, wherever they want to go. *At least Tobin's not with them,* I think, and it's a small comfort but at least there's that. "Well?" Ellington asks.

"I want to see him," I announce. When Ellington sighs, Ramsey starts towards me again and I tell them, "You can't make me talk. You can't *force* me to say shit, and you know it. Carry me if you have to but if I can't see Dylan—"

"Jesus *Christ!*" Maclin cries. "Can we get this over with already?"

Ellington looks like he wants to kill me, just take the knife from my hands and plunge it in my heart and tell the *Semper Fi* not to worry about landing here anymore, there's no reason to now. But he must see something in my eyes, something that tells him I'm not joking, I'm not saying a word on the radio until I see my boy, because he sighs again and throws his hands in the air. "Fine," he says. "Come on."

Tentatively, I take a step forward. "Without the knife," he says. I hesitate a moment, then let it fall to the floor, where the blade tings off the steel. "Come on."

He stands back, lets me step out into the corridor, and for the briefest of seconds I consider just running for it. The door ahead is open, I could be free, it'd surprise the hell out of them if I took off now—

But there's Dylan to think about. He's still here. I can't leave without him, I can't leave him here, I can't do that.

So I set one foot in front of the other, careful, and then Conlan steps in front of me to lead the way. When his eyes meet mine I can see the hope in them, the hope I put there. *If Shanley has it, he can come here,* I want to say. *There's no reason he can't. No reason Marie has to lose this baby, too.*

But then he turns away and I feel Ellington's hand on my back, pushing me after him, and the only thing I'm thinking about right this second is Dylan.

※　　　※　　　※

Conlan stops at the third door up the corridor from mine, on the left. There's a small keypad set into the wall, and I watch as he punches in a code, *23*—that's as much as I see before Ellington shoves in front of me, cutting off my view. "Jeremy, watch it," he growls as the bars slide apart. Someone behind me pushes me through the open door.

Empty cells line either side of the corridor. I force myself to walk naturally, fight against the voice inside my mind that wants me to run down the corridor and peer into every cell, call out my lover's name until I find him. But I have an audience, I'm not going to do that. "Last cell," Ellington tells me.

I ask, "Can I do this alone?"

Conlan glances up at Ellington, who shakes his head. "I don't think that's going to work," he says, but he motions for the others to wait in the main corridor, at least he does that much. Then he takes Conlan's arm, pushes him after me. He follows us at a distance, and with every step we take, Conlan falls further and further behind, until it's just me nearing the end of the corridor by myself. There two cells face each other and I try to look in them both at the same time, which one is Dylan's? Where's—

I see him, curled up on his bunk like a child, buried beneath the blankets as if he's hiding away from the rest of the world. Didn't Conlan say he's been mostly sleeping since they brought him here? A quick look behind me shows that Ellington is about halfway down the corridor, glaring at me. Conlan is closer, but still a whole cell's length away—he's turned his back to me for a little privacy, at least. The bars of Dylan's cell are cold when I wrap my hands around them and press my face against the steel. "Baby," I whisper. I don't want the others to overhear.

The blankets stir and then Dylan peeks out cautiously, like he's been dreaming of me and now he thinks he's hearing things, I can't be here, I'm not real. I smile at him, so damn beautiful, his hair disheveled and his eyes wide at the sight of me, and before I can say another word, he's tumbling from the bed, kicking his legs free from the blankets, falling over himself to reach me. "Neal!" he cries. He covers my hands with his, I never thought I'd feel his touch again so soon, and then he cradles my face in his hands, pulls me to him, kisses me hungrily, the bars adamant about keeping us apart. "Oh God," he moans, his lips insatiable against mine. He tries to pull me closer and can't, the bars stop him. "Jesus, are you okay?"

"I told you about calling me that," I murmur, but he licks the words from my lips. There's a coppery taste on his breath that I don't like, blood where that fucker hit him, and I pull back just enough to study him, run a thumb along his bruised lip, over the cut in the corner of his mouth. He kisses my thumb, then my palm, then sighs my name again. "Baby, I'm sorry—"

"I'm fine," he tells me, lowering his head as my hand pushes his long bangs from his face. "Did they hurt you? Did anyone touch you? I'll kill them, I'll kill them all."

"Shh." I place my hand over his mouth to quiet him and he kisses my palm again, holds my hand to his cheek. "I'm fine, Dylan, really." Now would not be the time to mention Tobin.

Dylan leans against the bars, trying to see down the corridor. "How'd you get out?" he wants to know. "What—" The look in my eyes stops him. "You're not free," he whispers. I shake my head, no, I'm not. "Where are they taking you?"

"To the comm center," I tell him, resting my forehead against his. "The *Semper Fi*'s called in." Behind me I hear Ellington clear his throat, anxious to get this over with, and Ramsey asks no one in particular if we're finished here yet. As quickly as possible, I tell Dylan what's going on, the sick girl and the lockdown on the colony. Then I tell him that I think Shanley might be infected, too. I raise my voice a little to include Conlan, even though he pretends he's not listening. "If he's already been exposed to it," I say, watching Conlan's stiff back from the corner of my eye, "then there's no reason he can't land. No real reason at all."

"They still might not let us go," Dylan reasons. "If we're all sick—"

I press my lips to his knuckles and whisper, "We're not. I'm not, I feel fine. You?" He nods in agreement. "We're not sick, baby. We haven't been exposed. If they keep us down here until the scare is over, that's understandable—"

"I want you here," Dylan declares. "With me. This separate cells shit is *not* understandable, not at *all*."

I silence him with a kiss. "If they let Shanley in," I explain, "then he might have something in that pharmacy of his to destroy the virus. At any rate, he can help Marie."

"What about us?" Dylan raises his voice, indignant, until he's shouting down the corridor because he knows there's someone with me, there has to be. "What the fuck about us? That's what I'd like to know. What—"

"Dylan, shh," I admonish. Ellington shifts uncomfortably and even Conlan glances at us over his shoulder—has Dylan been like this the whole time? Knowing my boy, more than likely. "With Shanley here, he'll talk sense into them. He'll run those tests of his and prove we're not carrying anything—"

Dylan groans. "Not *that* again," he says, rolling his eyes. "You know how sick I was."

I know, I start to say, and I even open my mouth, the words on the tip of my tongue, when I get it. The reason why the colonists have been so against us from the start. Not Shanley, they let him in the med lab, let him examine the expecting women. Not Parker, the hateful stares were never quite directed at him. Just the two of us, Dylan and me, and why? *Because they had our med files*, I think—why didn't it occur to me before? *Because they saw on Dylan's chart that he got sick from the HTS, and sickness to them means death. They don't care that it was a reaction to the treatment or that he recovered—he was sick before we landed and Ellington's wanted to lock us away since we got here. It's because he loves me, true, and they don't allow that here, sex is only for procreation and love doesn't exist, but it's also—*"Because you were sick," I murmur out loud.

Dylan frowns at me, confused, but I can't explain, Ellington starts my way, this little visitation is over. "I have to go, hon." I kiss him again, trying to imprint the feel of his lips against mine, to sear his touch into my memory. "I love you."

His hands tighten over mine, trying to keep me here. "Neal—" he starts, and I hate myself when I have to let go. "Don't leave me," he pleads. How can I possibly ignore the need I see in his face? The naked want, the love? "Baby, please—"

"Time's up, kids," Ellington says. When he reaches for me, Dylan's eyes narrow evilly—if looks could kill, Ellington wouldn't have to worry about the bleed anymore, he'd be dead on the spot. Seeing that look, he sighs, explains, "We might lose the transmission—"

I kiss Dylan one last time, hungry for him. "I love you," he whispers, his mouth against mine, his breath the air I breathe.

"We'll get out of this," I promise, even though I don't know how. "You'll see."

Conlan leads the way out of the depths of the ship up to the comm center. He walks with his head down but I can see him chew his lower lip, he's thinking over what I said. If Shanley's already exposed to the bleed, there's no reason he can't come back and help Marie. *And get us out of here*, I add silently. To tell you the truth, that's all I'm really hoping for right now, to get out of this. First thing I'll do is hold Dylan and never let him go. I don't like the memory of the steel bars keeping our bodies apart.

I can see the indecision play across Conlan's face—he's thinking of ways to broach the topic with the committee maybe, plead for Shanley to come back. How long has it been since they were supposed to land? Hours, and how much more time does Marie have before the terbute just doesn't work? It's not for late stage pregnancies, she needs the briox to carry to term, they *all* do. Whatever this bleed is, it somehow affected their ability to reproduce and if they don't stem that now, the colony will die. Can't they *see* this?

As we walk through the empty corridors, I try to catch up with Conlan to talk with him. Maybe my words will spark him to action. Maybe I'll be able to convince him to talk to the committee again and force *them* to see, as well. Maybe—

But Ellington cuts in front of me, keeping me from Conlan, and Henry takes my elbow like he thinks I might jet off any minute, just hightail it out of here, so he has to keep a tight rein on me. To my other side, Ramsey stares straight ahead at Conlan's back, his scowl so bitter that my step falters to see it and behind me Maclin walks so close, I swear he's just inches from me and I can feel him hovering, too close, too damn close. Together they form a vanguard around me, a prison of men to make sure I don't run away. *They don't want our help*, I think, glancing at their closed faces, amazed. *They're so damn sure they can survive this, they can get by the way they always have before, and they don't want anyone to even try to help them out. They're afraid we'll just ruin all they've worked so hard to attain. Ellington's afraid because he IS the colony, isn't he? He's only doing what he thinks is best.*

How can I hope to reason with that? I can't—I'm not part of them, I'm outside their unity and he'll never trust us, never trust *me*. My best bet is to appeal to Conlan, get him on our side, get him to talk some sense into his friends. Ellington will listen to him, if I can just get Conlan alone long enough to convince him that Shanley *can* land. *And we can go free*, I keep telling myself as I follow them into the comm center.

Two techs man the radio, the woman who was here when Ellington took us on his tour yesterday and a young blonde man I don't recall seeing before. "They're still standing by," the woman says as we enter. She speaks in clipped tones that leave no room for argument, and she doesn't quite look at me, just relinquishes her seat without a word as I'm led to the radio.

Trepidatiously, I sink into her chair. I look up at Ellington—what's he want me to do? Just hail them, say hi? Who's on the other end of this transmission? *A little help here would be nice*, I think, glancing from Ellington to Conlan, who's staring through me like he's still thinking over what I said before. "What…" I trail off, not even sure what I want to ask.

Ellington just motions at the radio. Taking a deep breath, I press the transmit button and speak slowly into the open channel. "Neal James to the *Semper Fi*." I hope my voice sounds stronger than it does to my own ears—at least it doesn't tremble. Thank God for that. "*Semper Fi*, do you copy?"

Vallery's voice comes in a rush as sweet as water in the desert. "Neal, my *God*!" she cries, and her laughter is bubbly and nervous but it sounds wonderful to me. "We've been so damn *worried* about you guys—oops! Sorry, didn't mean to say damn. Shit, I said it again. I mean—"

I can't help but grin as I cut her off. "That's okay, Val. I thought I'd never hear your laugh again. Where's the *Semper Fi*?"

"Just above the cloud cover there," she tells me. Beneath her words I can hear Johnson tell someone to get the hell off him, and then Leena's throaty voice over his, telling him to shut up, she can't hear, if he doesn't want her in his lap then he can get up and let her have the seat. *What I wouldn't give to be back on that nav deck,* I think, almost wistful. *With Dylan in the cockpit, calling me on the intercom, telling me to come on up and keep him company.* I wonder when I'll see these people, my crew, again.

Vallery disrupts my nostalgic train of thought. "What's going on down there, Neal?" she wants to know. Beside me Ellington tenses—what have they told her? I'm sure she doesn't know about our arrest, I'm almost certain of that, but what *does* she know? "Mike's touched base with Dixon, says all we need to do is map the signal's frequency and get you guys offworld, so why can't we land? Evan says those girls down there need his help."

"They do," I tell her. "But there's a virus going around and everyone's a little on edge, I guess you can say." That's putting it lightly. I'm learning the subtle art of understatement from Conlan, who keeps looking at Ellington like he has something he wants to say but he can't quite catch his friend's eye. Ellington studiously avoids him. "Remember that bleed I told you about earlier? The symptoms are the same. It's spreading—"

"Oh God, do you have it?" she asks sharply. "Jeez, you guys stay away from that scary shit. Oops! I mean crap, I'm sorry. Scary crap."

Despite the men towering over me, I have to laugh—she's so cute. A breath of fresh air in this stale colony, that's for sure. I don't want to tell her that she's probably already infected if it *is* the bleed, because we don't know that, no use terrifying her yet. So I try to keep my voice neutral as I say, "The bleed spreads quickly." I look up at Conlan for confirmation and he nods, yes, very quickly. "Shanley went over the records while he was here. I think the incubation period's something like a day or two, no more than that. They've got the girls quarantined but…" I don't want to say it. "Is the *Semper Fi* patched in? Maybe I can talk to Shanley directly—"

"What's up?" Vallery wants to know, but before I can reply, she says, "I'm hooking into them now, hold on."

I wait. Beside me I hear Conlan mutter, "He's right, you know. If they already have it, why *can't* they—"

"We don't know if they do or not," Ellington tells him, but he's glaring at me, it's my fault Conlan's thinking about this. "I can't take that chance."

"You're not the only one here," I remind him. "Why can't you—"

Static rips through the room, scratching the speakers, and then Shanley speaks. "Neal? Vallery tells me you're standing by."

I turn from Ellington's hateful gaze and focus on the incoming transmission. "I'm here," I tell him. Cutting to the chase, I ask, "Are you sick?"

"No." Relief floods through me, *thank you, Jesus*. "What's the status of the Thomas girl? Which woman miscarried? Do you know the symptoms—"

"I don't know anything," I admit. "It was Shauna?" Conlan nods again, yes, that's right. "They say another girl might be infected and since you were with her yesterday I thought maybe if it was going to spread, you might have caught it. But you say you're fine?"

"I'm not sick," Shanley repeats. "We need to land, Neal. I have some antibiotics with me. When Vallery radioed for the coordinates this morning, I was still at the carrier. I can help them." I turn to Ellington, motion towards the radio triumphantly. *See?* my gesture says. *Get them out of the sky already, let them IN.* "What's the holdup down there?" Shanley wants to know. "Kitt says we're just burning fuel. It's four hours from the carrier onworld and I don't want to waste more time than necessary, but no one will give us clearance to set down. Is this about the water supply?"

"I don't know what it's about," I grumble. "We're prisoners here, you have no idea—"

Suddenly Ramsey has me by the arms, dragging me back from the radio, out of the seat, away. "Hey!" I cry, struggling, but it's no use, he's much stronger than me. Over the radio, Shanley asks, "Neal? Are you still there? Prisoners? What—"

Ellington clicks off the radio, breaking the signal and cutting Shanley off in midsentence. "What the *hell* is your problem?" I want to know. Ramsey has his arms laced through mine, holding me back, but I strain against his grip, *let me at him,* I think, trying to lunge at Ellington. "He can *help* you! Only you're too goddamn stubborn to see—"

"Ben," Conlan starts, "he's right—"

Ellington whirls on his friend. "We discussed this!" he cries, anger humming through him, it's in the way he motions with his arms, the muscle that begins to twitch in his jaw. "I told you I didn't want them interfering here, none of us did. I didn't even want them to land but you assured me we wouldn't let them ruin what we have here. We're the only colony to succeed—"

"You call this success?" I shout. Conlan winces at my words. "Half of you die at the beginning, the rest of you can't reproduce, just what the *hell* are you trying to do here? You're too proud to admit that this isn't worth fighting for!"

With a single, fluid motion, Ellington turns on his heel and hits me, flat handed, across the mouth. My head snaps back against Ramsey's shoulder and through half-closed lids I see the look of horror on Conlan's face, the vindication in Ellington's sneer, everyone stops, watching us, waiting. I can hear rapid panting, Ellington's quick breath. I can feel the rough cloth of Ramsey's shirt against my cheek.

"This is our home," Ellington tells me, his voice dangerous and low. "We're doing this the only way we know how."

"You're dying," I mutter. I shouldn't have to point this out.

Behind him, Conlan tries again. "Ben—"

"We've made it this far," Ellington says. He straightens his shoulders, manages to look down at me even though I'm almost a head taller than he is. Then he laughs, a short burst that seems to surprise him. "You think I hadn't thought Shanley could be infected? Why do you think I don't *want* him coming back in here just yet? Everyone who was with Shauna yesterday, they're all in quarantine. I'm not taking any chances here."

"He's not sick," I remind him. "You heard him yourself on the radio. He's fine. They're all fine."

Ellington shakes his head, bemused. "You don't get it, do you? It takes forty-eight hours for the bleed to surface. He may still get it, we don't know yet. Right now what our women have, it could be anything. We won't know for sure—"

"Until they die," I finish for him.

"We don't know yet," he says again. "The last thing we need is the infection to spread. Shanley can't come back until we're sure he's clean."

"What about us then?" I ask. "Why are you keeping us locked away? Dylan and me, we're clean."

Ellington raises an eyebrow quizzically. "Are you so sure?" he counters.

"What the hell do you mean by that?" I ask, but he doesn't answer. Instead he nods at the men behind me. Henry takes one of my arms from Ramsey and together they lead me out of the comm center, back to my lonely cell.

※   ※   ※

The knife is gone.

I sort of figured it would be. Someone in the guardroom saw it lying on the floor and just picked it up, took it away. My only weapon, such as it was. I don't expect them to bring me another with my meals. I just hope they don't let Tobin down here again—he pulls another stunt like the one he did earlier and I'll carve his heart out with a spoon if I have to. Fucking queer, my ass. And they think *I'm* the deviant one. *I'm* the one who's behind bars here. *Whatever.*

Throwing myself down on the thin bunk, I stare at the ceiling and think about Dylan—what else? My baby in his blankets, hiding from his jailers, so eager to see me that he tripped hurrying to touch me. What am I going to do if we get out of here and he has to go back to his starmapping? How will I live without him?

If. I don't like that I used that word. It should be *when*. We'll get out of here, we *will*. We have to.

The distant sound of the corridor bars opening—is it dinnertime already? It feels like I just ate lunch, that soup sits so heavy on my stomach. Still, I swing my legs off the bunk as footsteps approach, and I'm surprised when Conlan steps into view. "They let you come down here?" I ask, rising to my feet.

"Lie down," he hisses. He stays at the corner of my cell, just out of sight of the camera. He doesn't have to say that no one's supposed to know he's here, *Ellington's* not supposed to know—it's written all over his troubled face. "Just lie down and listen to me."

Slowly, I lie back down. I prop my hands behind my head, cross my ankles, stare at a spot just above the sink. "I'm listening," I tell him.

From the corner of my eye I watch as Conlan leans back against the bars and sinks to the floor, hugs his knees to chest. "Marie's not doing too good," he murmurs.

I start to sit up before I remember I'm supposed to pretend he's not here. "I'm sorry." I don't know what else to say. "What's wrong? She doesn't have—"

"No." Conlan shakes his head for emphasis. "She's not showing any of the symptoms. Personally? I don't think it's the bleed. It's just a cold and Shauna's in a bad way right now so it just hit her pretty hard. The other girl, that's just fear." My opinion of Conlan rises a few points—he's smarter than I thought, if he can see through whatever Ellington's feeding him, see what's really going on. "I hoped maybe Ben would let your friend in," he continues. He talks so low, I have to strain to hear his voice. "Maybe after you talked with him on the radio, but that didn't go over too well, did it?"

Heh. "Don't remind me," I mutter. "What about Marie?"

"She's dilated half a centimeter," Conlan whispers. "And she's having contractions again, worse than before. I don't—" He sighs, buries his face in his hands, and I almost can't make out his muffled words. "Another four or five hours, that's it. Your friend said he can do that surgery of his, stitch her closed if he has to, but she can't be too far along. If the contractions get too frequent, he can't do it. She'll lose—" He chokes and can't finish the thought.

He doesn't have to.

Minutes pass like funerals between us, me on my bunk staring at the ceiling and him in the corridor curled into himself, trying hard not to break down and cry. *Go ahead*, I want to tell him, but I get the feeling crying's like love here, it's not an emotion worth having. So he struggles against tears that threaten to fall and I pretend like he's not even there, until finally he sniffles and says, "I hate this."

I want to ask him to elaborate but I don't. I'm not sure if he even knows what it is he hates—the colony? How could he? It's the only home he's ever had. The situation? The committee? Before I can ask, he pushes himself to his feet, turns and peers in at me, says, "I can't do this alone."

"Do what?" I ask.

He doesn't answer, just shakes his head and tells me, "Be ready. 23761, can you remember that? 23761."

I repeat it back to him. "23761, what's that?"

"Just be ready," he tells me. "I can't do this alone."
And then he's gone again.

Part 8

Be ready.

I lie on my bunk and can still hear Conlan's words, *be ready*, even though he's been gone for some time now. *Ready for what?* I wonder. *23761.*

I can't even guess what that is. Some sort of code? Something I'm supposed to know? A password, obviously, but for what? *23761.*

Marie's worse, and Conlan's at the brink now, the edge of his limits, he doesn't know where else to turn. He's thinking—I remember the way he chewed on his lower lip when we went to the comm center, he's thinking, hard, about everything I've said. About letting Shanley land, and getting us out of here, and maybe even about Ellington and what exactly he's doing, maybe he's thinking about that, too. *What IS he doing?* I don't know, can't begin to imagine. He's jeopardizing the future of this colony just because he's too damn stubborn to let outsiders help. He's so sure they can do it alone, thinks maybe if he doesn't think about it, everything will work itself out and they'll be fine.

Only Marie's going to lose the baby, I think to myself, *and Conlan's losing himself in grief.* He's already unsubscribed from the common mentality here—Maclin's *not mine* way of thinking, Ellington's *leave us alone* over-protectiveness, he's not concerned with any of that now. No more *good of the colony*. No more *it's for the best*.

One thing exists for him, one thing only—his child. That's all he cares about.

Not me, or Dylan, or Shanley. Not doing what's right. Just that child, and I think this might be the first time anyone in this whole damn colony has thought about someone other than himself since the S410 set down on this planet twenty years ago. It's understandable, to an extent. The virus killed so many, their friends, their parents, and those who survived found themselves pulling away from the sick, the infected, the diseased. It numbed them after a while, so much dying, you can't go through something like that and come out unscarred. So they closed down their emotions to block it out, block it all out, and they've gone through their lives here with just one thought—survival. Their own. For all the talk of the colony, it only boils down to one person in the end, doesn't it?

Like children, it's all *me me me*. But maybe it's easier that way. They don't let the pain in, the loss. It isn't personal. It's almost not even real. As long as it's not happening to them, they can pretend it doesn't exist—lock it away like they've done to us, keep it out like they're doing to Shanley. It's their way of dealing with things they don't understand, their way of coping.

And finally someone is ready to fight that.

So he needs my help. *Be ready.* Staring at the ceiling of my cell, I hope I'm prepared for whatever he has in mind. I wonder if he even knows what that is yet.

❦   ❦   ❦

Conlan brings my evening meal. I'm surprised to see him again so soon and a million questions press against my lips, anxious to be asked. Did he get in trouble for coming down here earlier? What did Ellington have to say about that? Did anyone hear what he told me? What's the code he gave me for? Ready for what?

But he doesn't look at me and I hold my tongue, afraid to say anything that might get him in trouble. He's going to try to get me out of here, isn't he? He needs my help, whatever he's planning, he can't do it alone.

The tray he carries is laden with salad and a thick slab of lasagna, a pile of napkins, a cup of water that still looks a little reddish to me. A spoon, a fork, a knife—that's unexpected. Conlan nods at the knife by the plate and mumbles, "I'm supposed to wait here until you're done. To take this back."

They don't trust me with the knife, imagine that. As he eases the tray into the slot, he points at the knife, the napkins, and I nod. *Give it back, yes, I know.* "That number you gave me earlier?" I ask. "What—"

Conlan jerks the tray, almost spilling its contents to the floor, then pulls his hands away quickly. He's looking at me with terrified eyes and shakes his head, an almost imperceptible gesture. He doesn't have to tell me to shut up, I get the picture—he's not alone. Leaning against the bars, I try to see down the corridor, but whoever's with him is out of sight. "Who'd they send with you?" I whisper.

"Ramsey."

The word is nothing more than a breath in my ear, but it's enough to make my blood run cold. *Ramsey.* So they don't trust Conlan anymore, is that it? They don't trust *me*, I know this, and they've sent Ramsey along to make sure I don't try anything funny. "Oh," I sigh, turning back to the lasagna. Suddenly I've lost my appetite.

I force myself to eat, though, knowing I'll be hungry later if I don't. I have to be ready, don't I? But I don't know why, and I can't ask, not with Ramsey just down the corridor, probably listening to every word we say. In an effort to fill the awkward silence between us, I ask Conlan, "How's Marie?"

"Holding," he says in that low, *can't talk now* voice I don't quite like. "She's..." He sighs. "She says she's fine and she's not sick but—"

From where he stands, Ramsey growls, "Shut the fuck up, Jeremy."

Conlan starts, "He asked—"

"I said shut up." Ramsey's tone of voice leaves no room for argument. Conlan ducks his head, picks at the front of his shirt, chews the inside of his cheek to keep quiet. "Jesus," Ramsey mutters, like he's looking for a fight. "Ben told you not to buddy up to him."

"I know," Conlan concedes quietly.

"Then get the hell over here." Conlan doesn't listen, just stands in front of me like he's rooted to the spot. "Jeremy," Ramsey warns.

Raising his head just enough to catch my eye, Conlan mouths the word, "Napkins," then looks at my tray, the napkin folded halfway beneath my plate. I brush my hand over the thin paper—"Take 'em," he whispers, barely audible. When I curl my fingers around the napkin, Conlan nods, yes, *yes*. There's something in here, something he's put here, something for me and he doesn't want Ramsey to know about it. *Be ready.* I imagine whatever's wrapped inside burning through the paper, warming my skin, and it takes everything I have in me not to rip the napkin open right here, right now, just to see what Conlan's managed to slip me.

But suddenly Ramsey's there, pushing Conlan aside, and as nonchalantly as I can, I lift the napkin from the tray. "Go wait down there," Ramsey says, angry. Conlan hesitates, but Ramsey gives him a hard shove down the corridor, away from me. "Go on."

Conlan doesn't argue, but he's still looking at my hand, the napkin I'm holding, and he doesn't move until I clench it tight in a fist. While Ramsey glares at him, I slip my hand behind my back, tuck the napkin into the waistband of my pants. "Jeremy," Ramsey warns again. "I said—"

"I heard you." There's no malice in Conlan's voice as he drifts further down the corridor, hovers where I can just see him if I turn. How can he talk like that to Ramsey, who *terrifies* me, and not have the balls to stand up to Ellington? *Who's like a big brother,* I think, *overprotective, he won't even let you make your own mistakes.*

Ramsey scowls at me. Crossing his arms in front of his chest, he stares until I can't even swallow, I can feel that livid gaze bore right through me, and I'm sure he knows about the napkin that presses into the small of my back, any minute now he's going to tell me to hand it over, he'll rip it to shreds and I'll never know what it is Conlan has gone to such great pains to get to me. The silverware in my hands trembles because I hold it too tightly and any minute I'm just going to hand the napkin over, save him the trouble of going through me to get it. When he speaks, I'm so sure he's going to ask for the crumpled paper that I'm already half reaching for it, but he just tells me, "Cut the damn noodles already so we can get the hell out of here."

I do as I'm told, handing the knife to him through the bars, handle first so he won't think I'm going to try something. He snatches it from me—there's so much *anger* in him, it scares me—and then snags Conlan's arm, pulls him away from my cell.

I hear the door at the end of the corridor slide shut. *The napkin*, I think, but I take another bite of the lasagna, pretend there's nothing else I'd rather do than finish this meal, just in case someone's in that guardroom watching me on the security vid. Each bite I take tastes like sawdust, dry, and I have to choke it down, wash it away with the brackish water. I count as I eat, each bite, each chew, each swallow, counting off seconds and minutes, until I'm sure that enough time's gone by that looking at the napkin now won't seem too suspicious.

So I retreat to my bunk, crawl beneath the covers, lie on my stomach with my back to the bars and my head at the foot of the bed, away from the camera in the corner of the cell. Pulling the blankets up over my head, I feel like a kid again, sneaking awake in the middle of the night to read comic books by the light of a small flash. Only it's dark here, the covers blocking the light from the corridor, but I don't dare inspect whatever it is Conlan's given me out in the open, where someone might see. Instead I pretend I'm sleeping, lie my head on my hand and reach behind me slowly, carefully, for the napkin. The paper's so thin, it threatens to tear when it catches on the waistband of my pants, but I manage to work it free. Conlan risked a lot to get this to me. I can't afford to give him away. He's our only hope.

The napkin is rumpled and folded. I lay it on the bed at eye level and smooth it out, feeling for anything he might have slipped inside. Nothing. Just the soft paper beneath my fingertips, that's it. No secret key to unlock these bars, no pill to slip into my drink to fake an illness, no tiny weapon to use in my escape. Nothing as exciting as that.

Gingerly, so as not to tear the paper, I unfold the napkin. I can see dark lines under the first layer, like the silhouettes of caterpillars hidden in their silk tents in the biosphere back at the station. Then I recognize cramped letters, written in black ink with a heavy hand, and excitement courses through me, *a note*. As quickly as I can, I unfold the napkin completely and sit up a little to read it better.

> *SF landed but can't get in. Marie doing poor. Tonight I have guard 10-2. Can cut breaker, lights, alarm, cell doors. Three minutes only, or Ben will know. Be ready.*

The message takes up one fourth of the napkin—folded, it's unnoticeable. The words are crammed together so tight, some of them run into each other, but I still manage to make them out. They give me more questions than answers, though. How did the *Semper Fi* land if Ellington didn't want to give Parker coordinates? He's still not letting them in, though. And Marie's getting worse. It occurs to me that I've never talked with her, I don't know her feelings on this whole situation. Is she as blasé as Maclin about the life of the child she carries? Is she xenophobic like Ellington?

I doubt it. If she's managed to break through the emotional barriers Conlan built around himself like all the other colonists, then she probably shares his anguish, his desperate hope. All the more reason to help her, help them both. Maybe this will be the start of a new family unit here, one that doesn't fall apart from death or disease, one that survives.

Only then will the colony—and Operation Starseed—truly succeed.

So Conlan will be in the guardroom tonight. And he's planning, what? *Cut the breaker.* And the lights out in the corridor, an alarm of some sort, the cell doors, all that goes down. He's going to open the doors? For three minutes, that's it, and he wants me to be ready. *Three minutes to get from my cell down the corridor, into the main hall. Then I have to find Dylan's corridor, find his cell, and get out.* Will that be enough time? Thinking back, I try to remember how long it took when Conlan led me down there. More than three minutes, I'm sure. I don't know how he thinks I'm supposed to sprint from here to there in that time, but I'm sure as hell going to try. And then there's that keypad lock—

23761.

That's the code, I remember Conlan entering the first two digits and then Ellington stepped in my way, didn't want me to see the rest of it. But if he's cutting the breaker that feeds the doors, won't that one open as well? I won't need the code, it should already be open.

Unless you don't make it there in the allotted time.

I tear the napkin up into tiny squares that litter my bed like confetti. Then I scoop the pieces into my hands, careful not to leave any behind, and I throw the blankets back, go to the sink, wash the napkin away down the drain. When it's gone, I lie back down on my bunk and stare at the ceiling and wait. That's all there is left to do now, wait.

Be ready. My whole body hums with the thought. I'm as ready as I'll ever be.

※   ※   ※

Some time later, I wake with a start. *Shit.* I didn't mean to doze off. What if I missed Conlan's opportunity? What if I slept through it? How would I ever know?

Then I hear it, the slight sound of the bars retracting into the wall, the sound that woke me from the light nap I didn't mean to take. Turning my head in what I hope looks like a casual gesture, I see that the door to my cell is opening like before, inch by excruciating inch.

Be ready.

I scramble off the bed, launch myself at the door, work my hands into the scant opening, try to hurry it along. There are no footsteps in the corridor this time, no one's coming, I'm free. As soon as these doors open completely, I'm free.

Six inches, a foot, a third of the way and suddenly an alarm sounds, an ear-splitting shriek that splits the silence, reverberates through the cell, freezes me in place. *Oh FUCK—*

The lights in the corridor wink out.

Before I can cover my ears, the alarm stops as abruptly as it began. My time starts now.

Now. But I can't see, it's so damn dark in here, pitch black, no emergency lights, nothing to show me the way. I grope blindly for the cell door and for a heart-stopping moment, I can't find the bars. Maybe I've become turned around somehow, I'm losing precious seconds, I can't waste time like this—

One of my hands finds cool, rounded steel and I sigh. *Thank you, Jesus,* I pray, squeezing through the partially opened door. Silently I start counting, *one Mississippi, two Mississippi, three Mississippi,* counting the seconds I have in the dark. Closing my eyes, I picture the corridor and hurry down its length from memory, keeping one hand on the wall beside me, one held out in front. I feel bars, the cell next to mine, then a cold span of wall, then more bars. It takes thirty-five Mississippi's to reach the end of the corridor.

When I feel the barred door in front of me, I open my eyes, but I still can't see anything. I didn't think it would be this dark. How much time did I lose disoriented in my cell? Ten seconds, maybe, which puts me at almost a full minute gone now, possibly more. I have to pick up the pace.

This door's only partway open, too, but it's larger and I manage to ease through into the main corridor with no trouble at all. Dylan's cell block branches off the opposite wall—I can sense an empty space in front of me, stretching out to either side. What if there's someone else in the corridor? Maclin or Henry, that Tobin kid? I shudder at the thought of running into *that* freak in the dark, with his lecherous hands and eager grin. *But you're wasting time,* a voice inside my mind whispers. *Don't worry about what you can't possibly know, focus on what you're after, on Dylan. Only him.*

Dylan. The first time we ever kissed, his lips tender and tentative on mine. The first time he touched me, his bare hands hesitant on my chest, my skin tremulous beneath his fingers. When Dixon sent him on short jaunts to map nearby stars, he'd come back to the station exhausted, and the only thing he'd want to do is crawl into my bed, beneath my covers, breathe in my scent from the sheets. I would sit beside him, massage his tired muscles, his neck, his back, his thighs, take each foot in my hands and knead until he moaned my name, a low, guttural sound that does horrible things to my stomach, makes me giddy and fluttery and so damn in love. I love him. I'm going to him, *him.* I can do this.

I hold my breath, and the first step I take feels like I'm walking out over an abyss, my heart hammering in my throat. The next comes a little easier, and once I've started, I don't let myself stop, arms stretched out for the wall. Another step, another, one foot in front of the next, and I imagine the wall moving further away from me, continuously out of reach, where is it? Four steps, five, how wide *is* this corridor? I don't remember, but I'm walking straight ahead, aren't I? If I'm angled a little one way or the other, it'll take me longer to get to the other side, but I'm going straight, right? It feels like I am, at any rate. Each shuffled step is another second I lose, another moment that disappears, *please*—

Just as I'm about ready to give into the panic eating away inside of me, my fingers brush against steel. *Thank you,* I think, relieved, pressing against the wall to assure myself that it's there, it's real, I've made it. I run my hands over the steel, feel the edge of a doorway, the cell block across from mine. *Four up,* I remind myself. Dylan's was four doors up from mine, on this side of the corridor. How much time do I have left? A minute, maybe. I've lost count.

The bars disappear and then there's an expanse of wall, several feet wide, then more bars, door one. Growing more sure of myself, I hurry along, one hand on the wall, one arm outstretched. More solid steel, more bars, door two. Another stretch of steel, another door, three. Another—

In front of me, my hand touches fabric, warmth, the nugget of a nipple sheathed in the linen shirt the colonists wear. *Oh shit.*

Before I can pull back, a hand clasps my wrist, pulls me closer, holds me prisoner. My throat locks over a scream that threatens to burst from me, terror, *someone's found me. Don't let it be Tobin, please God if you're listening don't let this be that kid, anyone else but him. Hell, Ramsey if you have to but not him, please oh please oh—*

Then warm lips find mine in the darkness, a soft mouth with a sweetness that shoots through me like Cupid's arrow, straight to my heart. I *know* this kiss, these lips, these hands that smooth down my arms and around my waist and this body holding me tight. "Dylan," I sigh, and he kisses the name from my lips. I've missed this, *him,* my body aches in places that long for his touch. "Oh God, Dylan—"

"I knew it had to be you," he whispers, his breath hot against my cheek. He trails tiny kisses down my chin, around the curve of my jaw, until his lips close over my earlobe, his teeth nip at me gently. "Baby," he breathes. "I'm going to hurt them for keeping us apart. I'm going to hurt them all—"

"Conlan did this," I tell him, "turned out the lights, opened the doors. He's helping us get out."

Dylan speaks over me, ecstatic to finally hold me again, and I'm almost delirious to have him in my arms. "I heard the alarm," he says, talking low, his voice urgent. "I woke up and saw the door and didn't stop, didn't even *think*, just ran to get to you. Are you okay? Did they hurt you? Did they—"

I kiss him quiet. "I'm fine," I promise him. "Conlan says the *Semper Fi*'s set down. We need to get Shanley in here, he's got to help Marie and the infected women, if he can."

Dylan slips his hand into mine, lets me tug him through the darkness in the direction of the guardroom. At least, I *hope* we're headed the right way, I *think* we are. "Is it the bleed?" he asks, walking so close, our hands are caught between our bodies and his chest is pressed against my arm, like he's afraid of losing my touch. His step falters, pulling me back against him. "Wait, Neal, no. If it's spreading—"

"Conlan says it isn't," I assure him. A part of me knows Conlan hasn't really said that in so many words, but he's not sick, is he? They have the girls quarantined, we should be fine.

"But—" Dylan starts, unsure.

Ahead, another voice cuts him off. "Mother*fucker!*" someone curses, and glass shatters in the darkness. It's Maclin's voice and I stop in midstep, they're here, the others, they're *here*. "Look what the fuck you did, asshole."

"I can't see shit," someone answers, and that's Tobin, I've got his voice tattooed into my brain. They're up ahead somewhere, in the guardroom maybe, no more than three or four yards in front of us. *If they didn't say anything,* I think wildly, *we would've walked right into them, smack dab into the center of their little party, and we'd be busted.* "Ow! Hey!" Tobin cries. "Get your hands out of my hair, Seth—"

"You two knock it off, will you?" Ellington. His voice comes from above the others, impossibly high for someone as short as he is. "Jeremy, where's that flash? Damn breaker."

When Conlan speaks, I can hear the stammer of a lie in his words. "It just blew. I don't know what happened."

"The flash?" Ellington asks again. A small cone of light clicks on, illuminating a free-standing ladder, a cluster of legs, pants bleached white in the flash. As the light's handed up, I can see the bars separating us from the guardroom. Conlan holding the flash. Tobin glaring at Maclin, who fakes a punch at him that makes me grin when Tobin flinches. Ellington on the ladder, his head and arms disappearing into an open panel in the ceiling. He reaches for the flash and angles it into the panel. The light falls down around the small group of colonists, diffused and faint but I can see them now, Tobin and Maclin and Conlan and Ramsey, he's with them, he's standing in the half-opened doorway of the barred wall, blocking the only escape.

Dylan eases back, pulling me along with him. His hands slide around my waist protectively and his lips press against my ear. I feel the shape of his words rather than hear them, he speaks so softly. "Now what?"

Good question. I'm about to answer when Conlan tries to ease past Ramsey, heading our way. As he steps into the prison corridor, though, Ramsey growls, "Where the fuck you going, Jeremy?" He's closer than the others, *too* close, and I don't dare answer Dylan with him right there in front of us. "Get the hell back here."

"I was just going to check on them," Conlan tells him, but Ramsey isn't having it. He grabs the back of Conlan's shirt and pulls him into the guardroom again, an almost rough tenderness in his gesture that in another time and place could have meant something more.

For the first time I realize these guys, his friends, they're as protective of him as Dylan is of me. Ramsey is, at any rate, he's all too willing to stand between Conlan and any imagined threat we might pose. And Maclin leaves Tobin alone, turns to Conlan, says quietly, "You're not going in there by yourself." Only it doesn't sound like he says it out of distrust but something else, another feeling, something deeper, something *real*. And Ellington frowns down at them, doesn't say a word but hasn't he been protecting Conlan since the moment we arrived? Didn't want him to get all excited about the briox, didn't want to get his hopes up, didn't want him to be devastated if the drug didn't work. Somehow Conlan's managed to make each of these men care for him in a way that goes beyond the apathy they have for everything else. He's gotten past their selfish exteriors, he's become necessary to them, if anyone's the colony then it's *him*, not Ellington but Conlan. Ellington runs things, keeps it on track, wants everything right, but Conlan's the heart of the ship, he's the one who ties these men together, he's the one fighting for their future.

So maybe, just maybe, there's hope for this colony after all. *If we can get out of this.*

※　　　　※　　　　※

I don't know how long we stand there in the dark, mere yards from freedom and trapped because Conlan's not alone. Ellington must have come running at the alarm, Conlan didn't silence it fast enough, and Dylan's right, now what? *Now they fix the breaker and the lights come back on and they find us here, just waiting to be led back to our cells. Separate cells.* I'm not going to let them do that to us again.

Nudging Dylan, I start to ease away, down the corridor, back the way we came. Maybe to one of the cells, I don't know, but I don't want to be standing here when Ellington's tinkering brings the lights back up. Dylan gets my drift and unwraps his arms from around my waist, takes my elbow, starts to lead me away from the scant light of the flash, when Tobin sighs lustily. *They're so damn close*, I think, amazed. If not for the cover of darkness, we'd have been seen already, we wouldn't be together right now.

I could tell Dylan what that fucker Tobin said to me and my baby would go into Godzilla mode, kick ass and take names, ask questions later. We might get out of here then. It's a tempting thought, but I remember Ramsey and Maclin, who managed to get Dylan down here in the first place, and I don't want him going up against them. I don't want them to hurt him, I don't want Ramsey to bloody his mouth again.

"This is all your fault," Tobin announces, and I stop, catch Dylan's hand to force him to stay by my side. *Whose fault?* Even though I know we shouldn't linger, I want to hear this.

Tobin's staring up at Ellington but I know he means Conlan. Ramsey stiffens at the comment—*he* knows the kid means Conlan, too. Hell, even *Conlan* looks uncomfortable, he knows the comment was directed at him. Tobin laughs like he's just thought of the funniest thing, and he asks Conlan, "How'd the breaker trip again? I don't quite get that part. I mean, it's fine all these years but we finally get prisoners and when you're in here by yourself it all of a sudden blows? How's that work?"

In a low, dangerous voice, Maclin asks, "Just what are you saying, Tobin?"

Tobin must not hear the threat in those soft words—God, how can he not? Or see the way Maclin's watching him, so carefully, just waiting, because he shrugs and says, "I'm just saying it's funny, that's all. Funny how it's *his* girl who needs that pill most, right? He's got the most to gain from letting those guys back in here."

"Stop talking like that," Ellington warns. His voice is muffled where he's half in the ceiling, but it's still audible. "We all gain if we get that pill and it does what they say it does."

"Then why don't we let them in?" Conlan asks. Dylan tugs at my arm, we shouldn't just stand here. "If you know it's what we need—"

"Because we can't," Ellington tells him. He sounds exhausted, like he's tired of talking about this, they've been over it enough already. "Another day or two, Jeremy, that's it. Then we can be sure they're not carrying anything and we can let them back in, okay?" Conlan chews on his lower lip thoughtfully in that way he has that makes him look like he's about to cry. When he doesn't answer, Ellington glances down at him, and even from here I can see the concern in his face. "Jeremy? Another day, that's all. Marie can hold out that long, I'm sure she can."

Maclin gives Conlan a playful punch in the shoulder, and Conlan forces a tight grin. "Yeah," he says, but he doesn't sound too convinced.

Tobin glances at Conlan. "Maybe he doesn't really believe that. Maybe he thought no one would hear the alarm, and he could bust these two queers out and no one would know." Dylan's hand tightens on my arm, squeezing almost painfully, it's that *queer* remark, he's going to hurt Tobin for that alone. *Wait til I tell you what else he's said.* "Maybe he even set the breaker off himself—"

That's as far as he gets before Ramsey has him by the throat, up against the ladder, pushing his head back between the rungs at an awkward angle until I'm sure the poor kid's neck's going to snap. "You watch what you fucking say," he growls. "The breaker blew—could've happened to anyone, could've happened to *you*. Heh, maybe *you* fucked with it. You rushed down here quick enough when the alarm went off. Maybe *you* wanted the lights out so you could stick it to Blondie back there and no one would know."

"Oh, he is so dead," Dylan murmurs behind me, his hands finding my waist again. "Tell me he didn't really try—"

I push against him, push him back down the corridor, away from the men in the guardroom, they'll hear him and now he's ready to fight at Ramsey's words. "Neal—" he starts.

"Just go," I hiss. "Dylan, please—"

Behind us, Tobin blubbers, "I didn't mean anything, really! Just talking shit, that's all. Ramsey—"

Something pops in the ceiling and Ellington curses as a shower of sparks erupts around him, rains down. Tobin twists in Ramsey's grip. "Let me up!" he cries, trying to shield his eyes from the sparks. "Ramsey, let me *go*! I didn't mean it. I didn't—"

Ramsey releases him abruptly and Tobin staggers away from the ladder, stumbles to one knee, gasping for breath and rubbing his neck. "I didn't mean it," he sighs. "Jesus. I didn't."

"Then watch what the fuck you say," Ramsey warns him, stationing himself in the doorway again.

From the electrical panel above comes another pop, followed by a sizzle and more of Ellington's low curses. "What are you *doing* up there?" Maclin wants to know.

Before Ellington can reply, the flash slips from his hand, splashing light on the walls, the men's faces, the ceiling. For a split second it shines our way, blinding me. Shadows dance wildly and then the flash tumbles to the floor, the bulb shattering on impact, dousing the light.

I blink in the sudden darkness, so complete I think I've gone blind. But I can still see the gray ghost of the flash, trailing in front of my eyes, and I can't seem to shake it away. When Dylan starts to pull at my arm again, Tobin whispers, "Did you see them? Did you? They're right there. Did you guys see them?"

He means us!

I shove against Dylan but he's already one step ahead of me, racing down the corridor, dragging me along behind him. "Go!" I breathe, but what's the use in keeping it down? They saw us, when the light fell they *saw* us, they know where we are, they're going to follow any minute and *they saw us.* I run alongside Dylan, hold his hand tight so we don't lose each other in the darkness, and pray nothing gets in our way.

"They're right there!" Tobin cries, his voice still too close, too loud for me. It spurs me on faster.

"Shut up," Ramsey says, and then, "Get back here! Where the hell do you think you're going?"

I almost stumble to a stop when Tobin answers and I realize Ramsey's talking to him, not us. "I *saw* them." Tobin sounds vindictive, triumphant almost. "They're right *there*—"

Not anymore, I think, widening the distance between us and the guardroom. How long *is* this corridor? In the dark, it's endless. The afterimage of the flash still hangs in front of me, a specter forever out of reach. Behind us Tobin argues that they should catch us, and Ramsey must have hold of him, keeping him back, because he doesn't follow. Ellington calls for a new flash, he can't see shit, Seth, Jeremy, *somebody* get him another goddamn flash so he can fix this fucking breaker already. "They aren't going anywhere, Tobin!" he cries out. "Get me another flash."

"The emergency exit—" Tobin starts. My heart skips a beat. *Yes! Thank you, God.*

"Hello?" Even as we run I can hear the sneer in Maclin's words. "The fucking power's out, dumbass. They ain't getting through that door."

Beside me, Dylan turns, his breath ragged in my ear. "There's an exit," he says, and I nod, a gesture lost in the dark.

"Locked, though," I tell him.

The colonists are arguing again, but their voices grow faint, we're finally widening the gap, they're fading behind us. A hot stitch rips through my side, just below my lungs, and I slow down a bit, press my hand against it, taking shallow breaths so the pain isn't too intense. When Dylan tugs at my hand, I pull him back and stop. "Wait."

His hands smooth across my stomach. "You okay?" he wants to know. My heart pounds in my ears, I can barely hear myself answer. "Neal?"

Fine. I don't know if I say the word out loud or not, but from the corner of my eye I see a dim light, someone's found another flash, they'll get the breaker back up any minute now. Swallowing the pain, I take off again, away from the faint light, Dylan right behind me. I'm out of breath, panting almost. "Come on, baby." The emergency exit Tobin mentioned can't be much farther.

It's not. Another dozen steps and we come up against a wall—the end of the corridor. Frantically our hands roam over the cold steel and I find the door before Dylan does. It's not a barred door like the rest but the kind that slides into the wall, and it must be on a different circuit than the cell doors, because it's not even open just a little. Maclin's right, we're not getting through it. Not as long as the power's out—

Suddenly the lights above us flicker to life, die out, flicker again and hold this time, accompanied by a high buzz like angry insects. "Hey!" It's one of the colonists, at the other end of the hall, I'm not sure who. All I know is I want to run and I can't, I want to hide and I *can't*. I can't.

Dylan glances behind us, grips my shoulder, pushing me against the wall as he steps in front of me. His hands find my waist, position me directly behind him so he shields me from the colonists. "Don't worry, baby," he murmurs. I can hear footsteps running down the corridor, towards us. "I'm not letting them take you from me again."

Then I see the keypad beside the door. Without thinking, without even wondering if it's going to work, I tap in the code Conlan gave me, *23761*. *Please,* I pray, feeling the raised Braille digits beneath my fingers. *Please.*

Nothing.

The door stays shut.

"Fuck," I mutter. I risk a glance over my shoulder, around Dylan, and they're coming closer now, Ramsey and Maclin, not really running because they know we don't have anywhere to go. They're like jackals advancing on a wounded animal, they're *enjoying* this, it's a game to them, I can see the gleam in their eyes and their evil grins and *please no, the code has to work, it just HAS to.*

Turning back to the keypad, I see a key at the bottom marked *Enter,* and God, can I be any stupider? When I press it, the door slides out of the way so fast, I tumble into the corridor beyond. "Dylan!"

He's right behind me, already through the door. I get a glimpse of the surprise on Maclin's face, the anger twisting Ramsey's features, and then Dylan hits the keypad on this side. The door starts to slide shut, is almost completely closed, when the lights cut out again.

On the other side of the door, Ramsey lets out a terrifying roar. His hands stretch through the space where the door doesn't quite meet the wall and before I can move out of reach, his fingers snag my shirt, yank me towards him.

And then Dylan's hand is in mine, pulling me loose. "Get the fucking power back on!" Maclin cries. "Ben, now!"

"Run!" Dylan tells me, giving me a push. I don't know where we are, where we're going to end up, and I don't even care. His hand is warm in mine, so strong and safe, and we race into the darkness, away from the prison and the colonists, together.

We run for hours in the dark, it seems, my side burning, my lungs on fire. The only thing keeping me going is Dylan—he's more athletic than I am and I'm only slowing him down, but he doesn't stop, doesn't falter. Instead he pulls me along after him, and when I start to lag, he's there with a hand on my arm to help me along, how much farther? I mean, really. My legs are starting to quiver, they ache so bad, and my feet—what I wouldn't give for my boots again, but I don't know what happened to them. I took them off before we laid down and never had a chance to put them back on before we were arrested, but this floor is hard on my feet and these slipper shoes the colonists wear aren't much at all. How long have we been running like this? "Dylan, wait," I gasp, trying to catch my breath. This time when I slow down, he doesn't make me keep going—he stops beside me, wraps his arms around my trembling shoulders, hugs me close. I bury my face into his neck, smell the sharp tang of his sweat, feel his damp muscles through the thin shirt he wears. "Just give me a minute," I ask. "Please."

He rubs my back, kisses my ear, breathes, "Sure, babe." But I can feel the energy still coursing through him, the desire to be off again, to put as much distance behind us as we possibly can. "Did that guy tell you where this passage leads to?"

I shake my head. "I didn't even know it was here," I sigh.

"You knew the code," Dylan points out.

True. "It's the same one for the door that led to your cell block," I explain. "I was only hoping it'd work on the exit, too." In a small colony like this, though, with no real threat from the planet outside their ship, chances are *all* the passcodes are the same—that'd be the easiest way to remember them. When Dylan kisses my cheek, I tell him, "I just got lucky."

"I'm hoping to get lucky," he murmurs against my skin, "soon as we get out of this damn place." His hands slip down to cup my ass, squeezing to emphasize his point.

I get it. But much as I love his hands on me, we're still not in the clear yet, are we? "Dylan," I start.

Above us the lights flare to life. We glance up at the dim bulbs, and when I look down the corridor, back the way we came, I can't see the partially opened door. *That doesn't mean shit,* I tell myself, taking Dylan's hand again. *Now that the power's back on, they'll be through that door in a heartbeat and they'll come looking for us.* "We gotta keep going," I tell him, breaking into a quick jog.

Dylan leads the way, through so many twists and turns, up stairways, down more corridors, until I'm completely turned around, all sense of direction shot. There's only one way, ahead, that's it. I don't even know where the hell we are—I'm surprised we're not back in the prison, or outside the ship by this point. Every time I look over my shoulder, I expect to see Ramsey racing to catch us. Every corner we take, I think Maclin's waiting just around the bend. In the stairwells, I hear the thud of a hundred feet trailing us. We're lost, chased by our own shadows, the echoes of our own shoes over the corrugated floors, and we're going to roam these corridors for the rest of our lives, ghosts haunting a dying ship. I even begin to think that maybe we should've taken our chances back in the prison, tried to fight our way to the guardroom instead of jumping for the other exit—what good is this passage in an emergency? It just turns you around and around and leaves you dizzy and tired and weak.

But we've come so far—we can't go back now, if we could even find the way. Still, I'm just about to give up—just sit down right here, right now, I'm through with walking—when Dylan pushes open a service hatch and we come out into another corridor, a larger one, a *familiar* one. "Neal," Dylan begins, "isn't this—"

"The airlock." I point past him and there, not a half dozen yards away, is the airlock door we first stepped through what, just yesterday? It seems like years ago now. "Dylan! That's the airlock!" Excitement replaces the exhaustion in my limbs, ignites my blood, and I race ahead of him to the keypad by the airlock door. "The *Semper Fi*'s just outside," I tell him, punching in the code Conlan gave me. "We can let the guys in and put this all behind us. Shanley can help Marie and the other women—"

Dylan's as excited as I am. "And we can finally get a room all to ourselves," he purrs, easing his arms around my waist.

I laugh—when's the last time I had him? I can't even remember, though it was just before we landed on this planet, not long ago at all, but it seems like an eternity and I can't wait to get him alone again, I can't wait to love him.

The airlock door doesn't automatically open, but I don't panic. "Step back," I tell him as I press the *Enter* key.

Only this time? The door *still* doesn't open.

🍁　🍁　🍁

No. I must have entered the number in wrong, *had* to have punched the wrong key, that's all. "Neal?" Dylan asks.

"It's okay," I tell him, but I frown at the keypad and watch my fingers this time, make sure I hit the right combination. *23761.* Then I hesitate, my thumb over the *Enter* key. I typed it in correctly, I *know* I did.

I press *Enter*, hold it a second to make sure it's in, then release the key.

Nothing.

"Fuck," I mutter.

Behind me, Dylan peers over my shoulder at the keypad like he's going to be able to help. "What's the problem?" he asks.

"It's not opening," I say. Can't he see that?

Dylan points at the keypad, his finger hovering above the *Enter* key. "Did you hit this?"

"Yes," I tell him, but he presses it again, just to make sure. Still nothing. "See?"

Dylan steps around me, his arm still on my waist. "Why doesn't it work?"

I sigh, roll my eyes, bite back the bitter words that leap into my throat—I'll only have to apologize if I set them free. So I just say, "I don't know," and hope he'll leave it at that.

But this is Dylan, he's not going to just drop it. He starts to punch the keys at random, hitting the keypad hard enough to break something, and I catch his hand, pull him away from the door. "That's not going to help us any, babe."

Twisting out of my grip, he starts pushing the buttons again. *How old are you?* I think. *Twenty going on two.* "Dylan, stop it. You might jam the controls and then it'll *never* open."

"What's the code?" he asks. "I thought you said Conlan gave it to you."

"It doesn't *work*." God, he can be so frustrating sometimes. I have to remind myself that I love him and he's just doing this because he's scared, we both are, this is his way of showing it, he hates not being in control of what's happening to him, to *us*. Smoothing a hand down his arm, I knead the bunched muscles and kiss his shoulder, savor the warmth of his skin through the thin shirt he wears. "Baby, please—"

"It should work," he tells me, like I don't know this. Before I can stop him, he balls his hand into a fist, punches the keypad angrily, once, twice—

"Dylan!" I grab his hand, work my fingers into his, uncurl his fist. "Okay, you know what? I have a feeling hitting it's *not* going to work."

"They changed the code," he announces bitterly, kicking at the wall. He's forgotten that he's not wearing his boots, just the shuffling shoes that the colonists have, and they weren't made to be kicking at steel. I know that had to hurt. But he's pissed, and when he gets like this, he doesn't feel the stupid shit he does to himself. Once, back at the station, Dixon told him he didn't want his best pilot sleeping on the tech level—didn't want him sleeping with *me*, in all honesty—and it ticked him off so bad, my hot-headed boy ran his fist through a glass radar screen on the nav deck and never even realized he was cut until I saw the blood on his knuckles.

But maybe he's not *too* mad right now, because he just glares at the airlock and mutters, "Fucking pricks," and he lets me rub his hand to keep it from fisting again. He doesn't bother to kick the wall a second time.

"I know," I tell him. I do, I know, I want out of here just as badly as he does, if not moreso, because when he gets in this Neanderthal mode of his, I think it's unbearably cute. It turns me on something fierce to know that I'm the only one who can calm him down, I'm the only one he listens to, and there's nothing that I want more right this second than to lie him down somewhere, kiss that pout from his lips, erase the creases in his brow, love him until the anger dissolves.

And I can't. It pisses *me* off that I can't do that, not here, not now. We're alone for the moment but this isn't the time, there are more pressing matters at hand. Like getting Shanley in here, and getting us out.

Looking around, I notice the corridor that leads to the colony. "Come on," I say, tugging on his arm.

"Where are we going?" he wants to know. I don't answer but he recognizes the corridor as I turn down it and he tries to dig his heels into the floor, tries to stop me. "Neal, we can't go back there—"

"Conlan got us out of those cells," I remind him. "We have to help him. He can't do this by himself."

"Do what?" Dylan asks, holding back, resistant. "Neal, there's nothing we *can* do."

I know this. Nothing tangible, anyway—it's Shanley's help Conlan *really* needs, not ours. But if our presence makes him stronger, if he knows we're sided with him, if we stand behind him and that's all he needs to help him stand up to Ellington and the rest of the colony, then we can't deny him that. He helped me, didn't he? He freed us, got Dylan back for me. I can't *not* help him any way that I can.

As we follow the corridor into the heart of the ship, Dylan asks, "How are we going to get back inside? Just knock on the door, say hey, let us in? Somehow I don't think that's going to work."

"We'll think of something," I assure him, though the last turn before we reach the colony is just up ahead and we better think of something soon—

"Ramsey, *listen* to me!" It's Conlan's voice, low and urgent and around the bend, just out of sight, we almost walked right into him and *Ramsey*.

God, I think, *how I hate that name*. I stop abruptly and Dylan runs smack into me. "Shh," I hiss before he can say a word.

Then I hear Ramsey's harsh voice, the anger clear in his words. "I *am* listening, Jeremy. I've heard every fucking word you've said." Can't Conlan hear that? The danger in that voice, running like a live current just beneath the words, waiting to lash out. "You're saying you cut the power back there."

Oh shit. I press against the wall, inch forward until I can peek around the corner. Behind me, Dylan fists his hands at my sides, holds me back. *Don't tell me you told him that, Conlan. Don't tell me you don't think he didn't run to Ellington with that info. You can't TRUST him.*

When Conlan doesn't answer, I have this horrible vision of Ramsey strangling the life from him. But when I glance down the corridor, I see Conlan squatting on the floor, his arms raised in front of his face, his hands tugging at his hair. His shoulders shake as if he's struggling not to cry or laugh, I can't tell which. Ramsey leans back against the wall, arms crossed in front of his chest, everything about him closed and foreboding and just downright *mean*. But despite the scowl on his face, he's watching Conlan with something akin to compassion in those stormy eyes of his, a foreign emotion that seems to make him look even angrier, more hateful. I expect him to swoop down on Conlan at any minute, tear him open, leave him wounded and bleeding because he just admitted to letting us go. *You can't possibly trust him*—"Fuck, Jeremy," Ramsey growls.

That's all he says.

"I know." Conlan's voice is muffled, indistinct. "I know."

For long moments neither of them says another word. They're trapped in a tableau, frozen in time, Conlan waiting for Ramsey to pass a judgment on him that never comes. "What's going on?" Dylan whispers. He tries to see around me but I keep him back. "Neal, what's—"

"Fuck," Ramsey says again, softer this time, defeated almost. Beaten by Conlan's silence, his open acceptance of what he did and why he did it. I don't think Ramsey knows what else *to* say. "Why—"

"I'm not like you," Conlan interrupts, his voice just as soft. He raises his head, presses the heels of his hands against his eyes, sighs and explains, "I can't give up hope, Ramsey. As long as there's a chance—"

Ramsey laughs, disgusted. "So you just believe whatever they say, is that it? Fuck the colony, right? What if they're lying to you?"

Anger runs through me. *Why would we lie?* I wonder. *What the hell do we have to gain by it?* But Conlan just shakes his head and counters, "What if they're not?"

Ramsey has no answer for that.

Lowering his hands from his face, Conlan looks up at Ramsey, studies him, until the older man has to look away. I see he's still clinging to that desperate scowl, the anger he's trying to keep between them, and it makes me wonder what kind of a dynamic they have together. What is it that gives Conlan this much control over an animal like Ramsey? *Another time,* I think, feeling Dylan's hand on my waist, *another place*—"You going to tell Ben?" Conlan asks.

"No," Ramsey grumbles. *No.* I almost can't believe it.

"So now what?" Conlan wants to know.

Ramsey pushes away from the wall. "Now you get your scrawny ass up off that floor." He grabs Conlan's arm, hauls him to his feet. "And go let that damn physician in here."

"But Ben—" Conlan begins.

Ramsey shoves him in our direction. "Let me worry about Ben." Conlan takes a few stumbling steps then stops, glances over his shoulder at his friend. "Go on," Ramsey tells him, his scowl deepening. "Before I change my mind." He holds up one hand and turns away. "Don't even fucking say it, Jeremy. Just go."

Conlan hesitates, but before he can say whatever it is Ramsey's afraid to hear, the older man punches a passcode into a nearby keypad, hitting the numbers angrily. The door at the end of the corridor slides open, out of the way, and Ramsey hurries through into the colony, leaving Conlan alone.

He waits until the door closes before sprinting to the other end of the corridor, towards us. "He's coming," I breathe, leaning back against the wall.

As Dylan opens his mouth to ask me who, Conlan bursts around the corner. He sees us as he passes, I know he does, but it takes another few feet before it registers. Then he cries, "Hey!" and skids to a stop. "Hey you guys, we've been looking for you two."

Dylan's lips twist into a sardonic smile. "I can imagine."

I elbow him in the ribs. "There's not much time," Conlan says, taking off again. Over his shoulder, he calls out, "Marie's holding still but—come on!"

Dylan and I exchange a quick glance. "Come on," he says, taking my hand. We hurry after Conlan.

"Ben changed the security code," he explains, breathless, as he leads us back to the airlock. "Claims he doesn't understand how you got it but I know he knows it was me. Seth saw me write that note, that's why Ramsey had to come with me to the cells. That's why they came running so quick when the alarm went off." Conlan laughs, nervous. "I didn't expect that. I was going to open the doors, then cut the breaker, give you enough time to get out, but apparently there's this bypass switch I overlooked and if you don't throw it and try to open *all* the doors at the same time, it sets off the alarm. I didn't even bother with the breaker, just tore cables til it shut down."

"Are you in trouble?" I ask.

Conlan laughs again. "I don't know," he admits. "I just don't know."

We stop at the airlock, where he enters a complicated code, one I don't catch because I can't follow his fingers, they're a blur over the keypad. "You know Ramsey's girl, Kelly?" he asks, motioning us to stand back as the airlock opens. "On the committee. She's dilated two centimeters, just like that." He snaps his fingers, an eerie sound that makes Dylan jump beside me. Leading us into the airlock, Conlan seals the door shut, begins the decon cycle. "After we get the lights back up, he and Seth go through the exit looking for you guys, but you must've taken a wrong turn—"

Dylan rolls his eyes. "You have *no* idea," he says, leaning against the wall. He pulls me into the space between his legs, holds me tight as a fine mist sanitizes the air around us with a clean and antiseptic scent.

At Conlan's confused look, I explain, "We got a little lost."

Conlan nods. "That's easy to do. There's a serviceway you have to take, brings you right out into the commons, but you probably ran past it in the dark."

"So then what happened?" Dylan prompts.

Conlan watches the light above the door—it's red now, but it gradually shifts to orange, then yellow. Green and the cycle will be complete. "Then we go back to the colony," Conlan says. He's excited, I can see it in the nervous way he twists his hands in the hem of his shirt. "And Tobin says it's all my fault—he wouldn't let up on that. Ben almost decked him for it, he just doesn't know when to quit. Me, I didn't say anything because, well, it *was* my fault, and I think Ben sort of knew that. He knows a lot of stuff you don't think he's noticed. Nothing slips by him, *nothing*."

I don't doubt it. The light above the door is a bright yellow now, and Conlan begins to shift from foot to foot, anxious. "I went to check on Marie," he continues, "just to see how she's doing. She's such a trooper. You have to meet her—she asks about you every time I go in there. *How are those boys?* she always wants to know."

"Breathe," Dylan tells him. When Conlan frowns at him, he flashes one of his sunny grins. "You're talking so fast, you're going to pass out."

Conlan laughs. "I'm fine," he says, and for once, I believe it. "But Kelly's not. When I went to see Marie, she told me Kelly started having contractions, nothing serious, but she wanted Ramsey to know. And so I had to find him and—"

The light turns green and he launches himself at the door. Leaning against it, he asks, "Can you help me with this?"

Together the three of us manage to shoulder the door open enough to squeeze through. Outside there's a steady drizzle, cold and wet and so gloriously *natural* that I turn my face up to the clouded sky, close my eyes, feel the rain course down my cheeks like tears. It slicks my clothing to my body like a second skin, and when I turn to Dylan, I laugh at his hair, damp and starting to curl at the ends, the rain beading in it like stars in the sky. Without thinking, I throw my arms around his neck, pull him to me for a hungry kiss. His hands mold to the curve of my ass and his body fits wonderfully against mine, this is where I'm meant to be, in his arms. I kiss him again, a man dying of thirst and he a chalice that holds the sweetest wine. I've missed this, I've missed *him*, and now that we're free from the ship, we stand in the rain and let it wash away all the doubt the colonists have managed to make us feel, all the insecurity, all the *wrongness* because he's mine and there's never, ever been anything more right.

In the shadow of the ship, Conlan eyes the rain distrustfully, then takes a deep breath and steps out into the light downpour. "Your friends," he says, pointing into the distance.

I turn and see the *Semper Fi*, dark against the bruised sky. "God," I sigh, hugging Dylan close. "That ship never looked so good."

Dylan laughs. "If Parker's so much as scratched her," he starts, but he doesn't finish the thought. Conlan's already trekking through the mud and rain to the battered hull and Dylan takes my hand, following him.

"So Ramsey just agreed to help you?" I ask as we near the ship. "Because his girl's in trouble now." How selfish is that? *But at least someone's helping. At least you don't have to do it alone.*

"This is his first child," Conlan explains. "You don't know him like I do. He's not so bad—" I laugh, and he smiles tightly at me. "He's not, really. Just a little rough around the edges."

"So rough, he could cut glass," Dylan mutters.

Conlan's grin widens at that. "Sometimes," he concedes. "But he's always been there for me. When Marie lost the baby the first time? I don't know what we would've done without him." Lowering his voice, he adds, "What *I* would've done."

You have to understand, I think, and it's so unexpected that I burst out laughing. "What?" Conlan asks. He smiles at me like I'm about to let him in on a great joke, and even Dylan looks my way.

I just shake my head. "Nothing," I tell them. Dylan squeezes my hand and starts to say something, but we step into the shadow of the *Semper Fi* and hear the slight creak of the hatch opening, that silences him.

"Hey hey!" Parker cries out, jumping out of the hatch before it opens completely. He grimaces at the soft mud like he forgot it was there, and then he takes in our soaking wet clothing, our clay-streaked shoes, and laughs. "You know I was hoping this shit would let up, right?"

"Did they give you clearance to land?" Dylan wants to know, frowning at the ship's struts, slowly sinking into the earth. "Did you remember to cut the thrust when you docked? Don't tell me you went in my room—"

"I didn't go in your room," Parker says, rolling his eyes. Winking at me, he jokes, "Your porno mags are right where you left them, don't worry. And that naked pic of your boy—"

"You *found* that?" Dylan asks.

"Hey!" I cry, indignant. "There better not be any naked pictures of me in there."

Dylan kisses my forehead. "Don't worry," he kids, "I hid them all." To Parker, he asks, "What coords did you use? I thought they weren't letting you down—"

Shanley steps out of the ship, a weather-proof case in his hands. "We're low on fuel," he says, nodding at us by way of hello. "There's just enough to jaunt back to the carrier, that's about it. Kitt used the same coordinates Neal programmed in when we first landed." He manages to look sheepish when he tells us, "We didn't really have clearance to set down, but we had to do something. We couldn't fly back and just leave you guys here."

Conlan nods at the case in Shanley's hands, his eyes wide. "That it?" he asks, awed. "The briox? That's what'll help Marie?"

"If it's not too late," Shanley tells him.

With a determined nod, Conlan leads the way back to the S410.

Part 9

Conlan's anxious to get this show on the road—we all are. But the colony's decon procedures are so ingrained in him that he starts the cycle in the airlock before he realizes most of us just went through this what, five minutes ago? If that. "Ben will ask," he explains, when Dylan points it out. With a wary glance at Shanley and Parker, he adds, "I don't suppose you ran through those tests again back at your carrier."

"I think it's safe to say we're still clean," Shanley assures him. "The whole crew underwent the procedures before we landed the first time."

"You were with Shauna," Conlan says, his voice low. "If she's contagious—"

"She was with Marie, too," I remind him. Conlan lets his gaze fall to the ground, he doesn't answer, but I can see he's thinking about that girl in Marie's room the other day. "If she *is* contagious, Marie's already got whatever it is she's carrying." Conlan shrugs helplessly. "I'm not saying she does." Looking at Shanley for help, I ask, "You're not sick, are you?"

Shanley shakes his head. "I'm fine. Marie's going to be fine, I promise you, Jeremy. If it's not too late—"

"It's not," Conlan says, stubborn. The earlier excitement that gripped him has worn off, leaving a grim determination in its place, but there's a helplessness in his eyes that scares me, like he's beginning to doubt himself, he's asking if he's doing the right thing and it's a moot point, he can't back down now. Shanley's here, the briox is in his case, we're just a few dozen yards from getting the drug to Marie—there's no way he can change his mind on this. *This is for the good of the colony,* I want to tell him, *no matter what Ellington and the others have to say.*

Only I can't find the words—what do you say to someone who's going against everything he's ever been taught? What's the comfort in hearing you're only doing what's right when you're not even sure you believe that yourself?

Conlan shakes his head as if to shake away the fears gnawing at him. His wavy hair curls below his ears, falls in front of his haunted eyes, and with one hand he combs it back out of the way roughly. "It's not too late," he says again, as if to convince himself.

Once the decon cycle is complete, Conlan keys in the clearance code to open the airlock door. He's the first through, followed by Parker and Dylan, who elbow each other like this is some sort of game here, let's see who can get into the corridor first. Parker pushes Dylan back, laughs when he stumbles into Shanley, and I manage to snag a handful of my lover's shirt before he can launch himself at the other pilot. "Dylan," I warn, holding him back so Shanley can pass.

"He pushed me first," he whines—yes, twenty and whining like an eight year old because he's got a streak of pride that runs like a river through his soul. "Give me a kiss," he demands. Before I can answer, his lips are pressed to mine, and it's just a sneaky ploy to distract me as he works my hand free from his shirt. But when he sighs, "Love you," and stares at me with those endless eyes of his, deeper than the reaches of space, my knees go weak and I don't have the strength to hold on. I let him loosen my grip, and then he kisses my knuckles, his gaze never leaving mine.

Behind us, Parker calls out, "Come on, you guys. Get your freak on later. This is why they threw your asses in jail, remember?"

"Shut up," Dylan growls. As he pulls me out into the corridor, though, the airlock door starts to slide shut. It hits his shoulder, bounces back into its frame, tries again. "Hey!" Dylan glares at Parker, smirking at us—he's the closest one to the keypad. Conlan's halfway down the hall leading to the colony, Shanley right behind him. I jump clear of the door's path when it tries to close again, and this time it slides shut. Advancing on Parker, Dylan pushes him back against the far wall. "You're just looking for a fight, aren't you?"

"Wasn't me," Parker says. He knocks Dylan's hands away and I step between them before they can start something. "Jesus, Teague, the door closed on its own. I didn't touch the damn thing."

A little ways off from us, Conlan stops. "We're coming," I tell him before he can ask, grabbing Dylan's arm to pull him along.

"The door closed on you?" he wants to know as we catch up with them.

I shrug. "It's no big deal—"

But he's not listening. Dread creeps into his features and then he's off, sprinting down the corridor. "They must've changed the code again," he tells us. Dylan races after him, tugging me along, Parker and Shanley right behind us. "Those doors don't shut by themselves," Conlan explains. "They stay open til you hit the pad on the other side. But they reset when you change the code. If somebody's done that…" He doesn't finish the sentence, he doesn't *have* to.

If they've changed the code again, we can't get into the colony.

Conlan tears down the corridor as if trying to outrace that thought.

Ellington is waiting for us.

Around the bend, where we overheard Conlan and Ramsey talking earlier, Ellington squats on the ground against the wall, his head leaning back against the cold steel and his arms stretched out, resting on his knees. When we round the corner, his head lolls to one side and he looks up at us, at all of us, and then his gaze finds Conlan. Something in his expressionless face makes the younger man stumble to a stop. "Ben," he sighs, breathless. "Did you change the security code again? He's got the drug—"

"Seth changed it," Ellington replies. "I don't know what it is."

Dylan looks at me, *Now what?* I see the question shining in his eyes. "You don't—" Conlan starts, confused.

"It's what's best," Ellington tells him. He doesn't rise to his feet, doesn't shift into a more comfortable position, just watches Conlan with that sad look on his face. "For the colony."

"The briox is what's best!" Conlan cries. He advances on Ellington, one step, two, but hesitates when his friend doesn't move. "Ben, we can't afford—"

"Shauna's dead."

He lets the words sink in. "Dead," Conlan echoes, and when Ellington nods, the fight goes out of him, his shoulders tremble, he hunches forward like he's caving into himself, *dead.* I reach for him but Dylan holds me back. *Dead.* "Alison?" Conlan's hands clench into useless fists at his sides. "Marie? Ben, please tell me, Marie—"

Ellington shrugs. "Maybe," he whispers. What the hell kind of answer is that? *Maybe.* Either she's sick or she isn't, there is no *maybe* about it. "We've quarantined eight others. Holly, she was with them yesterday, remember? Aaron, Leslie, Tobin—"

Against my will, I make a strangled sound in the back of my throat, *Tobin.* I touched him earlier, grabbed his nasty hair and yanked him against the bars of my cell, held a *knife* to his throat—"Oh God," I moan.

Dylan's hand tightens in mine. "Did that fucker touch you?" he wants to know. Numb, I shake my head, but I can't find the words to speak. Suddenly my throat is too dry, scratchy, my eyes burn, I fight off the panicky urge to cough. *I'm not sick,* I tell myself. *I'm NOT.*

"Marie's sick?" Conlan asks. He takes another step towards his friend. "Is it the bleed? I need to see her. You can't do this to me."

With a sigh, Ellington tells him, "She's not sick yet. But give her time. What's the use? Tobin wasn't even near the girl and he's got it."

And probably now so do I, I think, but I stifle the thought. Lowering his voice, Ellington whispers, "We should have never let them in."

He means us. "We had nothing to do with it," Dylan says hotly, but I quiet him with a hand on his arm. There's nothing we can say in our defense, doesn't he see that?

"The bleed." Conlan's voice is distant, haunting, and when he turns to look at us, there's a hunted look in his eyes that terrifies me. *They've given up hope*, I think wildly—that's what I see reflected in his tortured gaze. *First Ramsey, now Ellington, and not you, too, Conlan, you can't give up the hope you've been clinging to, you'll never survive without it. The colony will never survive without you.*

His gaze shifts to Shanley, who clears his throat, speaks in his comforting, almost feminine physician's voice, the kind of voice a doctor *should* have, the kind that lends itself to a good bedside manner. Professional and caring and distant and so damn compassionate, it makes your eyes tear up to hear it. "Jeremy," he starts, and that about does it, his name in that voice, because Conlan's face crumples like a used tissue and he struggles not to cry. "I've been thinking," Shanley hurries on, easily snagging our attention. Even Ellington's listening. "I'll have to get into the colony to study the disease and make sure, but from what you've told me, this sounds like a fairly straight-forward filovirus. It has all the classic symptoms. Now, I'm not set up here to do a hemoflush, all that stuff's back at the station, but there are alternatives—"

"Like what?" Ellington wants to know. He laughs, a harsh sound in the close corridor. "You want all of us to pile into your little ship? Go with you back to your station, abandon our home, open ourselves up to further infection on the chance that some of us might make it to your facility alive? I don't think that's a viable *alternative*, doctor."

Before Shanley can answer, I step forward. "Shut up," I tell him, that hateful man, sitting on the floor, staring at me. "Just shut up and listen to yourself, will you? For all your talk about the good of the colony and saving your home, have you ever stopped to think about what exactly it is you're *doing* here?" Dylan holds my wrist, keeps me from taking another step, and another—anger flows through me like the blood in my veins and I just want to grab Ellington, shake him until he opens his eyes and *sees*—"What kind of a place is this? That you're willing to turn a blind eye to any offered help, that you're willing to destroy everything instead of saving it?"

"It's our home," Ellington reminds me, his voice listless and dead. Glancing at Conlan, he adds, "The only one some of us—*most* of us—have ever known."

There's nothing here worth saving, I want to tell him—there's *not*. What's so wrong with admitting defeat? With leaving this place behind? Before I can ask, though, Conlan pulls himself together, resolve shining in his eyes and, turning to his friend, says, "You can't protect us forever, Ben. You can't just freeze time and hope—"

Ellington shakes his head, angry. "I'm not—"

Conlan raises his voice to speak over him. "And hope things will get better. They *won't*, not without some help here. We can't just turn back the years and pretend none of this ever happened. We can't go back to the way things used to be—we just *can't*."

Ellington sighs, covers his face with his hands, curls into himself there on the floor like he wants to disappear. I can hear the tears in Conlan's gentle voice when he says, "You want us to survive, I *know* you do. But maybe you want it too much? You want to control every single aspect of our future and you can't. There's no *way* you can hope to do that." Ellington doesn't respond—there's no indication he's even listening, though I suspect he's hanging on Conlan's every word. "We'll never be the colony you remember, Ben. Too much has happened to us, too many have died. But we've grown up now, *I've* grown up, and you have to let us move on."

"To more death," Ellington says bitterly, his voice muffled. "That's all that lies ahead, Jeremy. We'll all die anyway, we're dying now. Why should we even bother moving on? What kind of a future is that? Why bother?"

You can't think that. The only thing keeping me from saying the words is Dylan's hand on my arm, a comforting touch, I don't know how I could listen to this without him by my side. Conlan's stronger than he thinks, if he can stand there alone and face down his friend. *He's given up hope like Ramsey has,* I think, watching Ellington, his face hidden in his hands. *Maybe they all have.*

Except Conlan. "My child," he says softly. "And Ramsey's, and Seth's. They need this chance, Ben. There's still hope for those children, if there's still time. *They're* our future here. We're doing this for them."

I hold my breath, waiting. Dylan slips his arm around my waist, pulls me to him. Beside us, Parker has his hands on his hips, watching Ellington, and Shanley's waiting, we're all waiting. *If there's still time...*

Finally Ellington whispers, "I don't know the code. Seth changed it after I left. I'm sorry."

※   ※   ※

For a moment I think Conlan's going to just give up like all the other colonists. He kicks at the ground, his lower lip caught between his teeth, he's going to worry at it until it bleeds. Then Dylan squeezes my hand and tells me, "The emergency exit."

I don't follow. "What—" I start, but he's already off, dragging me along behind him. "Dylan!"

"We came out from the exit right near here," he reminds me. Looking over his shoulder at Conlan, he explains, "You said there's a passage from the exit leading into the commons. We can reach it from the serviceway we used. Those hatches aren't coded, right?"

Hope lights up Conlan's face. "Right," he agrees. He starts to follow us, then turns and looks back at Ellington, still squatting on the floor, defeated. "Come on, Ben."

"You're wrong, Jeremy," Ellington says without raising his head. He stares at a spot on the ground, something that's fascinated him, something from which he can't tear his gaze away. "*You're* the future of this colony, not the children, sure as hell not me. I'm the past."

Dylan sighs dramatically, rolls his eyes and opens his mouth to say something, something mean, I can almost hear it now. "Don't," I whisper, nudging him with my elbow.

"What?" he asks, like he doesn't know what I'm talking about.

I'm not buying it. "Just don't."

Ignoring us, Conlan walks over to where his friend sits. He takes Ellington's arm, tries to haul him to his feet. "Don't be like that," he says, his voice so quiet, I can barely hear it. "Come on, Ben. It's not too late. It *can't* be."

Either Conlan has a lot of strength in those sinewy arms of his, or Ellington really *has* given up, he just doesn't care, because he lets Conlan help him stand. He doesn't resist as Conlan leads him to where we wait, then past us—Ellington lets his gaze slide over Parker, Shanley, me, like we're not even here. But he sees something in Dylan's face, something that makes him turn away and mumble, "I'm sorry about…" He trails off, waving his hand in an obscure gesture. "About everything."

I give Dylan a shove to get him moving down the corridor before he can answer. "It's okay," I say, as if locking us up was no big deal. It's over with now, there's no use dwelling on it, no matter what Dylan thinks. I can tell from his creased brow that he won't forgive so easily, but we have other things to worry about first. Like getting Shanley into the colony's med lab.

We lead the way back to the airlock, the others following closely behind us. Even Ellington, though Conlan keeps a supportive hand on his friend's arm. At the airlock, we lose a few precious moments where Dylan can't remember which service hatch it was we exited—there are three or four down either side of the corridor, I didn't realize there was more than one, and I didn't pay much attention before. "Neal," Dylan says, thoughtful as he opens another door. It slides away to expose a supply closet. "Where—"

"There." Ellington points to a nondescript hatch a little further down the corridor, away from where we're looking. "That's it."

I don't want to trust him. But this is his home, he's lived here for most of his life, played in these corridors as a child—he knows this ship inside and out. Still, he's been so resistant to our help since we landed, I don't know if I can believe he's changed his mind at this stage of the game.

Why not? He has nothing left to lose. The bleed is back, or something so similar to it, it's already killed one colonist, infected eight others. The women can't carry to term. Conlan has sided with us—I think that's hurt Ellington the most, he was desperate to protect Conlan from us, from the disease, from pain and heartache and *it doesn't work that way*, I think, watching the indecision play across Conlan's face. He wants to believe his friend and doesn't know if he can. Ellington's kept too much from him already, tried to shield him too much, and Conlan doesn't know if he can trust him not to keep him in the dark any longer. *He's right, he's grown up now, you can't keep him in the shelter of your hands anymore, you can't bottle him like a captured butterfly, you can't hold onto him forever. You said it yourself, he's the future of this colony. You can't deny him that.*

Seeing the doubt in his friend's face, Ellington pleads, "Trust me, Jeremy. That's the corridor you want. It leads straight to the prison, branches off to the commons, that's the one."

Conlan doesn't hesitate any longer—he launches himself at the hatch, tears it open, doesn't even wait for the rest of us before he barrels through. He pulls Ellington after him, Parker on their heels. *Déjà vu* washes through me as I follow Dylan down the narrow passage, up stairwells, around blind corners, Shanley right behind me. "Hey, haven't you brought me here before?" Dylan jokes, but I don't laugh. This isn't funny.

The route back to the prison seems shorter this time, but maybe that's because Conlan knows where he's going. When the emergency exit door looms ahead and we can't go any farther, Conlan turns down a darkened hall, one Dylan and I missed when the lights went out before. The hall ends at a spiral staircase that twists up into the heart of the ship, short, metal steps with wide gaps between each riser. Dylan walks behind me, his hands on my ass, and somehow I suspect that's not just to help me up the stairs. "Baby," I tell him, taking his hands in mine. "That's not really helping me here."

A few steps below me, he looks up and winks bawdily. "It's helping me," he says, his hands slipping free from mine to curve around my buttocks again. He gives me a gentle push. "Keep moving, sexy."

The staircase ends in a short, unlit serviceway—the only light comes from the end of the hall, which opens out on the commons area. I can hear the faint rush of water, and the walls around us dance with red dappled reflections, cast from the fountain just beyond the doorway. I don't know what I'm expecting—angry colonists, maybe, armed with pitchforks and crying for our blood, I can't seem to shake that image from my mind—and my heart begins to race with each step we take away from the stairs. I have to fight the urge to turn and run away, back down the stairs, out the airlock door and to the *Semper Fi*, and I don't care if I don't know the new security code, I don't care if I don't know the route, it's *safe* back there. But with Dylan's hands on my waist, I can keep putting one foot in front of the other just because I know he's here with me, he's going to stay with me, we'll get through this together.

❦   ❦   ❦

Out in the commons, the colonists huddle together by the food counter. From where we stand they look like just a handful of people milling about, not so many after all. They form a half-circle around one end of the counter, standing back so there's an empty space in their midst and *it's a fight*, I think, that's the first thing that comes to mind—they look like children in a schoolyard, gathered around a bully and his hapless victim. No one notices us, no one turns as we approach. "What's going on?" Dylan whispers. The way he cranes his neck to see, I think he already suspects.

He starts to push ahead of the others but I grab his hand, hold him back. "We don't need to get in the middle of this," I remind him as he strains my arm, pulling me along.

Ahead of us, Conlan stops at the edge of the crowd, stands up on his toes to get a good look at what's happening. What he sees makes the color drain from his face and he shoves through the colonists. "Hey! Let me through. Ramsey—"

Ramsey. Oh God. I stop behind the gathered colonists and refuse to move. If that guy's fighting, I don't want to see it. I don't want him to see *me*, because there's something about him that I think is all too eager to take a swing at me and if I get too close to him now, when he's already in ass-kicking mode, I might find myself in his way. And Conlan—he can't hold his own against that man, what's he thinking? *Somebody stop him,* I want to shout, but who'll listen to me? Conlan's already through the crowd, Ellington right behind him, Parker and Shanley following, and I hold onto Dylan's hand and wrist as tight as I can so he can't join them. I can stand my ground when I have to, I don't want him getting hurt. *Anyone but you, baby.* "Get back here," I mutter.

A few of the colonists recognize Conlan, see Ellington behind him and stand aside, parting to let them into their midst. "Ramsey!" Conlan cries. "Seth, stop!" *Maclin.* I definitely don't want to see this.

But Dylan has other ideas. He gives up trying to pull me into the thick of things—instead he circles around behind me, a surprise move, and with his hands on my shoulders, pushes me through the opening in the crowd. He's not one to miss a good fight.

In the space between the colonists and the counter are Ramsey and Maclin. Ramsey's back is up against the counter, his nose bloody and broken, a livid bruise beginning to bloom above one eye, a trail of red beads scratched across his cheek. His eyes flash like the sea before a storm, flickering from Conlan to Ellington to Maclin, who's holding him at bay, the muscles in his thin arms taut with the effort. Conlan grabs Maclin's shoulder, tries to get him off Ramsey and can't. Despite appearances, Maclin is strong. "Seth, stop it, stop! What the hell is this all about? What—"

"Fucker here changed the code," Ramsey growls, kicking out at Maclin. His foot connects with Maclin's shin, I can hear the force of the blow, it should've buckled his leg and brought him to his knees.

But Maclin shakes it off like he doesn't even feel it. He pulls his fist back, hits Ramsey in the chest, a low punch that makes the other man gasp for breath. With wild eyes, Maclin glances around at us, his lips pulling back into a sneer when he sees me, and I feel Dylan's arms slip around my waist, tighten protectively. "You let them in," he says, his voice like the soft roar of a cougar on the prowl. Then he turns that awful gaze onto Conlan and his arm shoots out, his hand clenches in the front of Conlan's shirt, he pulls him close, off the floor and into his face, shakes him angrily, snarls, "What the *fuck* did you do that for, Jeremy? At a time like this?"

"My child," Conlan gasps, his hands trying to loosen Maclin's grip. "Seth, please—"

Ramsey lashes out again, only he's not fighting fair anymore. He goes for the crotch, an attack Maclin senses a moment before the crippling hit, and he turns just in time. Ramsey's knee glances off his thigh, but it's forceful enough that he lets Conlan go to refocus on the man he's got against the counter. Conlan stumbles back, his hands rubbing at his throat. "Ramsey," he chokes, and that's all he manages to get out before Ramsey shoves Maclin away from him and at the crowd, at *me*. Fingers claw in my shirt as Maclin staggers back, searching for purchase, but Dylan steps in front of me, knocks the grasping hands away.

Maclin rams into the colonists behind us and they scatter out of his way. I see surprise flit across his face as he lands on his ass, hard enough to knock the wind out of him, and before he can get his breath back, Ramsey is there, fisting a hand into his shirt, hauling him up, tossing him against the counter with a sickening *crunch* that sounds like splintering wood or bone. "Ramsey!" Conlan cries again.

Maclin sinks to the floor, an arm wrapped around his narrow chest, holding bruised or broken ribs, his head hanging in defeat, but Ramsey advances on him, kicks his leg aside and pulls him up again. When Conlan grabs his arm, tries to intervene, Ramsey shrugs him away. "Get out of here, Jeremy," he growls. He throws Maclin back against the counter a second time. "Take them to the med lab. Leave this to me."

"No," Conlan pleads. Maclin wraps his hands around Ramsey's, tries to break free, but another slam into the counter and his face clouds with pain, he seems to give up. "Ramsey, this isn't—"

Ellington steps forward. "Ramsey, stop." *Yeah, that's going to help,* I think as Ramsey turns an evil glare onto the older man. *He's never listened to you before.*

He doesn't now, but it's enough of a distraction that Maclin can land a punch in Ramsey's neck. A solid thud that I feel in my teeth, he hits so hard Ramsey stumbles back into Ellington, who barely manages to jump out of the way. Ramsey falls into the crowd and is already pushing away from them, launching himself at Maclin, when Conlan steps in between them. "Ramsey!" he cries, shielding Maclin. "Look at you two! This isn't helping, this isn't—"

Ramsey grabs Conlan by the shoulders and for a second I think he's just going to crush the man between his hands, ball him up like paper and toss him aside. There's a fear in Conlan's face that tells me he's thinking the same thing, and he grits his teeth, closes his eyes in pain as Ramsey crushes him in his grip. "Ramsey," he sighs. "What's this all about?"

I don't think Ramsey's going to answer. I don't think *he* thinks he's going to answer, but then he sees Conlan, really *sees* him, eyes closed, head back, waiting...waiting. It takes everything he has to force himself to stop—the struggle wars across his face, his arms tremble with the effort. But somehow he manages to let go.

With an angry roar, Ramsey turns onto Ellington. "This is all *your* fault, Ben," he spits, poking one forefinger into Ellington's chest, hard enough to push him back a step. "You *told* him to change the fucking code? Do you *want* us to die?"

"I thought it was the right thing to do," Ellington explains. He's a full head shorter than Ramsey and has to glare up into the other man's face, I don't know how he can stare into all that *hate* and not fall back, but somehow he manages to stand his ground. "I was wrong, Ramsey." He looks past him at Maclin, laboring to breathe as he leans against the counter, holding sore ribs. "Seth, I'm sorry. I was wrong." He looks around at the colonists, watching silently, waiting. "I was wrong."

Maclin forces a laugh. "Now you tell us," he moans.

"Seth, don't," Conlan admonishes softly. He eases Maclin's arm around his shoulders, helps him to his feet. "Evan, can you—?"

Shanley rushes to Maclin's side, already opening his medical case. "Sit him down," Shanley says, pulling out a chair from a nearby table, which Maclin sinks into gratefully.

"You were wrong." Ramsey's voice is dangerously low. "Marie's going to lose her baby and you were wrong. Shauna's dead and you were wrong." He lunges at Ellington, grabs his collar, shoves him back into the crowd. "Kelly's next and you were *wrong*? What the hell good does your apology do us now?"

Conlan speaks up from where he kneels beside Maclin. "Ramsey, there's still time."

Ramsey whirls on Conlan. "You stay out of this, Jeremy. I told you I'd handle Ben."

"*Listen*," Conlan says, rising to his feet. He looks around at the colonists to include them, too. "All of you, stop and look at yourselves. Standing here gawking when people are dying—"

"There's nothing we can do about that," a woman says, her face lost in the crowd, but her words start a low murmur that runs through the room, *yes, nothing we can do.*

Ellington glares at Ramsey as he shrugs to straighten his shirt. "Maybe they *can* help," he says, with a nod our way. Dylan's hands are on my waist, Parker is behind us, and when the colonists turn to stare at us, *through* us, I just want to melt into the floor. *Just let me disappear*, I pray. "All I wanted was for things to go back to the way they were," Ellington tells us, "and we can't do that, Ramsey. God, you remember. You out of all these people, you remember what it was like before the death, before the bleed." Ramsey scowls at the ground but I think he *does* remember, I can see in his eyes a wistfulness that makes my throat close up, it's so poignant. "I wanted us to get back to that, if we could. Hell, if we *couldn't*—I was willing to do anything at all to get that back."

"At the sake of the future?" Ramsey asks, incredulous. His eyes flash with an angry light—the hope he lost over the years, the hope Conlan gave back to him when he convinced Ramsey we could help, the hope that's now shaky and unstable, he thinks we might be too late, and the intensity of the gaze he turns onto Ellington suggests that he thinks this is all his fault. "You'd destroy us just because we can't be what you want. What kind of fucked up mess is that?"

Ellington doesn't have an answer. "I don't know," he mumbles. "I did what I thought was right. I didn't mean—"

Without warning, Ramsey closes the distance between them, snatches Ellington up by the collar again, shakes him until I'm sure he's going to snap in two. "You don't know?" he growls. "You don't *know?*"

"Ramsey."

It's the only word Conlan says, and it's so low, I'm sure the people at the back of the crowd didn't hear it, but it's enough to make Ramsey stop. Ellington grips Ramsey's hands, tries to work them free from his shirt, but the fingers are closed tight as if in death. He wants to say something and doesn't dare, Ramsey's pinned him with a withering look, another word and Ellington might not live to see whether or not our medicines work after all.

Conlan waits. We all do.

"Fuck," Ramsey growls, tossing Ellington aside. He rounds on Conlan behind him, who doesn't flinch when those stormy eyes turn his way. *Very brave,* I think, watching Conlan stare Ramsey down, *or very stupid.* I'm not sure which.

Or maybe he just trusts Ramsey. The thought surprises me—I can't imagine trusting someone like him, with that much unbridled anger roiling around inside. Someone that unstable, I couldn't do it.

When Ramsey speaks, his voice is filled with that anger and I take a step back, so much *hate* in those words, it staggers me. Only Dylan's hands on my waist keep me from running away. It's a voice that nightmares speak in. "He changed the passcode," Ramsey explains, as if Conlan might not know this. He points at Maclin where he sits, Shanley bandaging his ribs. "Ben asked where you were, I said none of his fucking business. Then Shauna dies and he panics, they all do." He glares around at the colonists, who shrink from his accusation. I try to back away but Dylan's behind me and he's not moving, and when Ramsey's eyes meet mine, fear rises in me, freezes me like a deer in headlights, if I even *breathe,* he'll hurt me, that's the promise I see in his face. How can Conlan stand so close to him and not feel the heat of this man's anger? It rises from him in waves, so intense, like searing air from a boiler. What is it about Conlan that keeps him from getting burned?

"Ramsey," Conlan says again, easily snagging the older man's attention. As Ramsey turns towards him, my knees go weak in relief, that terrible gaze no longer imprisons me. How Conlan doesn't bow before it, I'll never know.

"They changed the code," Ramsey snarls. "They wanted to keep you *out*—"

"I know," Conlan tells him. "But they had their reasons. They thought it was the right thing to do. *You* thought so, too, before Kelly started having complications." He lets Ramsey think that over. "You told me it was for the best, keeping them out, just until we get the sickness isolated. Remember? Right before the power went out in the prison. You came and told me—"

Ramsey growls, "I know what I said." There's something in his voice that warns Conlan not to continue, no one else needs to know what he said in the empty guardroom, and part of me hopes Conlan doesn't take the hint.

But he does. He nods, lowers his voice until he's almost whispering. "You said the same things Seth did, Ramsey, just a few hours ago. If Kelly were doing fine, you might have been the one to change the code on me when Ben asked you to. Don't shake your head like that, you *know* you would've done the same thing, Ramsey, *I* know you would have. Hell, *I* might've, in your shoes."

Ramsey shakes his head again. "You're not like us," he says, his voice a soft rumble like distant thunder. "You said it yourself, Jeremy. You never gave up hope."

"And I still haven't." Conlan takes a step closer to his friend, dares to place a hand on his shoulder. Ramsey's anger seems to deflate at the touch. "I'm not saying to pack up and leave this all behind. This is our *home*. I grew up here, I belong here—I'm not about to give in just because things aren't working out for us. I'm not saying we should give up."

From behind Conlan, Maclin asks, "Then what *are* you saying?" His raised shirt exposes a chest so thin, the muscles stand out like cords beneath his skin, and he winces as Shanley runs a handheld laser over the bruised flesh, mending cracked ribs. "Exactly," he adds, "in small words, so *some* of us can understand." He glares at Ramsey, who ignores the jab.

"I'm saying we let them help." Conlan watches the emotions flicker across Ramsey's face, as if he's trying to gauge how his friend will react. "They're offering a solution, and I know we've made it this far on our own, yes. I know we're the only colony from Operation Starseed to survive, I *know* this is personal to us, to *all* of us. We all want to survive. We want to go on, to have something here when we're gone, to have a *life* here—I want something real, something solid. I want years from now to look back and go *damn* but we did good." Ramsey glares at the floor, doesn't meet Conlan's eyes. "What we have now isn't *living*. We're breathing. We're existing. But we're not *alive*. And we won't be as long as we hold onto this fear that locks us into place. There's been too much death, too much disease, and if we don't take this chance now, if we don't let them help us, there's only going to be more."

I glance around at the colonists, at Ellington and Maclin, and I *am* invisible to them now, only Conlan exists. He's the only one alive here, in this landscape of pain, of suffering. He's the only light that illuminates this world—I can see it shine in his face, flash in his eyes, a new sun dawning inside of him, a new *life*. "If we do nothing," Conlan explains, "then we die. The children die, the bleed resurfaces, and that's it. This—" He sweeps an arm around, indicating the colony, the S410, everything—"this all dies. We're never going to be what you remember, Ramsey. We'll never be all that Ben wants us to be. But maybe, just maybe, we can become something more."

Ramsey frowns at the ground, scuffs his foot along a crack in the tile. "Marie's waiting," he mutters, his voice gruff with bottled emotion. He doesn't look at Conlan, just waves dismissively in the direction of the med lab. "Go. She needs you."

You all do, I think.

❦   ❦   ❦

Shanley insists on setting Ramsey's broken nose before he turns to other concerns. "Won't take but a minute," he says, and I can hear the crunch of cartilage as he pops it back into place. Ramsey grits his teeth and Conlan flinches, has to look away. But Shanley ignores the pain shining in Ramsey's icy eyes. *You're a stronger man than me, doc.* There's no *way* I'd be able to stay nonchalant with that man glaring at me like that.

With Maclin and Ramsey taken care of, Ellington claps his hands, breaking up the crowd. "Okay, people? We're still under alert here. Maybe we can go back to the quarters? Just until Dr. Shanley gives us a green light. What do you say?" A few of the colonists grumble, but when he glances around at them, they shuffle away in small groups, twos and threes, they've trusted him for so long now, it's easier to just let him tell them what to do. Easier to retreat into themselves again, more of their *me* mentality. Easier to sit on their bunks, watch their neighbors and friends with a wary caution, wait for the first cough, the first sniffle. Wait to quarantine them, to push them away. Wait for them to die.

But maybe Conlan managed to finally break through that selfishness—a few of the colonists laugh quietly together, there's no anger, no moping, no despair. When people file past me, they don't stare at me hatefully, they don't glare at Dylan's arm around my waist, his hand pressed flat against my stomach. There are no mumbled words, no barely breathed insults, no half-imagined mutterings. I don't believe things have changed—if Shanley's medicines don't work, I'm sure these same people will be all too quick to tear us apart again, throw us back into their jail, lock us away forever. But maybe, just maybe, there's a hope here that wasn't there before, an anticipation that isn't simply a death watch, an expectation of a future that might come true after all.

We race down another corridor, one I vaguely remember, heading for the med lab. It's just the four of us again—the crew from the *Semper Fi*—and Ellington, with Conlan leading the way. Shanley keeps Conlan's frantic pace while the rest of us fall back, clustered together, almost afraid. Even Ramsey and Maclin are gone, back to the quarters with the others, and I can't help but wonder just what we're rushing headlong into here. If no one else follows us…how contagious *is* this disease? Why hasn't Shanley gotten it yet? And, more importantly, will *we* get it? How can we not?

I spot the low window that peers into Marie's room and Conlan sprints ahead, runs up to the door, presses against it impatiently while it opens, too slow for him, he slips through before the cycle's complete. "Marie," he sighs, rushing to her side. We pile in behind him, my hand seeking Dylan's, a small comfort but something, at least. One glance at Conlan's face, twisted in sadness and hope, and I feel like we shouldn't be here, it's an intrusion, this is something private. I start to back out of the room but Dylan holds me still. Then the door closes behind us—I can't leave unnoticed now.

Marie lies on the bed, her skin pale against the white sheets. Her auburn hair fans out around her, dark curls that frame her face. Shadows pool in the hollows of her cheeks and her eyes are like large bruises, painful to see. "Jeremy," she says as he takes her hand in both of his, presses it to his chest carefully, tenderly, like she's made of the finest porcelain and he's afraid of crushing her fingers too tight. Looking past him, Marie smiles at Shanley. "Hey there, doc."

"Hey yourself, pretty lady," Shanley says with a smile. He sets his medical case on a nearby cart and wheels it over beside the bed. Taking her wrist, he glances at his watch to time her pulse and asks, "How are you holding up? Feeling okay?"

"I'm fine," she tells him. With a nod at the bulge of her stomach, hidden beneath the bed sheet, she adds, "Someone's getting restless down there, though."

"We'll take care of that," Shanley assures her. He reaches for a white lab coat hanging from a peg on the wall, slips into it, buttons it up over his damp jumpsuit. Then he turns to the monitor by her bed, begins setting up for an ultrasound. Nodding our way, he asks, "Have you met the rest of my crew?"

Marie flashes us a wan grin. "I've heard so much about you boys," she says, her voice husky and low. Now *that* has to beat out anything Conlan's ever said for understatement of the year. Since we've arrived, I'm sure she's heard of nothing *but* us.

Shanley eases down the covers to expose Marie's stomach, swollen with child. Out of decency I turn away, nudging Dylan to do the same. But he's like a little boy, all eyes, and I have to elbow him in the ribs to get his attention. "At least close your mouth," I whisper over the rapid *thub thub* of the baby's heartbeat.

"The cervix," Shanley explains, pointing to a small C-shaped image on the monitor. Dylan stares at the screen, enthralled, but when I touch his chin, his mouth snaps shut. "It shouldn't look like this."

"Is it too late?" Conlan asks in a hushed voice.

Shanley shakes his head. "I don't think so. It's not *too* bad. Just have to close it up again, until it looks like a ring, and we'll be fine. If the briox doesn't work, there's still that procedure I told you about. But if we can be noninvasive…"

Marie laughs uneasily. "Noninvasive is good."

While Shanley runs through the sonogram, Conlan introduces us to her. "You know Ben," he says, a lame attempt at a joke, but Marie smiles at that and Ellington snorts—it got a *little* something out of him, at least. He folds his arms across his chest and nods at Marie, but I notice he can't quite look her in the eye, like he thinks she should hate him. He was willing to sacrifice her child for the good of the colony, wasn't he? She *should* hate him, in my opinion.

But she's known him for so long, I don't think it's in her to hold anything against him, least of all for thinking of the colony before the colonists—it's just his nature. She knows this, she forgives him for it, it's in her eyes, her smile, her voice when she laughs and says, "Nice to meet you, Ben. I'm Marie."

Ellington ducks his head, embarrassed. "Hey," he mumbles.

From beneath the sheet she kicks at him playfully—he's too far from the bed for her leg to reach but the gesture makes him laugh, a real laugh this time, nothing faked. "Marie," Shanley warns. The image on the monitor shakes, unsteady. Catching her leg, he holds her down. "You have to stay still, beautiful."

"Listen to him," Conlan tells her. He stares at the monitor, the blurry lines just a suggestion of the life growing within her. In a low, awed voice, he asks, "What do you see?"

"Three heads," Shanley says. He's so deadpan that for a minute my heart leaps in my chest, my mind cries out, *triplets! You mean*—Then he smiles and says, "I'm only teasing. The baby's doing real well."

Relief floods Conlan's face. "Oh Jesus," he whispers. "For a minute there I thought—"

Laughing, I admit, "I did, too."

Marie looks up at the sound of my voice and smiles at me. "Let me guess. Neal?" When I nod, surprised, she explains, "Jeremy told me you talk from the bottom of your chest. What's a cute boy like you doing with a big, deep voice like that?"

Suddenly everyone's looking at me. I just shrug and find my lips pulling into one of my *aw shucks* grins that Dylan thinks are unbearably adorable. And there he is, touching a spot on my cheek where it dimples. "It's a rumbly voice," he murmurs, smoothing his thumb across my skin. "I like it."

"Dylan," Marie declares with an infectious laugh. "I'd know you anywhere. Jeremy told me you can't keep your hands to yourself."

I have to laugh at the look of consternation that crosses my lover's face, but he sees Marie's just kidding and kisses me quick. "Damn straight," he purrs. "With a boy like mine—"

"Dylan," I say before he can continue. "I'm sure they don't want to know."

Marie winks at us like she has a pretty good idea what Dylan was about to say. Something graphic, I'm almost sure of it, and I have to hold his hands in mine to keep them from curving into places I'd rather not let other people see him touch. "Jeremy clued me in," she starts.

But Conlan squeezes Marie's hand to quiet her, and his face burns with a bright blush, the pink rising into his cheeks before he turns away to try and hide it. "You don't have to tell them *everything* I said," he whispers.

"Just the good parts," she concedes.

Now I'm *really* curious what Conlan might have told her about us, but when he nods at Parker in an effort to change the subject, she lets the matter drop. "And this is Kitt. The pilot who went with Evan back to the carrier?"

Parker raises one hand, halfhearted. He looks as if he'd rather be anywhere but here, like the fact that she's lying pregnant on the bed makes him uncomfortable. Or maybe it's Shanley, finished with the ultrasound and now shaking a vial of clear liquid, a long syringe in one hand. Parker's keeping a close eye on that needle, and I notice he's standing the furthest away from the physician. Personally I don't blame him—I don't like the looks of that thing, either. The light winks off the tip like a flash of bright pain, and I tell myself if Parker bolts, I'm right behind him. I don't know how Marie can lie there and ignore the slight *pop* of the syringe breaking the seal on the vial, the liquid drawing into the needle's length slowly to avoid air bubbles. Conlan was right, she *is* a trooper. She doesn't even wince when Shanley pulls up the sleeve of her shirt and pokes the needle into the fleshy part of her upper arm.

"This should stabilize the cervix," he explains. "I have a small amount of liquid briox, which I'll give to you and Kelly. It's faster this way, believe me. The contractions will stop within minutes, and in an hour we'll take a look but you should be closing up by then." Marie lets go of Conlan's hand to clench the cotton ball Shanley presses to her skin. Holding up a bottle of pills, he tells her, "More briox. Two of these in the morning with food, every day for the next few months. After that, the baby's going to come whether we're ready or not."

"I'm more than ready," Conlan gushes.

"You?" Marie asks with a laugh. Patting her swollen belly, she asks, "What about me?"

❦ ❦ ❦

Shanley gives Ellington another bottle of the briox. "See that Kelly gets this," he says. "You can administer the shot?"

"I've done it before," Ellington says with a nod, grateful for something to do.

"If any of the other women are dilating, let me know." Shanley hands over another hypodermic needle, still wrapped in plastic, and a package of lancets. "When you're done with the shot, I want blood samples from all those who are sick."

Ellington nods again, clasps the medical supplies in tight fists as he leaves the med lab. "I'll go with you," Parker offers, following the older man. I think this room's getting too crowded for him.

Once they're gone, Shanley pricks Marie's finger with a lancet. "I have to run some tests, doll," he tells her, "just to see what we're dealing with here." A bead of bright blood fills the tiny needle, and he presses a small square of gauze into her hand, which curls into a fist to staunch the wound. "How are you feeling?"

"Tired," Marie admits. To emphasize her point, she yawns, lying back against the pillow. Conlan smoothes the hair away from her damp brow and frowns down at her. Seeing the concern in his eyes, she tells him, "I'm not sick."

"Shauna's dead—" Conlan starts.

Marie nods as if the news doesn't surprise her. "But I'm fine," she insists. Looking up at Shanley, she watches him extract a handheld hemoscanner from his case. He slips the lancet into the data port and clicks on the scanner, which beeps to life. "Shauna didn't stay long yesterday. I'm not sick."

"I believe you," Shanley assures her, but he keeps his gaze on the scanner's display and I wonder just how bad it would look if I covered my nose and mouth? Didn't Ellington say Tobin's sick? Self-consciously, I run a hand across my face. I'm not sick either. I'm not.

Speaking to Conlan, Shanley asks, "Ben mentioned that eight others have symptoms?"

From where he sits on the edge of Marie's bed, Conlan nods. Her hand, held tight in his, rests on his thigh, and he leans back against her pillow—it's a narrow bed and there's not much room, definitely not for two people to lie together comfortably, this place was *not* designed for love, but Conlan's thin enough that he doesn't take up much space and Marie doesn't seem to mind that his shoulder leans against hers. When she closes her eyes, Conlan sinks down a little on the bed, just until he can rest his head on top of hers. "They're in quarantine," he murmurs, blinking sleepily. He looks exhausted.

Shanley doesn't answer. I wonder how awkward it would be to just back out into the corridor now—Marie's tired, she said so herself, and Conlan's worn down, they need their rest. Suddenly I'm all too aware of Dylan's hand on my hip, his arm around my waist, the fact that I haven't held him in so long, in forever it seems like, and I just want to find a dark corridor like the one last night, I just want to hug him close to me, let his hands and lips erase the memory of the cell and the threat of disease hanging over us. We don't need to be here, right? We're not *needed* here, are we?

Maybe we can slip away for a few minutes. When I turn to suggest it, though, I find Dylan staring at me with glassy eyes, as if he already has me undressed and beneath him in his mind. The heat of his gaze burns through me, ignites my blood, stirs my groin, I get hard just seeing him like this, so eager in his love, so transparent in his desire. With a coy smile, I whisper, "Are you thinking what I'm thinking?"

He grins wolfishly. "Maybe," he purrs. "But do you really think they'll have whipped cream on this ship?"

Oh God. "What?"

Before he can say anything else, the scanner in Shanley's hands beeps again. "You're clean," Shanley announces, discarding the lancet. "No virus, Marie. I suspect Shauna became infected after she stopped by here to see you."

"She seemed fine yesterday," Marie murmurs sleepily.

"It makes sense," Shanley muses aloud. "This is a filovirus, it's carried in the blood. Ben mentioned she bled heavily when she lost the baby. She could've contracted the disease then."

"How?" I want to know.

Beside me, Dylan rests his head on my shoulder, blows gently along my neck, and to be honest? It's damn near impossible to listen to Shanley when he admits, "I'm not sure yet."

"What about the others?" I press. I take a step towards the bed to get away from Dylan's insistent, mind-numbing breath on my skin, and he stumbles after me, he didn't expect me to move. His hands find my waist and pull me back to him—he doesn't want me out of reach. How long has it been since we've had a moment alone? I know that's what he's angling for, just a couple minutes together, and the more he touches me, the more *I'll* want it, that's what he's thinking, I know how his mind works. But I want to know what Shanley suspects about this virus because what if it's as contagious as everyone fears? What if *we* get it, too? "They said Tobin has it," I remind Shanley. "How did *he* get it?"

Dylan's arms tighten around me possessively. "Did he touch you?" he wants to know. "If you're sick and it's his fault, I'll tear his arms off. Which one is he again?"

"Baby," I whisper, patting Dylan's hand, "hush."

He sighs. "Neal, tell me—"

"We got in a little…argument," I say. "Nothing major, don't worry. He didn't *touch* me." *But he wanted to,* I add silently. Still, I know Dylan well enough to know that if I tell him what happened, the way Tobin came onto me, the way he touched himself while looking at me—if I told him *that*, he'd be down in the quarantine ward in two seconds, ripping every single one of those ratty curls out of the kid's head. Much as I might like to see that happen, I don't think that would be a prudent course of action right this second, seeing as how these people are finally beginning to trust us.

Well, to trust *Shanley*, at any rate. "How do you think it spreads?" I ask him, trying to move on.

"I don't know," Shanley says. I didn't ask if he *knew*, but before I can rephrase my question, he glances at his watch and tells us, "I should check on the other women. Then I want to run another ultrasound on you, pretty lady—" He touches Marie's arm, smiles down at her, and even though she nods drowsily, she manages a bright grin. Beside her Conlan's already asleep, his head still resting on hers. "I'll give it a few more minutes and then see how the briox is taking effect. In the meantime, you stay here, you hear me? No partying just yet."

Marie laughs at that. "I promise," she says softly. *Yeah, right*, I think. Like these people know what a party is.

Dylan and I follow Shanley out into the corridor. As I close the door behind me, he gives us a tired grin and says, "I don't want to get your hopes up, guys, but I'm thinking we might be in the clear."

It's hard to follow his cliché-speak, *in the clear*. Just what is he referring to? The disease? Our leaving this planet? What? Next to me, Dylan takes my hand and asks, "That's a good thing, right?"

Shanley nods, starts off down the corridor, and we fall into step beside him. "Marie doesn't have it," he explains. "Her blood came up clean on the hemoscan, which is nothing more than a tiny version of the same apparatus in the HTS. It isolates and identifies cell signatures that variate from the normal blood cells. So it pulls up all intruder cells, not just viruses—cancer, sickle cells, bacteria. She's healthy."

With a laugh, Dylan squeezes my hand. "Well, *that's* a good thing, at any rate."

"I'll need to take samples from the infected colonists," Shanley continues, "so I'll know what I'm looking for, and I'd really like to autopsy the body—that's where a lot of the answers will lie—but I have a feeling that won't be possible."

"Why not?" I ask.

Shanley smiles sadly. "They have a practice here of incinerating the dead," he says gently. "To prevent the spread of infection. Jeremy told me about it before. They probably didn't think I was coming back into the colony, or maybe they weren't really thinking at all, I don't know, but I'm sure the body's already disposed of. It would be the sensible thing for them to do."

"They incinerated her?" Dylan asks, incredulous. "This planet's a nonstop downpour. How do they get a fire started hot enough to burn their dead?"

"The ship's power supply," Shanley explains. Dylan looks at me and nods, yes, that makes sense. "It's really the best thing, I don't blame them. But if I could've at least taken a look at Shauna, it might answer a lot of questions. Like maybe how it's spread? Evidence suggests it's airborne—how else would the others get it? And so quickly?" He frowns, speaks quietly as if he's forgotten we're here and he's just thinking out loud. "But if that's the case, why hasn't *everyone* gotten it yet?"

I shrug. "Maybe they isolated it fast enough," I suggest. "Lord knows they've had enough practice in containment procedures."

But Shanley shakes his head, unconvinced. "It would've spread through the duct system like wildfire," he murmurs. "A few hours and everyone would be sick. But they aren't. *We* aren't, and we've never even had the bleed before. We should be the first ones to get it, don't you think?"

I don't want to mention Tobin again, or the fact that I might already have it, even though I feel fine. A little tired, sure. My eyes burn but that's from lack of sleep, that's all, nothing more. I'm not sick. I *can't* be.

"So now what?" Dylan wants to know. "Marie's doing well, right?" Shanley nods, and Dylan continues. "That's all you really came back here for, isn't it? Make sure she has the medicine, make sure she'll have the baby. We can leave now, can't we?"

"What if you're infected?" Shanley asks, his quiet voice low in the empty corridor.

"We're not sick—" Dylan starts.

Shanley stops and looks at us, at our hands laced together, at the fear I know he sees in our eyes. "You *might* be," he says softly. "Either of you two might be carrying the virus. What happens when we go back to the carrier? When we head back into the station?" Dixon's station isn't as large as the S410 but it easily houses almost a hundred people at any given time, technicians and pilots, there's always a ship docking in the bay, always a crew taking off to map another sector. If we're carrying something that manages to get through the decontamination procedures—if it doesn't even register on the bioscans—then we stand the chance of infecting the whole station, all the pilots passing through, anyone at all. There's no *way* we can risk that.

As that realization sets in, Shanley nods. "I have to study this thing first," he says. "Nothing too in-depth, but we have to know what this is, how it spreads, and we have to make sure none of us have it before we head offworld. And there are the other women to worry about—I have to make sure they're going to carry to term. Then there's the whole question of delivering the babies when the time comes. These colonists aren't physicians—"

"I'm not staying *that* long," Dylan replies hotly. His hand clenches mine in a tight, angry grip, and I massage his fingers, try to loosen them from mine. "I hate it here, Evan. It's a nightmare world, I get jailed because I love him?" He points my way and Shanley glances at me, forces a sympathetic grin, one that makes his lips disappear in his face. "What the hell kind of shit is that?"

"I'm not saying you have to," Shanley tells us. "But I can't just up and leave right this instant. I'd be derelict in my duties if I did—I have to think of the rest of the crew. We can't just hop on the *Semper Fi* and possibly infect everyone back at the station. Dylan, Neal, you have to see that."

"We do," I say, placing a hand on Dylan's arm to keep him quiet. "We're just not happy about it."

Like Conlan says, I think, *you have to understand.*

Part 10

Shanley leads us to the quarantine section of the med lab. I'm expecting bubble suits maybe, decontamination chambers, something more than the plain steel door with the biohazard symbol strategically placed to cover the tiny window, blocking any view of the room beyond. "This is it?" I ask, as Shanley enters a passcode into the keypad beside the door. "Didn't they change the code?"

"These locks are on a dedicated server," Shanley explains. "They have a different passcode than the others. Jeremy gave it to me the last time I came through here." He presses the *Enter* key and the door slides away to reveal a white laboratory, much like the med lab back on the carrier. Shelves stocked with medical supplies line two walls while closed doors along the back lead off to supply closets, most likely, and a low counter runs around one side of the room. Two consoles are set into the counter, and a panel above them is filled with stainless steel instruments that gleam wickedly in the bright overhead lights. Sterile, that's the word that comes to mind. I'm afraid to touch anything, afraid to even *breathe* for fear of contaminating this place.

An examining table sits in the center of the room, chrome painted white, white paper sheets spread across the top, white everywhere. As we step into the room, the door closes behind us automatically, the first time in this place that's happened. A rush of air circles around me as if the conditioning system's kicked on and I'm right beneath a vent, but Shanley sees me glance up at the ceiling and explains, "The decon cycle. It comes on any time the door opens." Now that he's said that, I can smell the antiseptic scent I've come to associate with the S410's airlock, and my hands and face tingle where a fine mist falls on my skin.

"Hop up here," Shanley says, patting the examining table. Against the white paper, his skin takes on a dark tone, almost dull, lifeless. In all this light, we pale by comparison.

The decon procedure cycles down, the whoosh of air disappears, and Dylan doesn't have to be told twice, he jumps up on the table amid a crinkle of paper and starts to play with the stirrups that protrude from one end. "What're these for?" he wants to know, so childlike, that's one of the things I love about him. So unconcerned about the fact that we're not supposed to touch anything—he pulls the stirrup right off the end of its support bar. "Oops," he mumbles, slipping it back into place.

"Stop it," I whisper, climbing up on the table beside him.

"I'm not—" he starts, and then he finds the handle of a drawer beneath the stirrups and leans over, pulls it out to see what's inside. "Hey, this stuff is cool."

"Dylan," I warn. Without looking at me, he reaches back and eases a hand up my thigh in an effort to distract me so he can rummage through the drawer without further protest. Before he gets too far, though, I knock his hand away. "You shouldn't be rooting through their stuff."

"I'm just looking," he mumbles, resting his hand on my knee.

Shanley sets his case down on a nearby counter and laughs. "Just don't break anything," he says, opening the case. He takes out the lancets again, the hemoscanner, a handful of cotton swabs. "After you asked me if I was sick—over the radio, remember?" I nod, slap Dylan's hand away from me again, it's creeping steadily up my leg. Shanley pretends he doesn't notice and when it starts up my thigh again, I pretend to ignore it. "I thought it best to run a quick hemoscan on Kitt and myself, just to make sure we weren't infected. I ran two, actually, one while we were in the air and one after we landed."

Dylan looks up from the drawer, interested in spite of himself. "And?" he prompts. He gives me a quick wink before turning his attention to Shanley. "You're not sick."

"No, we're not," Shanley agrees. "I can't imagine you are, either, but we have to make sure." Standing in front of me, he holds up a lancet and says, "Give me your hand."

My stomach churns, suddenly queasy. The needle doesn't bother me—it's just a tiny pinprick, nothing more, an instant of sharp pain that's gone the moment Shanley pulls the lancet away. But what if I *am* sick? What if Shanley's hemoscanner finds something in my blood—what then?

I don't know. When Shanley hands me a strip of cotton to staunch the blood, I curl my hand into a fist, the cotton tight in my grip, and try not to think about what I'll do if that scanner of his says I'm not in the clear. Isn't that what Shanley said? He thinks we're in the clear? *Here's hoping*, I pray.

Dylan must see the nervousness in my face, because his hand slips into mine and he tells me, "It's just a needle, babe. You've been stuck by bigger things."

And there's his wink again. I must be blushing something fierce because he smiles, a grin as bright as the white light that reflects off the walls and counters and shelves. My cheeks start to burn and thank *God* Shanley is studiously keeping his eyes downcast, he *so* did not need to know that. *Stuck by bigger things*—Dylan doesn't know the meaning of the word *uncouth*. Shanley busies himself with inserting the lancet into the hemoscanner's data port and doesn't even look our way. "Dylan," I mumble. He can embarrass me so easily.

Before I say anything else, though, he kisses my cheek with a quick peck that leaves a wet smear on my skin. "Buck up and take it like a man," he says with a laugh.

The scanner beeps. Clearing my throat, I ask, "Well?" Anything to change the subject.

"It's not finished yet," Shanley says. "Give it a chance to run through the tests."

"How long?" I want to know.

Shanley shrugs. Preparing another lancet, he tells me, "A few minutes, that's all." To Dylan, he says, "Your turn, flyboy."

Dylan holds out his hand, the one holding mine, but when Shanley frowns at him, he lets me go. "Just kidding," he says softly. Shanley doesn't respond, simply pricks Dylan's finger with the lancet. Dylan yelps, pulls his hand back quickly, almost knocking the needle from Shanley's fingers. "Hey!" he cries, wiping his hand on his pants leg. The wound leaves a small bloody smear along his thigh.

"Buck up," I tease. "You've been stuck by bigger things."

"Shut up," Dylan mutters. He sticks his finger into his mouth and glares at Shanley.

"Marie didn't carry on like this," Shanley reminds him. "She's a much better patient than you are."

"Maybe she's more man than he is," I say.

Finger still in his mouth, Dylan punches my leg and mumbles, "I said—"

The hemoscanner beeps, interrupting him. My heart begins to hammer, I can feel my heartbeat pound in the finger where Shanley drew blood. "What's it say?" I ask.

No answer. *Oh God.* I have it, I know I do, I *have* to, I just know it. Shanley stares at the display, adjusts a few controls, keys in some information, waits while the scanner processes it and why is this taking so long? I have to have it. I'm sick, that's all there is to it. I'm sick. *Fuck.*

The scanner digests Shanley's input and beeps again. "You're clean," Shanley says, finally flashing me a quick smile. "I just had to coordinate with your profile back on the carrier. Sorry if I had you worried for a second there."

Sorry? Heh. Dylan nudges me and when I look up, I find him staring at me with wide eyes as deep as the sea, his finger still in his mouth. "You okay?" he asks, the words muffled around his fist.

"Fine," I sigh. Then I laugh, relieved. "I'm fine."

And because I am, I lean over and plant a kiss on the tip of his nose, which gets him smiling. "Do it again," he says.

With another laugh, I nod at Shanley, turned from us as he slips the lancet with Dylan's blood into the hemoscanner. "When he leaves," I promise.

"Evan," Dylan starts.

"No," Shanley says before he can even ask.

Dylan pouts so hard, I have to laugh. I don't think I'll stop, I'm thrilled, I'm not sick, thank the *Lord*, I'm not sick.

Dylan's blood comes up clean, too. "Why couldn't we have done that little thing instead of the HTS last time?" he asks as Shanley puts the hemoscanner back into his case. Dylan isn't sucking on his finger any longer, but he picks at the small scab unconsciously, until the skin around it is an angry red. I smack his hand to make him stop and he rubs his palm on his leg, smiles at me, and starts picking at it again without even realizing it. "It's a much easier procedure." Then something occurs to him, and he asks, "This won't make me sick, too, will it?"

"It shouldn't," Shanley tells him. "Though the way you carried on..." He lets the thought trail off and when he glances at me, I have to grin at the mischievous glint I see in his eye.

"What?" Dylan asks, confused. He looks from Shanley to me, sees my grin before it slips away, and says, "It *was* an easier process. You can't tell me—"

I lean towards him until our shoulders touch, stare up at him with that look, the one with the hooded eyes and the slightly parted lips that I know does terrible things to him, and his words dry up. He watches, fascinated, as I let just the tip of my tongue peek out to curl over the front of my teeth. "We're picking on you," I tell him, lowering my already low voice until I sound like I want him, I want *only* him, and nothing's going to hold me back. It's a voice I've perfected, because I like the effect it has on him.

Like now. His jaw hangs down, slack, and when he swallows, I can hear a hollow click deep in his throat. "Neal," he whispers, breathless, and then, without taking his eyes off me, he raises his voice to include Shanley. "So are you about done here, Evan? Or what?"

Shanley snaps his case shut. "I'm done," he declares.

I glance over at him and Dylan sighs, the spell broken. "Can you leave, then?" he asks. "Not to sound rude or anything—"

"Oh no," I say, shaking my head, "never."

Another sigh. Then Dylan slips off the table, drapes a brotherly arm around Shanley's shoulders, leads him over to the door. "Evan, listen, really," he says, watching Shanley enter the passcode for the door. "I don't mean it like *that*."

And that's all I hear before the door opens and they're out in the hall, Dylan leading Shanley away. He'll talk frankly, I know how he is, speak of need and lust and desire, so open about what he wants that I'm sure Shanley's going to say he'll leave us alone for a little while just so he won't have to hear it. *You know how guys are,* Dylan will say—I've heard him tell Tony the same thing, when he was trying to get him to leave the two of us alone for a few minutes. *And you have to admit, my boy is fine. Don't you think he's fine? Nice ass, big hands, strong arms—you have to have noticed.*

Shanley will shrug or mutter something incoherent, because Dylan doesn't want anyone to actually *agree* with him on that, he doesn't want another man looking at me and wondering what I would feel like in his embrace, beneath his body. He's jealous like that. And Shanley strikes me as the sensible type, he'll say something noncommittal, he's a smart one. *How long have we been on this planet?* Dylan will want to know. When Shanley tells him—I have the feeling he's the sort to say something along the lines of thirty-one hours, eleven minutes, twenty-three seconds and counting—when he tells him that, Dylan will say, *I can't live without him. I've gone long enough as it is. Thirty-one hours? I'm surprised I'm still breathing.*

Of course, he'll forget the two months we spent apart because he let Dixon convince him it would be for the best. Silly boy. I'm not going to let him do that to us again—when this is over with and we head back to the station, I'm going to tell him straight up, I'm happier with him, no matter how far away he is. If I go to bed alone, I want to know that he's out there somewhere dreaming of me, I want to know that he's looking forward to coming back to me, I want to know he's mine. Fuck Dixon. If he tries to talk Dylan into thinking we're better off apart...well, I just won't let him. That's all there is to it.

As I look around the sterile room, I almost hear Dylan's voice, seductive, convincing, urgent. *Evan, listen, really, what do you say? An hour, that's it. Make your rounds, do what you need to do, and let me have some downtime with my boy, what'll it hurt? Just some quality time, that's all I'm asking for here, that's it.*

And he'll come back and say, *We have to make this quick, babe,* but he's right, it *has* been a long time since we got together—those few stolen moments in the dark serviceway last night seem like eons ago. This isn't exactly the most ideal place to get a piece of him, though, even if it *is* clean and sterile and dry. That's the whole problem—it's *too* clean, *too* sterile, almost stale. In a room like this one doesn't make love, one has intercourse, and it's just a biological function, an act to continue the species, there's nothing emotional about it. I want more than just sex. I want him holding me tight, murmuring my name into my neck, moaning he loves me when he comes.

Looking around, I notice the row of doors along the wall behind me—closets, most likely, full of supplies, or maybe additional examining rooms, someplace where we can close the door and not have to worry about anyone walking in on us, someone like Shanley or God, heaven forbid, Ellington. I don't even want to *think* about that one. Jumping down from the table, I wonder if the doors are locked.

They aren't. There are no numbers on the keypads for these doors, just an *Enter* key, and when I press the first one, the door opens to reveal row after row of shelving units, stretched from floor to ceiling, stacked with bandages and medicines, scanner replacement parts, rubber gloves, needles, pills and bottles and vials, a regular pharmacy. The next door hides the same thing, supply closets, just as I thought. If they're *all* storage space, we'll just have to take our chances out here in the main room, despite the harsh lighting and the threat of discovery.

Luckily the next door is some sort of diagnosis room, but it has the same hard light, the same flawless surfaces, the same uncomfortable examination table set up against one wall. If we have to use this room, I guess it'll do, but we'll have to do it standing up—I'm not going to listen to that paper covering crackle in my ear with each thrust, that'll kill the mood right there. Next.

Another diagnosis room, an X-ray lab on the other side of that, another supply closet, and I'm thinking Dylan's going to be back any second now, ready for action, and I'm going to have to just take what I can get when the next door slides open onto a dimly lit bedroom. Soft, golden light comes from a single lamp beside a full-size bed, a *bed*, not a bunk or a table covered in plastic but a mattress and box spring and headboards, a comforter tucked in above a ruffled skirt, pillows that just beg to be slept on. It's so out of place in this sterile environment, so unexpected, that I don't even realize I've entered the room until I'm sinking down onto the firm mattress, tentative, like this might just be a holodeck and not real. But it *is* real—the pillows are cold against my cheek, the sheets smooth when I pull the comforter back and slip beneath it, the blankets a welcome weight that quickly warms to my body. When I close my eyes, everything washes away, everything disappears, the colony and the bleed and the jail, gone. Vaguely I remember Conlan mentioning rooms like this, though when he spoke of restricting sexual pleasures to a quarantined lab, I had envisioned something like the room beyond, something sterile, something utilitarian. I imagined men pacing the corridors, waiting for their girls to cycle just right, then the two of them coming together in a passionless fuck, rolling away from each other when it was through, dressing without meeting each other's eyes, she wouldn't even bother to fake an orgasm.

But rooms like *this*, with the soft bed, soft light, quiet and hidden from view, *these* rooms speak of a capacity for love, not just sex but something more, an emotion they've managed to dampen like the flames of a fire but haven't quite extinguished completely. Something *real*, and I can picture Conlan nervously taking Marie's hand, leading her to a place like this, standing above her awkwardly because he's not quite sure what to do. I can see her comforting smile, I can almost hear her whisper *it's okay*, and maybe they just laid together the first time, heads side by side on one pillow as they cuddled beneath the covers and talked in low voices. Ellington would be outside, tapping one foot anxiously, waiting, waiting, thinking only of the future and babies and moving on, while inside the two friends would giggle for hours, time would stop, nothing would matter and maybe, just maybe, Marie would let Conlan give her a kiss when their time was up.

In this room there is no future, no past, nothing but here, now, the cool pillow warming beneath my head, the warm blanket like a heavy hand above me, gentle and kind. *This* is where I want Dylan to love me, *here*, and somewhere between thinking of Conlan's blush the first time he brought his girl to a room like this and how beautiful my boy's going to look pressed naked against these sheets, I give into the exhaustion from all the excitement and rush of the past few hours and fall asleep.

🍁   🍁   🍁

A faint touch on my cheek, half-imagined, like a dream. Fingers feathered through my hair, warm lips soft on mine, a mouth insistent, a tongue probing, gentle, slipping into me with the familiar ease of a long-time lover. Deeper, hungrier, sure hands on my shoulders, laying me back. My shirt smoothed up, strong hands on my chest, nimble fingers tickling over my muscles, my stomach, fumbling below the waistband of my pants, moving lower. Lower. A moan lost in me, my name murmured like a prayer, kisses trailed over the slight growth of hair along my jaw, damp lips closing over my earlobe. The hand below my waist now, lower, cupping an erection already straining my boxers, a breathy laugh, a quick kiss on my ear, and the hand encircles me through the fabric of my shorts, kneads with a slow rhythm. The distant *pop pop* of snaps, followed by the low rasp of skin on skin, the blanket brushing across the tip of my cock. My name again, whispered, and then, "Wake up, baby."

Dylan. I stretch beneath him, open my eyes, and there he is above me, the lamplight spinning the hair that frames his face with burnished gold, a halo surrounding his sparkling eyes, his angelic grin. "I'm up," I mumble with a yawn—how long did I sleep? I feel renewed, ready to take on the world, my blood racing through my veins at the speed of light, but I doubt the short nap had anything to do with *that*. I think most of my sudden wakefulness stems from Dylan's hand rubbing the base of my dick, his fingers tracing small patterns into the soft skin of my balls. *That* has my whole body humming and alive, let me tell you.

Dylan's grin widens, if that's possible. "I know you're *up*," he says, giving me a squeeze that sends a burst of excitement through my groin. "We have about a half hour."

"That's all?" The words are out before I can stop them, and Dylan leers at me—who needs thirty minutes? I'm already halfway there.

"No interruptions," Dylan tells me, punctuating each word with a kiss. "Evan promised."

See? I think, triumphant. I knew he walked Shanley out just to ensure we got some time alone. *Told you so.* God, I know him so well. "Sit back," I say, and when he does, I scoot over, hold the comforter up to expose the sheets, and pat the bed beside me. "Here."

That leer again. Standing, he pulls his shirt up over his head, tosses it aside. Then he shucks off the pants he wears, kicks them away, hooks his thumbs into his boxers and takes them off, as well. He's already hard for me, thick red skin poking up from the patch of curls where his legs meet, and I can't keep from reaching for him as he slides between the sheets. My hand comes away slightly damp. "I want you," he breathes, lying down beside me. He props his head up on one hand and gives me a smoldering look I can't hope to resist. "Come here."

But we're alone. The door is shut, the rest of the colony is locked away, nothing else exists but me and him and we're not going to rush through this. I want him too much. So I stretch languidly, muscle by muscle, like a cat—my arms above me, my legs reaching for the foot of the bed. My shirt's still up, my pants down, the waistband biting below my balls with a sweet pressure, my hard length cool against my fevered skin. I arch away from the bed and watch Dylan's eyes widen. "You come here," I murmur.

I barely get the words out before he's crawling onto me, all hands and kisses. Somehow he manages to get my shirt off without seeming to remove his lips from mine, and my pants are gone, lost somewhere beneath the covers at the foot of the bed. "Neal," he sighs, his mouth on the hollow of my throat, my nipples, my belly button. His tongue trails along my erection, around my scrotum, over hidden flesh. He licks into me until I arch against him, and his hands cradle my buttocks, pull me to him. When he takes me into his mouth, I gasp his name and fist my hands into the sheets, his tongue swirling down around me, he's so hot, so soft, so wet and amazing and I thrust into him, once, twice, forever.

I come in a heady rush that leaves me trembling, but he's a gentle lover, he holds me tight until my heart stops its wild beating, whispers he loves me, he wants me, he needs me. *Me.* He's tender when he enters me, kissing my eyelids to wipe away the discomfort, easing into me as far as he can. I take him in completely, so tight I have to sink my teeth into the fleshy muscle of his shoulder to keep from crying out too loud. He moves in me with long, slow thrusts, and when he tries to speed up, I hold back, tighten my muscles, keep him in me until he's throbbing for release and I'm hard again between us. He fills me, in me and above me and all around me, whispering he loves me, sighing my name, thrusting into me over and over until he can't hold it any longer and he comes in a hot rush that burns through me, ignites my skin, sets the world aflame.

❦   ❦   ❦

"I love you," he whispers. We lie together, the sheets tangled around our legs, his arms around me and my body backed up against his. He laces his fingers through mine, hugs me tight, my arms crossed over my chest. He's draped around me like an expensive coat, wonderful and warm, mine. All mine.

I turn so I can press my lips to his chin, stubbly and unshaven—the hair's so light that I can only see it now, this close, it shimmers in the lamplight. "Dylan," I sigh. The way I say it brings a goofy grin to his face. "Love you, too."

He rests his head against my shoulder. "What time is it?" he asks.

As if I know. I hold up an arm to show him my bare wrist. "What time do you want it to be?"

That makes him laugh. He's so cute right after sex, all giggles and love talk, he's one of those guys who actually *likes* to snuggle up afterwards, he holds onto me and doesn't want to let go.

Only Shanley will be back soon and then this moment will shatter. We'll have to let the colony back in, and Conlan, and Ellington, and Shanley, Parker, the *Semper Fi*, the carrier and its crew and the station and *its* crew, and then Dylan will get back to his mission and I'll be back by myself, alone. Well, not *completely* alone. I raise one of his hands to my lips, kiss his knuckles, and tell him, "When we leave this place, you're going to radio in every night during my shift."

"I will," he promises. "You'll have to turn the backup off, though. I don't want Dixon hearing our dirty talk."

I don't think that'll go over too well. Knowing Dixon, he'll be watching over my shoulder every step of the way, and the minute I turn the backups off again, he'll have me pulled from the nav deck. *That* won't be good. "You'll just have to keep it clean," I joke.

Dylan grimaces. "Now you're starting to sound like *them*," he says with a laugh. I know who he means, the colonists. When I start to protest, he covers my mouth with his hand to quiet me. "I have to get you out of here. They're starting to rub off on you."

"They are not," I say. My words are muffled beneath his hand. "Dylan—"

"Shh." He raises his hand just enough so that he can kiss me, and then he lowers it, covering my lips again. Crawling on top of me, he says, "No talking. Just love me again."

Again. But this time we don't get very far—he's licking along my collarbone when someone knocks on the door. "I guess our half hour is up," I sigh.

He groans and rests his head on my shoulder, his breath fanning along my neck. "Go away," he calls out. I wrap my arms around his waist and pray whoever it is on the other side of that door listens to him, just this once. *Please.*

No such luck. The knock comes again, this time followed by Parker's voice. "I know you guys are in there," he says.

Dylan giggles against my neck. "No shit," he murmurs.

"Two seconds," Parker threatens, "and then I'm going to open this door and drag your naked asses out of that bunk. One—"

"Don't you dare!" Dylan cries, stumbling from the bed. Stepping into his pants, he pulls them up, hiding smooth, gilded skin. "You open that door, I'm gonna hurt you."

I kick back the blankets, find my own pants, lie down and slip into them. "He's just kidding," I say. Dylan should know by now that Parker likes to pick on him. He rises to a fight so easily, Parker can't *help* it.

But when I reach for my shirt, discarded on the floor, the door hisses open and Parker comes into the room, Ellington right behind him. "You *guys*! I didn't think you were *really*—" He doesn't finish, just covers his eyes and back-pedals out of the room, pushing Ellington out, as well. "God, my eyes," he moans. "I *so* did not need to see you in the buff, Dylan. I'm scarred for life."

"Shut up," Dylan scowls, tugging his shirt on roughly. He glances at me to make sure I'm dressed—I have my shirt on my arms and in another second it's over my head, I flatten it down over my stomach. "Was he checking you out?" he wants to know. His Mr. Hyde personality taking over, jealous because Parker might have seen my nipples. "I really *will* scar him for life."

Twisting one of the thin sheets up in my hands, I snap his butt with it. "Stop it," I say. He laughs and dances out of reach.

From the main room, Parker calls out, "Are you two decent yet?"

Climbing out of bed, I root for my slipper shoes, hidden in the folds of the sheets, and holler, "I am, but I don't know how decent Dylan is—"

"Hey!" Here comes that pout, the one I think is too damn cute for words, and I lean across the bed, snag a handful of his shirt, pull him back for a quick kiss. "Don't be mean," he tells me.

"I won't," I promise.

Parker peeks into the room as we kiss again, and he sighs dramatically. "I thought you said you were through."

I laugh. "I thought we were," Dylan purrs, one knee already on the bed. He's ready for more.

"We are," I tell them. Dylan pouts harder, if that's possible. "Later," I promise him. *Later.*

Like back on the *Semper Fi.* We'll be there soon enough, right? If Shanley's finished his rounds and none of us are infected, that just leaves the signal to talk about and how much longer do we need to stay here anyway?

🍁 🍁 🍁

"You're interrupting us," Dylan announces when we step into the main room.

Parker's stretched out along the examining table, hands laced behind his head, already dozing, and Ellington glares at us from where he leans against the counter, his arms crossed in front of his chest, a closed look on his face. He's thinking he'll have to sanitize that room now, I can almost see him spraying it down when we're finally gone. I have a feeling he's going to lay into us about having sex and I already have a reply ready for him. *It's called love when we do it, but you wouldn't know about that, would you? Why don't you ask Conlan if he understands the concept?* But before either of us can say a word, Dylan gives Parker a hard shove off the table and asks, "Well? What's so damn important that you had to go bust up our party for?"

Parker rolls away from him, landing on the floor nimbly like a cat. At Dylan's angry scowl, he laughs. "Looks like we just came in at the end."

"That's not the point," Dylan tells him, leaning on the examining table as if he's about to climb over it and go for Parker's throat, just because he interrupted us. Parker's right, we *were* done, though another round would've been nice.

I cross my arms like Ellington does and lean against the counter at the far end, where I can watch his face and jump in if he says anything hateful. Yeah, he might be letting Conlan run the show now, but I can tell he still doesn't like us, doesn't like *me*, and I don't want him saying shit to Dylan that'll mess up the already strained relations we have with this colony. Like it or not, once we're off this rock and back at the station, we're their neighbors for the next five years or so, however long it takes to map this sector, and the last thing I need is Dixon riding my ass because Ellington here doesn't like the fact that Dylan and I are together. In love. Heh, maybe he's just resentful I'm getting some and he's not.

Whatever his reasons, he's not talking, at least there's that. Maybe he's just tired of this, we all are, he just wants it to be over with already, and I understand *that* completely. Parker, on the other hand, is all about teasing Dylan, and it's quite cute to see the consternation that flickers across my lover's face when the other pilot asks him, "What *is* the point?"

"The point is," Dylan starts, and when he glances at me, I know he doesn't have a clue what he's going to say. He's the type to talk first, figure out what he said later, like that whole *I want you happy* stint he pulled when he left for this mission two months back. But he's quick on his feet, I'll give him that. "The point is that Evan said we could have a half hour—"

"Time's up," Parker says. He laughs when Dylan frowns at him. "Contrary to popular belief, though, it ain't you I came looking for." He turns to me and asks, "Where *is* the good doctor, anyway?"

With a shrug, I tell him, "I'm not sure. He brought us here to run a check on our blood—"

"And?" Ellington asks, eager for the answer.

I knew he would be. "We're clean," I say, smug. I give him a withering look and almost say something more, something along the lines of *I told you so*, but I'm better than that. I just add, "No infection," and drop the subject.

He nods but doesn't apologize for locking us up, for keeping our crew out, for anything he said or did over the past few hours. Maybe he thinks that halfhearted *I'm sorry* back in the corridor sufficed. He doesn't strike me as the overly contrite type.

Parker asks, "Then where'd he go?" He's still talking about Shanley.

Dylan answers. "You guys distributed the briox, right?" When Parker nods, Dylan tells us, "He said he was heading to the sick bay. I'm not sure where that is—"

"I know," Ellington says. He pushes away from the counter, heads over to the door. Parker follows him, but Dylan doesn't make a move—I know what he's thinking, if they leave we can pick up where we left off, it's written all over his face. At the door, though, Ellington glances over his shoulder at us. "Well?" he asks. "Come on."

Dylan sighs dramatically. "Do we *have* to?" he wants to know, but he lets me take his hand and lead him out into the corridor.

The infected colonists are housed in another section of the quarantine lab, not far from the room where Shanley left us. Two long, low windows are cut into either wall, facing each other, and Ellington stops, shoves his hands into the pockets of his pants, nods at the room beyond the glass on the left. "Sick bay," he says, his voice awed. "I don't think it's a good idea to go much further."

On the other side of the window, a series of beds stretch out of view, only a few of them occupied. Chairs are scattered around one end of the room and there's a small table stacked with vid-disks and gamepaks, even one or two print magazines, imagine that. And there's Holly, the pretty girl with the blonde curls from the committee, lying on her side on one of the beds, staring listlessly at the window, at the glass and not through it, not seeing us. Another colonist on another bed with her back to us, I can't see her face but I know it's a woman by the curve of her hips. Tobin sits in one of the chairs—I'd recognize him anywhere, that nappy ragtag hair of his a spray that hides his face—he's hunkered into himself, and as we watch he starts to cough. We can't hear it through the window but I can see his skin turn a mottled red, he doubles over with the spasm, pushes the hair from his eyes and for a split second my heart twists in sympathy. Then I remember the way he touched himself outside my cell, the way he rubbed up against the bars, and I turn away in disgust. I don't want to think this serves him right, that's a mean thing to wish on anyone, but what did he call me? *Fucking queer.* Maybe this disease is too good for him.

Dylan's hand slips into mine. "You okay, babe?" he asks, concern haunting his dark eyes.

I nod. "Fine," I mumble.

Suddenly there's a tapping on the window behind us, and we turn to see Shanley, knocking on the glass. The room he's in is a laboratory, that much is clear—monitors line the walls above counters laden with microscopes and various medical equipment, instruments that I can't even pretend to understand. I'm just a navigator, my expertise lies in coordinates and star maps, not this field of research.

But Shanley's in his element. He's wearing biohazard gear over his jumpsuit, which makes him look like he just came onboard after a quick space walk, a thin atmosphere suit with sealed gloves, boot protectors, the whole works—a large hood even covers his head, and from what we can see through the Plexiglas visor, he's taken the added precaution of wearing a surgeon's mask over his nose and mouth. "Hey!" Dylan shouts, crossing the corridor. He laughs as he bangs on the window, hitting the glass hard enough that Shanley jumps back. "Is all that really necessary?"

"I don't think he can hear you," I tell him. When he raises his fist to knock on the glass again, I catch his arm and pull him back. The last thing we need is Hercules here tearing apart the quarantine lab.

Shanley points at his hood, then down the corridor to a door I hadn't noticed before. His actions are easy enough to read—*I'll be right out.* "Knock the window down, Teague," Parker growls.

"Shut up." Dylan glares at Parker and crosses his arms, my hand trapped in the fold of his elbow. When I try to extract it, though, he covers my fingers with his and murmurs, "Don't."

The door opens with an almost imperceptible *whoosh* and I can smell the clean air of a decon cycle billow out into the corridor. Footsteps ring off the steel floor and as we turn, Shanley says, "I've been wondering when you guys were going to show up."

He's out of the biohazard getup now, wearing his jumpsuit with the station's logo embroidered across his left breast. "I liked your other costume," Dylan says.

"It's just a precaution," Shanley tells us. "I'm running some tests on infected cells and it's better to be safe than sorry, you know?"

A Shanley-ism if I've ever heard one. To Ellington, he asks, "Well? How did the injections go?"

Ellington digs the empty bottle of briox out of his pocket. "Good," he says with a frown—the guy is *always* frowning. He hands the bottle over to Shanley, careful not to actually touch the med tech, as if he believes whatever the colonists in the sick bay have, he might be carrying. Shanley doesn't seem to notice, just palms the bottle and nods. Gesturing at the lab beyond the window, Ellington asks, "You think all that's going to keep you safe?"

"I'm not sick," Shanley assures him. "And I have a feeling I'm not *going* to get sick." He looks at Parker, Dylan, me. "None of us are."

"You can't be so sure—" Ellington starts, but Shanley cuts him off.

"I haven't had a chance to really study the virus yet," he says. He looks across the hall into the other room, at the patients beyond, as if he's talking to them and not us. "But from what I've seen, I can tell you a little about it. It's a filovirus, like I suspected. Obviously airborne, this strain. The girl who was with Shauna when she miscarried, Alison? She says they were in the crash sector yesterday, on a routine systems check."

Ellington closes his eyes and sighs. "Shit," he murmurs. "I forgot about that."

"About what?" Dylan wants to know.

Ellington shakes his head, a despairing motion that almost makes me want to pat him on the shoulder, tell him it's okay, it's going to be alright. If Shanley knows what the virus is, he can treat it, right? The pregnant women are doing well now, right? So everything's going to be fine. "We run a systems check on the S410 every five weeks," Ellington explains, "just to see how the rest of the ship's holding up. Shauna was scheduled this time but we have strict laws here, you know that."

"Don't we, though," Dylan mutters under his breath. I squeeze his hand in mine to quiet him.

With an annoyed glance his way, Ellington continues. "Pregnant women are exempt from colony duties. She was supposed to find a replacement for her task. If I had known she'd gone…" He trails off, doesn't say what it was he would've done if he knew, but I get the impression it would've been something akin to throwing us in jail, and maybe that's why no one told him she had left the colony after she got sick.

"Regardless," Shanley says, "she went, and Alison says that at one point Shauna got dizzy and couldn't see straight. She wanted to sit down for a few minutes and rest. She said she would be fine."

"But?" Parker asks. "Apparently she wasn't."

Shanley frowns at the empty briox bottle in his hands, thoughtful. "They wear biohazard suits when they do these checks, don't they? Like the one I had on just now."

Ellington nods. "They're mandatory in the upper levels of the ship."

"Alison told me that Shauna took her hood off," Shanley says softly. "She was having difficulty breathing. This was near the crash site—"

"The what?" I ask, looking from Shanley to Ellington. "Where's this crash site?"

"Where the meteor hit," Ellington whispers. *Now* I remember, the meteor that killed some of the colonists twenty years ago, the crash that forced the S410 to land here in the first place. Incredulous, Ellington asks, "You're saying the virus is still up there? After all this time?"

Shanley shrugs. "It's a possibility," he admits. "I'm not sure how long the pathogen can stay viable, but it *does* have a hard protein coating, sort of a protective shell, that allows it to live in the air between hosts. You said everyone in the colony now was exposed to a non-lethal respiratory form of the virus as children—"

"We were all sick," Ellington confirms.

"This is obviously airborne," Shanley says, "and it infects the lungs first with almost flu-like symptoms, so it's definitely a respiratory disease. The thing is, it kills like the bleed, so I can only assume this is a mutated strain. Since we haven't gotten it—" he motions with one hand, including Parker, Dylan, and me in that statement—"I'm thinking it might just attack someone with antibodies to the original strain. So any of the colonists are susceptible to it."

Ellington pinches the bridge of his nose, as he tends to do when things are getting out of control, and he murmurs, "Fuck. Now what?"

"I have to study it more," Shanley tells him. Beside me, Dylan sighs. *I know, baby,* I think—researching the virus means staying here longer and neither of us wants that. "I've started them on a combination of adenosine and rifavir, which I'm hoping will inhibit the virus before it gets to the bleed out stage. I think we should put everyone else on the adenosine, though, just to cover all bases. That should keep the virus from replicating if they're exposed." He forces a compassionate smile, one Ellington can't return. "It's the best I can do at this point," he says softly. "Hopefully it'll be enough."

"And if it's not?" Ellington wants to know.

"Then I'll have to find something that works," Shanley says with a grim determination that I've never seen in him before. "I'm not going to give up here, Ben. So I don't want you to, either, you hear me?"

Ellington nods but it's not a convincing gesture. I just hope Shanley's right. I hope these pills he has, this research he's doing, *is* enough.

※ ※ ※

Marie's already awake when we enter her room—Conlan rests against her chest and she brushes the hair back from his brow, runs her fingers through the long, dark waves. She smiles at us and in a low whisper tells Shanley, "The baby's quieted down a lot since you left."

"That's to be expected," Shanley assures her. He sets up the ultrasound again but when he goes to pull up her shirt, Conlan is in the way. "Can you move him over a bit?"

"I'm up," Conlan replies, groggy. Sitting up, he stretches until I'm sure his arms will reach the wall behind him, his shirt pulling up to expose smooth, pale flesh and hip bones that poke against his pants at odd angles. That kid's nothing but bones. A night with him and Marie probably comes away bruised and sore.

Now when Shanley points out Marie's cervix on the monitor, I can see that it's begun to contract. It's not quite a perfect C-shape any longer, but more like one of those spoon bracelets that come in and out of fashion—the ends are drawing together, tightening, and that's a good thing, right? Conlan, awake now and still holding Marie's hand, chokes up when he sees the faint outline of the baby inside her. "So it's going to live," he sighs.

"I can't guarantee that," Shanley cautions them. "There's still the virus to contend with—the baby will have antibodies, so he'll be at risk for the new strain. And then there's the whole issue of actually giving *birth*. I'm not sure how your facilities are set up here—that might bring more complications further on down the line. I won't lie to you," he adds. "It's going to be touch and go for the next few months."

"What are the chances?" Marie asks. There's a quiet strength in her voice that makes Conlan sink down beside her on the bed.

"Honestly?" Shanley asks, with a glance at the rest of us, Dylan and me and Parker and Ellington, all crammed into one corner of the room, trying to be as unobtrusive as possible. Conlan watches Shanley closely, almost holding his breath, clutches Marie's hand so tight, her fingertips have gone white. She puts on a brave smile for them both, rubs Conlan's hand between hers, looks up as Shanley smiles and tells them, "His chances are better than they were an hour ago. When the cervix closes completely, they'll be a hundred times better than they were yesterday. And when—"

"His?" Conlan interrupts. He looks at us, at Marie, back at Shanley, hope shining in his eyes. "It's a boy?" Grinning, Shanley nods, and Conlan trips over himself when he stands, trying to see the monitor. "How can you tell?"

Marie sits up as Shanley points to the monitor, and Conlan blocks our view of the baby, leaning over the bed to see. "A boy," Marie laughs, clapping her hands together, such a happy sound, it lights up the whole room. Part of me wishes she didn't have to go through this, any of it—I wish she had been on the committee when we first made contact with the colony, I wish she had been one of the first people we met when we landed. Because then I'm sure none of this would have happened the way it did, the mistrust, the arrest, the lockdown. She would've told Ellington to loosen up, she'd have brought that smitten grin to Conlan's face. She brightens this whole place with that laugh, that smile, and I know I could've fallen in love with this colony from the start, if only we had met her first.

I don't realize how late it is until Ellington suggests we might want to head up to the sleeping quarters. He chases us out of Marie's room and into the corridor, and now he stares at the floor awkwardly, shuffles his feet, doesn't look us in the eye when he mumbles, "You know how it is. With the virus, a lot of people are scared, you can appreciate that. So I don't really think it'd be a good idea if you two…" He trails off, unsure of how to continue. I know what he's going to say. He doesn't want Dylan and me sharing a bed again. Hell, after what happened last time? I'm a little leery of it, myself.

"I know—" I start, but Dylan squeezes my hand almost painfully, he doesn't want to make this easy for Ellington, not after what he put us through. I fall silent.

"Maybe you two can stay on the *Semper Fi*," Parker suggests. He shrugs like it's no concern of his one way or the other and looks around the corridor. He wants to get some sleep.

But Ellington shakes his head, big surprise there. "I don't think that's such a good idea, either," he says. *No, you wouldn't.*

"Maybe that quarantine room," Dylan suggests. He leers at me like he hopes I'll get his drift, and in his eyes I can see the memory of the two of us earlier, writhing in passion beneath the thick comforter, him above me, pressing me back against the sheets. Now *that's* not such a bad idea—

Before Ellington can say no, the door to Marie's door opens and Shanley comes out, followed by Conlan, who still has a glassy look of disbelief written all over his face. "She asleep?" Ellington asks.

"Getting there," Conlan tells him. He can't seem to stop smiling, he grins at me and Dylan, at Parker, at Ellington like he wants to kiss him, he's so damn happy. *This is what the rest of you need,* I think, looking between Conlan and his dour friend. *Something to look forward to, someone to love. What good's the future if it's not worth living?* But maybe Ellington was right, maybe Conlan *is* the future, and he's going to teach the others how to love again, how to live as families again, how to grow up.

"The quarantine room," Dylan whispers to me, tugging at my hand.

"I don't—" Ellington begins.

Don't say it, I pray. "I want to radio the carrier," I announce, interrupting him so I don't have to hear his words, his *no, that's not going to work,* his *you have to understand.*

"It's late," Parker tells me, like I don't realize this.

I shrug. "I know. But someone's got to be on the nav deck." I smile at Dylan and tell him, "Maybe we can start mapping the signal's frequency. It'll get us out of here a lot sooner." He's still not convinced, so I add, "We should at least let them know how things are going down here."

"Not very well," Dylan mutters. I squeeze his hand in sympathy, *I know.*

Ellington shakes his head. "Can't this wait til morning? You can do the mapping then and be on your way—"

"I'll take them to the comm center," Conlan says. He bounds down the corridor—actually *bounds,* as if he's suddenly so full of energy that he doesn't know what do to with himself. I have a feeling that if he tries to sleep, he'll be like a kid on Christmas Eve, too damn excited to close his eyes. And he's got five more months of this? Poor Marie.

"Jeremy," Ellington warns, but it's too late. Conlan's already halfway down the corridor, and with a quick grin my way, Dylan pulls me along after him, Shanley following behind us. "Great," Ellington mutters.

"Well shit," Parker drawls. "I'm going to bed."

"You do that," Dylan calls out. We have to hurry to keep up with Conlan, he's walking so fast, practically sprinting for the commons. When the others are out of sight, Dylan lets go of my hand, jogs up next to our guide, asks, "Do you think we can maybe stay in that quarantine room tonight? Just Neal and me, you understand—"

"Dylan!" I laugh, surprised at his audacity. He glances over his shoulder at me, flashes that disarming smile of his. "No."

"I didn't ask you," he says, sticking his tongue out at me playfully.

Beside me, Shanley asks, "How old is he again?"

I laugh in reply. Dylan has such a childish streak in him, that ego of his, that stubbornness, that jealous nature. And he's like a teenager with his single-minded determination to get me alone and naked at any opportunity, a gangly boy in a man's body—thank God for *that*, and his strong arms, his sure hands, his hard muscles. I love him just the way he is, childlike, wonderful, amazing. *Mine.*

Dylan takes Conlan's arm, leads him on ahead, and I can almost hear the words he's whispering so low. *You know how it is, when you want some time alone with Marie? What say you talk to your friend, see if he can't bend the rules just this once, okay? It's the least he can do after all that shit he's put us through, you know?*

With a sigh, I glance at Shanley and shake my head, the hint of a smile toying at the corners of my mouth. Only Shanley's not right beside me anymore, he's hanging back, and I slow down to let him catch up with me. "Everything okay?" I ask. From the look on his face, I have my doubts.

"I've been thinking," he tells me, and the way he says it suggests that whatever it is has been eating at him for a while now. Shoving his hands deep into the pockets of his jumpsuit, he says, "These people aren't qualified physicians, Neal. The briox will help, true, but so many things can go wrong during delivery. What'll they do if it's a breech birth? What happens if Marie starts hemorrhaging? What if she has complications?"

"I don't know," I admit. Truth be told, I hadn't even really given it much thought.

"Then there's the virus," Shanley continues, as if I haven't spoken. "The adenosine will only work for so long. It treats the symptoms, not the bug itself. What the colonists need is a doctor here who can research the bleed, trace it down to the source, find out how it works and *then* get it under control. What they need—"

"Is you." I stop and turn to him, watch the indecision play across his features. He's exactly what this place needs. "They wanted you down here from the start," I tell him. "Conlan fought to get us in here just because of you."

Shanley sighs. "Rick's not going to like it—"

"*Fuck* Dixon!" I shout, angry.

Ahead of us, Conlan's step falters and Dylan glances back at us, frowning. "Neal," Shanley warns.

"These people need you," I say. "We're not talking forever here, just a few years. This colony's close enough to the station that we can jaunt over and pick you up when the sector's mapped. We have other med techs, Shanley. These people have no one, you've said it yourself."

"I know," he concedes, his quiet voice softer than usual.

"Do you want to stay here?" I ask him, curious.

He shrugs. "They need—"

I cut him off. "What is it *you* need?"

He doesn't answer right away. Instead he glances down the corridor, thoughtful. Dylan and Conlan are already out in the commons, stopping now to wait for us, Conlan shaking his head. *I don't know*, he's saying, I can hear the words by the shape his mouth makes. Tentatively I touch Shanley's shoulder, bringing his attention back to me. "Evan?" I ask. When he turns, I add, "What do you want to do?"

"I want—I *need* to stay here." There's a conviction in his voice that I haven't heard before, a sense of purpose maybe, a sense of destiny. What needs to be done. What he wants to do.

Smiling, I clap him on the back. "Then fuck Dixon," I say with a laugh. "You do what you need to do."

Outside the comm center, Dylan grabs my elbow, pulls me back from the door to let Conlan and Shanley enter. "What was that all about?" he wants to know.

With a nonchalant shrug, I tease, "He wants to know if we can do a threesome tonight. Did you get the room?"

The look on Dylan's face is priceless—his eyes go wide, his jaw drops, and I don't know if he wants to laugh or cry. Then his eyes harden, his mouth turns down into that determined scowl, and he starts towards the door after the others. "That fucker—"

"Dylan!" I catch his arm before he can disappear into the comm center and kick Shanley's ass. "Baby, jeez, I'm just kidding."

Now comes the confusion—he's so predictable. "What?" he asks, as if I've never joked with him before. He always takes me so seriously, I love that he puts that much trust in me. "Neal—"

"Kidding," I tell him, and then I kiss his mouth quickly, before he can react. I don't usually get a little kiss like that—he clues in two seconds before my lips touch his and then he's all over me, pushing me up against the nearest wall, licking into me with an insatiable desire that makes me weak to think about it. All that lust, all that emotion, for me. I love him. "I'm just playing with you."

"Kiss me again," he says. *See?* I think. *Did I call that one or what?* "I wasn't ready before."

But I shake my head no, wrap my arms around his waist, pull him to me and rest my head on his shoulder. His arms come up around me protectively and he kisses my forehead, though he wants more—I can feel how much more he wants when he rubs his hips into me. "He's staying here," I tell him softly.

"Why?" he asks before he can stop himself.

"Why do you think?" I counter. This is Shanley we're talking about here—the colony accepted him from the start. He didn't get sick from the HTS, he doesn't have a male lover, he's not *us*. "He wants to beat this virus if he can, and make sure Marie's baby comes into the world okay, and he knows we don't want to hang around for that—"

"We *can't*," Dylan whines, exasperated. "You don't know how *hard* I tried to get that kid to let us stay in the quarantine room tonight. *You'll have to talk to Ben,* that's all he'll say. Like that ass will even let us *look* at each other. Jesus, if I can't sleep with you—"

With a sly grin, I kiss his shoulder, leaving a damp imprint of my lips on his shirt. "I told you about calling me that," I murmur.

His arms tighten around my waist and his hands roam my back, my hips, lower, until they cup my ass. "Let him stay then," he laughs. "I don't care. As long as *we* don't have to…"

I raise my head to answer him but *now* he's ready, and he cuts off whatever it is I want to say with a tender kiss. One hand trails up my body to cradle my chin, turning me towards him, stroking my jaw until my mouth opens and his tongue slips inside, gentle, eager. Unconsciously I clench my hands into fists at his waist, bunch the material of his shirt in my palms, lean into him, hungry. One kiss does this to me. *He* does it.

From inside the comm center comes the familiar crackle of static, and then Vallery's bright voice. "Evan!" she shrieks—I can hear it from here, but everything else is just a rapid-fire barrage of questions that I can't follow.

Reluctant, I pull away, my whole body raging for more. Dylan holds onto me, doesn't want to let go, and when he does, he sighs like this is all a major inconvenience for him and he wants me to know what a sacrifice he's making here, holding back when we both want so much more. "Can't we leave tonight?" he asks, resting his forehead against mine and staring into my eyes until I'm sure I'm going to drown in his gaze.

"First thing in the morning," I promise him. He smiles halfheartedly, runs his hands up my arms, kneads my biceps until the skin tingles beneath his touch. "Tomorrow."

"Now," he counters. "I'm not sleeping alone tonight."

With a wry grin, I tell him, "You're not crawling into my bed, lover boy. Last time you did that, I woke up in jail."

"And we didn't even *do* anything," Dylan sighs. "I mean, damn. For all that you'd think I could've at least gotten a *little* loving."

"You did," I remind him. "Just what, a few hours ago? Don't tell me you're already hungry for more."

"I'm *starving*," Dylan says with a smile.

I don't have anything to say to that because in all honesty I am, too. "I love you," I murmur, kissing him again. Then happy laughter carries out to us, Vallery's bubbly giggles, and I take Dylan's hand in mine and pull him through the opened door, push Shanley aside, lean on the transmit and cut off the steady stream of her voice. "Val!"

She laughs again, a wondrous sound. "Neal!" Her voice echoes off the walls and Dylan laughs with her. "I hear you spent the night in jail. Tessa's all about playing the cavalry but I guess it's a little too late for that, eh? What are you boys doing up this late?"

"I want to get the signal frequency down as soon as possible," I explain. I take Dylan's hand in mine and wink at him, eliciting another laugh. "Then we're coming in."

"Tonight?" she asks, hope ringing clear in her voice.

"You're as bad as Dylan," I tell her. "He doesn't want to sleep alone tonight."

My lover's arms ease around my waist, and despite the radio techs in the room with us, despite Conlan and Shanley standing beside us, he pulls me back against him and kisses my neck. "What's so bad about that?" he murmurs.

I have to admit that I really don't know.

THE END

About the Author

J. M. Snyder: Virginian, owned by 3 very spoiled cats, drives a Saturn. Graduate of George Mason University (1992). Fantasy editor of *The Fractal* from 1994 to 1996, editor of the online webzine *Disenchanted* from 1998 to 1999 and the *Star Wars* fan-fiction online webzine *Avatars* in 1998.

Publications: poetry in *Ultimate Unknown*, short story "Bones of the Sea" in *Goddess of the Bay*, short story "Eyes Like Twins" in *Distractions*. Has a few more things to write before this gig is up, including a book of short stories already in the final stages of publication and a second novel to be released late 2002. For more information, be sure to check out the author's website at **jmsnyder.net**.

0-595-22262-5

Printed in the United States
16033LVS00001B/292